About the Authors

Brenda Jackson is a *New York Times* bestselling author of more than one hundred romance titles. Brenda lives in Jacksonville, Florida, and divides her time between family, writing and travelling. Email Brenda at authorbrendajackson@gmail.com or visit her on her website at brendajackson.net

A native of Chicago's southside, **Phyllis Bourne** began her writing career as a newspaper crime reporter. After years of cops and criminals, she left reporting to write about life's sweeter side. Nowadays her stories are filled with heart-stopping heroes and happy endings. When she's not writing, she can usually be found at a make-up counter feeding her lipstick addiction. You can find her on the web at www.phyllisbourne.com and www.facebook.com/phyllisbournebooks

Yahrah St. John is the author of thirty-one published books and won the 2013 Best Kimani Romance from RT Book Reviews for *A Chance with You*. She earned a Bachelor of Arts degree in English from Northwestern University. A member of Romance Writers of America, St. John is an avid reader, enjoys cooking, travelling and adventure sports, but her true passion is writing. Visit: www.yahrahstjohn.com

After Hours

After Hours: Boardroom Temptation

BRENDA JACKSON

PHYLLIS BOURNE

YAHRAH ST. JOHN

MIX
Paper from
responsible sources
FSC C007484

This book is produced from independently certified FSC™ paper
to ensure responsible forest management.

For more information visit: www.harpercollins.co.uk/green

Printed and bound in Great Britain
by CPI Group (UK) Ltd, Croydon, CR0 4YY

MILLS & BOON

First Published in Great Britain 2021
By Mills & Boon, an imprint of HarperCollins*Publishers* Ltd
1 London Bridge Street, London, SE1 9GF

www.harpercollins.co.uk

HarperCollins*Publishers*
1st Floor, Watermarque Building,
Ringsend Road, Dublin 4, Ireland

AFTER HOURS: BOARDROOM TEMPTATION © 2021 Harlequin Books S.A.

Bachelor Unforgiving © 2016 Brenda Streater Jackson
Moonlight Kisses © 2015 Phyllis Bourne Williams
Taming Her Billionaire © 2017 Yahrah Yisrael

ISBN: 978-0-263-29962-5

BACHELOR UNFORGIVING

BRENDA JACKSON

Do not judge, and you will not be judged.
Do not condemn, and you will not be condemned.
Forgive, and you will be forgiven.
John 8:7 NIV

Prologue

Kara Goshay knew she couldn't put it off any longer. After all, the main reason she'd attended tonight's event was to seek out Virgil Bougard. She owed him an apology and she intended to give it to him. Nothing would stop her. Not even the cold, hard glares he'd given her all evening.

She had no illusions about not being one of his favorite people. Four years ago while they had been in an exclusive affair she had accused him of doing something she now knew he hadn't. She was woman enough to admit when she'd made a mistake, and in this case, she had made a big one.

She drew in a deep breath as she watched him. He was standing in a group, talking to five other men. She knew them. They were his godbrothers. Virgil had told her the story of how, close to forty years ago, six guys had become best friends while attending Morehouse and on graduation day had made a pact to stay in touch by becoming godfathers to each other's children, and that the firstborn sons' names would start with the letters *U* through *Z*. And that was how Uriel Lassiter, Virgil Bougard, Winston Coltrane, Xavier Kane, York Ellis and Zion Blackstone had come to have their names.

She eyed the group of men. All six were extremely handsome, but there was something about Virgil that had captured her from the first moment they had met. He'd walked into the room at a charity event, much like this one, looking as if he'd strolled right off the cover of *GQ*. She was convinced every woman at the black-tie affair that night had done a double take and concluded that no man could be that gorgeous.

Later that night, when he'd approached her and asked her to dance, she'd gotten a close-up view, and she discovered that she was wrong. He had been *that* gorgeous. Standing over six-three with a muscular build that would make any woman's mouth water, Virgil Bougard gave greater meaning to the phrase *tall, dark and handsome*.

She continued to watch Virgil interact with his godbrothers. When he wasn't sending hard stares her way, he was smiling at something one of them said. He and his godbrothers were close, and no doubt he'd told them what she had accused him of doing. However, she appreciated that, whenever her path crossed any of theirs, they were always pleasant.

Virgil had come to the party tonight alone. And as if he still had radar where she was concerned, his gaze had unerringly found her when he had entered the ballroom. If looks could kill, she wouldn't have any life in her body right now.

Drawing in a courageous breath, she placed her wineglass on the tray of a passing waiter. Straightening her spine, she crossed the room to where Virgil stood. She would take her chances and ask to speak with him privately. She hoped that, although he felt nothing but loathing for her, he would grant her that request.

As if he sensed her impending approach, Virgil glanced her way. The blatant animosity she saw in his eyes nearly made her weak in the knees. The only thing that kept her moving forward was knowing any anger he felt toward her was justified.

Two of his godbrothers also noticed her approach. She saw a warning flash in Xavier's eyes, giving her a heads-up that to tangle with Virgil tonight wasn't a good idea, that maybe she should turn around and head the other way.

The look she saw in Uriel's gaze was unreadable. She figured he was curious as to how she could summon the nerve to come within ten feet of Virgil, given his propensity to hold a grudge. These men knew better than anyone Virgil's unforgiving nature.

Kara slowly blew out a strained breath when she approached the men. Six pairs of eyes were now staring intently at her. "Hello, guys. Good seeing you again," she said, fighting back her nervousness.

Not surprisingly, it was Uriel who responded. He was the oldest of the six and she figured he'd decided to take the initiative to be the spokesman. "Kara. It's good seeing you, as well."

"Thanks. And I understand congratulations are in order, Uriel, Winston, Xavier and York, on your marriages." Earlier she had noticed the women they were with. All beautiful women.

The four men said thanks simultaneously.

She then turned her attention to Zion. "And I want to congratulate you, as well, Zion. Your jewelry is beautiful and your success is much deserved." Zion, the youngest of the six, was a world-renowned jewelry maker who'd received international acclaim after being selected as the First Lady's personal jeweler.

"Thanks, Kara."

Everyone had responded to her in some way except Virgil. He just stood there and continued to stare at her. His eyes were so cold she felt the icy chill all the way to her bones. She took a deep breath and then said, "Hello, Virgil."

He didn't return her greeting, just continued to give her a cold stare. But she pushed on. "May I speak with you privately for a minute?"

"No. We have nothing to say to each other."

Virgil's tone was so hard Kara was tempted to turn and walk away. But she refused to do that. She would get him alone even if she had to provoke him into it. She lifted her chin, met his gaze and smiled ruefully. "I understand your not wanting to risk being alone with me, Virgil. Especially since you've never been able to control yourself where I'm concerned."

The narrowing of Virgil's eyes indicated she might have gone too far by bringing up their past relationship and reminding him of how taken he'd once been with her.

He continued to stare at her for the longest time. Silence surrounded the group and she figured Virgil was well aware the two of them had not only drawn the attention of his godbrothers but a few others in the room who'd known they'd once been a hot item.

Finally Virgil slowly nodded. "You want to talk privately, Kara?" he asked in a clipped voice that was shrouded with a daring tone, one that warned she might regret the request. "Then by all means, lead the way."

Virgil followed Kara as she made her way through the crowded ballroom. He thought she was headed toward the patio, but instead she turned and opened the door that connected to a hallway where several small meeting rooms were located. Evidently she wasn't going to risk their conversation being overheard.

Honestly, he didn't give a royal damn. She was lucky he hadn't called her out right in the middle of the ballroom and told her just what he thought of the comment she'd made. The only thing that had held him in check was the warning looks he'd gotten from his godbrothers to behave himself. He reminded himself that Kara Goshay meant nothing to him anymore. No matter what she thought, she was the last woman who could tempt his control while he was alone with her.

"I don't plan on going any farther, so say whatever you have to say right here, Kara."

She stopped walking, turned around and met his gaze. He thought the same thing tonight he'd thought the first time he'd met her almost five years ago. Kara had the most striking eyes of any woman he'd ever seen. They were a silvery gray and were perfect for her almond-colored complexion. That hadn't been her only asset to grab his attention the night they'd met. She was a bona fide female from top to bottom. Even now he couldn't keep his gaze from trailing from the soles of her stilettos, up her shapely legs, past a small waist and perfect breasts before pausing briefly to take in the mass of medium brown curls around her shoulders. Topping everything off was a very beautiful face.

And then there was the gown she wearing. The peach mermaid style made her resemble a goddess. He couldn't help noticing when she'd been walking ahead of him how it hugged every curve and flared around her legs at the bottom, giving her a graceful yet sensual appeal. It was as if the gown had been made just for her.

He drew in an angry breath. How was it possible that after all she'd done to him…to them…he could still find her extremely attractive and so desirable? At the moment, he refused to acknowledge that even with all the animosity he felt toward her, the air around them crackled with sexual tension and awareness.

Narrowing his gaze, he said, "You've got one minute."

He watched as she breathed in deeply, which made her breasts appear to press even more against the evening gown she was wearing. How he'd loved her breasts— He cut off the memory, frowning as he wondered why he was thinking about that now.

"All right," she said softly, breaking into his thoughts. "I wanted to speak with you privately, Virgil, to apologize. I found out a few days ago that Marti lied to me about you."

If she thought her apology exonerated her for not trusting him, then she was wrong. "It took you four years to find out just what a liar your sister is? Honestly, I could care less what you now know, Kara."

"Will you accept my apology?"

"No."

"No?" She actually sounded surprised.

"No. Why should I? I tried to convince you of my innocence and you refused to believe me. Instead you chose to believe your sister's lies. So now you've found out the truth and expect me to forgive you for throwing away all we had? No."

"I had no idea Marti would deliberately lie about you."

"You should have trusted me enough to believe I would not have betrayed you. Without trust, love is nothing and you proved what we shared was nothing."

He then glanced at his watch. "Now if you will excuse me, your minute is up."

Without giving her a chance to say anything else, he turned and headed down the hallway that led back to the ballroom.

Chapter 1

Six months later

"How was the wedding?"

Virgil glanced up when his father walked into his office. For a minute he had forgotten his old man had arrived in town that morning. While growing up Matthew Bougard had been his idol and he still was. Although it seemed that lately, as they both got older, father and son didn't always agree on things. He couldn't help wondering what had brought his father back to Charlotte that morning. All the text message he'd received last night had said was to expect him around ten. And like clockwork, he was here.

"The wedding was nice, although it's hard to believe another Steele got married. Tyson surprised all of us."

Matthew chuckled as he took the chair across from Virgil's desk. "I can imagine. But did you honestly think those Steeles would be die-hard bachelors forever? Take a look at your own godbrothers." The Steele family were good friends of theirs.

Virgil frowned. "I'd rather not." Doing so would make him recall how he and his five godbrothers had formed the Guarded Hearts Club almost four years ago, right after his breakup with Kara Goshay. At the time all six godbrothers had been going through their own personal hell with women and made a pledge to remain single forever. Now four had defected. He and Zion were the only unmarried members left and they were determined to keep the club going, no matter what.

"Well, I am proud of my four godsons and their decisions to settle down and marry. Look at your mom and me, Virgil. We've been happily married close to forty years now."

Virgil hoped his father wasn't about to start his never-ending sermon about love, happiness and the pursuit of marriage. He'd heard it enough over the years; hearing it again wouldn't change a thing. Yes, he knew his parents had a long and happy marriage. He knew his father considered his mother his queen and she considered Matthew her king. He even knew—although he'd rather not think about it—that they still had a very active sex life. He'd discovered that upon arriving in the Keys unexpectedly last summer to join them on their vacation. It was supposed to be a surprise for them but ended up being a shocker for him when he'd walked in on his parents making out like teens.

Matthew and Rhona had met while attending college in Atlanta. His father had graduated from Morehouse and his mother from Clark Atlanta University. Instead of returning to Houston, where he'd been born and raised, Matthew asked Rhona to marry him and they settled in her hometown of Charlotte, North Carolina.

Just in case a sermon was on his father's agenda, Virgil

quickly asked, "So, Dad, what brings you back to Charlotte?"

His father was still CEO of Bougard Enterprises, though he rarely came into the office anymore, leaving Virgil, as second in command, to make most of the day-to-day decisions. His parents were often busy traveling, and just last year they'd bought a home in Houston with the intention of spending more time there.

But Matthew Bougard was well aware of every aspect of BE's business. He was sharp and highly intelligent, which was how he'd taken a small financial company he'd founded right out of college and made it into one of the largest hedge fund corporations in the country. And thanks to a few recent deals, they could now even boast of going global.

His father remained quiet for a moment and then said, "I'm thinking about retiring, Virgil."

Virgil sat up straight in his chair. "You really mean it this time?"

Matthew chuckled. "Yes. Leigh informed us on Friday that she and Chad are expecting a baby," his father said, beaming heartily. "That means your mom and I will be grandparents."

Virgil couldn't help but smile. He knew how much being grandparents meant to them. His younger sister had married her childhood sweetheart a few years ago after they both finished medical school. Last year Leigh and Chad had opened a medical complex in Houston and were doing just great.

"I need to call Leigh and Chad to congratulate them. Congratulations to you and Mom, as well," Virgil said.

"Thanks. I'd like to spend more time in the Keys as well as in Houston. Plus I promised your mom we'd do more international travel. She really enjoyed that Mediterranean cruise I took her on last year."

His father leaned back in his chair and studied him. From the close scrutiny, Virgil got the feeling there was more to come regarding his father's pending retirement. "My decision to retire depends on you, Virgil."

Virgil lifted a brow. "How does your decision to retire depend on me?"

His father leaned forward and Virgil knew this would be one of those Matthew Bougard deeply serious moments. Virgil wasn't sure if he was mentally prepared for it this early in the morning.

"You have a reputation, Virgil."

He didn't have to wonder what his father was alluding to. It was well-known around Charlotte and the surrounding areas that Virgil Matthew Bougard was an ardent womanizer. As far as he was concerned, he had no reason not to be if that was the lifestyle he chose. He wasn't married, nor was he in an exclusive relationship with any woman. So in his defense he could do whatever the hell he wanted to do and with whomever he chose.

"I'm a thirty-five-year-old single man, Dad. There's no reason I shouldn't enjoy female company whenever I want it."

"Well, there's that incident with Whitney Hilton that won't go away as much as I wish it would. Marv Hilton hasn't forgotten about it."

Virgil released a deep sigh. That had been almost two years ago. Why couldn't the man get over it? Would that be the scandal that haunted him forever? Marv Hilton had been one of their biggest clients and Whitney was his twenty-five-year-old daughter. Her father had brought her along on one of his business trips to Hawaii when BE had held a meeting at the same time.

"She came to my hotel room. I didn't go to hers."

"I know but to Marv none of that matters. You slept with his daughter, and as her father, he was livid."

Virgil recalled the man had been so livid that he'd dropped his account with Bougard Enterprises. Drawing in a deep breath, he could now admit when he'd gotten out of the shower and found Whitney naked and stretched out on his bed, he should have tossed her out of his room. But that option had quickly left his mind when she'd proceeded to give him one badass blow job. Her father had found out about the incident, which Virgil suspected had been intentional. Whitney wanted to get back at her father for forcing her into an engagement with some rich, old oil baron from Texas.

"That was almost two years ago, Dad."

"Yes, but Marv Hilton still wants blood, especially since her fiancé called off the wedding. Marv blames you for that. He swears his daughter was a virgin up to that time and she was saving herself for her wedding. However, I'm sure you know better."

Yes, Virgil definitely knew better since Whitney had boasted about her very active sex life that night. And the only thing she was saving was herself—from being forced into marrying a man old enough to be her father.

"You've done a great job running things in my absence, Virgil." His father intruded into his thoughts. "And there's no doubt in my mind the company would be in good hands if I were to retire. But we have to do something about cleaning up your image, especially if we want Paul Wyman's business. He and I have talked. But he's heard about you from Hilton, and Wyman has three daughters he's concerned about."

Virgil's gaze narrowed. "You make me sound like someone who goes after anything in a skirt."

"Well, that's the impression that's out there and Hilton is milking it for all it's worth. Such an image could eventually hurt the company."

Virgil stood, walked over to the window and stared out at downtown Charlotte. It was the second week in August and already the sun was beating down, guaranteeing it would be another hot day. Drawing in a deep breath, he slowly turned around.

Knowing his father, Virgil was certain the old man had a plan, one he'd thought out thoroughly. That's the way Matthew Bougard worked. If there was a problem, he came up with a solution. Virgil just hoped it was one he could go along with. "Okay, what do you suggest?"

"I think we should hire a good PR consultant, one who will come in and clean up your womanizing image."

Virgil frowned. "Do you really think that's necessary, Dad?"

"Yes. Hilton is claiming that you seduced his daughter. So I hope you can see the need to take proactive measures."

Virgil walked back over to his desk and sat down. Like his father said, Marv Hilton was out for blood. His. Unfortunately the man ran in circles with people who were potential clients for Bougard Enterprises.

"Fine. Do what you think is best. If you think hiring a PR firm will work, let's do it."

"I figured you would understand, so for the past couple of weeks I've been checking out firms. The one I suggest using comes highly recommended."

"Great," he said drily. "What's the name of the company?"

"Goshay PR and Image Consultants."

Virgil was out of his seat in a flash. "That's out of the question. You know Kara owns that business."

"Yes."

Virgil was fuming. "Then why on earth would you want to hire her?"

"Calm down, Virgil. The reason I'm hiring Kara's company is because she's the best. Anyone who could clean up Senator Jack Payne's reputation after that scandal involving him and those women—and get him reelected—can surely clean up yours without a problem."

Matthew stared hard at him, and continued, "Why are you so upset about it? Are you admitting you've only been lying to yourself these past four years and that you do still care for Kara?"

"No! I care nothing for her." It had taken a long time for him to finally reach that point, but he had. At one time he'd thought it would be nearly impossible to ever get her out of his heart.

"Then working with her shouldn't be a problem for you."

"It will be a problem because I prefer not being anywhere near her."

"Then maybe you need to ask yourself why."

Virgil shook his head. "You don't understand, Dad."

"What I understand is, because of her lack of trust in you, you won't forgive her and you're still holding a grudge. But then so is Marv Hilton. That's why Kara's services are needed."

Virgil didn't say anything but walked back to the window to stare out. A few moments later he turned to his father. "I prefer we go with some other company, Dad."

"Unless you can give me a good reason why Kara can't do the job, Virgil, she's in."

Virgil drew in a deep breath. There was no need to tell his dad that Kara had been the only woman he had ever loved. Both his parents knew that. But they didn't know he had planned to propose to her the same week she had hurled her accusations against him.

"Level with me, Virgil. The last thing I need to worry about is you trying to seduce Kara. She's getting hired to do a job. So if you think you still feel anything for her then—"

"Oh, I feel something for her all right," Virgil said in an angry tone. "I feel so much dislike for her you can whip it into butter. So I honestly don't see how I'll be able to work with her."

"For Bougard Enterprises it's business, Virgil. For you, it sounds like a personal problem you need to work through. The way I see it, you could have sent Whitney Hilton from your room that night but you didn't. Instead you chose to let her stay. It was your decision and with that decision came consequences this company has to deal with. I would love to retire and spend more time with your mother and my future grandchild, but I'll hang around if I have to."

Virgil definitely didn't want that. As much as he loved his father and appreciated his wisdom and expertise, Virgil had gotten used to making the decisions. He was ready to handle things without the old man. If his father thought he needed an image adjustment, then fine. "You win, Dad. Go ahead and hire Kara's company."

Matthew stood. "It's not about winning, Virgil. It's about making the right moves to ensure that Bougard Enterprises will be around for a long time. I'll have my administrative assistant call Kara to come in so we can discuss our plan with her."

Virgil drew in a deep breath. He would have to put up with Kara…or die trying.

Kara hung up the phone with a shocked look on her face. Of all things… A call from Matthew Bougard's administrative assistant saying he wanted to meet with her tomorrow to discuss a possible job offer.

She leaned back in her chair. Just what did Bougard

Enterprises need? Considering her strained relationship with Virgil, which she figured Mr. Bougard had to know about, she was surprised he'd reached out to her company, despite its excellent reputation. She'd find out soon enough what Matthew Bougard wanted.

Will Virgil be at the meeting?

Tossing a paper clip on her desk, Kara thrust the question from her mind. Sure, he'd be there. And it was no big deal, she told herself. She recalled her last meeting with Virgil six months ago when she had apologized. She would always regret believing Marti's lie and what doing so had cost her. She had not spoken to her sister since finding out the truth. As far as Kara was concerned, they didn't have anything to say to each other. She loved Marti but Kara could never forget the day she'd arrived back in town early from a business trip. She'd gone to her sister's office to invite her to lunch only to overhear Marti telling someone on the phone how she had lied to Kara. Marti had claimed she had seen Virgil having a romantic dinner with a woman and had followed them all the way to a hotel and watched them go inside.

When Kara had confronted her, she had admitted lying and said she had done it for Kara's own good, as it would have been just a matter of time before Virgil hurt her. To Kara, that excuse was unacceptable.

The buzzing on her desk brought her thoughts back to the present. "Yes, Janice?"

"Your mother is on line one."

Kara drew in a deep breath. Her mother was the last person she wanted to talk to. To Lydia Goshay's way of thinking it was past time Kara forgave her sister.

"Tell my mother I'm in a meeting and I'll call her back later."

At the moment, Kara didn't want to talk to anyone.

All she wanted to do was to relax her mind for a minute. That call from Bougard Enterprises had definitely rattled her brain. Leaning back in her chair she closed her eyes and, it seemed of its own accord, her mind began reliving memories of that night five years ago when she and Virgil had met.

"May I have this dance?"

Kara's heart began pounding the minute she turned to stare up into what had to be the most gorgeous pair of brown eyes she'd ever seen. Bedroom eyes. They were an indulgent chocolate hue that made one think of something totally sweet and clandestinely sinful.

Although they had never been formally introduced, she knew who he was. Virgil Bougard. He had a reputation around town that would make Casanova look like a choir boy. His name was often whispered on women's lips followed by a salacious smile. She'd first heard about him in the locker room at her gym. Women claimed he was hot, both in and out of bed. They also claimed he was a man who got any woman he wanted. And she had a feeling that tonight for some reason she had caught his eye.

She'd seen him when he'd arrived and had watched how several women had put themselves in his path. It seemed he drew them to him like a magnet. But he hadn't danced with anyone. His attention had seemed targeted on her.

For most of the night their gazes had been meeting and holding from across the room. Each time she could feel her blood rush through her veins. She had noticed how impeccably he was dressed and how tall he stood, an imposing figure against any other man in the room. Talk about sex appeal.

She wished she could say it was all due to his ultra-handsome looks, consisting of an angular face that boasted a firm jaw, full lips and high cheekbones. And when he'd smiled her stomach did a couple of flips, and then she saw the dimples in those cheeks.

And now that same man was standing right in front of her, asking her to dance. Although she wished otherwise, she could feel heat swirling through her. She felt an intense sexual connection between them and couldn't understand how that could be. Although she knew better and was totally aware of his scandalous reputation around town, she was shamefully attracted to him.

"Dance?" she repeated.

The way his mouth curved in a teasing smile made more curling heat settle in the pit of her stomach. "Yes, dance. I would do just about anything to hold you in my arms."

Kara couldn't believe this stranger would be so audacious as to say that.

"Who are you?" she asked. She knew his identity but felt he should introduce himself nonetheless.

He gave her another smile. "Virgil. Virgil Bougard. And you're...?"

"Kara Goshay."

"Nice meeting you, Kara." He paused a moment and then asked, "So...are we going to dance?"

She didn't miss the desire smoldering in the depths of those bedroom eyes. The sight of it made her heart rate accelerate in her chest. "Yes, Virgil. I will dance with you."

Kara slowly opened her eyes and drew in a deep breath. They had danced. More than once.

Believing Marti's lie was something she would regret for the rest of her life. Because in doing so, she had lost the one man she would ever love.

Chapter 2

Virgil entered his home and tossed his jacket across a chair. At least his father's visit hadn't stopped him from sticking with his plan to leave work early. He needed to rest, relax and recover from too much partying this weekend at Tyson's wedding. Now he had another reason for needing down time. Namely to get his mind prepared for tomorrow's meeting with Kara.

She had done something no one had thought was possible, which was to literally bring him to his knees and show him there was a difference between love and lust. His womanizing ways had begun to morph into those of a man who wanted only one woman. Her. She had singlehandedly transformed his reckless heart into a thoughtful one.

That was then. This was now.

He was no longer a fool in love. And Kara was someone he could do without. He staunchly refused to give his heart to another woman, and he enjoyed his time as a single man who wore no female's heart on his sleeve. He was a card-carrying member of the Guarded Hearts Club.

Over the years the club had seen its membership dwindle. Uriel had dropped out when he married Ellie. A year later Xavier had married Farrah, followed by York marrying Darcy and then Winston tying the knot with Ainsley. The last one had been a shocker because no one had been a stronger advocate of bachelorhood than Winston. Hell, Winston even held the office of club president for a number of years. That left only him and Zion as lone members. As the president, he felt it was time they recruited new members.

Although the club started out exclusively for him and his godbrothers, that didn't mean it had to stay that way. There had to be other single men who felt the same way they did. Men who enjoyed the single life and intended to never marry. Mercury and Gannon Steele headed the list. It wouldn't be hard to convince them that bachelors needed to stick together and they needed to join the exclusive club. He'd heard the frustration in their voices this weekend at Tyson's wedding. Mercury and Gannon figured it would only be a matter of time before their mother eyed one of them as the next possible groom.

And then there was Xavier's friend Kurt. He would be another good candidate. And wasn't it just last week that Quade Westmoreland, who was an in-law of those Steeles, mention something about newfound bachelor cousins living somewhere in Alaska? A semblance of a smile touched Virgil's face. There was hope after all.

A frown replaced the smile when his thoughts shifted to Whitney Hilton. She had definitely been a mistake and one he was still paying for. It wasn't as if Whitney had been an underage teenager. Hell, the woman had been twenty-five. An adult. A consenting adult. Hilton was disillusioned if he thought his daughter had been a virgin that night. Nevertheless, for one night of lust, he would pay by having to put up with Kara. That was something he didn't look forward to doing.

As he headed for the kitchen to grab a cold beer out of the refrigerator, he couldn't help allowing his mind to recall a time when Kara's presence was the only thing he'd wanted.

And it had started with their first dance...

"So, Kara, tell me about yourself."

Virgil couldn't help looking into her eyes when he'd made the request. She was simply beautiful. Striking. Stunning. And the dress she was wearing showed off her body right down to every curve. He wanted to get to know her but there were other things he wanted to do to her, as well. Taste her. Touch her. But for now, dancing with her had to suffice.

He had noticed her the moment he'd entered the ballroom and had known then she was someone he had to connect with. Each time their gazes had linked, he'd felt stirring emotions he had never felt before. There was no way he could have not sought her out. They had introduced themselves and now he wanted to know everything there was to know about her. Then maybe he could figure out why she was having such an effect on him. No woman had ever rattled his senses like she was doing.

"There's not a whole lot to tell," she said.

"I was born in San Francisco twenty-five years ago. My parents are still there, both alive and well, and I have a sister, who is older than me by three years. I got my degree in marketing from Duke and landed a job here in Charlotte right after college. Last year I opened my own PR firm."

She felt good in his arms and he liked the way his arms fit around her waist. "Are you dating?"

"Sometimes."

"Seeing anyone exclusively?"

"No."

"Good."

She raised a brow and he could only smile. And before she could ask he said, "The reason I think it's good is because I want you for myself."

She tilted her head to study him and even raised her chin showing a little irritation at his audacity. His intent was unmistakable. His smile deepened, clearly unmoved that what he'd said might have possibly annoyed her. He believed in being honest with women. Game playing wasn't his style. "And what if I'm not interested, Virgil?"

"Then it would be my job to get you interested. But I think we can toss out that possibility. You're just as interested in me as I am in you."

He could tell her irritation increased. "What makes you think so?"

He shrugged. "A number of things, including body language. But primarily the way we've been flirting with each other most of night."

"Is that what you think? That I've been flirting with you from across the room?"

"Haven't you? But then I'll admit unashamedly that I've been flirting with you, as well. Now I think we should move beyond flirting."

"Do you?"

"Yes." *He held her gaze while she stared at him. The sway of their bodies in tune with the music was a no-thought process, and it was a good thing since they were so focused on each other. He especially liked the feel of their bodies touching while they danced.*

"And just where are we supposed to be moving to?" she asked. For her to have done so meant she was giving the idea some thought.

"I'm hoping I can entice you to leave here with me and..."

When he felt her tense, he said smoothly, *"Go to an all-night café not far from here and share a cup of coffee with me. That way we can get to know each other even better."*

She relaxed and he was grateful for that. The last thing he wanted to do was give her the impression all he wanted was to take her to the nearest hotel or back to her place or his. Doing any of the three would definitely work for him since he wanted her just that much. However, he had a feeling she was not a one-night-stand kind of woman, even though he had no problem being a one-night-stand kind of man when it suited him. He had a feeling he would have to work his way into her bed. He didn't mind that and figured she would be worth it in the end.

"I'll think about it...the part about the all-night café. But you haven't told me anything about yourself."

A smile touched his lips. He had no problem doing that. *"I'm thirty and the oldest of two. I have a sister who is four years younger. She's single but dates her high school sweetheart. I figure they'll get married one of these days. I work at Bougard Enterprises, a financial corporation founded by my father years ago. He's brilliant when it comes to finance and I'm learning all that I can from him. He's been hinting at retiring in a few years."*

"And when he does, that means more work for you, right?"

"Yes, but I love what I do. I guess it's in my blood."

Much too soon the music came to an end. Without questioning why such a thing mattered to him, he kept a firm grip on her arm. Instead of leading her back to where *she'd been standing before the dance, he led her toward the patio. "It's a beautiful night. Let's appreciate it, all right?"*

"Okay."

He couldn't help but smile as he led her through the huge French doors and outside. For some reason he felt tonight would be his lucky night.

Virgil took a huge swig of his beer, bringing his thoughts back to the present. Had it been his lucky night? It depended on how he looked at it. Yes, they'd left the party early to share cups of coffee at that café, and, yes, from that night and for a full year after that, they'd dated exclusively. He chuckled, thinking she hadn't been as easy as he thought to get into bed. She had made him earn that right and he'd felt it had been worth it. She had been worth it. And he had fallen hopelessly in love. Their time together had been happy times…till they were tinged with heartache when she'd accused him of being involved with another woman.

When he saw her tomorrow he would be as professional as he could, no matter how much he would hate every minute of doing so. He didn't want to give anyone, especially his father, the impression that he felt anything for her anymore.

He finished off the rest of his beer and was about to change into more comfortable clothing when his mobile phone went off. He recognized the ringtone. Each of his godbrothers had their own specific ring. "What's up, W? Calling all the way from Australia is probably costing you a pretty penny, isn't it?"

Over the years he and his godbrothers had shortened their names for each other to just the first letter. Winston, a marine biologist, and his wife, Ainsley, were currently living in Australia near the Great Barrier Reef on some project dealing with sea turtles.

"Just giving all of you a heads-up that I'll be home next month."

Virgil chuckled. "You were home six months ago. Getting homesick?"

Winston returned his chuckle. "No. Ainsley and I love it here. Six months ago we were home for her parents' wedding anniversary. This time it's for Uriel. Have you forgotten his birthday is next month? I talked to Ellie and she's throwing a party at the lake and would like all of us there." He paused a moment and then asked, "How are things going with you, V?"

He knew why Winston was asking. When he was home back in February, Virgil and his godbrothers had been together at the charity ball when Virgil had seen Kara. They knew what Kara had once meant to him and were glad she'd finally found out the truth about her sister. They'd also thought it had taken a lot of guts for her to apologize, considering how he'd been staring her down all night. And last but not least, they all thought he should have accepted the apology she offered. They felt he should be able to forgive Kara even if he didn't want to have anything to do with her ever again.

Virgil didn't see it that way. He saw no reason to release her from the guilt of accusing him of something he hadn't done. "Things are okay," he finally said. "Tyson's wedding went off without a hitch. In fact, he had that same lovesick look that you did at your wedding."

"It's the 'I'm in love' look, Virgil. I recall you once wore it yourself."

"That was when I didn't know any better. It was before I talked you guys into forming the club. The one you, York, Xavier and Uriel defected from."

"Only to pursue happier days."

"If you say so," Virgil said, shaking his head.

"Have you seen Kara since that night, V?"

Virgil frowned. "Why would I see her after that night?"

"Um, maybe you've had a change of heart. Called her. Asked her out for old times' sake."

"Don't hold your breath. But I will be seeing her tomorrow. Not my choice, believe me."

"Why? What's going on?"

He then told Winston about his father's plan to improve his image.

"Well, I hope you don't plan to be an obnoxious ass when you see her. She did apologize. And can you imagine having a sister like Marti?"

Most of his godbrothers knew Marti because she'd dated Xavier. According to Xavier, three weeks was all he could take of Marti Goshay, who thought a lot of herself. Even Virgil would admit it was hard to believe Marti and Kara were siblings. They were as different as night and day.

"Can you imagine how Kara must feel knowing her sister lied? If you can't trust your sibling, then who can you trust?"

Virgil decided not to answer that. In fact he really didn't want to discuss the Goshay sisters any longer. He deliberately got Winston to talk about something else—namely his work. Winston loved what he did for a living and went on to tell Virgil how his research on the turtles was coming.

When Winston began getting too scientific, Virgil decided it was time to end their conversation. "We'll get together when you arrive in town, W."

"You bet. Take care."

"You, too."

"And remember to be nice tomorrow, V."

"I'll try. Can't make any promises."

Virgil clicked off the phone. Dread filled him as he thought about tomorrow. Just like he told Winston, as far as being nice to Kara went, all he could do was try.

Chapter 3

Kara paused to draw in a deep breath, needing to calm her frayed nerves. She was ten minutes early so why were the Bougards already in the conference room waiting on her? And the thought that one them had seen her naked probably just as many times as he'd seen her wearing clothes was enough to rattle her.

Shaking off the memories of all those times, she thought about one of her favorite quotes. *You are more stronger than you think.* She certainly hoped so because at the moment she felt a little weak in the knees. And what were those sensuous shivers racing through her? Now was not the time to remember any of that. Straightening her spine, raising her chin and pasting a professional smile on her lips, she turned the knob and entered the conference room.

Both men stood and, although she hadn't wanted it to, her gaze immediately went to Virgil before shifting to the older Bougard. She liked Virgil's father and could easily recall when Virgil had taken her home to meet his parents. She'd been nervous then, as well.

Like Virgil, Matthew Bougard was handsome. He was also tall, standing way over six feet, and had a muscular build. She knew he liked playing golf and he'd been on the Olympic swim team while in college at Morehouse.

"I hope I haven't kept you waiting," she said, and with all the professionalism she could muster, she crossed the room and extended her hand first to Matthew. Instead of taking it, he pulled her to him in a hug. "No, you're early, in fact. We just didn't want to keep you waiting on us. It's good seeing you again, Kara."

When he released her, she smiled up at him. "Good seeing you again, too, Matthew. How's Rhona?"

"She's fine and sends her love."

Kara then shifted her gaze to Virgil. He was standing beside his father, impeccably dressed in a dark business suit. She wished she wasn't so intensely aware of him and wished more than anything that seeing him didn't remind her of how long she'd been without a man. After him and the pain she'd felt at the time, she had sworn off men.

His expression was unreadable when he said, "Kara, glad you could meet with us today." He extended his hand to her, letting her know that if she assumed he would pull her into his arms for a hug like his father had, then she was wrong.

Kara took the hand Virgil offered and tried not to show any sort of reaction when a frisson of heat raced up her spine. "Glad I'm meeting with the two of you, as well."

Although he didn't say anything, something in his eyes told her that her presence here today hadn't been his idea. She pulled her hand from Virgil's and then said to both men, "I'm eager to find out why you feel that you need my services."

"And we're eager to tell you so you can get started on our problem right away," Matthew said, smiling. "Please have a seat."

"Thanks." She sat down in the chair Matthew had pulled out for her, the one right across from Virgil.

She tried to ignore his intense stare or at least try to. "So what's the problem?" she asked, darting her gaze between the two men.

It was Virgil who spoke. "It seems my image needs improving."

She raised an eyebrow. "Your image?"

It was Matthew who then added, rather bluntly, "Yes, his image. Everyone thinks my son's behavior is that of a manwhore, and it's hurting business. We want to hire your company to improve his image."

Virgil frowned at his father. "Manwhore? I wouldn't go that far, Dad."

"I didn't say you were one, Virgil. I said that's the perception out there and it's hurting the company."

Virgil wished he could say "damn the company," but he loved Bougard Enterprises just as much as his dad did. He would do anything to make sure the company his father had started years ago did not fail under his watch. Even if it meant making sacrifices. Still, he couldn't help saying, "I enjoy women and like I told you yesterday, Dad, as a single man there's nothing wrong with my dating habits."

Okay, he would admit he dated a lot of women, but being thought of as a manwhore was a bit too much. The only good thing about his father's statement was that it was painting a picture for Kara that he'd successfully moved on and put her behind him.

But even with all the pain she'd caused him, he could say without a doubt that Kara Goshay was the most beautiful woman he'd ever met. Not too many could go from being a staunch businesswoman to a slinky seductress in the blink of an eye.

It had taken every ounce of strength he had to control himself when she'd walked into the room with that sensuous and graceful movement of hers. Six months ago when he'd seen her at that charity event, she'd been wearing an eye-catching evening gown. Today she was dressed in a tan business suit with matching pumps. He'd always thought he was a stilettos man but he had to admit her legs looked gorgeous in a pair of pumps.

Why was he thinking about that? And why was his mind filled with the memory of taking a business suit— similar to the one she was wearing—off her one night? Piece by piece. Bit by bit. And why was he remembering how good she looked naked, how smooth her skin was and how soft she was to his touch?

Her hair hung in soft layers around her shoulders and the little makeup she wore did what it was supposed to do, which was to enhance her looks and not cover them. And were those pearl earrings in her ears the same ones he'd given her when they had celebrated their first Christmas together? If so, why was she wearing them today? Did she think doing so would move him in some way? Make him remember the good times? Forget about the bad? If she thought that, then she was wrong. He was so over her.

"As far as something being wrong with your dating habits, our major investors apparently think so," Matthew said, breaking into Virgil's thoughts. "So what about it, Kara? Can he be helped?"

Kara didn't say anything for a moment. Matthew's words about Virgil's wretched reputation hadn't been a shock. Since their breakup she'd heard he had gone back to his womanizing ways.

Matthew and Virgil were waiting for her response…at least she figured Matthew was. Virgil sat there wearing one of those "I don't give a damn what anyone thinks" expressions. That made her wonder if he was willing to change his lifestyle for the sake of his company, which prompted her ultimate response. "I can only help if Virgil wants to be helped."

Virgil decided to speak up. It was time he let both Kara and his father know that this change in his image had limitations. "I'm a single man who's not in an exclusive relationship with any woman. I enjoy dating and if anyone has an issue with that then that's their problem and not mine."

Matthew turned to him. "But you would agree after the Whitney Hilton scandal that your image needs an overhaul?"

Not really, he thought. Whitney had gotten just what she'd come to his hotel room for that night. She'd been happy. He'd been satisfied. It was her father who refused to accept that his daughter had an active sex life—before, during and after Virgil Bougard.

"Is that something I need to know about? The scandal with Whitney Hilton?" Kara asked.

As far as Virgil was concerned it wasn't any of her business. But evidently his father didn't see it that way.

"Whitney Hilton is the daughter of one of my biggest clients," Matthew said. "At least I should say former clients. During a business trip almost two years ago, Whitney tagged along with her father. She took a liking to Virgil and ended up in his hotel room one night. It caused a little ruckus when her fiancé found out and broke their engagement. Her father was livid and accused Virgil of deflowering his daughter. Claimed she was saving herself for her husband. Since then Marv Hilton has tried to tarnish our company's good name with potential clients."

Kara looked over at Virgil, cocked her head. "Do you know if she was a virgin as her father claims?"

Virgil frowned. "No. That's the lie Marv Hilton wants to believe. But then that's the thing about lies. They are meant to be believed, especially by those who're gullible enough to do so."

Kara didn't have to wonder if what he'd said was meant to be a dig because she knew that it had been. "How old was she?"

"At the time Whitney was twenty-five."

"Twenty-five?" Kara asked, surprised. "So she wasn't a child but an adult who was old enough to make her own decisions."

"You tell that to her old man" was Virgil's flippant response. "It's my guess she would have done anything to get out of marrying the man her father had picked out for her. Some oilman from Texas who was old enough to be her father. And she used me to do it. She had a reason for coming to my room and then making sure both her father and fiancé found out about it."

"So what do you think, Kara?" Matthew broke in to her thoughts to ask. "Can his image be fixed?"

Before she could sufficiently answer that, she needed to make sure Virgil was 100 percent on board with an image makeover. If he wasn't then he would only be wasting her time and his company's money. "Not sure," she answered Matthew while holding Virgil's gaze. "Virgil still hasn't answered the question I put out there a while ago."

She watched Virgil's lips twitch in annoyance. "What question?"

"The one I posed as to whether or not you want to be helped. I need to know if you will allow me to do my job to improve your image."

The room had gotten quiet, and he knew that his dad,

as well as Kara, was waiting on his response. "Fine, knock yourself out."

"In other words you will do it and not give Kara a hard time doing so, right?" His father turned and asked him with those razor sharp eyes that all but said to leave the bullshit at the door.

"Yes, Dad. Right now my main concern is keeping Bougard Enterprises at the top."

"Good." As if what Virgil had said was enough to satisfy him, Matthew Bougard stood and looked at his watch. "The two of you can work out all the finer details of what needs to be done. As for me, I've kept my queen waiting long enough. Rhona and I are joining friends for lunch at the Racetrack Café."

The café, which was jointly owned by several drivers on the NASCAR circuit, including a friend of his by the name of Bronson Scott, had the best hamburgers and fries in Charlotte. "I hope you and Mom enjoy lunch with your friends, Dad."

"And we will, especially since I know this matter of your image will be resolved with Kara's help." Matthew then turned to Kara. "I appreciate your handling this for us."

He paused a minute and then said, "I'm going to tell you just what I told Virgil yesterday. No matter how the two of you feel about each other, this here is business. The reason you're being hired is because I believe you are the best person to do what needs to be done, Kara. I expect you and Virgil to put aside whatever differences you have and act like professionals. And I'm sure the two of you will."

With that said, Matthew Bougard opened the conference room door and walked out, leaving Kara and Virgil staring uneasily at each other.

Chapter 4

"Well, he certainly said a mouthful," Virgil said moments later, breaking the silence in the room.

"And I can understand his concern." Kara pushed back her chair and stood. "But I'm sure you and I will handle ourselves as the professionals that we are. What happened to end our relationship was unfortunate. It was a mistake on my part. I apologized. You didn't accept my apology. There's nothing I can do about that but move on and not worry about it. And I have."

She saw Virgil's body tighten as he gazed up at her. "Did you really expect me to accept your apology?"

She shrugged. "Don't know why you wouldn't. It was made in all sincerity. I admitted I was wrong. My conscience is clear."

He frowned as he stood, as well. "Your conscience is clear? I don't see how it can be," he said in a gruff voice.

Kara couldn't help but study the features of the man standing before her. He was handsome to the point where the word *eye candy* just wouldn't do him justice. But as she stared into his brown eyes, she saw something that made her swallow hard. His inability to forgive. It was there in the dark depths of the eyes gazing back at her, letting her know he was barely tolerating her presence.

"Well, let me tell you how that can be, Virgil," Kara said, staring him down. Frankly, she was sick and tired of his attitude. He acted as if he was the only one who'd suffered from Marti's lie.

"I am human. I make mistakes. Big and small. We all do. We also trust and believe in people that we should not. I did. I took Marti's word over yours. Something I will regret doing for the rest of my life. I loved you and—"

"No," Virgil said angrily. "There's no way in hell you can convince me that you loved me. No woman could love a man one minute and then assume the worse of him the next. You only thought you loved me."

She stared at him, knowing it would be a waste of her time to try to convince him otherwise. In his eyes, a woman who loved a man would not have believed the worst of him. But regardless of what he thought, she *had* loved him.

"I apologized to you, Virgil. But you didn't accept it. Great. Fine. That's your prerogative. Mine is to keep moving and keep living. I can't let your inability to forgive hang over my head. There's more to life than living in the past."

She paused a moment and then in a calmer voice said, "I'll start work immediately on a plan of action for your image makeover. I'll call you once it's completed so we can meet to discuss it."

With nothing else to say, she turned and walked out of the office.

Virgil's body stiffened in anger when the door clicked shut behind Kara. She had a lot of nerve. That was all fine and dandy that she could keep moving and keep living; he could make the same claim. But what she failed to take into account was what her belief in her sister's lie had done to him. Had done to them. And he couldn't help noticing she hadn't refuted his words when he said she'd only assumed she loved him. In not doing so, she'd all but admitted he'd been merely an infatuation. That thought angered him even more.

There's more to life than living in the past. Upon remembering Kara's words, it took every ounce of control he had not to go after her and let her know that although he wasn't living in the past, it was the past he'd shared with her that had shaped him into the man he was today. A man determined not to let any woman get close to his heart again. A man who'd been taught there was no such thing as the perfect love. A man who enjoyed being physically involved but emotionally detached from women.

She would never know how she'd nearly destroyed him four years ago. For months he hadn't been able to eat, sleep or function like a sane person. It was only when his godbrothers had talked him into taking one of those singles cruises with them that he'd returned to the land of the living. It had taken him almost a full year to get over Kara; put her behind him. And in doing so, he'd developed an entirely new agenda and game plan when it came to women. He refused to love one, and he lusted for plenty.

And she thought she could wipe the slate clean with just an apology?

Virgil shoved his hands into his pockets as he walked over to the window and looked out. And now they would be working together to improve his image. How crazy was that? He rubbed his hand down his face. *There's more to life than living in the past.*

He forced his mind to rethink Kara's words, this time

with deeper meaning and clarity. Maybe by carrying all this bitterness inside of him the way he had, he was living in the past, not letting go of what she had done.

Forgiving didn't mean forgetting. Nor did it mean reconciliation. What they once shared could never be regained. She was totally and completely out of his heart now, so wasn't it time he acted like it? There was no reason why they could not deal with each other on the professional level his father had alluded to. It wasn't about him or her but all about Bougard Enterprises.

Virgil figured one day he would eventually marry, especially since he needed heirs to continue the Bougard legacy. And when he did, it wouldn't be for love. Thanks to Kara Goshay he would know better the next time.

"Your father is on line one, Ms. Goshay."

Kara released a frustrated sigh but couldn't stop the smile that touched her lips. She figured since her mother's attempt to bring an end to her strained relationship with Marti had failed, Lydia had called in the big guns. Namely Byron Goshay. Kara had always been a daddy's girl and proud of it. Her father adored both of his daughters, but there had always been a special bond between the two of them.

"Put him through, please."

Leaning back in her chair, she waited for the connection while recalling her conversation with her mother when she returned her call yesterday. It was a discussion that hadn't gone over well. Lydia tried shifting the blame to Kara, saying she was allowing a man to come between her and her sister. She felt Kara should make up with Marti now that her sister was under a doctor's care for stress and anxiety attacks.

Kara had gotten royally pissed. She sympathized with whatever Marti was going through, but what about those four years Kara had suffered, thinking the man she loved had betrayed her? What about the stress she'd gone through? The heartbreak? The pain? How could one sister do that to another?

"Kara? How's my girl?"

The sound of her father's voice chased away the anger. She smiled. "I'm fine, Dad. What about you?"

"I'm doing okay. Looking forward to retirement in a few years. Just waiting for my daughters to pay off their student loans so they can take care of their old man."

Kara shook her head. "Our student loans are paid off. Besides, you wouldn't accept a handout from me or Marti even if your life depended on it."

She heard her father's chuckle. "True."

He then paused, and she knew what was coming when she detected him shifting to a more serious mode. "Your mom talked to me last night about the ongoing situation between you and Marti."

"And?"

"And I think we need to have a family powwow. A sort of bonding session. I'd like to fly both you and Marti home for the weekend."

As if flying out to San Francisco would magically make things better. "It won't do any good, Dad."

"Sweetheart, Marti's your sister."

So now her father was taking that approach? She couldn't stop the flare of anger. "Yes, and *my sister* deliberately sabotaged my relationship with the man I loved."

There was another pause. "I just want my daughters back together. I feel our family is breaking apart."

"Don't blame me, Dad."

"Of course I don't blame you."

Kara was glad to hear that. "Mom did."

"Lydia should not have said that. I told her we needed

to stay out of it and let you and Marti handle things. But I guess she saw that wasn't happening and figured she needed to step in. But that's no reason to blame you. You didn't ask for what Marti did. Have you seen Virgil and told him the truth?"

"Yes, for what good that did. I apologized but he didn't accept my apology. I can't blame him to be honest with you. I said some mean things to him back then. I think now he hates me more than ever."

"Sorry to hear that. I tried calling him to apologize, as well. He's changed his number from the one I had."

Kara lifted a brow. "Why would you need to apologize?"

"Because after the two of you broke up and Marti told me what he did, I called him and said a lot of not-so-nice things to him."

Kara's eyes closed for a minute. Her sister's lie had caused more damage than Kara had realized. "I didn't know," she said softly. Her father had liked Virgil a lot, and vice versa. Getting such a call from her father had probably only added to Virgil's anger. "Why didn't you tell me?"

"At the time I felt there was no reason to tell you. I thought he had hurt you and that was all I needed to know. Now I feel bad about what I said."

Welcome to the club. "That's okay, Dad. Like I said, Virgil is not in a forgiving mood right now anyway."

"So there's no chance the two of you can patch things up and get back together?"

Kara shook her head as she recalled Virgil's words. *Without trust, love is nothing and you proved what we shared was nothing.*

"No, Dad. There's no way Virgil and I will ever get back together."

The finality of what she'd just said overwhelmed her

and she knew she had to end the call with her father before he detected anything. "I've got a ton of things to do," she said softly. "Goodbye, Dad. I love you."

"I love you, too, cupcake."

It was only after he clicked off his phone and she clicked off hers that she gave in to her tears.

Chapter 5

"Mr. Bougard, Ms. Goshay is on the line for you."

Virgil tossed his pen down on his desk. "Thanks, Pam. Please put her through." When he heard the connecting click, he said, "Yes, Kara?"

"I told you I would contact you when I completed my action plan."

Yes, she had said that a week ago. He had pushed the thought of hearing from her out of his mind. At least he'd tried, but he had found himself thinking a lot about Kara whether he wanted to or not.

"I was wondering when we can meet," she added, interrupting his thoughts.

He checked the calendar on his desk. "I'm booked solid the rest of the week. It will have to be sometime next week." *Or the week after that*, he thought to himself. He was in no hurry to see Kara again.

"It's imperative that we meet this week, Virgil. I got a call from your father yesterday for an update. At that time he expressed that he wanted me to present my plan to you ASAP. I told him that I would."

"Now you can go back and tell him that you tried," he said. "Like I said, my calendar is full this week. To be honest it's full next week, as well."

"And there's no way you can squeeze me in *this* week?"

He heard the annoyance in her voice and figured she thought he was deliberately being difficult. "No, sorry. Unless…" he said, studying his calendar again.

"Unless what?"

"Unless we make it a business dinner. That will work for me. How about for you?"

He heard the pause, which lasted a little too long to suit him. Now he was the one getting annoyed. "Look, Kara. My time is precious and right now you're wasting it. Will you be able to meet me for dinner tomorrow or not?" Virgil snapped.

"Yes, I'm available for a business dinner tomorrow," Kara snapped back.

"Good. My administrative assistant will call you later today with details as to where we will meet."

"Fine."

"Goodbye."

When Kara heard the click in her ear, she leaned back in her chair, and she clicked off her own phone. "And goodbye to you, too, Mr. Obnoxious." Of course he hadn't heard her comment but it still felt good making it.

A business dinner? Why couldn't he just add her to his schedule? He couldn't be *that* busy. She guessed that in a way she should be grateful. He probably would not have agreed to meet with her at all if she hadn't told him about the telephone call she'd received from his father. Matthew had made it clear he expected them to work together, grudgingly or otherwise. She had no problem doing so but couldn't speak for Virgil.

Kara sighed deeply. It was obvious he was being difficult already. It wouldn't be the first time she'd had to do an image makeover on an unenthusiastic client. She couldn't let that be a deterrent to what needed to be done. She had a job to do and she intended to do it.

Arriving early, Virgil chose a table in the back of the Goldenrod Restaurant mainly for two reasons. First, the table sat beside a huge window and on a clear day you could see the mountain peaks of Chimney Rock. And, second, the location gave him a good view of the restaurant's entrance. For some reason he wanted to see Kara before she saw him.

No one had to tell him that he hadn't been pleasant yesterday while talking to her on the phone. She had a tendency to bring out the worst in him and she had been the last person he'd wanted to converse with, business or otherwise. And then for her to mention his father had called her, literally reminding him he had to toe the line, had annoyed the hell out of him.

If Virgil didn't know better, he would think his father was trying to play his hand at matchmaking. After all, his parents had liked Kara a lot. But he did know better because the one thing Matthew Bougard didn't do was play games. His father was too no-nonsense for that. The only reason his dad had insisted on hiring Kara was because she was the best and had a stellar track record to prove it.

Virgil saw Kara the moment she walked into the restaurant and knew his biggest challenge would be her. If he hadn't known Kara and had glanced up and seen her for the first time, he would have had the same reaction he noticed several men in the restaurant having now. Kara

Goshay wasn't just a beautiful woman, she was downright striking. Her entrance into any room drew stares from both men and women.

She was wearing an olive-green pencil skirt with a matching jacket and white blouse. Probably on any other person the colors would look drab, but on Kara they looked stunning. The skirt emphasized every single curve of her body as well as her long, gorgeous legs. Her hair was neatly tied up in a knot and he thought the style highlighted the gracefulness of her neck and the long, dark lashes fanning her eyes.

He thought now the same thing he did the very first time he'd ever laid eyes on her. She was a woman about whom fantasies—the hot and steamy kind—were made. Evidently others thought so, as well, and Virgil couldn't help noticing several men shift in their seats, probably wondering if they would get the opportunity to meet her. Get to know her better. And that, Virgil thought, was the kicker. He already knew Kara, better than most. Knew more than he wanted to remember knowing. Like how she looked underneath her outfit, the location of that half-moon tattoo and all about that little mole on her backside.

He knew where those long legs began and especially where they ended. And he was well aware of those curves—intimately. Every single one of them. And the firm breasts under her blouse…he knew them, too. Very well. He knew how they felt in a man's hand and how they tasted in his mouth.

She glanced over in his direction and their gazes met, then held much too long to suit him. He sighed deeply and wished he could break the connection and look away, focus his attention on something or someone else, but he couldn't. He could only sit there and stare at the woman now walking toward him. Stare and remember. However, for some reason he wasn't thinking about what had torn them apart, but his mind was remembering things they'd done together, especially in the bedroom. After a hard day at work, the bedroom—either his or hers—had been their playground. And they'd played a lot. He could vividly remember all the positions they'd tried, the games they'd played and the talks they'd had. Sexual chemistry had a way of overpowering them whenever they were together, and heaven help him, he was feeling it now with every step she took toward him.

Virgil was beginning to see that suggesting a business dinner might not have been a smart thing to do. He should have found a way to work her into his workday schedule. He tried not to notice how her hand was clutching a leather briefcase—the same one he'd given her for her birthday. He was surprised she still had it. He could remember the night he'd given it to her and how she had thanked him. Just remembering how she'd thanked him made his lower body ache.

Of its own accord his gaze lowered to her legs again, and he couldn't help but remember the last time they'd made love. And how those same legs had flanked him, locked him between her thighs while she rode him hard. Damn. That should be the last thing he was remembering. What he should be thinking about was how Kara had caused him so much misery and pain.

With the latter thought flaming through his brain, he stood to pull out her chair for her, pasted a smile on his face and said in a tight voice, "Kara. Glad you could make it."

"Thanks," Kara said once she was seated across from him. She immediately picked up on his mood and knew it wasn't good. Just her luck it would be a carryover from yesterday.

She glanced around. "Nice place."

At least he hadn't chosen someplace where they'd dined before as a couple. This restaurant had recently opened and was part of the new development on this side of town. Since taking office as mayor of Charlotte, Morgan Steele had kept his campaign promise to grow the city by attracting new businesses and major corporations. While driving here she'd passed a huge medical technology complex as well as several communications firms.

But it wasn't the town or the restaurant she was focusing on right now. It was Virgil. And he was staring at her. "Is something wrong?" she asked him.

"No. Why do you ask?"

She shrugged. If he hadn't realized he'd been staring then she wouldn't be the one to enlighten him. "No reason."

Kara averted her eyes, looking down at the menu that had been placed in front of her. Moments later she glanced back up at him. "If it's okay with you, we can skip the meal and just discuss my action plan."

He frowned. "No, it's not okay with me. I skipped lunch and I'm hungry. Have you eaten something already?"

"No. I haven't eaten since breakfast."

"Then what's the problem?"

She could give him a list but decided the less he knew the better. "There's no problem, Virgil. I just don't want to take up any more of your time than necessary."

Virgil's penetrating stare deepened. "Trust me, Kara. You won't take up my time, mainly because I wouldn't let you."

He caught the glare in her eyes as she stared at him and it didn't bother him one way or another to know she was irritated with him. In a way, it should. She had a job to do and he was well aware that his unpleasant attitude wasn't making it easy for her. But then why should he make anything easy for her?

Sighing deeply, he placed his menu down. Hadn't he decided last week that he needed to move on, and in order to do that he had to get beyond all this anger he had for her? He looked over at her. "Kara?"

She glanced over at him. "Yes?"

"That apology you made six months ago. I accept it."

For a minute she didn't say anything but continued to stare at him. "I'm curious as to why you've decided to accept it now," she finally said.

He shrugged. "That shouldn't be so hard to figure out. We need to work together."

"And can we try to be friends?"

"No, I wouldn't go that far. I doubt we'll ever be friends. Forgiving does not mean forgetting."

She narrowed her gaze at him. "Then why bother?"

"Do you prefer I not accept your apology?"

She rolled her eyes. "Do whatever you want to do, Virgil. I don't care anymore."

He really didn't care that she didn't care. "Now that I've accepted your apology, let's decide what we're having for dinner."

After giving the waiter her order, Kara took a sip of her ice water. While Virgil was telling the waiter what he wanted for dinner, she took time to think about his acceptance of her apology.

Did he honestly assume she believed just saying he accepted her apology meant his attitude toward her would change? She knew better and like she'd told him, she really didn't care.

So why are you letting it bother you if you don't care? a voice inside her head asked.

"So how are things going at the office, Kara?"

The sound of his husky voice intruded into her thoughts. Why was he asking her that as if he really cared? However, since he was making an attempt to be civil, she would tell him. "Everything is going fine. Cassandra no longer works for me. She and Eric moved to San Diego to be closer to his family. That way she could get help with the baby."

Cassandra was the young woman who'd been her administrative assistant during the time they'd been a couple. But Cassandra had been more than just an employee, she had been her friend, as well. Cassandra and Eric had been two of the first people she'd met upon moving to Charlotte. The couple had lived in a condo a few doors down. Kara had been looking for office help at the same time Cassandra's job had been downsized.

"Baby? Cassandra had a baby?"

Kara couldn't help the smile that touched her lips. "Yes, a beautiful little girl named Regan. Regan is about two years old now."

Virgil smiled and Kara knew this smile was genuine. "I'm happy for her."

"So am I." Kara knew he would be happy for Cassandra because her former administrative assistant would bend the rules for Virgil. Like allowing him to sneak into her office when she was away to leave special notes on her desk, drop breakfast off for her or personally deliver her flowers…no matter how many times she would tell Cassandra she didn't want to be disturbed. And Kara would also admit Cassandra had been the one person who hadn't believed Marti's lie about Virgil.

She banished the thought from her mind. She was here for a business dinner, she reminded herself, so best to get to business. "I sent copies of my proposed action plan to both you and Matthew. I assume you looked over it."

"Can't speak for Dad but I haven't had the chance. So please enlighten me. What kind of strategies did you come up with, Kara?"

She wished there wasn't a tingling sensation that moved up her spine each and every time he said her name. Leaning back in her seat, she said, "Usually when I take on a client, I have three areas to concentrate on for improvement. What I consider the ABC's. Appearance, behavior and communication. There's nothing wrong with the way you dress and your communication skills are excellent. That means we need to zero in on your behavior."

"What do you suggest?"

"I note that, although your company is involved in a lot of worthwhile causes and is a huge benefactor to a number of charitable organizations, you're rarely seen supporting them."

He frowned. "I beg to differ. Just last week I was seen at that banquet for cancer research."

"Yes, you were. It was a black-tie affair. What about the cancer walk?"

"What about it?"

"You didn't participate in that. Your senior and junior executives did but you didn't. You only make appearances at the galas and balls, as if to court your clients there. You never appear where people in the community can see you, get to know you."

When he didn't say anything, she pressed on. "My recommendation is for you to be seen at a lot more of those types of events. Several of the major corporations around town will be getting together for a back-to-school extravaganza. I believe your company will be giving away book bags. I suggest you put in an appearance there instead of sending one of your executives."

Again, he didn't say anything, as if mulling over her suggestion. "Okay, I can do that."

"And there's a 5k walk for cancer research next month. I suggest you sign up for that, as well."

"Fine. Prepare a list of such activities you think I should participate in and pass the information on to my administrative assistant to add to my calendar."

Her next recommendation wouldn't go over so well with him. "I did my research and you've garnered quite a reputation around town with women."

She quickly held up her hand. "And before you try giving me that same spiel you gave your father about being single and dating whomever you please and not being accountable to anyone, you might want to rethink that assumption."

"Why should I?" he asked coolly.

"Because your image as a womanizer is hurting your company. It's giving Marv Hilton the ammunition he needs to make you seem worse than you really are. I agree that as a single, unattached bachelor you should be free to date whomever and whenever you want. However, to curtail what Hilton is saying, you need to tone down your social life."

"What do you mean 'tone down my social life'?"

"I strongly suggest that, for the next few months, you're seen around town with the same woman and no one else."

Chapter 6

Virgil's glacier-cold eyes narrowed. "That's not going to happen. There's no way I'll establish an exclusive relationship with any woman. Ever again." And he figured she knew the reason why. She had been the first and the last woman he'd claim exclusivity with and look where it had gotten him.

"It won't be permanent, Virgil. You've dated a lot of women over the years. I'm sure there's one you wouldn't mind being seen with for a while on a regular basis."

"There's not a single one. Besides, I don't want to give any one of them ideas that our relationship might one day go somewhere."

"Then we can hire a woman from a legitimate escort service. I happen to know someone who owns such a discreet company out of DC. She only hires educated women, some who speak several languages. They are poised, classy, sophisticated and—"

"No. There has to be another way. I just won't date as many women as I've done in the past."

She shook her head. "In order for this plan to work, Virgil, you will need to restrict yourself to being seen with one woman. It's a lifestyle change you temporarily need to make. Men feel threatened by you and want to keep their wives, sisters and daughters away from you. Some of those same men are potential clients. Is that what you want?"

"No. Hilton has become a pain in the ass that I plan to take care of."

Kara lifted a brow. "Take care of how?"

"Two can play his games."

"What do you mean?"

"I'm using York's investigative firm to dig into Whitney Hilton's past. Like I said. Two can play Hilton's game." Marv Hilton hadn't known the mistake he was making by messing with him. Virgil had never hesitated to retaliate before and he certainly wouldn't now.

"Digging up information on Whitney might serve your purpose of stopping Hilton from spreading his lies, but it won't help the issue of your image. You need to do something now even if it's nothing but a temporary fix."

He leaned in to make his point clearer. "Dating any woman exclusively for any amount of time is out of the question." He sat back when the waiter brought their meals and quickly departed.

"All I'm saying, Virgil, is you should think about my suggestion."

He picked up his fork and put an end to the conversation. "There's nothing to think about."

Virgil had finished his steak before he noticed conversation between him and Kara was nonexistent. And he was okay with that. He'd needed to gather himself anyway. As much as he didn't want them to, memories of other times they'd shared a meal were nearly suffocating him. Granted they'd never dined at this particular restaurant, but there had been others.

He glanced over at her and saw she was looking everywhere but at him as she ate. That was fine because he had no problem looking at her. And he did so as he took a leisurely sip of his drink. A spike of intense awareness shot up his spine. He wasn't surprised by the sudden reaction, just a little annoyed. How could he still desire a woman who'd hurt him the way she had? Slowly inhaling a deep breath, he drew her scent into his nostrils and the lower part of his gut ached with the familiar scent. And why was he concentrating on her lips?

She glanced over at him and caught him staring. She didn't say anything for a minute and then she smiled and asked, "How are your godbrothers?"

Virgil placed his glass down. Her smile was unexpected and for a quick second it threw him off-kilter. He rebounded quickly.

"Everyone is fine. Even the married ones."

"Why wouldn't they be? Even the married ones?"

"No reason."

"They seem happy."

He lifted a brow. "You've seen them with their wives?"

She shrugged and his gaze moved to her shoulders. He recalled the times he had kissed those shoulders and how they had felt beneath his lips and hands.

"Only from a distance," she said. "At that party six months ago."

Virgil nodded. "Yes, they are happy and I am happy for them. They married good women." He figured he would leave it at that, deciding not to add that his godbrothers had married women who trusted them. A hell of a lot more than she'd trusted him.

"And how are your parents?" he asked, trying not to recall the last time he'd spoken to her father and the names the man had called him.

"They're fine. In fact I talked to Dad last week. I hadn't known he'd called you when we broke up. He said he tried calling to apologize but couldn't reach you. You'd changed your number."

"Yes, I changed it." He didn't explain that he did it to end all ties with her.

"Yes, well… Dinner was great, Virgil. I hope we were able to agree on a number of things."

"We did. Once my personal assistant provides me with that list of events you prepare, I'll see how many I can add to my calendar." He gestured to the waiter for the check, then turned back to her. "As far as the other suggestion, I think there has to be another way, so cross that one off your list."

Virgil had barely made it inside his condo when his cell phone rang. It was Xavier. "Yes, X?" he asked after clicking on the line.

"Just checking in with everyone about next month when Winston comes home. He's arriving a week before the party so all of us can hang out. You game?"

"Yes," Virgil replied, pulling the tie from around his neck and removing his jacket. "Zion and I should be asking if you, W, Y and U are game since you four are married and have to check in with your wives."

"Don't be a smart-ass, V."

There was a pause and then Xavier asked, "So what's this I hear about your company hiring Kara to do an image makeover for you?"

Since he hadn't mentioned it to anyone but Winston, he figured Winston must have mentioned it to the others. "It was Dad's idea."

"Um, makes perfect sense. She's good at what she does. Cameron has used her firm to do group training for his employees on more than one occasion. He thought she did a fantastic job. Has she come up with a game plan?"

Cameron Cody was the founder and CEO of Cody Enterprises. Xavier was not only the executive attorney for Cody, he was considered Cameron's right-hand man and the two were very close friends. "Yes, she came up with a game plan," Virgil said, kicking off his shoes. "Her recommendation that I become more visible around town during charity events is doable."

"You do that already."

"Not to the extent she thinks that I should. I do a lot of black-tie affairs. I'm never seen walking marathons for charities or in the soup kitchens helping to feed the homeless. She thinks that's a good way to improve my image in the community."

"I agree. Cameron and the Steeles are always visible that way. It's good PR. There're a lot of new businesses moving to town, and when they're new to the area and want to size you up, their best level of measurement is how well you're thought of in the community. What else did she recommend?"

"The other thing she suggested is something I won't go along with."

"And what's that?"

"To began dating exclusively for a while to give the impression that my bachelor days are winding down."

"That might not be a bad idea, V. If you did that then you'll appear to be more focused on your company and not so much on seducing women."

Virgil put the phone on speaker as he removed his shirt, frowning. "I'm a single man with a healthy appetite for women, X. Why should I change my routine?"

Xavier's deep chuckle sounded through the phone. "Healthy appetite for women? Admit it, V, since your breakup with Kara you've taken the word *player* to a whole other level. Granted, you're up front with the women and let them know you're not into anything serious, but still, you're out there quite a bit. It's like you're afraid to give another woman the time and attention you gave Kara."

"I'm not afraid, just cautious. Once you get burned you're smart enough not to play with fire again." He picked up the phone again. "Anyway, I offered Kara a compromise."

"What was your compromise?"

"That instead of dating one woman exclusively, I decrease the number of women I'm seeing."

"What did she think of that?"

"I could tell she wasn't thrilled with the idea."

For a moment Xavier was quiet, and then he said, "Do me a favor, V, and let Kara do her job. I agree with her that total exclusivity would work better in your case, especially with that Hilton guy trying to be an ass. Fathers get real crazy when it comes to their daughters. In this case the justification for the craziness isn't there, but still. We all agree you need to clean up your act for a while. You're not talking about forever."

"Forever or not, like I told Kara, there's not a woman I can start seeing steadily who won't get crazy ideas she might become permanent. I'd rather not deal with that kind of foolishness."

"I know just the woman who might fit your needs. You've dated her before and the two of you hit it off. You won't have to worry about her getting any crazy ideas and she's definitely a looker."

Xavier had piqued Virgil's curiosity as well as his interest. "Who is she, man?"

"Kara."

Virgil nearly dropped the mobile phone out of his hand. "Kara? Are you crazy? Why in the hell would I want to start seeing Kara again? For any reason?"

"Dammit, V, I'm right here. You don't have to yell. What are you trying to do? Destroy my eardrums?"

"Better than getting in my car and going to your place to kick your ass."

"Calm down and think about it, V. First of all, according to you, there will never be anything between you and Kara again."

"There won't be."

"In that case, what are you worrying about? Kara is a well-respected and well-liked young woman in the community, who also happens to be a savvy businesswoman. When people see you together, they will think it was a smart move on your part. And like I said, she's a looker so it will squash any man's notion that you'd be after his wife, sisters or daughters. There wouldn't be a need when you have a woman like Kara who has both looks and brains. Besides, the two of you know it's only for show, to clean up your image. You don't have to worry about Kara getting any designs on you or you on her."

Virgil knew Xavier had made some valid points. But... "I don't know, X. I could barely tolerate being with her at dinner tonight."

"Why? You claim you don't feel anything for her."

"And I don't. I finally told her tonight that I accept her apology. But before you get any crazy ideas about me and

Kara rekindling anything, forget it. I'm telling you the same thing I told her. Forgiving doesn't mean forgetting."

"It should. You need to forgive and forget, V."

"Don't think that I can. She believed her sister's lie."

"We all make mistakes. Farrah doesn't have a sister but she and Natalie are best friends. Had Natalie told Farrah she saw me checking into a hotel with another woman, I can bet you Farrah would have believed her."

Farrah was Xavier's beautiful wife and regardless of what he said, Virgil knew she would not have believed her husband guilty of being unfaithful. "Kara should have known I would not have cheated on her. Hell, I gave up that lifestyle for her and gave her no reason to think I would be unfaithful. I loved her, X."

Virgil wasn't sure why he was trying to convince Xavier of anything. He'd had similar conversations with all his godbrothers. They had liked Kara and felt he'd been too hard on her.

"Kara loves her sister and she had no idea what Marti was capable of doing. Fortunately, I did. If you recall, Marti and I dated for three weeks. That's all the time it took for me to see Marti Goshay was bad news. I honestly think she has this thing against men."

Virgil shook his head. "I can't believe you'd suggest Kara as the woman I should be seen with exclusively."

"Think about it. It would sure piss Marti off royally if she thought you and Kara had gotten back together. It would serve her right."

Yes, it would, Virgil thought. Whenever he had run into Marti she'd smiled at him as though she'd taken great pleasure in ruining things between him and Kara. To this day Virgil didn't have a clue as to why. How could one sibling do something like that to another? It was crazy.

"Now that I think about it, you and Kara as a couple might not be a good idea after all," Xavier said.

Virgil lifted a brow. "Why?"

"You might run the risk of falling for her again."

"That won't happen."

"It might."

"It won't, X. I could never love Kara again." There was no need to tell his godbrother that the only thing he felt whenever he saw Kara was lust. The same degree of lust that he felt for any other good-looking woman.

Virgil glanced at his watch. His favorite television show would be on soon. "I need to go, X. I'll talk to you later."

"Hey, wait! There's a reason I called."

"It better be good. You've wasted twenty minutes of my time already talking about that Kara foolishness."

"It's good," Xavier said chuckling. "Farrah and I are having another baby."

Chapter 7

Frowning in irritation, Virgil stepped off the elevator to the executive floor of Bougard Enterprises. Why had he allowed Xavier to put that foolish notion into his head about Kara stepping into the role of his exclusive love interest? And what bothered him more than anything was that he'd been giving it serious consideration. How crazy was that?

He hadn't been able to sit and watch his favorite TV show for thinking about the possibilities…especially how the thought that he and Kara were back together would irk Marti to no end. But what really had him twitching in the gut was his attraction to Kara. Last night's dinner showed she could still raise his desire to an unprecedented level. It had taken every bit of control he had to concentrate on the taste of his steak and not allow his mind to be flooded with memories of the taste of her.

However, like Xavier had pointed out, such a move had its advantages. But just like there were pluses, he could think of several minuses.

He walked into the lobby adjacent to his office. "Good morning, Pam."

His administrative assistant gave him a huge smile. "Good morning, Mr. Bougard. Your father is waiting for you in your office."

Virgil's smile faded. "He is?"

"Yes."

Virgil assumed his parents would stay in Houston for at least another month. In addition to Leigh and Chad, his father's family still lived there as well as a few high school pals he'd stayed close to over the years. That was one of the reasons his parents had purchased a second home in Houston.

"Hold my calls for a while, Pam."

"Sure thing."

He walked into his office to find his father standing at the window staring out. "Dad, I hadn't expected you back in Charlotte for a while."

His father turned around and smiled. "And I hadn't expected to come back. Rhona remembered she agreed to be commencement speaker next weekend at UNC Charlotte. She wanted to return early to concentrate on writing her speech."

"I see." Virgil wondered if that meant his father would be hanging around Bougard Enterprises while he was in town. His father's next words gave him hope that would not be the case.

"Rhona suggested I fly back to Houston tomorrow. A few of the guys—former high school classmates of mine—planned a fishing trip this weekend." Matthew chuckled. "Your mother needs to work on her speech and claims I'll be a distraction if I am here."

"And I agree," Virgil said smiling. "You know how

quiet Mom likes it when she's in her Dr. Rhona B. Bougard mode, Dad."

In all honesty, Virgil was proud of his mother, who had
earned her PhD in education before he had started high
school. She had been the president of Johnson C. Smith
University for years before retiring two years ago.

Matthew nodded. "I definitely don't want to distract
Rhona and there's really no reason to hang around here. I
got a copy of Kara's action plan. It seems the two of you
have everything under control."

Virgil moved toward his desk to place his briefcase on
top of it. If his father assumed that was the case then he
would let him. "I take it you looked over what she proposed."

"Yes. Her recommendations are on point. I can see how
they will improve your image. Having a steady woman and
making yourself more visible in the community where it
counts are good strategies."

Virgil figured now was not the time to tell his father
that, although he intended to be more visible in the community, he had no intention of having a steady woman of
any kind.

"Well, I'll be going now. I'm flying back to Houston tomorrow for that fishing trip." Before heading for the door
Matthew said, "I'll see you when I get back next week,
and I'm looking forward to meeting your lady."

Virgil raised a brow. "What lady?"

"The one you select to be seen around town with on a
consistent basis. And it would be nice if you brought her
to UNCC's commencement to hear your mom's speech. I
anticipate a lot of people will be there and it will be a
great place to be seen with her. For you to bring her around
your parents will give the impression the two of you are
serious."

Matthew glanced at his watch. "I need to run. Can't keep my queen waiting." And then he opened the door and was gone.

Virgil sat down at his desk and stared at the closed door for a long moment while thinking that some days it didn't pay to get out of bed. He built a steeple with his fingers while leaning back in deep thought. His father naturally assumed he would fall in line with every one of Kara's recommendations since he expected his son to put the needs of Bougard Enterprises before his own.

Virgil knew there was no good reason for him not to go along with everything Kara had suggested. And taking everything into consideration, he also knew Xavier was right. Kara would be the logical choice if he did so.

He stood, walked over to the window and shoved his hands in his pockets as he looked out. How would she feel if he suggested such a thing? For all he knew she was already in a relationship with someone. He hadn't made it his business to keep tabs on her since their breakup. As far as he'd been concerned, the less he knew about what was going on with her, the better.

He had to admit that rekindling an affair with Kara would seem more believable to people than for him to suddenly develop a deep interest in one of his lovers. Why did the thought of having to spend so much time with Kara twist his insides into knots? Considering their strained relationship, could the two of them even pull such a thing off?

His cell phone rang and from the ringtone he knew it was York. He and his wife Darcy lived in New York. Pulling the phone out of his pocket, he clicked it on. "Yes, Y?"

"Just giving you an update. I've been gathering information on Whitney Hilton's past as you requested, but you might want me to take a look at her old man's, as well."

"Marv Hilton? Why?"

"I'm finding stuff on him that's rather interesting."

Virgil nodded. "Interesting enough to use as leverage to make him back off?"

"Possibly. He's a businessman. One who's well thought of in the community. I'm sure he wouldn't want anything from his past to resurface that could tarnish his image like he's trying to do to yours. What's the saying? Don't try cleaning up somebody else's house unless yours is spotless."

"I see what you mean. Let's see what we can find that could possibly stop him in his tracks."

"Will do."

After hanging up the phone, Virgil leaned back against the windowsill. If York was to find some damaging information on old man Hilton, then…

Virgil knew he couldn't get his hopes up on that possibility. Even if York was onto something, it might take weeks before Virgil received a final report. So he was back to square one. The action plan Kara had devised.

He knew what he had to do. Drawing in a deep sigh he walked back over to his desk and picked up his phone. "Yes, Mr. Bougard?"

"Pam, please get Kara Goshay on the line."

Kara looked up from her documents. "Yes, Janice?"

"Someone is here to see you and he doesn't have an appointment."

Kara raised an arched brow. "Who is it?"

From the tone of Janice's voice, it was apparent whoever had dropped by without an appointment was standing within listening range of their conversation.

"Mr. Virgil Bougard and he says he needs to speak with you immediately."

Kara frowned. Virgil had called twice today already, but at the time, she hadn't had the inclination to talk to him and had told Janice to tell him that she would call him back by the end of the day. She'd taken as much of him as she could at dinner last night. Dealing with him had left her emotionally drained and she wondered what was so important for him to seek her out today.

"Okay, Janice, please send him in."

Kara stood, not wanting to remember Virgil's last visit to her office and all the scandalous things they had done in here. It had taken months, or rather years, to wipe the memories from her mind and the last thing she needed was for them to resurface. But they were doing so anyway.

She had been working late one night and Virgil had surprised her with takeout dinner. She would never forget the moment she had looked up from the stack of papers on her desk to find him standing there with a delivery bag in his hand. The aroma of the food had gotten to her, but it was the look of heated desire in his eyes that had really set everything inside her throbbing.

She wasn't sure how they got through their meal. Needless to say, after finishing off the food, they had then proceeded to finish off each other. She wasn't sure who'd made the first move that night, nor had she cared. The main thing she remembered was that they'd both stripped naked and made out all over this room. After that night she hadn't been able to sit down at her desk and not remember the time he'd made love to her on top of it.

The door opened and Virgil walked in. Her breath caught with every step he took into the room. He had a serious expression on his face but that wasn't the primary thing holding her attention. As usual he was male perfection, immaculately dressed and handsome as sin. She really didn't like the way her body was responding to him and fought hard for control.

She watched Virgil close the door behind himself and glance over at her. "Thanks for seeing me, Kara."

Coming around her desk, she leaned back against the front of it. "What's this visit about, Virgil? What's so urgent that it couldn't wait until I could return your call later today?"

He shoved his hands into his pockets. "I've changed my mind."

She lifted a brow. "Changed your mind about what?"

"Your recommendation that I date a woman exclusively."

She was definitely surprised to hear this. But she also knew him well enough to know there was something more to it than him having a mere change of heart. "What made you change your mind?"

He didn't say anything for a moment. It was as if he needed to make sure whatever words he spoke were given much thought. "I realized nothing is more important to me than Bougard Enterprises, and that I would do just about anything to ensure its continued success. Even if it means making sacrifices."

She nodded. "I think you're making the right decision. And like I said yesterday, if you're not comfortable with dating someone you know already, I have a friend who owns a legitimate escort service. One that has a good reputation for being discreet. I can call—"

"That's not necessary. I have someone in mind."

She really shouldn't be surprised that he did, although he'd claimed otherwise yesterday. "Fine. Then I'll let you take care of that part of things. You don't need me for that."

"Oh, but I will need you."

She was confused. "Why would you?"

He crossed the room to stand in front of her. "Mainly because I want *you* to be that woman. The one I will be dating exclusively."

Chapter 8

Kara stared at him. She figured he had to be joking but the intense look in his eyes indicated he was dead serious. And considering his attitude at dinner last night and the things he'd said, that made her angry. "You have some nerve coming here and suggesting something like that. If I remember correctly, although you accepted my apology, you made it clear you would never forget about what I accused you of. You stated without batting an eye that we could never be friends. And I know the only reason you're even tolerating me is because of Matthew."

"Will you at least hear me out?"

She raised her chin. "Why should I?"

"Because I'm the client, and although you presented my company with a good action plan, there's an aspect of it that won't work unless modifications are made."

She narrowed her gaze at him. "I will work with any modifications you suggest as long as they don't include me."

"But they do include you, because this idea of yours can only work with you."

She rolled her eyes. "That's the most ridiculous thing I've ever heard. Why on earth would you, of all people, think that?"

"Because it's true. I will only feel comfortable with a woman that I know for certain won't get any ideas. You won't, since you know our relationship will never go back to the way it was before. And you know the arrangement is strictly a strategy to improve my image. I prefer not sharing such personal details with anyone else."

"And you wouldn't have to if we used that escort service that I told you about."

"It's too risky. What if someone was to discover it's nothing but a sham and that I'm paying someone to be seen with me?" He held up his hand when she opened her mouth to speak. "Before you say that there's no way anyone will ever find out, think again. Even with all the precautions and safeguards you put in place, can you guarantee that won't happen, Kara? Think about the consequences if it does. That would be a scandal Bougard Enterprises could never recover from."

Kara knew he was right, but—

He cut off her thoughts. "Your company was hired to fix my image, Kara, not make a bigger mess of it."

Virgil's words momentarily froze Kara and she held his gaze with her glare. "I know what my company was hired to do and I know what I'm doing, Virgil. Don't treat me like I don't."

She saw the agitation in his face when he said, "Bougard Enterprises would not have hired you if we didn't believe that you knew what you're doing, trust me. All I'm saying is that for this plan of yours to work, all players have to be in the game. I know what I'm capable of doing and I doubt I can pretend interest in some woman."

"But you can pretend interest in me? Knowing how you feel about me, that doesn't make sense," she countered.

"Think about it, Kara. It makes perfect sense. First of all, you and I have a history and a lot of people remember that history. When they see us together again they will assume we've worked out whatever differences kept us apart."

He paused a moment then added, "And as far as pretending interest in you, that will be easy, because that's all it will be—pretense. And I won't have to worry about you getting the wrong idea about anything."

Kara hated admitting it but everything he'd said was true. They had dated exclusively for a full year and had been known as a couple in the community. They'd gone to events together and were always seen together. Everyone had speculated that eventually a wedding date would be announced. Some had even considered them the darling couple of Charlotte. At least that's how the society pages had pegged them thanks to a popular news column called *Flo on the Ro*.

For some reason the editor, a woman by the name of Florence Asbury, a romantic at heart, enjoyed keeping readers abreast on the romantic lives of some of Charlotte's prominent singles. Originally her column was called *Flo on the Romance Scene*, but later the title was shortened and became known as *Flo on the Ro*. Flo enlisted what had become known as Flo's Posse and the group would roam around town keeping their eyes and ears open for any newsworthy romantic gossip. A few years ago Flo and her posse had decided Kara and Virgil were newsworthy and she enjoyed writing about them in her weekly column, which had quite a following.

Then their breakup happened and it had fueled rumors as to what had caused it. It didn't help matters when Virgil reverted back to his old ways of being Charlotte's number-one womanizer.

"And you honestly believe people will assume we've reconciled our differences and are back together?" she asked him.

"I don't see why not. They only speculated as to why we broke up. Besides, it doesn't matter. It's been years and people love a good make-up story."

Although Kara knew that to be true, she just wasn't sure that she and Virgil should be in the starring roles of one. He indicated he could pretend, but could she? And why should she? She wasn't responsible for his less-than-stellar image. However, she had been hired to fix it. And for that reason, a part of her refused to let his company be the one she failed to make into another success story. But still...

"I have to think about this, Virgil. There has to be another way."

"If there is, you need to come up with it by next weekend. Mom is keynote speaker at UNCC's graduation and Dad wants me to bring whatever woman I've decided to date exclusively. He figures it will be the perfect time for us to be seen together."

Kara agreed with Matthew that it would be the perfect time—if the plans didn't include her. "Like I said, I have to think about it. I'll get back in touch with you."

He nodded and, without saying anything else, he turned and walked out of her office.

"So let me get this straight," Cassandra Gilbert said to Kara through the phone line. "You found out Marti lied so you apologized to Virgil. He didn't accept your apology at first but has since come around, although grudgingly.

And now his image needs repairing because of some scandal with another woman. Your company has been hired to fix it. And in doing so you'll be presented as his exclusive love interest."

"Yes, that's about it," Kara responded, setting her wineglass on her coffee table. She had needed someone to talk to and couldn't wait to get home to call her friend.

"In a way it's a rather smart move. Everyone will simply think the two of you have made up and gotten back together."

"That's the plan."

"Okay, so what's the problem?"

Kara rolled her eyes. "We're talking about Virgil Bougard, Cassandra."

"I know who we're talking about, and the way I see it, there shouldn't be a problem unless…"

"Unless what?"

"Unless you're not as indifferent to him as you claim you are."

Kara frowned. "What do you mean by that?"

"I think you know what I mean, Kara. You loved Virgil too much not to feel anything for him now."

"Have you forgotten that I thought he betrayed me? When that happened, I stopped loving him," Kara reminded her.

"Yes, I know how hurt you were, but did you really stop loving him?"

"Of course I did. I moved on."

"Moved on? Who are you trying to fool? You never allowed yourself to get seriously involved with anyone else. Yes, you dated after Virgil but you never let anyone get close. I was there, Kara. I know. Besides, Virgil isn't a man a woman can fall out of love with easily."

Kara defended herself. "Considering that I thought Virgil had betrayed me, falling out of love with him would have been understandable."

"Understandable, yes, but it would not have been you. Like I said, you loved Virgil too much. You were hurt, devastated, but you can't convince me that you fell out of love with him completely."

Kara wanted to argue with her friend, but Cassandra moved on to another topic. "I just can't believe Marti did that to you."

"Sometimes I can't believe it myself. I probably would never have found out if I hadn't overheard that phone call."

"Did she say why she did it?"

"She claims she was looking out for my best interests and felt Virgil would have eventually hurt me."

"That's crazy. Virgil loved you. Anybody could see that. I guess that's one of the reasons I never thought he was guilty even when you did."

Kara drew in a deep breath. "And now he hates me."

"I doubt if he could hate you, Kara."

"Trust me, he does. I can see it in his eyes whenever he looks at me."

"Yet he wants the two of you to pretend to be lovers?"

"Only to serve a purpose," Kara said drily.

"So what are you going to do?"

"I don't know. It's my proposed action plan that he's using. I just didn't think he would involve me personally. I'll sleep on it and hopefully I will make the right decision tomorrow."

"If I were in your shoes do you know what I would do?"

A part of Kara was afraid to ask. "What?"

"I would use that opportunity with Virgil to your advantage and remind him why he fell in love with you in the first place. I would make him remember how good the two of you were together."

Kara shook her head even though her friend couldn't see her. "I'm not even sure I wish that was possible."

"Regardless of what you're saying, I believe you and Virgil should be together. Your love just needs rekindling. A love as strong as the two of you had will never die."

Kara wasn't as convinced as Cassandra seemed to be. "He's changed. It's like his heart is made of ice and it's my fault for not trusting him."

"If his heart has turned to ice then you owe it to yourself to melt it."

Kara fought back her tears. "I honestly don't think I can."

"And I believe that you can. There's something you've omitted from your action plan, Kara. It's the only thing that can really help improve Virgil's image and behavior permanently. It will require that you and Virgil work out your differences and get back together for real. Otherwise, all you'll be doing is applying a temporary fix to the problem. Virgil might not know it, but he needs you back in his life. You were able to change him for the better once before and I believe you can do it again. The man loved you. He was happy back then. You owe it to yourself… and to him…to make him happy again."

Cassandra's words echoed in Kara's thoughts long after they'd said goodbye. Later that night after she had taken her shower and slid between the sheets, Kara couldn't stop thinking about everything Cassandra had said. Her friend was such an optimist, yet… *If his heart has turned to ice then you owe it to yourself to melt it.*

Cassandra was right on point about the changes Virgil had made after they'd begun dating. When she'd met Virgil, he'd had a reputation of getting any woman he wanted. Yet she had made him earn his way into her bed. His entire outlook on life had changed and she knew for certain he'd given up his entourage of women just to be with her. She had been his one and only...until Marti's lie had made her believe otherwise.

And now he was back to his old womanizing ways. And she of all people was hired to clean up his image. Cassandra was right. All her company would do was put a bandage on the problem and not provide a permanent solution. It would be just a matter of time before he resorted back to his womanizing ways.

Could she be Virgil's permanent solution as Cassandra thought?

By the time sleep had lulled her to close her eyes, she had at least admitted something to herself. She was still in love with Virgil Bougard.

Chapter 9

"Mr. Bougard, Kara Goshay is—"

"Put her call through," he interrupted.

He hoped Kara had made a decision about what he'd proposed to her yesterday, especially after he read the article appearing in that morning's newspaper. And then there was the phone call he'd received from Thomas Fortner.

Fortner had informed Virgil that he was considering taking his business elsewhere after playing golf with Marv Hilton this weekend. Virgil could just imagine what embellishment Hilton had added to the story to make Fortner consider doing such a thing.

"Ms. Goshay is not on the phone, sir. She's here and would like to see you."

Kara was here? "Please send her in."

He clicked off the phone and adjusted his tie as he stood. In the old days Kara rarely read the morning paper before noon so chances were she was unaware of the article. In that case, was she here to turn down what he'd suggested yesterday? Fearing that possibility, last night he'd tried coming up with a plan B and had even gone so far as to make a list of other women. Not a single one he'd considered a strong candidate.

The door to his office opened and Kara walked in. He wondered if there would ever be a time when her entrance into any room would not take his breath away. As usual she looked beautiful. Professional and sexy rolled into one. Her chocolate-brown business suit emphasized her small waist and curvy hips. However, it was what was beneath that business suit that he was remembering so well.

It wasn't even ten in the morning, yet she looked as radiant as any woman had a right to be this early. She had a graceful, fluid walk, something he'd always admired watching, and he wasn't surprised at the sexual chemistry that surrounded them. It had always been that way and always would, regardless of how they barely tolerated each other.

"Kara, to what do I owe this visit?" He studied her. There was something about her that looked different this morning and he wasn't sure what it was.

"I've made a decision regarding your request yesterday. The one about us dating exclusively just for show."

"And?"

"And like you said, there could never be anything between us again. But letting people assume there is might work in our favor. Your image will improve and I'll get another success story to boast about."

So in essence she would be using him like he would be using her. Why did the thought of that bother him? There was no reason for it. Like she said, in the end both of them would benefit.

"Are you willing to attend that commencement with me next weekend?" he asked her.

"Yes. I'm sure your father will explain things to your mother so she'll know the truth."

"I'm sure he will." He paused a minute then asked, "This plan will also require us to be seen together on occasion, around town, having dinners, going to movies. Do you have a problem with that?"

"I should be asking you that, Virgil. Will you have a problem with us being seen as if we're getting back together?"

Virgil knitted his brow for a second as he contemplated. "No, I won't have a problem with it. Those I care about will know the truth."

"Fine. Then I'll see you next weekend," she said, turning to leave.

"Meet with me later today."

She turned back around. "Why?"

"To plan our strategy. Did you see the newspaper this morning?"

"No."

He picked up the copy off his desk and handed it to her. "We've drawn interest already."

Kara read the headlines in the *Flo on the Ro* column.

Has Charlotte's Biggest Womanizer Finally Come to His Senses?

Virgil Bougard was seen having dinner last week with Kara Goshay. It's been almost four years and the big question on this editor's mind is...are these two on again? I certainly hope so and think it's about time. Stay tuned.

A frown bunched Kara's brows. Below the article was a photo of her and Virgil enjoying dinner together that day at the Goldenrod Restaurant. Shaking her head, she handed the paper back to Virgil. "Who took that picture?"

"No telling. Smartphones can turn anyone into a photographer these days. Now we have to deal with everyone speculating. For us that might be a good thing. We need to keep the momentum going by being seen together often."

"We'll be seen together next weekend at UNCC's commencement ceremony."

"I think a couple of times before then wouldn't hurt. Let's meet later to discuss it. Plan strategies."

Kara was inwardly elated he'd suggested meeting with her later; especially after she'd awakened that morning to decide Cassandra's suggestion last night had merit. She would use this opportunity to remind Virgil how good things used to be between them. Even if it didn't work, she felt it was a risk worth taking. The key was to not let him suspect anything, which meant she couldn't appear too eager for them to spend time together.

She gave a half-hearted protest. "I have a full day today, Virgil. I'm not sure I'll have time later."

His eyes narrowed. She could tell he didn't like to be denied. He was a man who was used to getting whatever he wanted. "I suggest you squeeze me in somehow, Kara."

She held his gaze and wondered what was there in the penetrating depths staring back at her. Cockiness? Anger? Lust? She hadn't missed the latter when she'd entered his office. He might be mad at her but she had clearly seen lust in his eyes when she'd arrived. That had given her hope. "Fine," she finally said. "We can meet somewhere later this evening. Have your administrative assistant call and—"

"I will be the one who calls you," he said, taking his phone out of his pocket. "What's your number?"

"It didn't change."

He nodded and then punched in her phone number. She

couldn't help being pleased that he remembered it. When her cell phone rang, he said, "Now you have my new number. Use it to reach me if you need to."

"I doubt I will." Turning back toward the door, she was surprised to hear him say, "You never know." Then she walked out.

When the door closed shut behind Kara, Virgil sat down at his desk and leaned back in his chair. He'd figured out what was different about her today. Her hair. It still hung to her shoulders but instead of being curly it was straight. He always liked the curly hair style on her but thought he liked this one even better.

He then frowned. The fact that he'd noticed such a thing didn't sit well with him. Why would it matter to him one iota how she wore her hair? But he couldn't help remembering those times he would run his fingers through the thick strands and how he would enjoy gripping a handful of her hair whenever they made love.

He muttered a curse under his breath, knowing he had to get control. Regardless of the picture they would be painting for others, there was no going back. He would tell himself that a million times a day if he had to.

Kara entered the Racetrack Café. Unlike the last time she'd met Virgil for dinner and he'd taken her to a place they'd never dined in before, this was the very place they used to hang out most of the time. She was immediately flooded with memories of how they would meet here after work before heading to her place or his.

Instead of calling, he had texted her instructions to meet here. At first she'd found it odd he would choose this place since it had such a history for them. Then again, she figured if he wanted to make it seem as if they were getting back together, this was the perfect place.

The first thing she noticed was that the café wasn't crowded, which was unusual for a Thursday night.

She glanced around and saw him. When their gazes met, she suddenly felt a little breathless and forced her feet forward to where he was now standing. Unlike her, he'd taken the time to go home and change into jeans. Since she had a late business meeting, she was still wearing her two-piece suit and heels.

"Sorry, I'm late," she said, trying to ignore the rapid beating of her heart. "Late meeting."

"No problem," he said, sitting back down after she slid into the booth across from him. "Glad you could make it. I saw you when you parked so I went ahead and ordered your Arnold Palmer."

"Thanks." She tried not to smile at the thought that he remembered her favorite drink. "You said we needed to meet to plan a strategy." She could tell he'd showered because her nostrils picked up the clean scent of man as well as his familiar aftershave. It had always been her favorite.

"Yes, but that discussion can come later. I thought we'd eat first," he said, breaking into her thoughts.

Kara tried to avoid looking at him by glancing around. "Not a lot of people here tonight."

"There's a big Panthers pep rally going on at the stadium. They're gearing up for tomorrow's preseason opener against the Eagles."

"Oh."

He chuckled. "You're still not a football fan, I see."

"No. Some things never change, I guess." Their gazes connected and she couldn't help but feel the chemistry. The same one they'd always shared. Despite how much he disliked her, that hadn't changed, which was a good thing.

He finally broke eye contact with her when the waitress delivered their drinks. She quickly took a sip of hers and appreciated the feel of the cold liquid moving down her throat. She felt hot and needed to cool off. Sitting across from her was the one man who had the ability to make her burn, both inside and out.

"So how was your day, Kara?"

She glanced back over at him. "Do you really want to know or are you just being nice?"

Virgil held her gaze. "Both." Bougard Enterprises was the only reason he was sitting across from her now and not at that pep rally like everyone else. But still the man in him appreciated a good-looking woman, which was why he'd felt a tightening in his gut when he'd seen her walk into the café. "So tell me, how was your day?"

He watched her shrug her shoulders before taking another sip of her drink. "It went rather well, actually. I was hired to do a series of leadership seminars at Lufton Financial Services. And I also found out that I've been nominated by our local league of women voters for Businesswoman of the Year."

A smile automatically touched his lips. He was genuinely happy for her. "Congratulations for both achievements."

"Thanks."

"We need to celebrate this weekend."

She lifted a brow. "We do?"

"Yes. It will be a good excuse for us to be seen together. I'll make the arrangements."

She reached out and the touch of her hands on his sent stirring sensations ricocheting all through him, sensations he was sure she felt, too. But she didn't let go. "No, let me make the arrangements, Virgil."

While gazing into her eyes, he thought like he always had that they were the most beautiful pair any woman could possess. Tonight he saw a determination in them that he hadn't seen in a long time, if ever.

"All right. You make all the arrangements," he said, giving in and not having a problem doing so. He liked the way her touch was making him feel, although he wished otherwise.

She smiled and released his hand, and damn if that smile didn't make his gut tighten even more. "You won't be disappointed," she said.

A short while later Kara pushed her plate aside. Virgil had invited her here to discuss strategies but so far they hadn't done that. Over dinner she'd asked questions about his family and when he'd told her his sister was pregnant, she couldn't help but smile.

She'd met Leigh and liked her a lot. Right before she and Virgil had broken up Leigh and Chad had gotten engaged. Kara had been surprised to get an invitation to the wedding but because she'd known Virgil would not have wanted her there, she hadn't attended. But she had sent a wedding gift. And now to hear that Leigh and Chad would be parents was wonderful news.

And when she'd asked, he'd told her about his father's family, some of whom she'd gotten to know when she had attended one of the Bougard family reunions with him in Houston. Matthew had come from a large family that consisted of seven brothers and three sisters. Of all his siblings Matthew had been the only one who hadn't attended college in Texas. Leaving home to attend Morehouse had been a big step and then settling down in Charlotte instead of returning to Houston after graduation had been another one. To compensate, he'd made certain both his son and daughter had been Texans by birth by making sure a pregnant Rhona had been in Houston when it was time for her to deliver.

Sitting here with him, chatting amiably, she couldn't help remembering the last time they'd dined together. She'd mentioned the possibility of them becoming friends and he'd flat out rejected the idea. She hoped he'd change his stance on that since they'd be seeing a lot of each other in the coming weeks. But she had to be realistic and remember Virgil was merely playing a role, one he intended to play to the hilt to benefit his company.

When their dishes had been cleared away, Virgil asked, "Have you noticed a couple of people looking over here at us?"

His question made her discreetly scan the café. It wasn't as empty as it had been, which meant the pep rally had ended. Virgil was right. Several people were openly staring at them, and Kara wondered if it had anything to do with the article appearing in this morning's newspaper. Thanks to *Flo on the Ro*, they were now the couple to watch.

"Give me your hands."

She looked back at Virgil. Not understanding his request, she complied anyway. He took her hands and entwined their fingers. She raised her brow while keeping her gaze trained on his face, trying to ignore the warmth of his fingers interwoven with hers. She was sure every cell in her body was heating up.

"Now we're giving them something to look at," he said in a deep husky voice that sent shivers down her spine.

"Are we?"

A smile touched the corners of his lips. "If you don't believe me just watch." And he then leaned and kissed their joined hands.

Kara couldn't stop the tremble that immediately coursed through her. She licked her lips when a familiar sensation stirred in the lower part of her body. "Do you think this is necessary?" she asked, letting out a slow, controlled breath.

"Don't you?" he asked softly. "Tell me what you think since you came up with the action plan. Was this not what you had in mind for the woman I was to date exclusively? Were we not supposed to give people the impression that we're all into each other?"

"Yes, but I wasn't supposed to be that woman, Virgil."

"But unfortunately, Kara, you are now that woman. Now lean toward me a bit. Don't ask why, just do it."

Drawing in a deep breath, and with their hands interlinked and heat spreading up her thighs, she leaned in closer. And that's when he leaned in and brushed his lips softly against hers. She figured the kiss was meant to be quick, however, instead of either of them leaning back, their lips remained mere inches from each other. The most logical thing was to kiss again. So they did. This one lasted longer than the last, and when he swept his tongue across her lips, she felt fire curling in her stomach.

When their lips parted he tilted his head and looked at her and said in a deep throaty voice, "I think that will do for now."

"Will it?" she asked in a breathless whisper.

"Yes," he said, slowly releasing her hands. "Now it's time to leave."

"But I thought we were here to plan our strategy."

A smile touched the corners of his lips. "We just did. Come on and let me walk you to your car."

Chapter 10

The next morning Virgil gazed out his bedroom window and thought back on last night at the café with Kara. For the umpteenth time he tried convincing himself that kissing her had served a purpose. They'd had an audience so it had been the perfect time to put on a show.

But did he have to kiss her a second time and taste her with his tongue?

There was no doubt in his mind that he had felt something in those kisses, something he hadn't counted on. It was not intended to mean anything. He'd been merely acting out a part and nothing else. However, the moment his mouth had touched hers, emotions he hadn't expected had flooded him. Those emotions should have been buried long ago, never to resurface again.

Some emotions were to be expected, he told himself. After all, regardless of the reason they'd broken up, Kara had been the one and only woman he'd ever loved. Not feeling something would have been impossible.

He had walked her to her car and, when he'd opened the door and she'd slid her body onto the leather seat, exposing a luscious thigh in the process, a pang of desire had shot through him. He'd been tempted to act on it so he'd given in to temptation and placed a kiss on the side of her throat. He'd gone even further and used his tongue to cop a taste when he licked her skin there.

Kara's sharp intake of breath had let him know she'd felt it. There had been no logical reason for his tongue to come into contact with her skin, and now he was paying for his actions. He was convinced the taste of her had somehow saturated his insides. After she'd driven off, he had quickly walked to his car, gotten inside and driven home totally aroused. He still was.

He didn't want to be sexually attracted to Kara. It had taken only a kiss to show that she could still get under his skin. And if that wasn't bad enough, the taste of her had him thinking of nothing else but tasting her again. And why on earth had he suggested they spend the weekend together? What had he been thinking?

The cell phone on his nightstand rang but he didn't have to answer it to know who was calling. It was Uriel. Uriel and his wife, Ellie, were spending the summer on Cavanaugh Lake, which was located a few miles from Gatlinburg.

Crossing the room, he picked up the phone. "Yes, U?"

"I came into town yesterday to attend the pep rally. Afterward a group of us went to the Racetrack Café and I heard you'd been there earlier with Kara. I also heard the two of you were all lovey-dovey." There was a brief pause before Uriel asked, "So, what's going on, V? Are you and Kara getting back together?"

"Not in a million years," Virgil replied in a gruff voice.

"In that case you have some explaining to do."

Virgil rolled his eyes. "Do I?"

"What do you think?"

Virgil drew in a deep breath. He didn't want his god-brothers getting the wrong idea about him and Kara. "Have you had breakfast yet?"

"No."

"Good. Join me, I'll explain everything."

"Okay. Where?"

"Meet me at the Racetrack Café in a half hour."

Kara stretched her body, not ready to get out of bed just yet. She glanced over at the clock and thought since she didn't have any appointments this morning there was no rush to get to the office. She would just lie here a minute longer and bask in her memories from yesterday.

He had kissed her. She would admit by Virgil Bougard's standards both kisses had been rather chaste. She knew from past experiences that Virgil had the ability to plow you with a kiss that could make your head swoon for days. But the lasting effect had been just as powerful. Then when he'd walked her to her car, he had licked her throat. The feel of his tongue on her skin had stirred something deep within her.

And then he'd suggested they spend some time together this weekend, to be seen in public as a couple. She would plan the activity and she already had an idea what she wanted them to do. They would—

Her cell phone rang, interrupting her thoughts and quickening her pulse. Virgil had her number. Was he calling her?

Reaching for the phone, she glanced at caller ID and felt her heart sink. It was Marti. It had been months since the two of them had communicated and she couldn't help wondering what her sister wanted. She sat up in bed and clicked on the phone. "Yes, Marti?"

"Is the article I read in yesterday's newspaper true?" Marti asked excitedly. "Are you and Virgil really back together?"

Kara frowned. Why would Marti sound happy for them after all she'd done? "And what if we are?"

"Then I'm happy for you. I know you don't believe me but I truly am. I was wrong about Virgil, and in trying to protect you, I went too far. I know you hate me and—"

"I don't hate you but you had no right to do what you did and then to brag about it to the person you were talking to on the phone. You know the pain I went through when I thought Virgil was unfaithful. You let me go through that. You even had the gall to give me your shoulder to cry on when you deliberately lied about him."

"I thought I was protecting you, Kara. Why can't you believe that? Why can't you forgive and forget so we can move on?"

Kara drew in a deep breath. Hadn't she wondered the same thing about Virgil when he hadn't accepted her apology? But there was one difference. "Because I don't believe you regret what you did. Don't forget I overheard that conversation you had with that person on the phone. You were bragging and boasting about how you screwed up my relationship with Virgil. If I didn't know better, I'd think the reason you did it was because you wanted him for yourself."

"That's not true! I told you why I did it. I didn't believe he really loved you and thought he would eventually hurt you. You're my baby sister and I didn't want you to go through the pain that…"

When Marti didn't finish what she was about to say, Kara asked, "What? What were you going to say, Marti?"

"Nothing," Marti said, much too quickly to suit Kara. "I was wrong about him and I'm sorry. But it's not about us anymore, Kara. It's about Mom and Dad."

Kara frowned. "What are you talking about?"

"They're on bad terms because of us. It's all my fault that there's a rift between me and you, and I hate that Mom and Dad are involved. Please let's meet this morning for breakfast. We need to at least talk, Kara."

Kara didn't say anything for a minute. She hated how the disjunction between her and Marti was affecting her parents. Maybe she should take Virgil's lead and forgive but not forget. She doubted she could ever trust her sister again.

"I need to shower and get dressed. It will take an hour."

"Great!"

Kara tried not to notice the excitement in Marti's voice. "You decide where."

"You know I'm going to say Racetrack Café. Their waffles are to die for."

She shook her head. Unknowingly Marti had selected the place where she'd dined just last night with Virgil. How could she sit there this morning and not be swamped by memories of his kisses?

"So there you have it, U. The only reason I'm coming within ten feet of Kara is for business."

Uriel Lassiter lifted a brow. "You sure about that? From what I heard, your mouth was playing around hers pretty damn good."

Virgil frowned. "That kiss was just for show."

"Whatever you say," Uriel said in a tone suggesting he didn't believe him. "Did you finally come around to accepting Kara's apology?"

"I told her I would forgive her but I wouldn't forget."

"People make mistakes. Even you, V."

Virgil's frown deepened. "You're right. My biggest mistake was ever falling in love with her."

Uriel shook his head. "I'd be wasting my time if I told you to let it go. I've suggested it before and you haven't. You recall how for all those years I avoided Ellie."

Yes, Virgil remembered. Ellie had played a teenage prank on Uriel that had taken him nearly ten years to forget. Eventually he had and the two were now married.

"I told you that I accepted her apology."

"But you're still holding a grudge."

"I am not holding a grudge. Doing so would require too much time and effort, and I don't intend to give Kara any more of either than I have to."

Uriel took a sip of his coffee. "I'm surprised Kara agreed to go along with pretending to be in an exclusive affair with you."

Virgil shrugged. "She wasn't happy about it. But Kara is getting paid to improve my image, no matter what it takes for her to do so."

Uriel gave him a hard glare. "I hope you don't have any sort of revenge on your mind, V."

Virgil didn't say anything as he took a sip of his coffee. He would be lying if he said the thought hadn't crossed his mind. As far as he was concerned if Kara hadn't believed her sister's lie they would still be together now. Possibly even married with a kid or two. Her lack of trust in him had ruined everything, including his belief in love.

"V?"

He met Uriel's gaze. "No, but I don't intend to make things easy for her."

"So in other words, you intend to be difficult."

A wry smile touched Virgil's lips. "Maybe. Maybe not."

"Well, I hope you don't plan to be difficult today."

Virgil raised a brow. "Why?"

"Because Kara just walked in and Marti is with her."

Virgil held Uriel's gaze in a hard stare. Then he slid his chair back, stood and said in a deadly calm voice, "Then by all means, U, let's go say hello to the Goshay sisters."

When the waitress placed the menu in front of them, Kara knew before they shared a meal, there was something she needed to ask her sister. For some reason she thought there was more to it than what Marti had told her.

"Marti, I need to know the truth as to why you lied about Virgil."

"Why are you bringing that up again, Kara? I told you I was sorry and why I did it. Why can't we move on? It's not like you and Virgil haven't worked things out and aren't back together."

Kara didn't say anything, knowing her sister would be the last person she told the true nature of her and Virgil's relationship. "Regardless of whether Virgil and I are back together, Marti, I feel there is more to it. Something you aren't telling me."

"You're wrong. I told you my reason so can we just drop it?"

She heard the annoyance in Marti's voice and wished she could drop it, but for some reason she couldn't. And another thing... She needed her sister to understand that rebuilding their relationship would take time. The only reason she was even here now was because of what Marti had shared about their parents.

Kara suddenly felt a rush of heat travel up her spine. When she glanced around she saw him. Virgil. And he, along with his godbrother Uriel, was headed straight toward their table. Virgil's features were unreadable so she had no idea of his mood. The one thing she did know was that Marti definitely wasn't one of his favorite people.

She inhaled sharply. Would Virgil confront Marti? The café was crowded and the last thing Virgil needed was make a scene. She could just imagine the article that would appear in *Flo on the Ro*. Virgil's image would go from bad to worse.

Knowing she had to take quick action, she stood, pasted a huge smile on her face and reached out to embrace Virgil when he reached her table. "Virgil, I didn't know you were having breakfast with Uriel here this morning," she said, wrapping her arms around him and looking up at him with a pleading look in her smile.

And then she leaned up on tiptoe and brushed her mouth against his in what was intended to be a quick kiss. When she was about to pull back, Virgil wrapped his arms around her and despite where they were, slanted his mouth across hers.

Virgil figured two could play whatever game Kara was playing for Marti's benefit. Although it irked him that they had her in their audience, at the moment he didn't give a damn since an opportunity was an opportunity, especially if it was for the media's sake. There was no reason he shouldn't take advantage, so he gave her a short, hot, tongue-stroking kiss.

It hadn't been the kiss he'd he wanted to plow her mouth with, but for now it had been effective. When he released her, he said softly, "Good morning to you, sweetheart. Uriel called this morning and we decided to get together for breakfast."

With every degree of control Virgil had, he turned and looked at Marti, fighting hard to keep the glare out of his eyes and the sting from his voice. "Marti."

"Virgil."

And then Kara gave Uriel a hug. "Hi, Uriel."

Uriel smiled. "How are you, Kara?" He then looked over at Marti. "And you?"

"I'm fine, Uriel. Thanks for asking" was Marti's response.

With pleasantries, even fake ones, out of the way, Virgil took Kara's hand, lifted it to his lips and kissed it. "Made plans for our weekend yet?"

Kara nodded. Her body reeled when she felt his tongue swipe across her fingers. "I'm working on them," she said, trying to keep her voice normal as sensations swept through her mind. What he'd done had been deliberate. Just like when his tongue had swept across her neck last night. When they'd been a couple, he'd had a penchant for using his tongue to lick her all over.

He smiled at her. "Good. I'll call you later."

"You guys leaving already? You're free to join us," Marti invited.

Kara frowned. Did her sister really think Virgil would? Marti had to know the high degree of disdain he held her in.

Virgil looked down at Marti and said politely, "No thank you." He then turned his attention back to her. "Have a good day."

"You, too," she said, knowing his patience with Marti had probably worn thin by now. As a way to thank him for not losing his cool with her sister, she leaned up and brushed her lips against his cheek.

When Kara stepped back, she knew they'd given a good show to anyone watching...and it seemed a number of people were. "We'll definitely talk later," he said softly.

She deciphered the underlying message in his words. They would talk and she had a feeling it was a conversation she'd prefer not having with him.

Later that day Kara had finished a survey on a potential client when her cell phone rang. When she picked it up off her desk and saw it was Virgil, her breath caught in her throat. She had deliberately put off calling him, and Virgil, probably sensing as much, had decided to contact her instead.

She braced herself for the conversation they were about to have. "Yes, Virgil?"

"What are our plans for this weekend?"

Kara drew in a deep breath. She wondered if he remembered that was the question he would call and ask her every Friday when they were dating. During those days it was a foregone conclusion that their Saturdays and Sundays would be spent together. She wished she could go back in time and relive those days when the two of them had been so much in love and enjoyed being together.

"How does spending the day at Carowinds sound?" she asked him.

Of all things, she hadn't expected the sound of his rich chuckle. She was so surprised by it that she held her phone away from her a minute just to stare at it, to make sure the sound had actually come from her phone. She fought off getting all emotional because she hadn't thought she would ever hear the sound of laughter in his voice again.

"Why aren't I surprised?" he asked with deep amusement in his voice.

"I don't know. Why aren't you?" Even if he wasn't surprised by what she'd planned, she definitely was surprised by how well he was taking it.

"Well, for one thing, I know how much you enjoy amusement parks, particularly those scary rides."

His words made her smile. "You enjoy them as much as I do."

He chuckled again. "That is true."

She leaned back in her chair and recalled how they both had a thrill for the wild side, especially those crazy roller coasters that could send your heart racing and your mind spinning. For them, the scarier the better. Carowinds, a four-hundred-acre amusement park that boasted over fifteen such rides, had been one of their favorite places to visit on the weekends. They'd found those heart-stopping rides the perfect way to relieve stress.

Thinking she owed him a reason for her choice, she said, "I figured since it's local, we'll be seen and that would be good."

Virgil didn't say anything for a minute. Kara's words had reeled him back in and made him remember that the trip to Carowinds, like everything else they would be doing together, was to serve a purpose.

"You figured right. So what time do you want me to pick you up in the morning?"

"Um, what about ten?"

"That will work." There was no reason not to end their conversation so he said, "I'll see you then. Goodbye."

"Virgil, wait!"

"Yes?"

"About Marti…"

His jaw tightened. "What about her?"

He noticed the slight pause before she replied. "Thank you for handling things the way you did this morning, considering everything."

Tossing the pen on his desk, while trying not to recall the pen had been part of a set she'd given him for his birthday, he said, "Your sister is your problem, Kara, not mine. This morning wasn't the first time I've seen Marti since finding out about her part in our breakup."

"So you knew? Even before I told you six months ago?"

"Yes."

"But how? I never told you how I'd come across the information."

No, she hadn't told him, he thought, standing to stretch his tall frame. "You didn't have to tell me. I figured it out. I was never one of your sister's favorite people, although around you she pretended otherwise."

"I never knew."

He paused a minute before he continued. "Like I said, Kara, Marti is your problem. How you deal with your sister is your business. But just so you know, I can barely tolerate being around her. You might have apologized but she never has, which makes me believe she doesn't regret what she did."

"She says the reason she did it was because she thought you would eventually hurt me."

"I never gave her reason to think that, Kara. You and I had been happy together. For her to tell such a lie is unacceptable. Who would do what she did to their sister, no matter what they thought?"

Kara didn't answer his question and Virgil knew there was no logical way for her to do so anyway. "Look, I have a lot of work to do before I can leave here. I'll see you tomorrow morning, Kara."

"All right."

When he disconnected their call, he shoved his hands into the pockets of his pants and walked over to the window. Bringing up the past with Kara would serve no purpose. She had always looked up to her sister and thought she could do no wrong. It must have been hard on her to find out that had been a lie, as well. But then why should he care?

Glancing at his watch, he got back to work. He still had a lot to do before he could go home, and he wanted to get to bed early. He'd need a good night's sleep to be ready for Carowinds in the morning. And for a day with Kara.

Chapter 11

Virgil arrived at Kara's home at precisely ten o'clock on Saturday morning, punctual as usual. Glancing at herself in the mirror one final time, she was satisfied with the shorts set she'd purchased a few weeks ago and never worn. As she moved toward the door, she told herself it was just a coincidence it was purple, Virgil's favorite color on her.

The weather forecast indicated it would be a beautiful day with no chance of rain, perfect for the amusement park. But the closer she got to the door, the more nervous she felt. Truthfully it had nothing to do with the weather and everything to do with the man. She tried reminding herself this date was for business purposes only. Still, he was the man she had once loved, still loved, so being around him and keeping her emotions at bay wouldn't be easy. She had no other choice but to try.

When she opened the door, a bright ray of sunlight came through almost blinding her, but not before she got an eyeful of the man standing on her doorstep. He was wearing a pair of jeans that tapered down muscular thighs, and a Carolina Panthers T-shirt that covered broad shoulders and a masculine chest. She of all people knew how he liked spending time at the gym and she could definitely see it was time well spent. Every bit of Virgil Bougard looked sexy and could make any woman drool. Like she would be doing if she didn't get a grip.

She angled her head to look up at him. He had an unreadable expression on his face so she had no idea what kind of mood he was in. "Good morning, Virgil."

"Good morning. You ready?"

"Yes, I just have to lock up. You can come in."

"I'd rather not. I can stay right here until you're done," he said.

"Yes, but if anyone is watching they might find your actions odd."

Virgil knew what she'd said was true. If anyone was watching, he figured they would expect them to greet with a kiss. He had no problem carrying that out, so he leaned forward and brushed a kiss across her lips. At her surprised expression he said, "Just in case someone is looking." Then he walked past her to enter her home.

He came to a stop in her foyer and, since her home was an open concept plan, from where he stood he could see her huge living room, dining area and large eat-in kitchen. All the rooms had high ceilings, and wall-to-wall windows provided a brightness he'd always loved.

He wished he didn't remember all the times he'd spent here with her. How many times they'd shared wine and kisses while sitting at her breakfast bar or made love on her sofa or in front of her fireplace. Or how many times he'd stood here, in the same spot, just seconds before sweeping her up in his arms to carry her to the bedroom.

"I won't be but a minute," she said, moving past him.

When she walked by, he couldn't help drawing her scent into his nostrils. She smelled good. She looked good, as well. He couldn't stop his gaze from roaming across her backside as she headed for the kitchen. She still had the best-looking ass of any woman he knew. And her legs—long and gorgeous—looked good in shorts.

When she'd opened the door, one of the first things he'd noticed was that she was wearing purple. She had to remember how much he enjoyed seeing her in that color. To him, it did something to her silver-gray eyes. It also did something to his libido like it was doing now.

"I'm all set."

While he'd been buried in his thoughts, she had returned and was standing in front of him. Too damn close as far as he was concerned. For the past few days, he'd played around with her mouth, brushing his lips across it, and even getting a lick or two on occasion. But what he really wanted to do was pull her into his arms and kiss her like they used to kiss. It would be the kind of kiss that would make her purr and make him moan deep in his throat.

The kind of kiss he needed right now but was fighting like hell to do without.

"Virgil?"

He'd gotten lost in his thoughts again. "Yes?"

"I said I'm ready to go."

He drew in a deep breath. "Okay, let's not keep all those rides waiting."

Kara would be the first to admit it was a fun day. It was as if she and Virgil had put the reason they were spending time together to the back of their minds. Like kids, they were excited to try a new ride, one scarier than all the others. It didn't matter that the lines had been long; they agreed the wait had been well worth it.

With the thrill of the rides also came complications. Packed tight into the compartment together, she tried not to notice how his thigh would rub against hers or how, on a few of the rides, she had to practically sit in his lap. And then there were the times he wrapped his arms around her, to make sure she was okay during the rides when she would scream her lungs out. At one point she recalled gripping his thigh when one of the rides seemed to nearly topple them over.

More than once she had glanced over at him to see him staring at her and wondered what he'd been thinking about. During one of those times their gazes had held and then he had leaned down and brushed his lips against hers. There hadn't been a reason for him to do so, but she had let him, a part of her even wishing it could have lasted longer.

At the end of each ride it seemed the sexual chemistry between them skyrocketed. She wasn't sure if it was because of the thrill left over from the rides or the sensuous energy they seemed to generate whenever they were together. And as if it was the most natural thing to do, they began walking around the amusement park holding hands.

They had just ridden their last ride of the day and were headed to the parking lot, and they were still holding hands. He only let go of her to help her into the car. A new car, she noted, since it still had that new car smell.

"Hungry?" he asked when he was seated beside her.

She couldn't help but grin. "I shouldn't be after all that junk food I ate. I hadn't realized just how much I missed eating a Carowinds hot dog." She paused a minute. "Thanks for bringing me here today, Virgil."

He chuckled. "Need I remind you it was your choice?"

She smiled. "No, but you didn't have to do it. In fact

you really didn't have to suggest that we do anything this weekend."

Kara was right, Virgil thought, he didn't have to. So why had he? He had convinced himself if they broke the ice with this weekend then spending time with her next weekend around his parents wouldn't be so awkward. Because he didn't want to explore any other reasons, he changed the subject. "How are things going at work?"

"Do you really want to know?"

When he stopped the car at a traffic light, he glanced over at her. "I always supported you and your work, Kara," he said.

She nodded. "Yes, you did. And I appreciated it."

When the traffic light changed, he resumed driving. It was on the tip of his tongue to say he didn't want her appreciation. He wanted her. There, he'd admitted it to himself because deep down he knew that he did. At some point his anger toward her had transformed into lust for her. When it came to Kara, over the years he had learned how to deal with his anger, but he wasn't sure how to handle this high degree of lust. Being around her today had reminded him of how things used to be. And in trying to put his animosity behind him and move on, he'd somehow rekindled his physical need for her. And it had gotten restored to a level he wasn't sure he could handle.

What he should do here and now was tell her that hiring her had been a mistake and there was no way they could continue to work together even if it meant improving his image. His father would just have to deal with that decision. But to be honest, he doubted that even he could deal with that decision. Mainly because just hanging around Kara for the past few days had accomplished the one thing he hadn't wanted to have happen. It had overwhelmed not only his common sense but also his self-control. If he licked her one more time he was liable to detonate.

"Virgil?"

He glanced over at her. "Yes?"

"If you're hungry, instead of stopping somewhere, I could make a pot of chili."

Now she wasn't playing fair. No matter what time of year it was—fall, winter, spring or summer—he loved her chili. His grandmother in Houston had shared the family recipe with her when Kara had gone with him to one of his family reunions. He didn't know how she'd done it, but hers was just as good as the chili Hattie Lee Bougard was known to make.

"I would hate for you to go to the trouble," he said, while inwardly hoping she didn't mind. He hadn't been to Houston in a year and missed his grandmother's home-cooked meals. His mother could cook, but when she'd gone back to college to get her master's and then her PhD, his father had taken over cooking duties. Although the meals had been all right, they hadn't been anything like his mom's. And now his parents enjoyed dining out, so there was no hope of ever getting invited over for dinner.

"No problem at all," she said. "In fact I've got all the ingredients I need. Won't take but a minute to prepare it."

When he came to another traffic light he glanced over at her. "You sure?"

"Positive."

He continued looking at her. When he held her gaze a little longer than he knew he should have, he broke eye contact but figured it had been too late. In that space of time, something intensely sexual had passed between them. He was certain that she was aware of it as much as he was. In the year they'd dated, he'd discovered that Kara was a very passionate woman. On top of that, she was as sensual as she was passionate.

And he was well aware that Kara knew just how much he enjoyed sex. More specifically, sex with her. Eventually he had stopped thinking about it as just sex and that's when he'd known he had fallen in love with her. But those days were over and anything they did now would be nothing more to him than sex. And he didn't even want that with her. Engaging in any kind of physical relationship with her was too risky for his peace of mind.

He quickly glanced back over at her and wished he could focus on something else. Why did he find her so captivating? So damn appealing? He wished like hell he didn't remember how good she looked naked. Drawing in a deep breath, he forced his gaze back on the road. He decided to get on the interstate to avoid the traffic lights so he wouldn't be tempted to seek her out.

A short while later she said his name. "Virgil?"

He glanced over at her. "Yes?"

"You okay?"

He drew his brows together. "Why wouldn't I be?"

"You just passed my exit."

He glanced at the interstate markers and saw that he had. "Sorry about that. My mind was occupied. I'll turn around at the next exit."

Virgil knew that he needed to concentrate on what he was doing and where he was going and not the woman sitting beside him. It was easier said than done.

Kara didn't have to wonder where Virgil's mind had been. She knew him and knew the look she saw in his eyes each and every time he had looked at her today. He wanted her. That was obvious, just like it was probably as obvious that she wanted him. But she knew him well enough to know he would fight the desire for her tooth and nail. In his mind he didn't love her anymore, which meant that he didn't want to share any kind of relationship with her ever again, sexual or otherwise. It was too bad his body wasn't getting the message.

During the year they'd dated she'd learned a lot about men in general and about Virgil specifically. When he loved he loved hard. When he hated he hated just as hard. Over the past four years she figured he had convinced himself he detested her with every bone in his body. Yet over the past few days he was beginning to discover that although the love might be dead, the lust was not only alive and well but had taken on a life of its own. And she figured that was the crux of his problem. It was a problem that he would have to figure out how to deal with on his own.

Kara had figured out hers. She still loved him and would always love him. It would be up to him to decide whether he was dead set against letting her have a place in his life and heart again. She was determined not to make that decision easy for him—this bachelor who was so unforgiving.

He had exited the interstate and was easing his car to a stop at a traffic light. She kept her gaze focused ahead, knowing as soon as he brought the car to a stop he would be looking over at her. Let him look, she thought. Hopefully he liked what he saw.

She could feel the heat of his gaze move up and down her body, lingering on her bare legs before slowly moving up past her hips and waist toward her breasts. He wasn't blind, so she was certain he was fully aware that her nipples had hardened and were pressing against her shirt. It was her guess he was thinking of just what he would like to do with those nipples. Oh, how she used to love the feel of him sucking on them.

She had timed it perfectly to when his scanning eyes

would move upward from her body to reach her face. That's when she turned her head and their gazes met. She felt a stirring in the pit of her stomach when she read desire in the depths of his eyes. The penetrating stare was having a hypnotic effect on her, and unlike him, she wasn't trying to fight it. In fact, she was embracing it, just like she intended to embrace him when and if he ever made a move.

The driver of the car behind them blasted his horn, letting them know the light had changed and they were holding up traffic.

Without saying anything Virgil broke eye contact with Kara to concentrate on his driving again. He found it hard to believe time hadn't eradicated the urgency he was feeling for her, a sexual hunger so deep he could feel it in his bones. Even more so in his groin. Evidently, even after all this time, she was either not out of his system like he'd thought or she'd miraculously managed to wiggle her way back in. His mind went into a tailspin because that was the last thing he wanted to happen.

Virgil knew at that moment that agreeing to have dinner with her was not a good idea. Chili wasn't the only thing he would want once he was inside her home.

"I've changed my mind about dinner," he said. "As much as I would love to eat some of your chili, I just remembered something I need to do."

"Okay, I understand. Perhaps some other time."

Not if he could help it, he thought. He would make sure when their paths crossed again that he had his head screwed on right. Being overwhelmed by lust was the last thing he wanted or needed.

The rest of the drive to her house was done in silence and he couldn't help wondering what she was thinking. No conversation was taking place between them, and the quiet caused every primitive male instinct he possessed to be on full alert. He was aware when she shifted her body, making her skin slide against the leather seat, and when she stretched out one of her legs to a more comfortable position. When he slowed down for traffic, he glanced over at her. She was looking straight ahead out the windshield and he thought her profile was simply beautiful.

It was his opinion that no woman should look this good after going on over a dozen or so crazy rides. She should look sweaty, ruffled and exhausted, not cool, refreshed and relaxed. His gaze lowered to her hands, which were resting in her lap. He wished he didn't remember those hands and what they could do when they touched him all over, especially in certain places. Those hands had the ability to stroke him to dizzying heights. Make him moan. Render him hard just thinking about it.

He shifted his gaze from her hands to her lips, recalling how on several occasions her lips and hands worked together to drive him as wild as those rides had done today. Even wilder.

The car horn that blasted behind him was a reminder that, once again, he was paying too much attention to her. He refocused on the road and moved the car forward, feeling a tightness in his crotch. Hell, his desire for her wasn't going away. It was getting worse.

When he turned onto her street, she said, "Thanks for today, Virgil. I enjoyed myself." And when he pulled into her driveway, she added, "And you don't have to walk me to the door."

She was wrong. Yes, he had to walk her to her door. And it had nothing to do with any playacting but everything to do with the fire burning inside him. His control had abandoned him, taken a leap and at this point he couldn't get a grip even if he wanted to do so. He should be putting distance between them but he was too aware of the sexual need building with force inside of him. A need that just wouldn't go away. He knew his limits when it came to Kara and today they were being tested.

He brought the car to a stop and she proceeded to unbuckle her seat belt and he did the same. Intense heat had spiked in the area below his waist and was quickly spreading through other parts of him.

She glanced over at him with a questioning look after seeing he had removed his seat belt. "Really, Virgil, you don't have to walk me to the door. I'm okay."

She might be okay but he wasn't. "Yes, I do have to walk you to the door, Kara."

Evidently something in his tone told her he was serious. She merely nodded before opening the car door, not waiting for him to do it for her. But she did pause and wait for him before she got out of the car.

When he reached her, she studied his face a second before extending her hand to him. Without hesitating, Virgil took it and then they moved toward her front door.

Kara knew he was determined to put distance between them, which was the reason he had changed his mind about staying for chili. But she couldn't help but be reminded of other times she and Virgil would return from a date and stroll up the walkway holding hands. During those times there had been no doubt in her mind that he wouldn't stop at her door, but that he'd follow her inside and then take her into his arms the moment the door closed behind them. She suddenly got weak in the knees remembering the intensity of the passion they would share, right there in her foyer. His kisses didn't just leave her breathless, they left her wanting more and more and more.

Upon reaching her door, she opened her cross-body purse, the very one he had given to her when they'd dated. It had been for no special occasion, he'd said when he'd done so. The card that he'd given her with the purse simply said, *I am so grateful that you're mine.*

When she took out the key, his finger reached out to trace along the intricate design of her purse. If he hadn't noticed the purse before, he was definitely noticing it now. Was he remembering that he was the one who'd given it to her? Did he remember what he'd written on the card, as well?

She turned to him before inserting the key in the lock. "Thanks again for a wonderful day, Virgil."

His dark, penetrating eyes stared down at her. "Aren't you going to invite me in, Kara?" he asked in a deep husky voice, one that sent sensual chills all over her body.

"I thought there was something you had to do."

"There is."

She frowned, finding what he said confusing. But instead of asking him to elaborate, she opened the door and he followed her inside.

"This is far enough," Virgil said when they stood in the foyer.

She turned to him questioningly. "For what?"

"This."

His mouth came down on hers, needing what he'd only gotten swipes of the past few days. The quick tastes of her had been silky and warm, but now he wanted the intensity of the real thing. A tongue swipe across her lips just wouldn't do anymore. He needed to take the plunge. So he did.

Tipping her head back with the palm of his hand, he claimed her mouth as his tongue boldly swept inside, reacquainting itself with the special brand of intimacy they'd always shared. A deep sexual hunger, the same one that had been gnawing at his insides most of the day, stirred to life in his midsection. As if he'd opened some kind of erotic box, all the memories of their kisses came flooding back, arousing him in ways he wasn't used to.

Virgil wasn't sure if it was because of the length of time since he'd shared a kiss of this magnitude with her. Whatever the reason, jolts of sexual energy were rocking him to the bone, causing his tongue to dominate hers. The kiss was making him ravenous for her taste.

He was devouring her, and at this point, slowing down didn't seem to be an available option. And when he heard her moan, the sound compelled him to deepen the kiss even more. Swirling his tongue inside of her mouth, his mated with hers while coiling arousal settled deep in his core. He'd always enjoyed using his tongue to do all kinds of naughty things to her. They were things he'd been dreaming about doing since the day she had walked into that conference room to meet with him and his father.

He knew he needed to reel in his senses and pull back, but kissing her had always been his downfall. He'd never been able to get enough of her taste. It appeared that nothing had changed. He growled deep in his throat when fire seemed to spread through his veins.

Wrapping his arms around her waist, he urged her body closer to the hard fit of him. His hands moved from around her waist and shifted lower to cup her backside. Touching her this way felt good. And it reminded him that he'd always enjoyed touching her here on her bottom every chance he got.

Then there was the feel of her breasts pressing against his chest. The swollen buds were hard, causing his entire body to sizzle. He would love to strip her naked right here and taste her all over. Feed the flames of the heat he was feeling.

Kara had missed this. She had missed him. His tongue

had taken control of her mouth while his hands were making all kinds of erotic designs on her backside. She needed this. She wanted this. It had been years since she'd felt passion like this. Four years, to be exact. Every part of her body was like a live wire sending all kinds of electrical currents through her.

He'd always been a master kisser and that hadn't changed. His lips were stroking her mouth in a way that had her reaching up, gripping his shoulders with her determination to match his kiss with the same hunger and intensity. She felt blood rush fast and furious through her veins and could feel her panties getting wet. Like always, their mouths fit together perfectly, while his tongue continued to explore every crevice of her mouth, using strokes so sensual, her stomach began spinning at the same time as her senses reeled.

She could taste the hunger in his kiss, the passion and desire. And when he plunged his tongue even farther into her mouth, sensations she could no longer contain began smoldering out of control and effectively blocking every single thought from her mind.

Suddenly he snatched his mouth from hers. Drawing in a long and deep breath, he stared down at her, holding her gaze but not saying anything. She could imagine what he was seeing. Half-lidded, liquid eyes. Flushed cheeks. A pair of well-kissed lips. When neither of them said anything, she was tempted to lean up and kiss him again. But his next words stopped her cold.

"This should not have happened." Removing his hands from around her, he took a step back. "Kissing this way could lead to things we don't want, Kara."

It was on the tip of her tongue to say *speak for yourself* because he had no idea what she wanted. But evidently he knew what he wanted and it wasn't her.

"You're right and I suggest you leave," she said, trying to keep the anger and hurt from her voice.

Obviously he heard it anyway and he reached out to grab hold of her hand. She pulled it back. "Don't, Virgil. You're right. Why should you waste good kisses on a woman you'll never love again? A woman you can barely tolerate being around? I get it. Thank you for looking out for my best interests."

Reaching behind him, she opened the door. "Goodbye, Virgil."

He stared at her a minute before saying, "I'll be leaving town this week for Orlando to meet with investors there. I get back the day before we're to attend that UNCC commencement ceremony together. I'll call you."

Tilting her head she pasted a smile on her face. "Have a safe trip."

He nodded, hesitating for only a second before walking out the door.

Chapter 12

Virgil gazed out of his hotel-room window to scan the grounds of one of Disney World's most prestigious resorts. It had been years since he'd visited Orlando, yet he could easily recall the times his parents had brought him and Leigh here as kids. Those had been fun days. And more than once when they'd been together, he'd thought of bringing Kara here.

Kara.

Drawing in a deep breath, he couldn't stop remembering this past weekend. Somehow he'd been able to let go of his bitterness and enjoy the day with her. It had been fun… until his desire for her had begun overruling his mind and taking hold of his body. He had immediately recognized the tormenting heat for what it was. And considering everything, the intensity of his attraction to her annoyed as well as mystified him.

Leave it to him to make matters even worse when he'd taken her home. Why had he walked her to the door and then suggested she let him inside? The torture of wanting her had gotten so great that he'd given in to intense desire and kissed her. And he'd kissed her the way he'd been longing to for days. Even though her presence back in his life was temporary and strictly for business, his libido didn't seem to care.

Nor did his mouth give a damn since the taste of her still lingered there, even after five days. She'd always had the sweetest mouth but it seemed that over the years it had gotten sweeter and so satisfyingly delicious.

Leaving his place by the window, he moved to sit down at the desk in the hotel room, deciding he needed to get some work done. Already he'd held a number of meetings with potential investors. The International Investors Summit had a tendency to draw hedge fund corporations from all over the world. For that reason, it was always a good policy to have appointments scheduled way in advance, like he'd done. He'd gotten positive feedback from the six investors he'd met with so far.

His thoughts shifted back to Kara and that kiss he couldn't stop thinking about. And tasting. He leaned back in his chair and recalled the outfit she'd been wearing Saturday. It had been purple, his favorite color. Strolling around the amusement park, he'd noticed more than one man checking her out. She had legs that made any man want to take a second look and several had. More than once a streak of jealousy had raced through him. Why had he felt such possessiveness for a woman who wasn't his?

He had forgotten how tight the compartments were for the rides, and more than once their bodies had been crammed together, which had kicked his testosterone into full gear. Then his horny mind had looked forward to the times he'd been squeezed against her backside or when their thighs had been all but plastered against each other.

Virgil figured that had to be the reason he'd gone crazy once he'd gotten hold of her mouth. He had kissed her like hers was destined to be the last mouth he'd ever taste. And she had kissed him back, meeting him greed for greed.

And then somehow through all that ravenous pleasure, he'd found his senses and pulled back. Surprising himself as much as he'd probably surprised her. There had been no logical reason for him and Kara to stand in the middle of her foyer and go at each other's mouths like they'd been doing. No logical reason whatsoever.

That didn't stop his body from yearning for her every day since. Or stop his mouth from feeling like it was missing something vital. Or stop his erection from swelling each and every time he thought about her.

Like now.

And although he hated admitting it, he would give anything to have another such opportunity to take her into his arms and kiss her. Unfortunately, he was finding out the hard way that when it came to Kara, out of sight and out of mind didn't seem to work.

What he needed to do was what any successful businessman would do—come up with a game plan, some strategic move to eliminate the problem without alienating the source. He could tell before he'd left her place on Saturday that she hadn't appreciated what he'd said about kissing her being a mistake. Had she considered that a blatant rejection of her? And why should it bother him if she had?

He knew the answer without thinking about it. It bothered him because it was far from the truth. As much as he wanted to continue to convince himself he was completely and totally over Kara, there was still this sexual connection between them. At times it was so strong it cloaked them in an air of intimacy so thick he felt as if he was smothered by it.

So the question of the hour was this: just what exactly was he going to do about it? Since seeing her was basically part of *her* plan—the one she'd put together to improve his image—he needed to come up with a plan of his own. One designed to save his sanity.

Kara looked at herself in the full-length mirror and smiled, pleased with what she saw. She didn't think twice about why she had put so much time and effort into her appearance. If Virgil thought he could continue to resist her, then let him try. She would do everything in her power to make sure he didn't succeed.

After spending time with him on Saturday and after that kiss he'd given her when he brought her home, she was convinced he wasn't as immune to her as he claimed. Granted, initially she had been slightly peeved at how he'd abruptly ended their kiss and left her home last weekend, but her annoyance had dissipated when she realized what had happened. He had been running scared.

Virgil had enjoyed the kiss; she was sure of it. But something had made him pull back and break off the kiss, then go even further by saying crazy stuff like kissing her had been a mistake and wasn't anything either of them wanted. He had tried replacing desire with logic. A person could do that only so many times, and she was determined to make sure the clock ran out on him. Her goal was to make sure he took off the blinders and realized they deserved another chance to get it right.

She turned slightly in the mirror and smiled again. The sophisticated-looking purple dress was one she'd purchased this week when she'd gone shopping. At first she'd thought that wearing his favorite color again might be a bit too much. However she decided, just in case he hadn't realized her intent on Saturday, that today should leave no doubt in his mind what she was about.

Pleased by that very thought, she tossed her head, sending her shoulder-length hair swinging around her face. When she looked at herself again in the mirror she didn't miss the seductive gleam in her eyes. Granted, she would behave herself around his parents, but later, when she got him alone, she would make it her business to find out just how scared he could run.

She hadn't heard anything from him all week while he'd been in Orlando, but last evening she had gotten his text message advising her he would pick her up at nine this morning. A second text had followed a few hours later, indicating his parents had invited them to join them for brunch at Hammer's, a popular restaurant in town, following the commencement ceremony.

Kara had texted him back to say she had no problem doing that and that she thought it was a great strategic idea that the four of them be seen together that way. He hadn't responded and, if her guess was right, he might not have liked being reminded of their business arrangement. Oh, well.

The doorbell sounded. Quickly moving from her bedroom, she grabbed her purse and jacket as she headed for the door. It was time to put Operation Virgil Bougard in full swing.

"Welcome back, Virgil," Kara said, smiling before placing a quick kiss on his lips. "I'm ready." She then closed the door and strolled past him, moving briskly down the walkway.

Virgil almost stopped breathing for the thickness of the air settling in his lungs. Dammit, where was the fire?

Why was she moving so fast? He quickly reached out and grabbed her hand. "Whoa. What's going on?"

She glanced back at him. "What do you mean what's going on?"

"Usually when I pick you up there's a last-minute item you've got to grab and I have to wait inside a minute or two," he said. Come to think of it, that's how it worked with most women, he thought.

"Not this time. I've got everything and I'm ready. No need for you to have to wait on me for anything."

"Oh," he said, releasing her hand to walk beside her toward the car. He tried not to check out her dress. She was wearing purple again and he liked it. But it wasn't the color of the dress that had grabbed his total awareness of her this morning. It was the style. On anyone else it probably would look okay, but on her it elicited some thoughtful cravings. Not only that, a hot rush of desire was sending shivers through his body.

It wasn't that the dress was too over-the-top for the event they would be attending because it wasn't. In fact it was perfect for the occasion. But did it have to emphasize the svelte lines of her curves and the gracefulness of her long, gorgeous legs? And did it have to show off her small waist and generous breasts? The effect was so mind-blowing that he felt it all the way to his groin.

"Is there a problem?"

A frown marred his brow. "No, there's no problem," he said, opening the car door for her.

A spike of heat exploded in his gut when the dress flashed a portion of her thigh as she slid down into the car seat. Seeing her naked flesh could arouse him in a way nothing else could. And speaking of arousal...she could pretend nonchalance all she wanted, but he hadn't missed that crackle of sensual energy that flowed between them when they'd walked beside each other. And he was certain she felt it, as well.

"You can close the car door now."

He'd been caught staring. Trying to keep his features neutral, he closed the door and walked around to the other side of the car. After getting in and buckling his seat belt, he glanced over at her. "You look nice."

"Thanks."

"And your dress is purple."

She looked over at him, tilted her head back a little as if she needed to study his face. "I know what color my dress is, Virgil."

He stared at her, unable to figure out if she meant anything by that. Grabbing his sunglasses off the dash, he said, "Mom is looking forward to your joining us today."

"She knows the truth, right?"

"Yes, she knows the truth."

"Good."

As he backed the car out of her driveway, Virgil wasn't sure if it was a good thing or not.

"Rhona's speech was simply wonderful," Kara said to the two men at her side.

"Yes, it was," Matthew agreed. "She did an outstanding job, but then she always does," he added proudly.

Kara had always admired Virgil's parents' close relationship. It was obvious from the huge smile on Matthew's face that he was very proud of his wife. And, although she was certain Virgil was equally as proud, he hadn't said anything. In fact he hadn't said much to her since leaving her place. He had taken her hand as they had found their seats beside his father. The entire time her hand had been encased in his, she felt flutters that stirred deep in the pit of her stomach. When they sat down and he released her hand, the stirrings continued for a while. More than once she had glanced over at him to find him staring at her, making her wonder if he'd had a similar reaction.

It was hard not to stare back at him. He exuded that Virgil Bougard level of charismatic and sexual power. He looked good in his charcoal-gray suit. Blatantly sexy would be one way to describe him but not the only way. There was this indescribable masculine aura surrounding him and Kara was certain she wasn't the only female who noticed it. More than once she'd observed several others looking his way.

"There's my queen," Matthew said in a joyous tone, interrupting Kara's thoughts when Rhona could finally be seen among the throng of graduates and their families. Kara had always thought Rhona was a beautiful woman, one who didn't look a day over forty. Her honey-brown complexion was flawless, not a wrinkle in sight. And Kara knew Rhona credited her young features and slender form to a healthy diet and regular exercise.

"Come on, let's go meet her," Matthew said, leading the way.

Virgil surprised Kara when he captured her hand in his again. It took everything she had to ignore the spike of hot sensuality that raced up her spine. There were a lot of media in attendance, so she knew they had to play their roles convincingly.

When they met up with Rhona, Kara wasn't sure what to expect. She and Virgil's mother had run into each other several times over the past four years, either while out shopping or attending various social functions. The Bougards had always been kind to her whenever their paths had crossed. So kind that for a long while she'd wondered if Virgil had told them why they'd broken up.

After accepting a kiss from her husband, Rhona then

turned smiling eyes toward Kara, reached out and gave her a hug. "Kara, it's good seeing you. Glad you could join us today."

Kara returned the smile. "I'm glad, as well."

Rhona then turned to her son. She placed a kiss on his cheek. "Thanks for coming, Virgil."

He smiled down at her. "There's no way I was going to miss it. You did us proud as usual, Mom."

"Thanks." She then glanced back and forth between Kara and Virgil before leaning over and whispering, "Play-acting or not, the two of you look good together."

Before either of them could say anything—Kara wasn't sure what she would have said anyway—Matthew spoke up. "We might as well beat the crowd and head over to Hammer's."

"I agree," Virgil said, taking Kara's hand once again. And when he did, he felt it. That tingling sensation whenever he touched her. He was sure she felt it, too, which was why she glanced up at him. Their gazes connected and held until she broke eye contact when his father spoke.

"We're parked on the other side," Matthew said. "We'll see you guys at the restaurant."

"Okay." Virgil glanced around. Just as he'd figured, eyes were on them. More than a dozen people he didn't know had approached him and Kara, unashamedly confessing they were ardent readers of Flo's column and basically giving them the same compliment that his mother had given about how good they looked together.

"Don't forget about next Saturday, Virgil," Kara said as they walked to where his car was parked.

He looked down at her. "What about next Saturday?"

"The back-to-school drive. Your company is one of the major sponsors and is giving away over three hundred book bags. You agreed to be there to help give them out."

He nodded, remembering. "Will you be there?"

"There's no reason why I should. Your company has been doing it for years but this will be the first time you've made an appearance."

She was right. It would be. His father had always participated in such community events and more times than not, his mother had been there, as well. His parents had made a great team and always worked well together for the benefit of Bougard Enterprises.

He glanced at the woman walking beside him. He was still holding her hand, and for the time being, he had no inclination to release it.

Chapter 13

"I had a nice time with your parents, Virgil," Kara said the moment he brought his car to a stop in her driveway.

He turned toward her. "And I'm sure they had an equally nice time with you since they've always liked you."

He sounded a little annoyed by that, Kara thought. "I take it you think that's a bad thing."

He shrugged. "Doesn't matter one way or the other to me. Since you were the first woman I ever brought home for them to meet, it would make sense for you to have made a lasting impression."

She decided not to remind him that, according to his mother at dinner, she had been the *only* woman he'd ever brought home for them to meet. She could tell from the expression that had crossed Virgil's face that he hadn't particularly appreciated Rhona's mentioning that to her.

"I agree, it doesn't matter," she said. *What does matter, Virgil Bougard, is that you pretty much haven't taken your eyes off me all day.*

"Again, thanks for a nice day and you don't have to walk me to the door."

Her front porch was bathed in moonlight and she could clearly see his frown by the light shining into the car. "I wish you wouldn't do that," he said gruffly.

"Do what?" she asked, unbuckling her seat belt.

"Tell me what I don't have to do. I intend to walk you to your door, Kara."

"Okay. I was just trying to save you the bother."

When she reached to open her car door, he said, "And I'll get your door."

She pulled her hand back. "All right."

He unbuckled his seat belt, got out of the car and walked around the front of it to the passenger side. Sexiness was oozing from every part of his body—it was in his walk as well as his clothes. Earlier he had removed his suit jacket and she enjoyed looking at his broad shoulders and tight muscular chest outlined in his fitted dress shirt. Kara would admit that she'd kept a close eye on him today, just as he'd been doing with her.

He opened her car door and extended his hand out to her. She took it and immediately sucked in a deep breath when a hot, raw and sensual spark of energy passed between them. That had been happening a lot today, especially when their hands touched.

Because he didn't step back, her body was nearly plastered to his when she got out of the car. Desire quickly soaked into her skin in a heated rush and she didn't have to be told what he was doing was deliberate. If his intent was a plan of seduction, she was one up on him. She had a plan of her own.

"You're blocking my way, Virgil."

He held her gaze. "Am I?"

"Yes."

"Sorry." He took a step back and then strolled beside her to the front door.

When they reached their destination, she turned to him. "Well, this where we say goodbye. It was a longer day than either of us anticipated."

She was certain neither of them expected his parents to suggest at dinner they go back to their place for dessert since Rhona had baked her famous chocolate cake the day before. They had sat around laughing and talking while eating dessert, and the next thing she knew they were watching several movies on Matthew's new ninety-inch flat-screen television. Although the additional time spent with Virgil's parents had been unexpected, she had definitely enjoyed herself.

"You're not going to invite me in?"

"Why, do you want to come in?" *Like I don't know.*

His gaze slid down her body before moving back up to her face. His eyes met hers. "What if I told you I think we need to talk?"

From the look in his eyes, she knew talking was the last thing on his mind. She recognized that I-want-some-of-you look in his eyes. "Talk about what?"

"How to proceed in our relationship."

What relationship? They had a relationship? If they did it was news to her. "We don't have a relationship, Virgil. We have a business arrangement. You've made that pretty clear more than once."

"And that's what I need to talk to you about."

She gazed at him thoughtfully for a minute and then said, "Fine, we'll talk but only because you have me curious." She then took the key from her purse.

When she found it, he took it from her hand. And the moment their fingers touched, a jolt of sexual desire rocked her to the bone. She glanced up at him and a tight smile touched the corners of his lips.

"I felt it, too," he said, his eyes flaring with the same intense desire that she felt. "I've been feeling it all day and that's why we need to talk."

If he thought talking would solve their problem, then he was not thinking realistically. But instead of saying anything, she nodded.

He unlocked the door and then stood aside for her to enter.

Virgil followed Kara inside, and the moment he stepped into the foyer, he couldn't help remembering what had happened the last time he was here. He had given Kara a kiss in a way that should be outlawed. And nothing would satisfy him more than to do it again. But like he'd told her, they needed to talk. While in Orlando he'd come up with a plan, one he hoped she would go along with.

"Would you like something to drink?" she asked him.

He reined his thoughts in and noticed she had paused to remove the high heels from her feet. "That would be nice."

"You know where the refrigerator is. Help yourself. I need to grab my flats."

He watched her walk off toward her bedroom and his gaze was fixed on her backside with every step she took. She damn sure looked good in that purple dress. He hadn't been able to keep his eyes off her most of the day. And he'd wanted to touch her every chance he got, which was why he'd taken hold of her hand a lot. Spending time at his parents' place had reminded him of other times they'd joined the folks for movie night. When she went into her bedroom and closed the door behind her, he rubbed a hand down his face and quickly walked to the kitchen. He definitely needed a drink.

Moving through her living room, he glanced around and noticed a number of changes she'd made. Several new pieces of furniture, more artwork on her walls. When he stepped into the kitchen, he immediately noticed new stainless-steel appliances. She had talked about getting rid of her old appliances but had kept putting it off. He was glad she'd gotten around to replacing them.

Grabbing a beer out of her fridge, he quickly popped the tab and took a huge swig. Today had been one hell of a day and spending a lot of time around Kara hadn't been easy. His parents had to know that, yet it seemed they'd intentionally prolonged the day.

"Virgil?"

"I'm still in the kitchen," he called out. "Want anything?"

"A cold bottle of water would be nice."

"A cold bottle of water coming up," he said, reopening her refrigerator and grabbing a bottle of water. He walked out of the kitchen, stepped into the living room and suddenly stopped. Not only had she changed shoes, she'd also changed clothes.

"Is anything wrong?"

"You changed clothes."

She smiled, glancing down at herself. "Yes, I decided to get comfortable. Anything wrong with what I have on?"

The fact that it wasn't purple was the first thing he noticed, although she did look good in the silky black shirt dress. What he liked most was how it was showing off her legs as well as how the outfit buttoned up the front with a shirttail hem that fanned across her backside. She wasn't wearing a bra, he was sure of it, and for some reason he had a feeling she wasn't wearing panties, either. She was taking "comfortable" to a level he definitely liked.

"No, nothing is wrong with what you're wearing. Here's

the water," he said, handing the bottle to her in a way that ensured their hands wouldn't touch. He wasn't sure how much control he would have if they did.

"Thanks."

He watched her uncap the top and tilt the bottle up to her lips. Immediately his gut clenched. It was almost too much temptation. Renewed desire throbbed all through him, nearly overtaking his senses. Knowing he needed to get a grip, he glanced around the room and then said, "I like the changes you made in here."

"Thanks. My next project is removing all this carpet and replacing it with wood floors."

"That will be nice."

"Yes, I think so."

She placed the half-empty water bottle on the coffee table and eased down on the sofa, tucking her feet beneath her. Doing so gave him more than a flash of bare thigh. He could feel the pounding of his heart in his chest.

"You said we needed to talk."

Yes, he had. He settled into the chair across from her, wondering about the best way to approach what he had to say. He figured the best thing to do was to come right out and not beat around the bush. "I want you, Kara. And you want me."

She raised a brow. "You think so? About me wanting you?"

"Yes." He paused a moment and held her gaze. "Are you going to deny it?"

She didn't say anything for a minute, and then she said, "At some point in our lives, Virgil, we all want things we can't have. Things we don't need. Things that can cause us more harm than good. Things that—"

"Don't get all philosophical on me, Kara," he interrupted in a tense voice.

He drew in a deep, shaky breath when his gaze left her face and scanned down her body before returning to her face again. She had a way of stirring up his emotions and passions that could do him in if he wasn't careful. "Just answer the question."

She broke eye contact with him to glance around the room, deliberately looking at everything but him. When she returned her gaze to his, she began nibbling at her lips before she finally spoke. "And if I do want you, Virgil, then what?"

He swallowed against the massive lump in his throat. He could tell her about a lot of ideas he had in mind. And all of them hot, raw and sexual. Instead he said, "Then it's time to present my own action plan."

Kara arched a brow. Virgil was sitting across from her taking another swig of his beer as if giving her time to digest what he'd said. She was doing more than digesting it. Her imagination was going wild with ways she could use whatever action plan he'd come up with to her advantage.

When he had walked out of her kitchen minutes ago, he had stood tall, broad shouldered and sexy. She could remember his muscular chest very well. Remember all the times that naked chest had rubbed against her breasts, causing her nipples to tighten.

"And what if I said I'm not interested?" she asked, studying him intently.

He stretched his long legs out in front of him and his mouth slanted into a sexy and seductive smile. "You haven't heard it yet."

"Don't have to, Virgil. I know how your mind works."

His smile widened and it made her pulse race. "You probably do, but I still want you to hear me out. I think I have a plan where we can both benefit."

She didn't say anything for a long moment. Instead she sat there and continued to hold his gaze. They were looking at each other with unflinching directness, even while she felt waves of sensual heat rippling between them. She could even feel the tightening of her nipples beneath the silk of her dress. And from his position in the chair, she could see the huge bulge pressing hard against the zipper of his pants. He wasn't even trying to hide his erection. Rather he seemed to be intentionally letting her see the proof of what he'd said earlier. He wanted her.

Kara knew Virgil was fully aware of what he was doing to her with his gaze. It was deliberately warming her, caressing her and sending throbbing need shooting through her. She'd discovered long ago that, when it came to seduction, Virgil's gaze was a mesmerizing force to contend with. It had the ability to break down her defenses. But for her it was about more than rolling in the sack a few times. She wanted to be back in his life. Totally and completely. She knew he couldn't fathom such a thing happening, but she had to believe she could pull it off. She was putting her heart on the line. But the big question was, would he ever feel secure enough to put his on the line again?

"Kara?"

"Fine, let's hear it," she said in a tone that made it seem as if she'd gotten annoyed, when in truth she'd gotten aroused just thinking about what he might have in mind. Like she told him, she knew how his mind worked.

He placed his beer can on the table. "I propose we become lovers."

"Why?"

He chuckled and the sound sent sensuous shivers down her spine. "Do you really have to ask me that?"

No, she didn't, but she wanted him to spell it out to her anyway. Every single detail. She needed to hear it. Feel it.

Imagine it. "Yes, I think I have to ask. I want to make sure I fully understand what you're proposing, exactly what I'll be getting myself into."

Virgil nodded. "Fair enough." He paused a minute before he continued. "What you'll be getting yourself into, Kara, is me. And I will be getting myself into you. Your action plan requires us to spend a lot of time together for the next several weeks. I see no reason why we can't make it worth our while. We're still attracted to each other so we might as well do something about it. Enjoy each other, both in and out of bed. Mix business with pleasure. Stir up mind-blowing passion the way we used to do."

He paused for a moment and Kara knew what his next words would be even before he spoke them. "But be forewarned, Kara. What we share will be sex and nothing else. There will never be anything of substance between us ever again."

"Don't you think I know that, Virgil?"

"Just making sure that you do. I need to be sure you understand that sex is all we can ever share. I have to know you can be satisfied with that."

"Yes, I'd be satisfied because that's the way I'd want it, as well." She could tell he was surprised by her words.

"I'm curious why you feel that way."

She shifted in her seat and watched his gaze move from her face to the glimpse of bare skin on her thighs, just like she had wanted it to do. When his gaze had slid back to her face, she said, "You make it clear how things stand between us every chance you get. I've decided I wouldn't want to get back with you even if the possibility was there."

She forced back her smile from the glare that came into his eyes. "And why is that?"

"Because I could never love a man with such an unforgiving nature. A man who expects me to be perfect, thinks he makes no mistakes, when I know he's certainly made a few of his own."

"You think I want a perfect woman?"

"Doesn't matter what I think. And to be honest I no longer care, Virgil." She eased off the sofa. "Now if you don't mind, it's getting late and I plan to go to early-morning church service tomorrow."

He eased up out of his chair, as well. "So you're in agreement that we should be lovers?"

"I'll think about it and let you know," she said, heading for the door to let him out. She knew he thought he would be staying a little longer, but she would do things on her time and not his.

"When will you let me know?" he asked when he stood across from her in the foyer.

"Soon."

"How soon, Kara?"

She thought he sounded pretty anxious. "Before the end of the week."

He was silent for a minute before saying, "Then maybe I need to leave you with a little persuasion."

"You can try." She knew Virgil Bougard didn't like to be dared.

He reached out and placed his arms around her waist to bring her closer to the fit of him. "I presented you with my action plan, Kara. Now for a sample of that action." And then he lowered his mouth to hers, kissing her with a desperation that made her toes curl and shot arrows of pleasure throughout her body.

When she parted her lips on a breathless sigh, he took advantage of the opportunity and swept his tongue inside her mouth in a smooth delicious stroke. She settled into his kiss, pressing the lower part of her body against him. And when he deepened the kiss, she could feel her heart stir in the pit of her stomach as their tongues tangled, mated voraciously, ravenously and urgently.

He was doing more than giving her a sample. Virgil was trying to erode her senses while kissing her with pure, unadulterated possession. Hadn't he said that any affair between them would be nothing more than sex? Then why was he kissing her as if he intended for her to be a keeper?

He finally broke off the kiss, and then as if he needed to catch his breath, he pressed his forehead against hers. That was good because she definitely needed to catch her breath. But then, before she realized what he was about to do, he eased back and reached out a hand to open the first few buttons of her dress, exposing her breasts. He stood quietly for a moment, not saying anything as his eyes simply feasted on her bare breasts. She felt her nipples harden even more before his gaze.

He reached out and cupped her breasts in his hands, running his fingers across the budded tips. When he lowered his head and sucked a nipple in his mouth, Kara's breathing escalated and she got weak in the knees. Reaching up she grabbed hold of his shoulders for support. And when he licked the nipple he was holding hostage, she forced back a moan.

To her detriment he didn't stop there. Reaching down he finished unbuttoning her dress all the way to the hem to find her naked. Without breaking from his torment of her breasts, he slid his hand between her legs.

Perfect, Virgil thought, when Kara parted her legs for him. When it came to multitasking, he was a pro. With his mouth on her breasts and his hands stroking her between the legs, he was proving just how much of an expert he was. He'd always enjoyed this, priming her with foreplay before getting down to the real business of easing inside her. He would stroke her back and forth, over and over again, while enjoying the sounds of the moans she would make, the way her breathing escalated and her body trembled.

His mouth moved to her other breast, and without letting up, his fingers continued to stroke her below. He loved the sounds of her purrs. It had been a while since he'd heard them and hearing them now made him realize what he'd missed. To be honest, he had missed her. He would admit that. They had been good together and could be good together again. At least this way, which was the only way he wanted. Sex, sex and more sex.

When he heard her groan his name, he knew his fingers were about to push her over the edge and he wanted his tongue to join his fingers when she toppled. He quickly released her breast and dropped to his knees, widening her legs in the process. She screamed the moment his tongue replaced his fingers and he gripped tightly to her thighs while his mouth locked down on her. He greedily began lapping her.

"Virgil!"

And then it happened for her and nothing, not even the feel of her fingernails digging into his shoulders, could make him stop and pull back. He needed her taste like he needed to breathe. It was only when he felt the last spasm pass through her body that he slowly released her thighs and reluctantly pulled his mouth away. But not before getting in one final intense lick. And he couldn't pass up the chance to place several nips around her womanly folds.

Leaning back on his haunches he looked up at her. Holding her gaze, he licked his lips, wanting her to know just how much he'd enjoyed her taste. Her face glowed from the effects of her orgasms and he thought she looked utterly beautiful.

Virgil recalled a time when seeing such a look on her face would make him crazier in love with her, so crazy he couldn't think straight. He blinked and quickly pushed that particular memory from his mind.

Slowly easing up from the floor, he didn't say anything but proceeded to button up her dress, ignoring the way his fingers trembled while doing so. More than once he had to rework a button when it kept coming back open.

When he had refastened all ten buttons he met her gaze and said, "Let me know your decision soon, Kara," in a voice that sounded husky to his own ears. "What we just shared was merely an appetizer. Let me know when you're ready for the full-course meal."

And then, after giving her lips one final lick , he leaned closer and whispered in her ear. "Sleep well tonight."

And then he opened the door and left.

Chapter 14

Kara woke up the next morning and for the longest time she just lay there and stared up at the ceiling. Last night had been round one and of course Virgil hadn't played fair. In fact she was convinced he hadn't been playing at all. He was deadly serious in his conquest of her, and all in the name of sex. But then, it didn't take much to recall that's how things had been the last time. He'd started out wanting nothing more than sex from her, but in the end they had fallen in love.

A part of her wanted to believe, had to believe, that it could be that way for them again. Virgil might think he wanted just sex, but it was up to her to show him she wasn't a just-sex kind of woman. Never was and never would be. He had his guard up and would continue to keep it up, but a part of her felt she'd been able to jump the first hurdle.

That meant she had to be on top of her A game because he was definitely on top of his. Even now her body was still stirring in passionate bliss from last night. While standing in the middle of her foyer, he'd taken her breasts, drawing them into his mouth, tugging, laving and sucking on them, torturing them with his tongue. He had pleasured her and made her remember things she had tried to forget. And if that wasn't bad enough, he'd used his mouth between her legs and made her come not once but twice. The man's mouth was definitely a weapon of deadly seduction.

Knowing Virgil, he would expect her to call him today, but she had no plans to do so. Nor would she call him tomorrow or the day after that. He thought the ball was now in his court but he was wrong. She would keep it in hers even if it killed her. It was her intention to let him think about what he was proposing, because if he thought she wouldn't come up with a few plays of her own then he was in for quite a surprise.

"Pam, did you receive that call I'm expecting from Kara Goshay?" Virgil asked his administrative assistant.

"No, sir, not yet. Do you want me to give her a call?"

Although he was tempted to take that option, he said, "No. That's not necessary." It had been three days and as far as he was concerned it was three days too long. He needed her to make a decision but, knowing Kara, she was probably trying to make a mountain out of a molehill. Personally, he didn't see the big deal, especially after what happened at her place Saturday night. She either was for them becoming lovers or not. He had a feeling she was stalling and that was unacceptable.

He glanced up when he heard the knock on his door. "Come in."

He stood when his father walked into his office. "Dad? I thought you and Mom were leaving for Houston today."

"We are but our flight doesn't leave until late this evening," Matthew said, easing into the chair in front of Virgil's desk.

"Would you like a cup of coffee?"

Matthew waved off the offer. "No thanks. Your mom and I had breakfast with Anthony and Claire at the Racetrack Café."

Anthony Lassiter, Uriel's father, was dating Claire Steele, aunt to Mayor Morgan Steele. A few years ago, Anthony's wife of over thirty years had asked for a divorce so she could date younger men. Virgil knew the divorce had left his godfather Anthony emotionally damaged. Virgil was glad he seemed happy now. Anthony and Claire had been seeing each other for about three years now and everyone was hoping for an announcement of something permanent. Evidently a second chance at love was possible for some people.

His father sat forward in the chair, a hand on Virgil's desk. "I understand Ellie is giving Uriel a birthday party next month at the lake and that Winston and Zion are coming home to attend. It will be nice to have all my godsons in one place again. Your mom and I were on that cruise when Winston and Ainsley came home in February."

"Yes, it will be good for all of us to be together. Do you know if all the godfathers will be there, as well?"

"Yes, we all plan to be there."

Virgil nodded. "Good. Then it will be like old times."

When Matthew didn't say anything for a minute, Virgil had a feeling there was something on his father's mind, so he decided to ask. "Dad, is anything wrong?"

Matthew shook his head. "I wouldn't say anything is wrong, Virgil—it's just, your mom and I are concerned."

He arched a brow. "About what?"

"You and Kara. In fact, we're more concerned about Kara than about you."

"What do you mean?"

"What I mean, Virgil, is that when you told us last week that Kara would be the woman you would be seeing exclusively while she worked on improving your image, we had our concerns. And after this weekend, our concerns have increased."

Virgil didn't understand. "What concerns?"

"You and Kara have history and I hope you're not using this as an opportunity to get back at her. To deliberately hurt her like she hurt you."

He remembered Uriel had thought the same thing. "I wouldn't do anything like that," he said, annoyed his parents would think that he would. "My seeing Kara has nothing to do with revenge. She was the most logical woman to make what needs to be done believable."

"I agree, but we don't want you doing anything out of line with her."

Virgil had to fight back the temptation to tell his father that whatever he did to Kara was none of his business. He wasn't a teenager who needed his parents meddling in his affairs. Out of respect, however, he decided to speak his next words carefully, but still make sure his father got the message to back off and let him handle the situation without any interference. When it came to business, because his father was the CEO of Bougard Enterprises, Virgil had no choice but to let him take charge, but when it came to his personal life, Virgil had no problem drawing the line.

"Dad, there's no reason for you and Mom to be concerned about anything that goes on between me and Kara. She knows where we stand and what will never be between us again. She apologized for believing the worst of me and I accepted her apology. We've moved on and we're only pretending interest in each other for Bougard Enterprises' sake."

Matthew nodded. "Your mother and I know what the plan is, but we also saw how you were looking at Kara on Saturday."

Virgil blew out a breath. There was no need to pretend ignorance because he was well aware he'd been caught checking out Kara a few times. "She's a good-looking woman."

"We know that and your mom feels she will make some man a good wife. And since it won't be you, when this is over she intends to introduce Kara to Dr. Alvin Lynwood. Your mother just hopes that the time Kara is spending with you, trying to improve your image, doesn't tarnish her own."

Virgil sat up in his chair. He'd never met Dr. Lynwood but knew he was the man who'd replaced his mother as president of the college when she'd retired. His mother liked the man a lot and had mentioned on more than one occasion what a great job she thought Dr. Lynwood was doing. But Virgil couldn't believe his mother would try setting Kara up with another man. And how could they think being with him could mess up Kara's image?

As if Matthew saw the questions in his eyes, he said, "Your mother sees nothing wrong with introducing Kara to Dr. Lynwood since you've made it known on several occasions there will never be anything between you and her again."

"Yes, but that's not the point."

Matthew frowned. "Then what is the point, Virgil? You've certainly moved on with other women and I'm sure Kara has dated other men since the two of you parted ways four years ago."

"I'm sure none of those men were anyone my mother introduced her to," Virgil said, trying to curtail his anger.

"And why would Mom think the time Kara and I are spending together could have any bearing on her image?"

"Think about it, Virgil. I'm sure you've seen the article and photos in *Flo on the Ro* this morning. From the looks of it, Flo's posse was out in full force at the commencement ceremony on Saturday. The two of you are linked back together. That's good news for you, but what happens when, in a month or so, your image has improved and then it appears that you've broken things off with Kara?"

Before Virgil could respond, Matthew stood. "Well, I'd best be going now. Your mom gave me a list of errands to do before we can get to the airport later. We'll text you when we get to Houston to let you know our plane landed safely."

Moments after his father left, Virgil was still sitting behind his desk. How could his mother think about hooking Kara up with Dr. Alvin Lynwood? Didn't the man just get a divorce from his wife sometime last year?

The buzzer on his desk went off. "Yes, Pam?"

"Kara Goshay is on line two."

Virgil ignored the increased beating of his heart. "Thanks."

He quickly went to his second line. "Kara?"

"Virgil. I was wondering if you'd like to join me for dinner."

Right now he wasn't interested in dinner. He needed an answer to his proposal. "And what about what I suggested to you Saturday night?"

"I'll give you my answer at dinner."

If he thought she was deliberately stalling before, he was even more convinced of it now. "Fine. Where do you want us to meet for dinner?"

"My place at seven. And bring a bottle of wine. Goodbye."

And before he could say anything he heard the definite click in his ear.

* * *

Kara glanced down at herself one more time before heading for the door. Virgil had arrived. When she'd called him today, she had decided she'd made him wait long enough for her decision. The goal was to not appear too eager and she would certainly continue that trend tonight.

"Who is it?"

"Virgil."

Dismissing how much she liked hearing the sound of his voice, she steeled herself and then opened the door. The man standing there holding a bottle of wine in his hand nearly took her breath away. How could any man look so insidiously handsome and utterly sexy?

"Kara."

"Virgil."

When she didn't move and just stood there and stared, he smiled and asked, "May I come in?"

Too late she'd realized what she'd been doing. "Yes, of course." Standing aside as he entered, she caught the scent of his aftershave and immediately thought he smelled just as good as he looked.

"Here you are," he said, handing the wine to her.

"Thanks." She walked ahead and said over her shoulder, "I hope you're hungry. I prepared lasagna." She knew how much he loved lasagna, especially hers.

"I can't wait."

And before she knew what he intended to do, he reached out and pulled her to him. "Hey, not so fast," he whispered against her lips. "What have you decided?"

She looked up at him, stared into the penetrating dark eyes. "I'll tell you over dinner."

"I want to know now."

She raised an arched brow. "What's the rush?"

That, Virgil thought, was a good question, and one for

which he didn't have an answer. He had been anxiously awaiting her decision since Saturday and saw no reason for her to delay it any longer. Since she had asked him, he knew the response he could give her that would have credence. Pulling her closer to him, plastering himself against her, he said, "Feel me? Now ask me your question again."

He figured the huge boner practically poking into her pretty much spelled things out for her. They were standing in her foyer again and he had no problem stripping her naked and taking her here and now. Although he liked the outfit she was wearing, a cute floral-print sundress, he'd rather see her wearing nothing at all.

She pushed back from him and smiled. "Okay, I feel you. Let's eat." She walked off and he frowned as he followed her toward the kitchen.

"You know where the bathroom is to wash up," she said, moving over to the stove after setting the wine on the table.

He glanced across the breakfast bar at her, trying not to recall that he'd taken her before right there. She was moving around her kitchen as if she'd completely dismissed him for the time being. Had she forgotten about the screams his fingers and mouth had elicited from her the last time he was here? If so, then maybe he needed to remind her.

Instead of moving in the direction of the bathroom, he moved around the breakfast bar and headed straight toward her. She looked up at him, surprised. "That was quick."

He smiled. She thought he'd washed up already and was definitely wrong about that. Instead of saying anything, he took the spatula out of her hand and placed it on the kitchen counter.

"Virgil? What do you think you're doing?"

Instead of answering, he swept her off her feet and into his arms.

"Put me down!"

Refusing to do what she asked, he headed toward the living room. Once there he eased down on the sofa with her cradled in his arms. Tightening his hold he kept her firmly planted in his lap when she tried to wiggle out of it. "Stay still, will you?"

She glared over at him. "Why should I?"

"For this."

And then he lowered his head and before she could draw her next breath he slanted his mouth across hers. At that moment he needed her taste more than he needed to breathe. As he intended, the kiss was quick, hot but thorough. It got her attention just as he'd meant for it to do.

And now that he had it… "So what's it going to be, Kara? Are you willing to accept my terms?"

She surprised him when she leaned up and licked across his lips causing his groin to tighten. She wrapped her arms around his neck and captured his gaze. "It depends."

Her calm response had his gut tightening. "Depends on what?"

"On whether you accept *my* terms."

A funny feeling settled in the pit of his stomach. "And what terms are those?"

She didn't say anything for the longest time and then she finally spoke. "It's a favor, actually. I mentioned to you last week that I would be replacing the carpeting in here with hardwood floors. They're ready to get started. That means I'll need a place to stay for at least a week or two while it's being done. So in other words, Virgil, I need to move in with you."

Chapter 15

Kara recognized that look in Virgil's eyes and knew what he was thinking. He'd never shared his space with any woman…except for her. And now she was asking him to share it again. And from the hard, penetrating stare he was giving her, he wasn't having it.

"There has to be someplace else you can stay," he said gruffly.

"If there was I wouldn't be asking you" was her quick comeback.

His gaze hardened even more. "What about your sister?"

"I'd rather not. Marti and I aren't on the best of terms."

"Could have fooled me from that day Uriel and I ran into you two at the Racetrack Café. You looked pretty chummy then."

"I'd rather not talk about Marti, Virgil. You just have to take my word for it when I say I don't have any place to go."

"Then postpone having your floors done. I'm sure you have that option."

"Yes, but I don't want to take it. Why should I?"

"Because you need somewhere to stay."

He was being a smart-ass. "And you have plenty of room at your place." That was an understatement. In addition to a huge master bedroom, his two-story home that sat on a huge lake had four guest rooms—each with their own full baths—a living room, dining room, family room, eat-in kitchen, a screened-in patio and a three-car garage.

Virgil slid her off his lap and she sat beside him on the sofa. She knew that already he was trying to put distance between them. "I don't share my space, Kara."

She decided not to call him out and say he had once. With her. Although he had never asked her to move in with him permanently, there were a lot of times she'd stayed at his place more than she'd stayed at her own. He'd even given her a key.

"I need you to share your place with me, Virgil."

"No."

"Fine," she said, easing from the sofa. "You need to eat before you leave."

He grabbed her hand before she walked off. "Why, Kara?"

Kara lifted her chin. She knew she was taking a gamble, but she had to break through that solid wall he'd erected. "Like I said, I need a place to stay for just a week or two. You want us to be lovers but I'm not good enough to sleep in your bed."

"You can sleep in my bed all you want, but you can't stay at my place. Temporarily or otherwise."

"Fine. Evidently you don't want me as much as you claim you do. I'll find somewhere else to stay." She tried pulling her hand away but when she did he tugged her back down in his lap.

He tightened his arms around her, and his lips were mere inches from hers when he said in a husky voice, "There's no claiming about it, Kara. I want you."

"Prove it."

Virgil looked at Kara intently for a second. He had no idea what was going on in that pretty little head of hers, but he had no problem proving anything. If she hadn't gotten the message before, then by the time he left tonight, there would be no doubt in her mind about the degree of his desire for her. As far as staying at his place, it wouldn't be happening. There was no way he could handle her invading his space. Not even for one or two weeks.

He drew in a sharp breath when she shifted positions in his lap, causing her backside to rub against his hard, throbbing erection. Heat began building up inside of him. He couldn't resist planting featherlight kisses around her lips before using the tip of his tongue to lick around the edges. She had to feel him harden against her, so how could she think he didn't want her just because he refused to let her move in with him?

"Don't waste my time, Virgil," she said against his mouth. "Either prove it or leave."

He leaned back, held her gaze and his stomach clenched in heated lust. He would prove it all right. "I think dinner will have to hold for a while," he said huskily. Then he stood with her in his arms and headed toward her bedroom.

Kara felt the mattress beneath her back and when Virgil stepped away from the bed, she felt the erratic beat of her heart. She had pushed him and now she knew he wouldn't let her leave this bedroom until he had proven everything to his satisfaction.

As well as to hers.

She'd known exactly what she was doing in taunting him. Now she had him in a place where she intended to rekindle a lot of hot and steamy memories. By the time he left tonight, she would have proven a few things of her own. Their lovemaking had always been passionate, but they had been pretty emotional, as well. He'd once told her that he'd never made love with a woman until her. Up until then for him it hadn't been anything but sex.

She wanted to believe that the Virgil who had felt that way then would feel that way now. Although he thought her believing the worst about him was unforgivable, a part of her wanted to believe that spending quality time together would eventually wipe away all the hurt and anger. She was taking a big risk, probably the biggest gamble of her life. But she had to believe that what the two of them once shared had been so special there was no way it could have been totally destroyed.

He returned to the bed and before she could blink an eye, he had tugged her up and within seconds had whipped her sundress over her head, leaving her bare except for her panties.

He tossed the dress aside as his gaze scanned her body. It was as if he needed to recapture in his mind what his eyes hadn't feasted on in four years. Granted, he'd tasted her pretty well Saturday evening, but now he was taking his time to look his fill. And she had no problem with that.

Already Kara could feel a deep tingling sensation between her legs. She hadn't slept with another man since Virgil. When she'd thought he had betrayed her, she hadn't wanted to become involved with another man. She'd dated on occasion but could never give her heart or body to anyone else.

"When did you start wearing thongs?" he asked her, intruding into her thoughts. She saw that his gaze was concentrating on the area between her legs and the little scrap of almost nothing lace covering her there.

"Why do you want to know? Do you have a problem with what I have on, Virgil?"

"No. Just curious."

Virgil recalled that she preferred wearing hip-hugging briefs. The thong fit her long legs and curvy hips perfectly and he liked seeing her in it…mainly because it exposed more of her body. And speaking of exposure, she wasn't wearing a bra. The last time he'd seen her breasts she hadn't been wearing a bra, either. Had this become a habit?

He shifted his gaze back to her face. "Have you stopped wearing bras?"

"What gave you that idea?"

"This is the second time I've seen you without one."

She smiled. "I don't wear one…whenever it suits me."

Hell, it definitely suited him. She had a pair of the lushest breasts any woman could own. Seeing her lying there, tempting and adorably hot, made him want to make love to her real bad. He had to fight hard for control. But then, hadn't she dared him to prove just how much he wanted her?

And he knew just where to start. Reaching out, he lifted her hips and slid the thong down her legs. After tossing it aside, Virgil felt his guts twist into knots as his gaze raked over her entire body. Never had he seen a woman more beautifully made. His fingers trembled when he touched her skin. It felt soft and smooth, almost like velvet. He could recall the days, right after they'd broken up, when his body had gone through withdrawal just thinking how perfect she was and how much he'd wanted her.

He pushed those memories to the back of his mind. That was then. This was now and she was here. He was here and for whatever reason they were back together in this place. He forced the thought that it was a temporary arrangement to the back of his mind. Right now he didn't care. All he could think about was that he was actually touching her again.

"Virgil?"

He lifted his head and met her gaze. "Yes?"

"What are you waiting on? Christmas?"

He couldn't help but throw his head back and laugh. Only she could make him laugh at a time like this. She always had the ability to keep things lively in the bedroom. "That mouth of yours will get you in trouble," he said, stepping back to start removing his clothes.

"Then I suggest you use that mouth of yours to keep me out of trouble."

"Mmm, I like you naughty," he said, sliding his pants down his legs and liking the look of appreciation in her eyes when she gazed at his erection. That look reminded him of times when she'd definitely been naughty.

Returning to the bed, he sat beside her, needing to touch her some more. As much as he wanted her, and no matter what she said, he would not be rushed into pleasuring her. For some reason, their first mating after all this time needed to be slow and painstakingly meticulous. It might annoy her at first, but in the end she would appreciate it.

He held her gaze as he began stroking between her legs with methodical detail, letting his fingers recall every inch of her, reacquainting his hands with the feel of her and needing to see the play of emotions crossing her face as he did so.

Virgil always thought she was the most passionate of women and pleasuring her had always been an honor as well as a privilege for him. He'd never felt that way with any other woman. Kara could arouse him to unprecedented heights. Even now her feminine scent was enveloping him, eliciting a need that all but crackled with the highest voltage of sexual energy.

He loved the sounds she made while he was getting her ready for what was to come. He wanted her to feel the heat, to desire it and need it as much as he did. His gaze was transfixed on her as he continued to stroke her and he wondered if she detected an air of shimmering sensuality surrounding them.

"Virgil…"

It had been a while since he'd heard his name whispered from her lips just that way. He'd missed hearing it. He leaned close to whisper, while keeping his fingers planted between her legs. "Tell me what you want, Kara."

"You."

Sexual tension thickened the blood in his veins and a rush of desire seized his groin. At that moment he couldn't hold back any longer. He had to have her.

Grabbing his pants off the floor, he retrieved a condom packet from his wallet and quickly sheathed himself, knowing she was watching him. Easing back onto the bed, he slid his body in place over hers while gazing down at her.

Needing to touch her, he reached up and tangled his hands with hers by the sides of her face, fighting deep emtions that tried resurfacing. He simply refused to let them. "I'm about to prove just how much I want you, Kara," he whispered when the hard ridge of his erection fit snugly at the entrance of her womanly core.

As if she couldn't wait any longer, she lifted her hips and he slid inside her. He kept going until he was totally embedded and couldn't go any farther. In the past, with him planted so deep inside of her and staring deep into her eyes, he would tell her how much he loved her, and he would feel the very existence of those words deep in his soul. But he was convinced all he was feeling now was the stirring sensations of heated lust combined with sexual excitement curling around in his stomach. There was no way he could love her again. He was convinced of it. But tonight he intended for the sex between them to be good.

Nothing, Kara thought, could ever equate to the feeling of being taken by Virgil. Nothing could compare to the feel of his engorged erection sliding inside of her all the way to the hilt. And then there were the sinfully erotic movements of his hips as he began thrusting hard. The steady rhythm rocked through her veins. She could even feel a throb of desire in the hands holding hers hostage near her head.

And when Virgil increased the pace, making his thrusts even more powerful, she couldn't stop herself from moaning his name. The intensity of their lovemaking was tripping her pulse, sending her heart rate off kilter and setting every inch of her skin on fire. And the look in his eyes held raw, sexual heat.

Then she felt it. The beginning of a thrumming sensation started low in her belly, compressing her inner muscles, making them clench him tight and begin milking him all the way into her womb.

That's when he lowered his head and kissed her, using his tongue to make swirling strokes inside her mouth. She pulled her hands free to grab hold of his shoulders, needing to feel her fingers digging into his muscles. An explosion erupted inside her that shook her, had her bucking her body upward at the same time he shouted her name and slammed downward in one deep, powerful thrust.

He kept kissing her, taking the kiss deeper while thrusting inside of her, running his hands all over her as if he needed to touch her, make sure she was real and not a figment of his imagination. And she kissed him back, needing him as much as he seemed to need her.

He was back in her bed. It would be up to her to make sure passion prevailed over caution, desire superseded Virgil's unforgiving nature and love conquered all.

What the hell happened?

Virgil slumped down beside Kara, totally spent, feeling raw, his muscles unable to function, and his emotions totally exposed. Why did making love to her always leave him with a feeling he couldn't explain? And how, after all this time and everything that had transpired between them, could he feel that way?

He thought that he could make love to her, desire her, yet keep a part of himself detached. But Kara had a way of making him give all or nothing. He'd given his all, and with each and every thrust into her going deep into familiar territory, emotions he'd tried holding at bay—the same ones he'd convinced himself were nonexistent where she was concerned—had overtaken him. In the end, he'd been powerless to fight it. Why?

He quickly concluded the reason had everything to do with being back inside of her after all this time. That coupled with the fact that over the past few weeks he'd been horny as hell. Yes, that had to be the reason why he'd lost it, and why even now he was getting aroused all over again.

Although he was no longer lying on top of her, their limbs were still entwined and his arms were thrown over her waist while they faced each other. She was breathing deeply and her eyes were open, but instead of looking at him she was staring beyond him at a painting on her wall.

So far she hadn't said anything. He couldn't help wondering what she was thinking. Did she regret letting him make love to her? Or, like him, was she thinking what they'd shared had been so mind-blowingly perfect, it had left them both at a loss for words?

He continued to lie there and gaze at her. She had to know he was staring yet she wouldn't look at him. That was fine since he needed to get his mind back on track, although that wouldn't be an easy thing to do. Not when he was thinking about how good it was to lie here beside her like this. He'd always enjoyed this, the aftermath, when they would lie naked in each other's arms and savor what they'd done together. They would talk, more times than not, and confess their love for each other. Telling her the first time that he loved her had been hard because he hadn't spoken those words to any woman before. But after he did it, and knowing she was so deserving of his love, the words had flowed easily and had come frequently... especially whenever they made love. For him it had been important that she know he was not confusing love with lust and that he knew the difference.

Tonight had brought back memories of how it felt being inside her, feeling her inner muscles squeeze to clench him and then proceed to milk him dry. She had a way of doing that perfectly, getting every single drop out of him. He had to force back the growl in his throat just thinking about it.

Virgil literally held his breath when Kara shifted her gaze to look at him. He was certain he wasn't mistaken about the look of total sexual fulfillment he saw in her eyes.

He held tight to her gaze and asked, "You okay?"

Instead of answering him, she reached out and caressed the side of his face and smiled softly. Then she finally said, "Yes. I'm okay. I had to take a minute to get myself together. What we did just now felt simply amazing."

Virgil would have to agree with her and was about to tell her so when she leaned in and placed her mouth over his. He needed this kiss just as much as she apparently did. Possibly even more. And when her tongue entered his mouth he greedily captured it with his own. Their tongues mated for the longest time before she finally lifted her mouth from his.

He was totally aroused all over again and from the way her hands began stroking him, so was she. "I want you again," he whispered, straddling her body and gazing down into her face.

"And more than anything, Virgil, I want you to want me" was her soft response.

He pushed to the back of his mind the possibility that she meant anything by what she'd said. Instead he turned his entire focus, his full concentration on making love to her again.

Chapter 16

It looks as if Virgil Bougard is trying to turn over a new leaf. About time. He was seen this weekend with his sleeves rolled up at his company's back-to-school charity event. I might be wrong but it looked like he was enjoying himself while giving out those book bags to all those kids. Can we credit his on-again love affair with Kara Goshay for his change of attitude? Stay tuned.

Kara tossed the newspaper aside to take another sip of her coffee. Thanks to Flo's article in the paper that morning, the strategy to improve Virgil's image was definitely off to a good start. And the photograph of him surrounded by some of the kids who'd attended the book-bag giveaway was priceless. He didn't look like an ordinary executive but, rather, like one who cared. And a part of her truly believed he did. Just like a part of her believed what they'd shared in her bed last week had meant something to him... although from the look of things, he'd run scared again.

Getting out of her chair, she took another sip of her coffee as she walked over to the window in her office and gazed out, remembering that night. After making love two more times they'd dressed and gone downstairs to eat the dinner she'd prepared. By then it was after midnight, but she doubted either of them cared. They had worked up a voracious appetite and the lasagna, tossed salad and strawberry cheesecake had hit the spot. He had offered to help clean up the kitchen but she declined his offer. However, he had refused to leave without helping her clear off the table. That was when he'd mentioned he would be out of town for a few days. Without saying when they would see each other again or whether he'd changed his mind about her moving in with him, he had kissed her goodbye and left.

That had been nearly a week ago, and she hadn't heard from him till an hour ago. Out of the blue he'd called to ask her out to dinner. When she'd informed him that tonight wouldn't be good for her because she was in the process of moving out of her condo, he'd said nothing for a minute before saying he would touch base with her later this week. He hadn't even asked where she would be moving to.

Since there was no doubt in her mind that making love with her had meant more to him than just a roll between the sheets, she believed he was fighting it. She couldn't force from her mind how he'd looked down at her, deep into her eyes, when he'd positioned his body over hers. Although Virgil refused to utter the words of love he'd once said, she had felt his resolve breaking with every stroke into her body. Why did he have to be so stubborn, unforgiving and determined not to put his heart on the line again?

She had taken tomorrow off to get settled into the hotel

where she would be staying for the next two weeks. There was a lot on her plate and she hoped she would be too busy to think about Virgil.

When Virgil pulled into Kara's driveway he saw several lights were still on, including the one in her upstairs bedroom. He had intentionally not contacted her for almost a week, feeling the need to put distance between them. Making love to her had affected him more than he'd figured it would and he'd needed time away from her to screw his head back on right.

But that hadn't stopped him from going to bed each night thinking of her, wanting her and desiring her in a way he could never desire any other woman. It had taken him all those restless and sleepless nights to figure out that even after four years, Kara wasn't out of his system like he thought and making love to her last week had only complicated matters.

He hadn't wanted to remember how good things used to be when they'd been together but he couldn't help doing so. Nor did he want to think about how, after playing several games of tennis with Donovan Steele, he had rushed home to come here. He couldn't hold out any longer. He wanted to see her again. He *needed* to see her again. He wanted to kiss her. Taste her all over. Make love to her again.

He'd suggested they have an affair and although they'd made love, she hadn't consented to his terms. Instead she'd asked a favor of him, one he'd quickly turned down. Now he wasn't sure where they stood and he needed to find out.

No matter what her ultimate decision would be about the affair, they would still have to be seen together in public for a few more weeks. He, more than anyone, would feel the sting of having to be around her and pretend romantic interest in a woman he wanted to take to bed.

At least he'd spoken to his mother earlier today and convinced her to drop the crazy idea of introducing Kara to Dr. Lynwood. Although he could tell his mother had not seen his point, since nothing serious would ever develop between him and Kara again, she'd agreed to leave it alone.

He had left his parents' home somewhat satisfied and had convinced himself all the way to the tennis courts that his visit with his mother had nothing to do with any jealousy he'd felt. He just didn't want to think about Kara with any other man after him. He knew it didn't make sense but since Kara had reentered his life nothing he did seemed to make much sense anymore.

Like the decision he'd made that morning…

It had taken him a while to come around, but he had convinced himself of the merits of having her at his place. That would be a logical move, especially since the two of them were pretending to be exclusive lovers. And he would get what he wanted. Lover's rights. He would go to bed with her and wake up with her. In other words, they would have access to sex whenever they wanted it. And with Kara he had a tendency to want it all the time. He would just have to be diligent in making sure he didn't start thinking with the wrong head. Not the one aching in his jeans at this very moment, but the one attached to his neck. He had to remember that whatever he and Kara shared was short-term and nothing more.

Getting out of the car and closing the door behind him, he headed for her door.

Kara was on her way down the stairs when she heard the ringing of her doorbell. She didn't have to wonder who was at her door. The deep pounding in her chest gave the identity of her visitor away. Why was Virgil here? To help pack up her things for her move to the hotel? A booty call?

The thought of the latter caused a heat to stir in the pit of her stomach. She really should be upset that sex was the only thing to bring him here, but pathetic as it might sound, she wanted to believe that making love to her would eventually come to mean something to him again.

She opened the door and stepped aside for him to enter. "Virgil, how was your trip?"

"Productive."

She thought he smelled fresh. And when he strolled by she picked up the scent of his aftershave and thought it was a turn-on. Instead of stopping in the foyer, he kept walking to her living room. She followed and saw him staring at her packed luggage.

She went over to the sofa and sat down, crossing her legs. "Any reason you're here?"

He moved his gaze to her, especially to her legs, which were exposed because of the short skirt she was wearing. Every time his eyes moved up and down her body, she could feel the sensual pull between them. "I had wanted to take you to dinner."

"And I told you what I'd be doing. Didn't you believe me?"

He shoved his hands into his pockets. "Yes, I believed you. In fact I came by to see if you needed my help."

"No thanks."

"You sure?"

"Positive."

Why did he have to stand over there, looking so perfectly male? And why was she looking at his sensuous mouth and recalling how it could take hers, make love to it, mate with it as if it was something he had every right to do?

He walked over to where she sat and he came to a stop right in front of her. She couldn't miss his aroused state. The huge bulge pressing hard against the zipper of his jeans was something that definitely caught her attention. And then he said in a voice that was deep and husky, "I want you."

She fixed her mouth to tell him the last thing she needed was for him to make a booty call now, but the words couldn't part from her lips. He was still fighting her, battling with emotions. Only someone who'd known him as well as she had could detect the struggle. Even now, he didn't want to want her, but something was driving him to do so anyway.

She knew how Virgil's mind worked. He stood there with his focus directly on her, trying to figure out why he wanted her so much. Why, considering their history, he wanted to strip her naked and make love to her, right where she sat. There was a dark intensity in the depths of his gaze, and the lines around his mouth were deep and drawn. She wondered if he was remembering the night they'd made love, right here in this house, under this roof. Of the time he had dropped to his knees, in the middle of her foyer and tasted her.

Kara was remembering those things and had to believe he was remembering them, as well. She had to believe this wasn't just another booty call but that it was one with a purpose. One that could bring her closer to her goal of cracking through the wall he'd erected around his heart.

She slowly eased from the sofa and stood in front of him, so close their bodies touched. She could feel his hard erection pressing against her middle. Just as she was certain that he could feel the hard buds of her nipples pressing into his chest.

At that moment she decided that although he'd made the booty call, she would be the one to take ownership of it.

"So you think you want me, Virgil?"

From the arch of his brow she knew her question surprised him. Evidently he figured any other woman would take what he'd said without question. In the end he would see she wasn't just any other woman. She was the one who loved him. The one he'd once loved. The one who was fighting hard to regain that love.

"I know I want you, Kara."

Hearing the words spoken so huskily from his lips should have been enough for her but it wasn't. She was fighting to hear him say different words, words that went deeper than just desire. "I'm glad you want me. Now let me show you just how much I want you."

She tugged her blouse over her head and shimmied seductively out of her skirt. And before he could catch his next breath, she reached out and whisked his T-shirt over his head.

Virgil's gaze scanned Kara as she stood there in a skimpy pair of panties. Evidently this was one of those times it suited her since she wasn't wearing a bra. Honestly, she didn't need one. Her breasts were beautiful, firm and full. While he watched, she slid out of her panties.

He was convinced there was not another woman with this much sensuality who walked the face of this earth. Would there always be this sensuous pull between them? One so strong it could create such an intense yearning that it threatened his control? And then there was her gutsiness. It had a way of increasing sexual tension between them to the point where he wanted nothing more than to make love to her all night and most of the next day—nonstop.

She pulled his belt through the loops of his jeans and tossed it aside; however, what made him get harder was when she slowly eased down his zipper. "Take off your jeans, Virgil."

Virgil had no problem doing what she asked and quickly

kicked off his shoes and removed his socks before lowering the jeans down his legs. When he tucked his fingers into the waistband of his briefs to tug them down his legs, as well, she placed her hand on his. "I can manage from here."

He nodded as he fixed his gaze on the lushness of her mouth, and he couldn't fight the heat that flared inside him when she licked her lips. And when she knelt in front of him and began easing his briefs down, he swore he could feel the floor beneath his feet shift. Awareness of what she was about to do filled his every pore with sexual greed. Even the air he was breathing seemed to thicken.

When she darted her tongue out of her mouth to moisten the head of his erection, it provoked a deep pounding right there in his crotch. He knew the shape and fullness of her lips, knew what her mouth was capable of doing, and he prepared himself for what was to come. No sooner had that thought entered his mind than she opened her mouth and took him all in. His breath caught while his entire body began to sizzle. He reached out and buried his fingers in her hair and released a torturous moan when a surge of hot, sharp sensation rushed through him.

Then she began sucking on him, just the way she'd done in all his dreams. Just the way she used to do when they'd been a couple. Just the way she knew he liked. Desire twisted his gut and every nerve in his body flared with the intensity of what she was doing. He could feel his erection enlarging and throbbing right in her mouth. She didn't let up and at the rate she was going, he would soon shatter into pieces. But he wanted to be inside of her when he did. And he wanted to be looking into her eyes when their bodies joined.

Ignoring her protest, he reached down and pulled her up and together they tumbled to the sofa. To cushion the impact he made sure she landed on top, straddling him.

She glanced down, flashed him a sexy smile and said, "Perfect landing."

Quickly taking advantage of their positions, she opened her legs wider and lowered her body down onto his shaft. Staring up at her, he gritted his teeth, but that didn't stop the moan from escaping. And when she began riding him, emotions he'd conditioned himself not to feel ripped through him and he grabbed her tight. This wasn't the first time they'd made love on her sofa, but it was the first time they'd done so with her on top.

Every bone in his body quivered with each and every erotic movement of her hips. He felt sexual sensations in every pore, every nerve. When frissons of heat raced up his spine he cupped the back of her head and lowered her mouth down to his. He needed this kiss as much as he needed everything else she was doing to him. The taste of her consumed him while at the same time thickening the blood in his veins.

And when sensations of a magnitude he'd never confronted before seemed to slam into both of them at the same time, they were pushed over the edge together. He had to hold on and maintain balance for the both of them, otherwise they would have tumbled to the floor. She broke her mouth free of his and screamed his name, and the sound seemed to pulverize every bone in his body.

He could feel his release exploding inside her, jetting all the way to her womb. It occurred to him then that he wasn't wearing a condom, and he hoped like hell she was still on the pill. But at that moment he didn't want to think about any possible risks of an unplanned pregnancy. He just wanted to think about how she'd made him feel.

They lay there as pleasure continued to flow through them, even when they were too tired to move. He loved her nakedness and gently stroked her back. Moments later she finally lifted her head to gaze down at him.

"You need to leave. I still have a lot of packing to do," she whispered in a tone he didn't think was too convincing. Not when he could feel himself getting hard inside of her again.

"I told you I would help."

"I don't want your help, Virgil."

"Tough," he said, leaning up and swiping his tongue across the pout that had formed on her lips. "Oh, and I forgot to mention that you're moving in with me."

Chapter 17

Kara stretched out her legs and when they came into contact with a muscular and hairy one, she recalled where she was and whose bed she was in. She slowly opened her eyes as memories from last night assailed her. After making love a second time at her place, that time in her bed, she and Virgil had dressed and he had helped her finish packing. It was way past midnight when they'd arrived at his home. By then she was too exhausted to unpack anything. Not even a nightgown.

They had showered together and he'd given her one of his T-shirts to sleep in. For all the good it had done. Once in his bed, he'd immediately taken the shirt off her. And they'd made love again. That was probably why he was still sleeping beside her. She glanced over at the clock, saw it was past eight and hoped he didn't have any meetings planned at the office this morning.

She snuggled back up to him as a feeling of happiness

washed over her. A part of her truly believed that no matter what Virgil said or how much he wanted to deny it, he loved her. The fact that she was here, under his roof, in his bed and nestled in his arms spoke volumes. She was certain he still thought it was about nothing more than sex, but she knew better and would be patient until he realized that fact, as well. There were still a lot of roads they would have to travel, more mountains they would need to climb. Trust and faith had to be rebuilt, but she believed they could do it and would do everything within her power to show Virgil that they could, as well. It would take one step at a time.

She believed being here with him this way was a start. It was more than what she'd had a few weeks ago. Even when she remembered his attitude toward her six months ago and where she was now, it was almost akin to a miracle. Somehow she had managed to put a crack in his wall of defense, but that wasn't good enough. She wouldn't be totally satisfied until that wall came tumbling down.

Still feeling totally exhausted, she closed her eyes when sleep overtook her again.

Virgil awakened to Kara's scent. It surrounded him and he would be surprised if it hadn't permeated his skin. He liked it. Always had. And the thought that she was here in his bed was simply unreal.

He glanced down at her. She was snuggled close to his side with their legs entwined. Her head was resting on his chest and one of her arms was thrown across his midsection. It was like déjà vu, reliving how things used to be, on those mornings when he would wake up beside her. Things could never be that way again so he would enjoy this while it lasted.

He glanced over at the clock and was glad he'd cleared

his calendar for the morning. Besides, he needed to work on that proposal for Stan Nelson, the wealthy Canadian who'd come highly recommended by a college classmate and friend. He'd been courting the Nelson Group for almost a year now and when he'd met with the man this week in Toronto, Virgil had felt it was almost a done deal. But he wasn't ready to mention it to anyone just yet. Not even to his father. He figured pulling something like this off would definitely make his dad a happy man. Hopefully happy enough to actually retire this time. And what Virgil liked about Nelson was that the man—who was known as a womanizer—didn't give a damn about Virgil's reputation. He wanted a man he could trust his money with.

Virgil knew he had to keep the deal quiet until everything was finalized, which hopefully would be in a couple of weeks. He glanced down at Kara again. On the drive here he had asked if she was still on the pill and had been relieved to find out she was. But then why had the image of a little girl with her features flashed through his mind?

As much as he wanted to wake Kara up so they could make love again, he knew he couldn't. She needed her rest. He glanced around the room and his eyes lit on her luggage, which he'd brought in after she'd fallen asleep. For someone who was only staying a week or so, she'd certainly packed a lot of stuff. But then, he would have to admit he didn't know of any woman who traveled light.

There were a few calls he needed to make this morning, so he slowly detached himself from Kara and eased out of bed. Already he felt a sense of loss with their bodies no longer connected. Grabbing his bathrobe off a chair he slid it over his naked body, remembering every single detail about the times they'd made love at her place and his. Before heading for the bathroom, he glanced back over at

Kara and put the thought out of his mind that she looked as though she belonged in his bed.

Kara awoke and she pulled herself up in bed to find she was alone. Where had Virgil gone? The smell of coffee was a dead giveaway. He had to have a cup first thing in the morning while he read the newspaper.

Easing out of bed, she couldn't help but smile when she saw he'd brought all her luggage into his bedroom. Last night they had left everything downstairs, and although she had slept in his bed, she wasn't sure if that's how things would be or if he would expect her to use one of his guest rooms. It seemed he'd made the decision for her to share this room with him.

When she heard her cell phone, she quickly rushed across the room to dig it out of her purse. She answered, not recognizing the caller ID. "Hello?"

"Where are you? I stopped by your place this morning and a group of workers were there. They said you had moved out to have some work done on your floors."

Kara eased into the wingback chair upon hearing her sister's voice. She hadn't talked to Marti since the day they'd had breakfast together at the Racetrack Café. Kara was trying hard to find it in her heart to forgive Marti and move on, but each time she tried doing so, she had a funny feeling about something that wouldn't go away.

"Why did you stop by my place?" Although she'd never told Marti she wasn't welcome there anymore, she certainly hadn't invited her sister over, either.

"To invite you to lunch and to give you my new cell number."

Marti had had her old cell number for years. "Why did you change it?"

"I started getting weird calls from a man I didn't know. Not sure how he got my number so I decided to change it."

Kara's concern for her sister kicked in. No matter what, she loved her and didn't want anything to happen to her. "Did you report it to the police?"

"No. Hopefully, changing my phone number will do the trick. If not, I'll go to the cops." There was a pause and then Marti asked, "So where are you? If you needed a place to stay, you could have crashed here with me."

Kara knew there was no way she could have done that. "Thanks, but I'm living with Virgil for a while."

"He's letting you do that?"

Kara raised a brow. Why was there surprise in Marti's voice? As far as Marti and anyone else knew—except for Virgil's parents and possibly his godbrothers—they had gotten back together.

"And why wouldn't he, Marti? Virgil and I are back together again." The lie was part of their ruse, but she couldn't help hoping it would eventually be true.

"No reason. Well, you have my number now. I hope we can do lunch soon."

Maybe they should. She didn't like the thought of Marti having to change her phone number because of harassing calls. "Yes, let's. I'll call you next week and we can plan something then."

"Thanks, Kara. I'll await your call."

Virgil turned from the stove when he heard Kara enter his kitchen, trying not to remember what happened the last time she'd done so. He remembered as if it had been yesterday. He was doing the same thing then that he was doing now, which was fixing breakfast, when he'd turned around. Instead of being fully dressed like she was now, she'd opted to wear just his dress shirt, unbuttoned, with nothing else on underneath. He recalled sweeping her into his arms to carry her back upstairs, but they hadn't made it that far and had ended up making love on the stairs.

"Something smells good."

He started to tell her that she smelled good. Frying bacon had nothing on her. He'd also liked her scent right before they'd made love. It was always a good indication of when she wanted it as much as he did.

"I wondered when the smell of bacon would bring you down here. It's almost lunchtime."

"I noticed, and why aren't you at work?"

"I decided to play hooky today and hang out with you."

Kara liked the sound of that. She tried not to notice how good Virgil looked shirtless, shoeless and with a pair of jeans riding low on his hips. He was one sexy man who knew his way around the kitchen, thanks to two grandmothers who knew the meaning of good food.

"If you do, then I'll put you to work helping me unpack."

He laughed. "You're not afraid I might see all that girly stuff?"

"Nothing you haven't seen before, although I have picked up some new things over the years." She thought about the purple negligee she'd recently purchased.

"Like those thongs?"

She chuckled. "Yes, like those thongs. You like them, don't you?"

He leaned against the kitchen counter while his gaze roamed all over her as if he had X-ray vision to see beyond her jeans and top. "Yes, I like them. Go on and sit down. Breakfast is almost ready."

"You didn't have to cook breakfast for me, you know," she said, doing what he said by taking a seat at his table. The same one she had helped him pick out when he'd decided to replace his last one. She loved his kitchen since it had a good view of a golf course and lake. "And don't you dare try to convince me it's something you do all the time because I know you don't," she added.

"You're right. But I knew how much you like grits, scrambled eggs and bacon and decided after all we did last night, you deserved energy food," he said, bringing several platters over to the table.

"That was kind of you."

He smiled when he joined her at the table. "It's the least that I can do." And he meant it. He'd been a greedy ass last night as far as her body was concerned, and although he'd made sure she got her pleasure, as well, he had kept her from getting a good night's sleep.

"By the way, I noticed your phone ringing a couple times while I was shaving. You were sleeping so soundly, I didn't wake you. I hope you didn't miss an important call."

The missed calls had been from Marti, and Kara decided mentioning her sister right now wasn't a good idea. "No, it wasn't important."

She hadn't realized just how hungry she was until she began eating. They shared conversation over breakfast and Kara was surprised how relaxed and unguarded Virgil appeared to be around her, and she was grateful for that.

After breakfast she helped him with the dishes and then they went upstairs to unpack her things. Of course they got waylaid several times, with several showers in between. What should have taken them less than an hour ended up taking them all afternoon.

She offered to cook dinner but he suggested they go out instead. They decided to go back to the Goldenrod. They both agreed the food had been delicious the last time they'd gone there. And just like before, they enjoyed their meal. After dinner he took her by her place to pick up a few items she had forgotten to pack.

Before returning to Virgil's place they had dropped by his parents' home to check on things while the older couple were in Houston. Virgil and Kara arrived back at his place, and no sooner had the door closed behind them than Virgil pulled her into his arms and kissed her with the passion of a man who enjoyed what he was doing. And she proved to him she appreciated all the attention. Later that night while he held her in his arms, a satisfied Kara thought the day had been simply wonderful and wished their remaining days together would be just as special.

She had only two weeks to completely tear down the wall Virgil had built around his heart.

Chapter 18

Xavier Kane leaned back in his chair and studied the man sitting across the table from him at the Racetrack Café. "You've certainly been in a good mood lately, V."

Virgil glanced up from his plate. "Have I?"

"Yes."

"Just your imagination."

"Um, I don't think so. Uriel mentioned it, as well. So did Winston. Although, he did say when he called last week you rushed him off the phone."

"Like you, he's imagining things," Virgil said, taking a sip of his coffee. "And when is Bronson's next race? I think I'm—"

"Don't try changing the subject. I want to know why you're in such a good mood. You have a tendency to be an ass at times, although you don't curse as much as you used to. If I didn't know better I'd think…"

Xavier didn't finish what he was about to say. He merely stared at Virgil.

"You'd think what?"

"That you and Kara are back together—for real, and not for any pretense."

Virgil pushed his plate aside and leaned back in his chair. "But I hope you do know better."

Xavier chuckled. "Can't say that I do. Couples are known to get back together. Farrah and I did. So did Uriel and Ellie. York and Darcy. Winston and Ainsley."

"I'm happy for all of you but that has nothing to do with me."

"I understand Kara has moved in with you."

He didn't have to wonder how Xavier knew that. Uriel had dropped by his place and Kara had been there. "Doesn't mean anything. I'm sure the person who told you that she was there also mentioned it's only temporary."

"Yes, he did mention it, but…"

"But what?"

"Like I said, you've been in a good mood. Maybe Kara should become a permanent fixture at your place."

"That won't be happening. She has another week and then she's out of there."

"You sure?"

"Just as sure as I know my father's name is Matthew and my mom's name is Rhona."

"I hope you aren't making a big mistake."

"I'm not. Now will you tell me when Bronson's next race is?" He told himself he wasn't changing the subject, that he just wanted to ensure he didn't miss his friend's car race.

An hour later while driving back to his office, Virgil thought about his conversation with Xavier. So what if he'd been in a good mood lately? Was that a crime? And although he wouldn't admit it to Xavier or anyone else, Kara *was* responsible.

Virgil tightened his hands on the steering wheel. The last thing he needed was to fill his mind with foolish thoughts. He and Kara were having no more than an affair. He had affairs all the time so why should this one be any different? It was different because he was her client. He couldn't lose sight of the fact that this was a job for her—a job that she was getting paid to do with the goal of improving his image. Not one to miss an opportunity, he'd simply capitalized on a good thing and he had no regrets about doing so.

If he was telling the truth, he would also admit that the thought of her returning to her place in a week didn't actually fill him with joy. He'd gotten used to waking up with her in his arms, her leg thrown over his or his over hers. Making love to her in the mornings and going to sleep after making love to her at night. Sharing breakfast and dinner with her. Being seen around town with her. It was beginning to feel just like old times—

He stopped himself right there. That was the one thing he couldn't allow to happen. Those days were over and done with. He'd told Kara that, and as far as he was concerned she had no reason not to believe him.

But what if she thought he'd changed his mind? What if she'd gotten it in her head that they could be a couple again just because they were enjoying each other in and out of bed? He hoped she hadn't, because she'd be in for a rude awakening if that was the case. As soon as her house was ready, she would be returning to it.

"You truly look happy, Kara."

Kara glanced over at Marti. They were enjoying lunch at her sister's condo. This was the first time she'd been here since finding out what Marti had done. She couldn't help smiling over at her sister. "I am happy."

"Because of Virgil?"

She held her sister's gaze. "Yes, because of Virgil. I know you don't like talking about what you did four years ago, Marti, but in order for our relationship to move forward, you truly need to regret what you did, and I don't honestly think that you do."

"I apologized, didn't I?"

"Yes, but was it sincere? I'm not sure it was."

Marti looked down and didn't say anything for a long time. Then she met Kara's gaze and said softly, "I honestly thought Virgil would hurt you, Kara, and I couldn't let him do that. I've been out there a lot longer than you have. I know the players, the heartbreakers, the men women trust only to find out how wrong they are, the men who don't mean a woman any good. And I didn't like the thought that one of those had targeted you."

"But Virgil changed while we were together. Surely you could see that."

"Yes, but still. I couldn't risk my kid sister getting hurt by a man the way I was."

Kara didn't say anything as she saw the pain in Marti's eyes, pain she was seeing for the first time, which meant her sister had done a good job of hiding it over the years. "Tell me about him," she coaxed.

When Marti shook her head, Kara reached out and took her hand. "You have to tell me. Maybe telling me will not only cleanse yourself of him but also help me to understand."

Marti didn't say anything for a minute, as if she was debating whether to share her story. "His name was Malcolm Edwards," she said finally. "He was already living in Sacramento when I moved there after college. I was twenty-four. Young. Naive. Too trusting. And my head was filled with romantic ideas of love and forever after.

Why wouldn't it be? Our parents loved each other and set a good example for us to follow. So naturally, I assumed that one day I would marry a man who loved me and I would have his children. I'd heard about Malcolm's reputation with women, but when we were together he made me feel special. And I honestly thought he had fallen in love with me. Like you and Virgil, we dated for almost a year. Things were going great and I definitely wasn't prepared for what he did."

Kara's heart pounded in her chest. "What did he do?"

Kara could see the pain in her sister's eyes deepen. "One night he had four of his closest friends over to watch a football game. We hadn't moved in together yet, but I figured it was only a matter of time since I was spending more time at his place than my own."

After a momentary pause Marti continued. "I knew about the football game and since none of the guys brought their girlfriends, I figured I would hang out in the bedroom and study for my CPA exam."

Kara watched her sister and knew she was fighting back tears. She wanted to reach out and take her hand, but she remained still, letting Marti set the pace.

"I honestly don't know what happened. The only thing I remember was Malcolm coming into the bedroom and offering me a glass of wine. He said I was studying too much and it would relax me. I thanked him for being thoughtful and drank it. Everything else is kind of woozy after that. All I remember is waking up sometime during the night in bed with five men. And I could tell from the way my body felt that all five of them had taken turns with me."

"They raped you?"

Marti wiped a tear from her eyes. "Yes. And just to make sure I knew what they had done, when they saw I was awake, they raped me again."

She stared with teary eyes at Kara. "Malcolm watched while his friends gagged my mouth and tied up my hands and had their way with me before he took his turn. He said he and his best friends shared everything."

Kara was indignant, angry beyond belief. "Did you call the police?"

"That's what's so sad. One of them was a cop. And he threatened to do all kinds of things if I reported them. All five of them said they would make my life a living hell if I told anyone."

Kara got up and went to her sister and hugged her tight, fighting back her own tears. "Oh, Marti. I'm so sorry they did that to you. I am so sorry."

Marti released a flood of tears while Kara held her. Kara wondered if this was the first time her sister had allowed herself to cry.

Moments later Marti said, "When they left that morning for breakfast and to play basketball, I cleaned myself up and left. I went back to my own apartment and packed. I flew home to San Francisco that night."

"Did you tell the folks?"

Marti shook her head. "No. Can you imagine what Dad would have done had he known? I couldn't risk it. Mom suspected something when she saw bruises on my arms and thighs. She'd walked into my room when I was getting dressed after my shower. She'd assumed I was out by the pool with Dad and was putting more towels in my bathroom. She asked me about the bruises and I told her that I had taken a fall. But I don't think she believed me."

"So you let those guys get away with what they did to you?" Kara asked with indignation in her voice.

"Yes, because of their threats. But you know what they say about payback being a bitch. Well, I became that bitch, Kara. A few years later, all five of them eventually married, had good careers and were highly respected in the community. However, being the evil men that they were, I believed if they did it once they would do it again. So I hired a private detective to dig up what he could on them. He discovered they were involved in child pornography— they used the children of immigrants. Once we had enough evidence, we sent what we'd gathered to the state attorney's office. The five of them were arrested and convicted. And as far as I know, they're still serving time."

Kara didn't say anything as she thought about what her sister had just told her. The thought of Malcolm Edwards, the man her sister loved and thought loved her, actually raping her with his friends made her sick to her stomach. "Did they ever find out you were connected with their arrests?"

"Yes, I paid a visit to each of them individually in jail and told them they had me to thank for their current situation. It made me feel good to look into their eyes and let them know they hadn't gotten away with what they did to me. I also told them that, since they shared everything, I hoped they enjoyed sharing jail time."

Kara nodded. In a way justice had been served, but at what cost? She'd often wondered why Marti could be so cold and heartless at times when it came to men. Now she knew. But there was still one question she hadn't answered. "Why did you think Virgil would be anything like Malcolm?"

"Because he was so close to his godbrothers. They're thick as thieves, just like Malcolm and his friends were. I didn't trust them."

Kara frowned. "But you dated Xavier for almost a month."

"It was just sex. Good sex but just sex. In the end I tested him. I lied and told him I wanted marriage and that's all it took for him to drop me like a hot potato. None of those godbrothers were marriage material. I didn't think Virgil was, either. I thought he was just feeding you lies."

"Four of them are married now, Marti. Including Xavier. So there is hope. I want to believe Virgil and I would have eventually gotten married. I loved him and I believe in my heart he loved me. I think you misjudged Virgil as well as his godbrothers. They are nothing like Malcolm and his friends."

Kara went back to her seat and looked over at her sister. "I regret what those guys did to you and I hope they rot in jail. But what you did to me and Virgil was wrong. You apologized to me but not to Virgil. I think you owe him an apology, as well."

The buzzer on Virgil's desk sounded. "Yes, Pam?"

"There's someone here to see you. A Marti Goshay."

Virgil leaned back in his chair, wondering what the hell Marti Goshay could want with him. She was the last person he wanted to see or talk to. But if she was up to something, he needed to know what. "Send her in."

"Yes, sir."

As the door opened and Marti walked in, he arched a brow. She was known to make a grand entrance whenever she walked into any room. But the woman who walked into his office looked...defeated. He tossed that opinion of her aside and asked, "What do you want, Marti?"

She looked everywhere other than at him. Another first. Marti was known to look any man straight in the eye and state what she wanted or didn't want. She glanced back at him. "I came to apologize for lying to Kara about you."

Her apology surprised him because he didn't think she would ever make one. Not that it mattered one way or the other now. Besides, he figured she was only apologizing to get back in Kara's good graces. "Fine. You've apologized. If there's nothing else then you can leave."

Marti turned to leave but then she turned back around. "I know I'm not one of your favorite people, Virgil. But I hope for Kara's sake the two of us can get along. What I did was wrong. I truly didn't think you loved Kara. I made a mistake. She loves you and I now know that you love her, as well. She's happy and I'm glad the two of you are back together." And then she walked out the door.

Virgil didn't say anything for a long while. Marti was wrong if she thought he loved Kara, but then, like everyone else who read *Flo on the Ro*, she assumed they'd gotten back together. That's all it was, he told himself. The gossip column made her think they were in love.

Pushing Marti's visit to the back of his mind, Virgil got back to work. He picked up the file York had overnighted to him. He was elated that he had enough goods on both Whitney and Marv Hilton. First of all, there was no way Marv could have thought Whitney was a virgin when there had been a porn video of her floating around—one that Hilton had dropped a lot of money to keep out of circulation. And Marv Hilton wasn't so clean himself. He had an expensive mistress he was trying to keep happy, not to mention his involvement in a couple of shady deals.

What the Hiltons did in their spare time was their business, but when they tried to ruin his reputation based on lies, then it became his. Leaning back in the chair he picked up the phone on his desk. "Pam, get Marv Hilton on the line."

Chapter 19

A smiling Virgil walked into his home later that afternoon with a bottle of champagne in his hand. Kara, who'd arrived a few minutes before, was in the kitchen. She was going to surprise him with another one of her dishes that she knew he liked—chicken and dumplings. It was another recipe his grandmother had shared with her.

"What's the occasion?" she asked, glancing at the champagne bottle he placed on the kitchen counter. Virgil pulled her into his arms.

"As usual, York came through, this time with his report on Marv Hilton as well as on Whitney. I had a conversation with Marv and told him that unless he backed off, I would send copies of what I had to the media."

"Did he agree to do it?"

"I left him no choice. He knew I meant business and he wants to keep his secrets secret."

"Good for you."

He sniffed the air. "Mmm, something smells good."

Her smile brightened. "Chicken and dumplings. I know how much you like it."

"Yes, and I like you better," he said, leaning down for a kiss. The moment their mouths touched, she felt a rush of need travel up her spine. By the time he ended the kiss, she felt totally weak in the knees.

"I'm hungry, baby."

Her heart began pounding at his use of the endearment. It had been years since he'd called her that. "For dinner?"

"No. For you."

And then he swept her into his arms and carried her up to the bedroom.

"It's a good thing dinner was finished cooking or it would have burned by now," Kara said, sliding back into her dress.

Virgil lay there, sprawled naked on top of the covers as he watched her, feeling himself getting hard all over again. It had always been this way with her. It didn't take much for him to want her. Desire her. Lov—

He shook his head, refusing to go there. Did he need to give himself another prep talk, the same one he'd been giving himself a lot lately? The one where he swore he'd never love her again?

"Virgil?"

He blinked. "Yes?"

"You were daydreaming."

He nodded. "Yes, I guess I was. What did you say?"

A smile touched her lips. "I said don't take too long coming down. I think we can both say we worked up an appetite."

"Okay. I'll be down in a minute."

When she left he continued to lie there for a minute as

he glanced around. He was just noticing the changes she'd made to his bedroom. Granted, he had moved her into his room but he hadn't expected her to take it over. It wasn't as if she was staying permanently. And where did that vase of flowers on his dresser come from? He doubted they were real but still, he never had flowers in his bedroom.

As he stood up to get dressed, a lot of crazy thoughts started flowing through his mind. What if Kara assumed she would be staying? But there was no way he could have given her that idea. Things were good between them and he enjoyed having her around, but he'd always known that in two weeks she would be gone. So had she.

Come to think of it, her two weeks were up in a few days. Then he realized something. She'd stopped giving him updates on the progress of her floors. Why?

Picking up his clothes off the floor, he went over to the closet to hang up his suit. The first thing he noticed was Kara's clothes next to his. Had they always been there? If so, then why was he just noticing them? And why was he beginning to feel crowded as though she was invading his space?

He pulled a pair of jeans off a hanger and slid them on when he heard his phone ring. Moving to the nightstand, he picked it up, knowing the caller was Uriel. "Yes, U?"

"Hey, Ellie is getting the last-minute details for my birthday party together and I need to—"

"Hey, wait a minute. I thought it was supposed to be a surprise."

Uriel laughed. "Man, you know it's hard for anyone to surprise me, especially my wife. Anyway, she wanted to know if you were bringing a guest?"

Virgil frowned. "A guest? You know I always come alone. Why would you think I'd bring someone?"

"Well, you do have a houseguest."

"Who will be gone by the time your party comes around, trust me."

"Oh."

Virgil knew the sound of that "oh" and what it meant. "All right, Uriel, get it out because I know there's something you want to say."

"I just thought things were going good between you and Kara."

"They are, considering how I felt about her this time last year. I've moved her to my 'friends' category."

"Can you do that?"

Virgil raised a brow. "Do what?"

"Just be friends with a woman you used to love?"

"I don't see why not not. Like I've told you a number of times, I can't love a person who doesn't trust me."

"And like I told you, you need to let it go."

"I have."

"Not if you're still feeling that way. I hope you open your eyes before it's too late."

Kara was placing the last platter of food on the table when Virgil walked in. She smiled over at him. "You're right on time."

He sat down at the table and she immediately picked up on a change in his mood. Had something happened since she'd left him in the bedroom? He had arrived home in a festive mood and their lovemaking was, as usual, off the charts. Afterward, he had held her as he told her about his conversation with Marv Hilton.

She couldn't help wondering if anything was wrong. So she asked him. "Virgil, is everything okay?"

For some reason she felt the smile he gave her didn't quite reach his eyes when he said, "Yes, everything is fine." Then he took a seat at the table and uncovered the platters. "Everything looks good and smells delicious. Let's eat."

Over dinner she told him how her day had gone and the new clients she'd taken on. She also mentioned the article about them that morning in *Flo on the Ro*. He brought up the charity 5k walk that he was participating in next weekend and she told him she would be participating in it, as well. She suggested they walk together, but when he didn't agree right away she let it go.

For a brief moment things got quiet and when they began talking again, she couldn't help noticing he only contributed to the conversation when asked, otherwise she did most of the talking. Till after dinner, when they were doing the dishes.

"You haven't mentioned anything lately about how things are going with your floors. They should almost be finished, right?" he asked, handing her a plate he'd just rinsed off.

For some reason, she didn't think he was asking her that for conversational purposes. She arranged the plate in the dishwasher and looked up at him. "I got a call from my contractor today, in fact. They finished early."

"It's all done?"

"Yes."

He nodded. "I don't have a problem taking off Thursday to help you move back to your place."

Kara's breath caught in her chest. "You trying to get rid of me, Virgil?"

"No, just making sure we stick to our agreement that your stay here was only temporary."

She drew in a deep breath. "But I thought…"

When she didn't finish what she was saying, Virgil prompted her. "You thought what, Kara?"

Kara didn't want to make a fool of herself, but she hon-

estly thought they had been making strides in their relationship. They enjoyed being together. It was just like
old times. "I thought," she said slowly, wanting to choose
her words carefully, "that we'd moved beyond all the animosity."

"We have."

"Then why can't you…"

Again she wasn't able to get the words out. But it
seemed he had no problem filling in the blanks for her.
"Fall in love with you again?"

He leaned back against the counter with his hands
shoved into his pockets. The man she loved with all her
heart. The man she'd been convinced loved her back—
she'd thought that all it would take was them spending
quality time together to relive the memories. Had she been
wrong?

"I told you, Kara. I could never love anyone who doesn't
trust me."

Kara felt her heart breaking. He hadn't moved on. He
couldn't move on. He didn't love her anymore and probably never would again. "I see."

"I hope you really do see it, Kara, because I don't want
to hurt you and I refuse to lead you on by making you
think there could ever be something between us again."

"But I don't understand. The time we've been spending
together, our lovemaking…"

He didn't say anything, but in a way he didn't have to.
The answer was written all over his face. To him it had
been nothing more than sex.

She knew at that moment she had to leave. She refused
to break down in front of him. "I think it's best if I go."

"Go where?"

Anyplace but here, she thought, moving toward the
stairs. "Home. Don't worry about helping me move my

stuff on Thursday. By the time you get home from work all traces of me will be gone." And then she rushed up the stairs.

Virgil stood at the window in his office and looked out. It was hard to believe it was September already and Monday would be Labor Day. He looked forward to the long weekend. *Doing what?*

One thing he could do this weekend was to celebrate. That call he'd gotten an hour ago from the Nelson Group should have him on top of the world. The deal had been finalized.

He walked back to his desk and sat down as his thoughts shifted to Kara. Returning home was for the best for her. That's what he wanted. She had started taking over the place and everybody knew he preferred his space. Women didn't spend the night at his place and they sure didn't stay for days, weeks. He'd made her an exception because of their past history but there had been no reason for her to stay any longer.

Then why was he feeling like crap?

He looked up at the knock on the door. "Come in."

His father walked in, smiling. "I just heard the news." He paused and studied his son. "For a man who just landed the company one of our biggest deals yet, you don't seem happy. You should be celebrating. Go home and take Kara someplace nice. You deserve it."

He met his father's gaze. "Kara is no longer staying at my place."

"Oh, where did she go?"

"Back home."

His father frowned. "Why?"

Virgil leaned back in his chair. "Because that's where

she lives. She was only with me temporarily until her floors were done."

"Yes, I know, but your mom and I had hoped…"

Virgil arched a brow. "Had hoped what?"

His father met his gaze directly. "That you would finally come to your senses."

"Come to my senses about what?"

"About what Kara means to you."

Virgil shook his head. Initially when he'd suspected his father's motives for hiring Kara, he'd dismissed them. But now…

"Dad, can I ask you something? And I want a truthful answer."

"What?"

"Did you have ulterior motives when you hired Kara to clean up my image?"

"Yes."

"Why?"

"Because your mother and I could see what you refused to see. You're in love with the girl. And the only reason you returned to your womanizing ways was because that was your attempt to forget her. To prove to yourself you didn't need her. That you didn't love her."

Virgil stared at his father. "How could you and Mom even think that?"

"Like I said, Virgil. We saw what you refused to. Besides, I know firsthand how a lie can tear two people apart. It happened that way with Maurice."

"Who's Maurice?"

"Maurice Grant. He's a childhood friend of mine in Houston. He has a daughter named Gina and a son, Trevor. Trevor's an ex-Marine."

Virgil nodded. It had been years but he recalled Mr. Grant. He remembered that Mr. Grant would bring Gina and Trevor around whenever his family took vacations to Houston when Virgil was a kid. He also recalled that Trevor and Gina were a few years older than him and Leigh.

"Yes, what about Mr. Grant?"

"Maurice and his wife, Stella, broke up over some woman's lie and they were apart for nearly twenty years. They were able to put the past behind them a few years ago and move on. But all those wasted years. To see Maurice and Stella together now, you wouldn't think they'd spent any time apart."

Virgil shook his head. He was getting sick and tired of people thinking he should be in love with Kara. Didn't they understand how he felt? "And your point, Dad?"

His father stared hard at him. "My point, Virgil Matthew Bougard, is that I don't want it to take twenty years for you to realize that Kara Goshay is the best thing that's ever happened to you." With that, he turned and walked out.

Kara left work and walked quickly to her car. Not because she was in hurry to get home but mainly because she wasn't sure she would be able to hold it together much longer. It had been a struggle remaining at work with a broken heart.

She had been so certain of her abilities, so hyped in the belief that Virgil still loved her. That all she had to do was spend time with him to rekindle what used to be. But in less than ten minutes he had squashed that notion and destroyed all her hope.

But there was one thing about Kara Goshay that couldn't be destroyed. Her ability to survive. She had survived four years ago when she'd thought Virgil had betrayed her and her world had come to an end. It hadn't and she'd moved on. And although she was hurting inside, she was determined to survive once more.

She knew she had to spend time with him since he was still her client. Although Marv Hilton was off his back, the business agreement between her and Virgil was for them to pretend an affair for six months. Now she knew where she stood and where she would never stand again. Namely by his side.

She had gotten into her car and buckled up her seat belt when her cell phone rang. She figured it was probably Marti, but she didn't want to talk to anyone right now, not even her sister. Since Marti shared her story with Kara, she had tried to talk Marti into getting counseling. Her sister had waved off the notion, saying it was too late, but Kara didn't agree. She felt there were issues Marti still needed to resolve so that one day she could enjoy a loving relationship with a man.

Kara figured she was a good one to talk when she didn't have that kind of relationship for herself. What was more pathetic than being in love with a man who didn't love you back? A man who couldn't forgive and let go? A man who refused to love her even though she believed that he could if he just allowed himself to do so. But he wouldn't and he had proven that. So now she had to move on. She'd done it before and would do it again.

She felt bad about not taking Marti's call. She hadn't spoken to her sister in a couple of days, but Kara had texted her, claiming she was extremely busy working on an important job-related project. She didn't want Marti to think something was wrong. The last thing she wanted was for her sister to know about her current situation with Virgil. Marti would blame herself for everything, and she needed to move on, as well.

Marti had shared with her that she had sought Virgil out and apologized. For her sister to do what she did and face Virgil was a start. It didn't surprise Kara that he hadn't been receptive. She knew all too well that he was not a forgiving man.

Like she'd told Virgil two days ago, today all her stuff would be gone when he came home. It hadn't taken more than three hours that morning for her to pack up, load the car and make two trips to her place. She hadn't realized how much extra stuff she'd purchased, assuming she was there to stay.

And when she had walked out the door of his house, she hadn't looked back. Nor had she looked around to see if Flo's posse was about. At the moment she truly didn't care.

Virgil entered his home and immediately felt a sense of loss when he glanced around. True to her word, Kara had made sure any traces of her were gone. It was as if she'd never been there. The pillows she had put on his living room sofa, the green plants she'd placed by his fireplace and that rug that had been on the floor near the breakfast bar were no longer there.

Needing a beer, he headed for the refrigerator and paused when he saw she'd left his extra key on the breakfast bar. His gut clenched. Why did he suddenly feel so lonely? It wasn't as if he'd never been alone before. For him, that was the name of the game. The only reason he could think of for his melancholy mood was that, during the days she'd been there, Kara had made her presence known, not just in his kitchen, but in every single room in his house.

It had become a common thing to come home and find her here in his kitchen, standing by the stove in her bare feet, smiling when she saw him, and then crossing the room to give him a big hug. Why had that hug been so easy to get used to? Why did he feel the need for one now?

Opening the refrigerator, he pulled out a beer, popped the tab and took a swig, needing it. Lowering the can from his lips, he thought about other times, not only in this kitchen, but throughout his house…both recent and when they'd been together years before. He doubted there was any room where they hadn't made love. Hell, he even remembered them making out in several of the closets, so overcome with desire for each other that they couldn't even get dressed without more heated kisses.

He couldn't help smiling at those memories. Then another memory suddenly flared in his mind. The one of how she'd looked when she'd realized he was ready for her to leave and go back to her place. He felt a tightening in his gut. He had hurt her and he'd known at that moment she'd been hoping things would turn out differently between them.

In his defense, that had been her assumption, not his. But then he couldn't help but think of how things would be without her in his life. Being the professional she was, she would honor the terms of the contract between her company and his. That meant they would still be seen together around town. Nothing had really changed. If questions came up as to why she'd moved back to her home he would just say it was closer to her job, which wasn't a lie. As long as he and Kara continued to see each other on a regular basis, no one would have reason to question their relationship.

He took another swig of his beer, knowing he was wrong about that. A lot had changed. But he refused to deal with that now. He had something else on his mind that should be taking precedence. His business deal with the Nelson Group. He would be flying to Toronto next week to finalize the paperwork between him and Stan Nelson. And earlier that day Pam had reminded him of the charity 5k walk for cancer research next weekend. In a way he was looking forward to it as a way to relieve his stress.

He frowned. When had he ever been stressed? He had a feeling he was beginning to find out just how it felt.

Chapter 20

Marti looked over at her sister. "Are you sure things are
okay between you and Virgil?"

Kara paused in the middle of sipping her tea. She
and Marti were having lunch at the Racetrack Café. She
would have chosen another place but dining here had
been Marti's idea. The last thing she needed was to run
into Virgil like they'd done the last time she and her sister had been here together.

It was hard to believe but it had almost been a week
since she'd seen or talked to him, although he had sent
her a text message a couple of days ago to let her know of
his trip to Canada. She knew the only reason he'd gone
to the trouble was because of the ruse of them pretending
to be lovers. It wouldn't look good if she didn't know his
whereabouts if someone were to ask. She figured he was
probably counting the days until he would no longer have
to pretend interest in her.

She forced a smile as she answered her sister's question. "I'm positive. What makes you think otherwise?"

Marti shrugged as she picked up a French fry off her plate. "He hasn't been around."

Kara lifted a brow. "How do you know that?"

"Because you haven't mentioned him. You said you moved back to your place and didn't say why, so I assumed the two of you had a disagreement or something."

Kara didn't say anything for a minute as she took another sip of her tea, knowing Marti was watching her closely. She couldn't let Marti or anyone else know her relationship with Virgil wasn't for real. Or that she'd tried winning his heart back and failed miserably. So she said, "Everything is fine, Marti. Virgil is in Toronto finalizing an important business deal."

"I'm surprised you didn't go with him."

She wasn't. Kara knew she was the last person he would have taken, even for appearances' sake. "I have a business to run here, besides I knew he would be busy most of the time."

She knew Marti still had her suspicions, but at least she hadn't asked any more questions. Kara was glad of that. Virgil had mentioned he would be back in time for the walk on Saturday and she had to prepare herself to see him again. That was one meeting she wasn't particularly looking forward to.

Virgil entered his hotel room thinking his meeting with the Nelson Group had gone off without a hitch. All the necessary papers had been signed and it was a great day for Bougard Enterprises. He had talked to his father on his way back to the hotel, and Matthew had made plans to take Rhona out to celebrate.

Speaking of celebration, Nelson had invited him out

on the town, stating he knew where they could meet up with a couple of beautiful women. But Virgil hadn't been interested and had turned him down. For some reason, he wanted to be alone tonight.

Removing his jacket, he tossed it aside and that was when he noticed the bottle of champagne that had been delivered to his room. He read the card and smiled. It was from his five godbrothers. They'd known about his trip to Toronto and were happy for him. He appreciated that.

He slid down into the chair, thinking he needed a woman. But not just any woman. He needed Kara. He'd gotten her text message that morning letting him know that, due to an impending rainstorm, Saturday's 5k walk had been postponed.

He had texted her back and thanked her for the information and she hadn't responded. There was no reason for her to have done so, but a part of him was aching and it was an ache that wouldn't go away. His eyes lit on the bottle of champagne on the coffee table. Why was he thinking about the day he'd brought champagne home to share with Kara? Champagne they'd never gotten around to drinking because she had left that evening.

She had left because he was too stubborn, too bull-headed, too damn full of himself to accept that nobody was perfect. People made mistakes, even the people you hadn't counted on making them. Sometimes those mistakes hurt. You forgave and forgot. Life moved on. No one should live in the past.

Then why was he?

Why did the thought of what he was not allowing himself to share with Kara leave an emptiness in his stomach? A hard ache in his chest and an intense longing in his heart? Closing his eyes, he thought of her—all those times she had smiled at him, made him laugh. He realized he had shared more good times with her than bad. And those good times had been the best. He smiled as he thought about them, but he couldn't help the tightening in his groin when he especially thought of their bedtime activities.

He thought of how he would make love to her, ease into her body, feel the way her muscles would clench him in possession, how her hands would stroke him with love. Love…

Although she hadn't said it, he believed she still loved him. And Marti believed it, too, not that he gave much credit to her opinion. Still…

What about him? He'd wanted to believe all there was between them was sex. He'd held on to that conviction steadfastly…till now. Now he knew it had been more than that. He had only been fooling himself by claiming there was no emotional component to their lovemaking. Now was the time to admit the truth. He was in love with her.

He opened his eyes as he remembered his father's words. *My point, Virgil Matthew Bougard, is that I don't want it to take twenty years for you to realize that Kara Goshay is the best thing that's ever happened to you.*

Virgil drew in a deep breath. His father was right. She was best thing to ever happen to him. A deep sensation stirred in his gut when he remembered the pain he'd seen in her eyes the day she had left his home. Pain he had caused when he'd allowed her to believe it had only been sex between them. Now he had to convince her otherwise. He had to prove to Kara that he loved her.

He wanted to go back to Charlotte and not only tell her but show her what she meant to him. Then after spending time together rekindling what they once had and never lost, he wanted them to plan their future. He wanted to offer what he'd planned the last time. Marriage. He wanted Kara as his wife.

It didn't bother him that in making that happen he would no longer be a bachelor. He hoped Zion would understand since that would make him the lone bachelor in the club. But he figured Z could handle it.

But what he himself couldn't handle was not having Kara be a permanent part of his life. Now he understood how U, W, X and Y felt about the women they'd married. Now, more than anything, he wanted to be included in that group.

Standing, he headed toward the bathroom to take a shower and to plan. He would do whatever he had to do in order to make sure he was no longer a man who held a grudge. He was no longer a bachelor who couldn't forgive.

The forecasters had been right, Kara thought, glancing out the window. She'd awoken to the sound of pouring rain and it was still going strong. She wondered if it would lighten up any. Not that she had anywhere to go, which was why it was close to noon and she was still in her PJs. She intended to make this a lazy weekend. She'd downloaded a new book on her e-reader and, if she finished the novel in record time, she would check out a flick on the movie channel.

She refused to think about Virgil. Unless his plans had changed, he should have gotten back into town last night. Now that the walk was postponed, he had no reason to call or text to let her know. They didn't have that kind of relationship. He'd made that clear.

An hour later, after eating a grilled cheese sandwich for lunch, she was about to settle on her couch with her e-reader when she heard her doorbell. Who would be visiting her in this weather? As much as she loved her sister, she didn't need Marti right now. She had a feeling her sister still suspected something was up and that Kara wasn't being completely honest with her about her relationship with Virgil.

Easing off the sofa, Kara padded in her bare feet toward the door, loving the feel of her new floor beneath her feet. She tightened her bathrobe around her waist the minute she glanced through the peep hole. Her breath caught when she saw it was Virgil.

What was he doing here? The obvious answer came to mind and that fired her anger. Did he think it was still the status quo between them? That he could practically ignore her for over a week then show up on her doorstep for a booty call?

Snatching open the door, she glared at him. "What are you doing here, Virgil?"

"May I come in, Kara?"

She noticed then that he was wet. Rain water was dripping off him. "Yes," she said, moving aside.

Virgil paused to take off his shoes as well as his wet jacket, which he tossed across a chair on her covered porch. "Do you have a towel? I don't want to mess up your new floors," Virgil asked, not entering her home.

"Okay. I'll be right back."

Virgil stood there and watched as Kara walked off. That gave him a chance to pull himself together. How could he not have known he still loved her? And that no matter what happened in the past he was ready to move forward? The thought of not having her in his life was something he couldn't accept. He wouldn't accept.

"Here you are."

She had returned and was handing him several thick towels. "Thanks."

He dried himself off while holding her gaze. He could feel the sexual chemistry flowing between them. He also detected something else. Love. He doubted if she could feel it yet because she was returning his stare with apprehension in her gaze.

It was only after he felt he'd sufficiently dried himself off that he crossed over her threshold, handing the towels back to her as he closed the door. When she walked off to take the towels to her laundry room, he looked around at her floors. The workers had done a nice job.

She returned and saw him still standing in the foyer. "You still haven't said why you're here, Virgil."

"I hope we can talk."

She rolled her eyes. "Talk? Yeah, right."

"You don't believe me?"

"Should I? When have you ever come here to just talk?"

Come to think of it, he couldn't recall a time he hadn't come here with sex on his mind. "Well, this time I only want to talk."

"About what, Virgil? What could we possibly have to talk about? I think you've made it clear—you accept my apology but will never forget how I didn't trust you. That you feel there can never be love without trust. I get that. I believe you're wrong but what you think is your prerogative. I don't care anymore."

He knew it was his fault she felt that way and it would be up to him to help her care again. He leaned against the closed door. "That might have been true then, but not now. And I think we have a lot to talk about."

He could tell from the look in her eyes she was slightly confused. "Like what?"

"Like how I've been a fool. How wrong it was to be so unforgiving. How wrong I was to deny the one thing I want and need in my life. You."

When she didn't say anything and just stared at him, he decided to keep talking, spilling his soul and speaking from his heart. "I love you, Kara. I guess you can say I always have, which is why that episode hurt me so much. I allowed the pain to harden my heart, and I vowed never to love anyone again. Problem was that I loved you too much to stop loving you."

"You said you'd forgive me but wouldn't forget," Kara said, tears misting her eyes.

"No more. I'm willing to forgive and to forget," he said, slowly walking toward her. "I don't want to live in the past anymore, Kara. Instead I want to start planning a future with you. I want to pick up where we left off, to rebuild our lives together, to learn from our mistakes but not dwell on them."

Coming to a stop in front of her, he added, "I want us to dwell on each other." He wiped away her tears. "Will you forgive me for being such a stubborn unforgiving ass?"

She nodded. "Yes, I forgive you."

"And will you accept me as a man who loves you?"

She nodded again. "Only if you accept me as the woman who loves you."

"Oh, baby." And then he pulled her into his arms and kissed her.

Virgil tried not to let his hunger for Kara take over, but he loved her so much and he wanted her. It was a deadly combination. When she parted her lips to give his tongue entrance, his arousal went into high gear. But he knew what he had to do. He broke off the kiss.

The confused look in her eyes drove him to sweep her off her feet into his arms and head for the sofa. Sitting down, he cradled her in his lap. "I love you so much, baby. I never stopped loving you. Everybody could see it but me." He leaned down and brushed a kiss across her lips. "I don't want to lose twenty years with you."

Kara didn't know what he was talking about with the

twenty years, but she didn't want them to lose any more time together, either. Nor was she exactly sure what had brought about this change in Virgil, but she didn't care. He was where he belonged, where she always wanted him to be. With her.

"Will you permanently improve my image by marrying me, Kara?"

She couldn't help but smile as happiness spread through every part of her. "Yes, I will marry you. I love you so much, Virgil."

"And I love you. Thanks for not giving up on me, baby. Thanks for loving me during those times I didn't deserve to be loved."

She could hardly believe she was hearing those words from Virgil now. She'd waited so long to hear him say I love you. She leaned up, wrapped her arms around his neck and pressed her mouth to his.

Virgil couldn't resist taking over the kiss, deepening it, tangling his tongue with hers. If he didn't pull back, he knew where things would lead and like he'd told her, he only wanted to talk. Pulling his mouth away from her moist lips, he said, "We need to finish talking."

A smile touched her lips. "I think we've said enough for now. We've said what's most important, don't you think?"

Instead of answering, he stood with her in his arms and headed straight for her bedroom.

He laid her down in the middle of her bed and began removing his shirt, but she put her hands on his to stop him.

"Let me."

He dropped his hands to his sides while Kara continued unbuttoning his shirt. "I can't believe you came out in this bad weather," she said softly as she worked the buttons.

"I came here straight from the airport."

She leaned back and met his gaze, surprised. "I thought you got back late yesterday afternoon."

"Flight was cancelled due to bad weather in Toronto. Had I gotten into town yesterday as planned, I would have come here before going home. Like I did today. I needed to see you just that bad."

Those words coming from him meant all the world to Kara. "When did you realize you loved me?"

"After you moved out. My house felt so lonely. And then while I was in Canada, I missed you like crazy and the more I thought about you, the more I knew."

She was going to ask him another question, the one about his twenty-year statement. But when she pushed the shirt from his shoulders and saw his hard-muscled chest, she couldn't say anything. His chest always was a turn-on for her. She liked touching it, running her fingers through the thatch of curly hair covering it. She looked down and saw how the hair tapered to a thin line as it trailed beneath the waistband of his jeans.

She looked up at him. "Remove your jeans, please."

He stepped back and did as she'd asked, dragging the jeans slowly down his hips and muscular thighs, knowing she was watching him. He did the same with his briefs. Her heart picked up a beat when she gazed upon his engorged sex. Just thinking about what it would do to her, imagining the feel of it sliding in and out of her, sent heated sensations rushing all through her. Virgil Bougard was such a masculine man and seeing him naked made her appreciate being a woman. The woman he loved. The woman who loved him in return.

At that moment she couldn't help saying the words again. "I love you."

He smiled and cupped her cheek, meeting her gaze.

"And I love you. I intend to spend the rest of my days showing you how much and how deeply."

Virgil then joined her on the bed. Skimming his hands down below her waist to the area between her legs, he felt her hot and ready. That was good because he was more than ready for her. All through the flight back to Charlotte, he'd thought of nothing but professing his love for her and then making love to her. Now that he was here, beside her, his entire body quivered in anticipation.

Positioning his body over hers, he glanced down at her and said the words he'd held back from saying all the times they'd made love this past month. "I love you, Kara."

He lowered his head to kiss her at the same exact moment he slid inside of her. He deepened the kiss as he began moving, thrusting in and out of her, setting into motion a rhythm that had her digging her fingers into his shoulders. But he was too far gone to feel any pain. The sensation of her inner muscles clenching him made him break off the kiss and close his eyes and moan.

No woman had ever made him feel like this. As though he was ready to blast off to parts unknown, a galaxy not yet discovered. One that only Kara could take him to in a blaze of heat and desire. He felt his insides trembling, and when she arched her body and opened her thighs just a little wider, he convulsed in pleasure.

A growl of deep satisfaction escaped his throat as his body was wracked with intense spasms. When she screamed his name, he knew she had joined him over the edge. Perfect. She once said no one was perfect. Well, he had news for her. She was.

Years ago she had done something no other woman had done and that was getting him to fall in love with her. Not with manipulations, deceptions or schemes. She had made it clear that she would not let him or any man compromise her principles. Lord knows he'd tried. But in the end she had won him over and he'd fallen head over heels in love with her. And he would love her until the day he died.

Kara snuggled close to Virgil after having thoroughly been made love to. She felt his arms tighten around her as if he never intended to let her go. She had no problem with that because she never intended to let him go, either.

She heard his even breathing and for a minute she thought he'd dozed off, until he leaned over and placed a kiss on the side of her face. "I love you," he whispered close to her ear. "And I intend to say it every chance I get."

Kara shifted her body to look up at him and smiled. "I definitely don't have a problem with that." She paused a moment then said, "Now tell me what you meant earlier about twenty years."

He told her about his conversation with his father, about his dad's childhood friend Maurice Grant.

Kara sat up in bed and looked down at him. "Let me get this straight. Your father had ulterior motives for hiring me?"

"Yes. Granted, my image did need improving and you're the best in the field, but I believe that I could have handled things my way. York was already on it."

Kara was so filled with love for Virgil. They'd been given another chance at love and she knew moving forward their love would only get stronger.

He pulled her into his arms and captured her mouth in a long and drugging kiss. When he released her mouth, he said, "This is the perfect weather to eat, sleep and make love."

Kara snuggled closer to Virgil, thinking that she definitely agreed.

Epilogue

"Welcome to our home and congratulations," Ellie Lassiter said with her husband, Uriel, by her side. "And I love your ring. It's beautiful."

"Thanks." Kara couldn't help glancing down at her engagement ring. The one Virgil had slid on her finger two nights ago. It was a Zion exclusive and she thought it was beautiful, too.

"Have the two of you decided on a wedding date?" Uriel asked, grinning.

"In March. That gives you and the other godbrothers six months to clear your calendars," Virgil said, pulling Kara closer to his side.

Virgil's parents had been ecstatic when they were told of their engagement. Her parents had been overjoyed, as well. Marti—who had finally confided to her parents what Malcolm had done years ago, had entered counseling and was doing well—had agreed to be Kara's maid of honor.

Kara had told Virgil what had happened to Marti and she'd appreciated his understanding in her wanting to rebuild a relationship with her sister. Florence Asbury had been thrilled to get the exclusive about the engagement for her *Flo on the Ro* column.

An hour later Kara decided she liked all the wives of the four married bachelors as well as Virgil's five godfathers and their wives. Most of them she remembered from the last time she and Virgil had dated. All of them were still married except for Uriel's parents. They had gotten a divorce.

"I wonder where Carolyn's boy-toy is tonight. She looks out of place without him," Virgil said.

"What do you mean?"

Virgil then told Kara how, after over thirty years of marriage, Carolyn Lassiter had shocked her husband and son when she announced she didn't want to be married anymore and had begun seeing a man twenty-six years her junior.

From the looks of things, Kara thought Carolyn Lassiter might be regretting those actions. Kara noticed how every so often Carolyn would glance over at her ex-husband and the beautiful woman by his side. According to Virgil, Anthony had begun dating the widowed Claire Steele, the aunt to Mayor Morgan Steele, around three years ago. She was an extremely beautiful woman. When she stood with her daughters—Vanessa, Taylor and Cheyenne— she could pass for their sister. Like her youngest daughter Cheyenne, Claire's Native American features—the dark eyes, high cheekbones and straight black hair—gave her a distinguished look.

"May I have everyone's attention?"

Kara turned to see Anthony Lassiter stand in the middle of the room.

"He's probably about to toast Uriel for his birthday," Virgil said as he leaned over to her.

"Before I toast the birthday boy," Anthony said with a grin. "who I think is the best son any man could have, I want to acknowledge that another one of my godsons will be getting married in six months, and I just want to say, Virgil, all your godfathers are proud of you. And, Kara, welcome to the family."

They accepted the applause and Kara could hardly believe her good fortune. She had to look down at her shiny new ring again to believe she'd actually become Virgil's fiancée.

Anthony then glanced around, spotted Zion across the room and chuckled. "You can't be in that club by yourself, Zion."

Zion laughed. "Want to bet?"

That caused everyone to burst into laughter. It seemed Zion Blackstone had no problem being the lone bachelor in the Guarded Hearts Club. The last bachelor.

Then, while everyone watched, Anthony reached out his hand and Claire joined him. "I'm happy to tell you that we've decided to take our relationship to another level, and with the blessings of my son and Claire's daughters, we've decided to marry. It will be a Thanksgiving wedding. We felt that day was appropriate since the two of us have a lot to be thankful for."

When he leaned over and kissed Claire on the lips, everyone clapped and cheered. Everyone except for Anthony's ex-wife, Carolyn. Kara wondered if she was the only one who noticed the regret in Carolyn's eyes before she slipped off to the ladies' room.

Before anyone could approach the couple to offer more congratulations, another godfather took center stage. This time it was Matthew.

"May I have everyone's attention?"

The noise level lowered as a beaming Matthew held up his hands. "You aren't the only one with good news to share, Anthony. I just want to announce that as of January first, I will be officially retiring from Bougard Enterprises and leaving the company in my son's capable hands. I know he will do well, especially since he'll have a good woman by his side."

Virgil, who hadn't known about his father's decision, was momentarily speechless. When he finally found his voice, he crossed the room to his father and gave him a bear hug. The torch had officially been passed. He then crossed the room back to Kara and pulled her into his arms. He could hardly believe the way things had worked out. He'd gotten the helm of Bougard Enterprises and, more important, the woman he loved. Overcome with emotion, he leaned down to give his future wife a kiss, not even hearing the cheers of their audience.

"I can't wait for March to get here," Virgil said later that night with Kara snuggled up close to his side.

Uriel and Ellie had put most of the attendees up for the night at their lake house. But Virgil and Kara had decided to stay at a hotel in Gatlinburg a few miles away.

"I can't wait, either," Kara said, staring up at him.

Last week they decided for Kara to move back into his home. He loved waking up with her each morning and going to bed with her at night. They had flown to California to talk to her parents and decided the wedding would take place at Kara's home in San Francisco. He and Marti were trying to build a better relationship. After all, they would be in-laws.

Unable to help himself, Virgil lowered his mouth to

Kara's and began kissing her with all the love he felt in his heart.

When he finally released her mouth, she smiled up at him. "What was that for?"

"No reason. That's my way to say I love you."

She wrapped her arms round his neck. "In that case you can use that way to tell me anytime."

He chuckled. "I'm glad."

He then proceeded to kiss her again.

* * * * *

MOONLIGHT KISSES

PHYLLIS BOURNE

For Byron

Chapter 1

"Who put the scowl on your face?"

Cole Sinclair looked up from the newspaper he'd been absorbed in to see his stepfather standing in his office doorway.

"No, don't tell me. Let me guess." Victor Gray raised a finger in a halting gesture. "Stiletto Cosmetics."

Folding the business section in half, Cole slung it across his desk in disgust. "How'd you guess?"

"If you're frowning, it usually has something to do with them."

Cole pushed away from his desk and began to pace in front of the wall of windows offering a panoramic view of downtown Nashville. He'd known when he'd returned to his hometown that reviving his family's troubled cosmetics company would be a monumental task.

The widely held opinion that Espresso Cosmetics was old-lady makeup was firmly entrenched. Moreover, an upstart cosmetics company had set up shop in town, grabbing both headlines and Espresso's dwindling customer base.

"The media's handing out good press to Stiletto like candy on Halloween," he muttered. "Meanwhile, we can barely get a reporter to return a phone call."

Victor hovered in the doorway. "They're just capitalizing on their fifteen minutes of fame since that singer mentioned them on television. It won't last much longer."

Cole wasn't so sure. Stiletto had been generating buzz on the web even before pop star Crave gave them a shout-out on national television. He stopped midpace to glance out the window. An electronic billboard in the distance stood out against the gray January skies. It flashed continuous images of a cheeseburger with toppings stacked nearly as high as Espresso's aging eleven-story building.

He stared blankly at it, his mind on how Stiletto was gaining ground with a generation of young women Espresso was desperate to attract. Unfortunately, an article in today's paper had pushed that demographic even further out of their reach.

"I stopped by to see if you wanted to go to lunch with me later," his stepfather said. "I saw a billboard of the most mouthwatering burger I've ever seen on the drive in this morning, and I've been drooling ever since."

That burger did look good, Cole thought. Real food. A lot better than the upscale dining experiences he'd endured while handling Espresso business these past months.

He also recognized that Victor's invitation was for more than lunch. His late mother's second husband, the only father he'd ever known, was extending another olive branch to help rebuild their once-close relationship after eight years of estrangement.

"Another time, Vic. I doubt I'll have an appetite by lunchtime. Dinner, either."

"So are you going to tell me what's going on or keep frowning until your face gets stuck like that?" the older man said, still hovering in the doorway.

"There's something you need to read."

Cole watched his stepfather hesitate before venturing beyond the doorway into the overhauled office that no longer bore the feminine traces of the company's founder.

Cole snatched the copy of *America Today* off the mahogany executive desk he'd brought in to replace the elegant Queen Anne writing table his mother and Espresso founder, Selina Sinclair Gray, had ruled from. Snapping it open, he pointed out the article responsible for his current mood and handed it to Victor.

He watched his stepfather's eyes narrow as he zeroed in on one of the photos accompanying the story. The older man drew the newspaper in until it nearly touched his nose.

"Wow!"

"Exactly," Cole said, still steaming over it. Then he caught an uncharacteristic gleam in Victor's eyes. It lit up his entire face. In fact, he was practically ogling the newspaper.

What the...?

"God knows I worshipped the ground your mother walked on," his stepfather said, "but would you take a look at those long legs in that short skirt and those high heels. I don't see a thing here to put a frown on a man's face."

Cole snatched the paper back from him.

Victor shook his head and a sly grin spread over his lips. "She's got a young Angela Davis thing going on with that wild Afro, too. Yes, sir! If I were five or ten years younger, she'd be your new mama."

Cole stared at the smaller photo he'd ignored before, the larger one having grabbed his attention and earned his ire.

"More like twenty-five to thirty years younger," he grumbled. "She could be your daughter."

Cole frowned at the photo of the woman sitting on the edge of a desk. So this was Stiletto's owner. His gaze drifted to the untamed mane of kinky coils surrounding a no-nonsense face and full, unsmiling lips. Sage Matthews looked exactly like what she and her company were—a pain in his ass.

He shoved the newspaper back at his stepfather and pointed. "This photo is the problem."

Victor re-examined the newspaper and then looked up at him. "The young lady in this one is okay, but not nearly as good-looking as that Matthews woman. She's smoking hot."

"Enough about her."

"Okay, okay," his stepfather said, still examining the photo. "You know, the old woman standing next to the young one in this picture looks kind of like…"

"A man in drag." Cole finished. He jabbed his finger toward the offending photo of an attractive young woman juxtaposed against an older one presumably representing Espresso. "Not only are they relegating us to the brand for senior citizens, they exaggerate the point with one of the ugliest old ladies I've ever seen."

"Well, as you just said, he's no lady."

A vein on the side of Cole's head pulsed. "You think?" Sarcasm permeated the question. "What gave it away, the hot mess of a gray wig or the damned goatee?"

"Hmm." Victor tilted his own graying head to one side, then the other as he continued to study the grainy color photo. "Not really a goatee. I'd say it was more of a five o'clock shadow."

"Are you actually defending that photo?" Cole asked.

The corner of his stepfather's mouth quirked upward.

"You know he kind of looks like the guy who stars in those Maw-Maw movies."

"Who or what is a Maw-Maw?"

Victor looked up, an incredulous look on his face. "Wow. You have been out of the country a long time. Maw-Maw is the star of a slew of movies about a wisecracking, busybody matriarch, who can't stop sticking her nose in her family's business." He chuckled and shook his head. "Can't believe you never heard of them. I have a couple on DVD. I'll let you borrow them."

"No, thank you," Cole said firmly, his patience waning.

"Oh, come on. You have to at least see *Maw-Maw Passes the Plate*. It's the one where Maw-Maw puts an envelope containing a thousand dollars into the church offering plate by mistake." His stepfather burst into a fit of laughter, slapping the newspaper against his thigh. "The old girl starts leaping over the church pews, like a sprinter clearing hurdles in the summer Olympics, trying to get it back. She even tackles a deacon. It's hilarious!"

Cole cleared his throat loudly.

"I'm not interested in any movie featuring a grown man wearing a dress. Right now, all I care about is this article and the damage it's doing to Espresso's image, which isn't one bit funny."

"Sorry about that, son." Victor dabbed at the tears that had gathered in his eyes from laughing. "I guess I got sidetracked." He extracted a pair of reading glasses from his shirt pocket and resumed studying the article.

A few minutes later, he shrugged. "Okay, so they took a bit of a dig at us. Try not to get so bent out of shape over it. It's not that big a deal."

"Not a big deal?" Cole fumed, the headline imprinted on his brain—Not Your Granny's Makeup: Stiletto Cosmetics Puts Its Spiked Heel in the Competition. He quoted the article, "As Cole Sinclair makes a last ditch attempt to rescue his family's declining Espresso Cosmetics from near extinction, an edgy new brand is poised to pick up the torch."

Victor removed his glasses, folded the paper and tucked it under his arm. "We just had our first successful collection in nearly a decade thanks to you," he said.

"And there wasn't a single word in the press about it, despite the efforts of our public relations team."

"Still, it was a huge boost to Espresso employees who haven't had much to celebrate in a very long time," the older man said. "You should be patting yourself on the back, not worrying about a ridiculous photo in some rag."

"*America Today* has a nationwide circulation. Not to mention online and international editions."

"My point is Espresso is finally making a comeback," Victor said.

"Comeback?" Cole leaned against the front of his desk and folded his arms. "We're a long way from what I'd consider a comeback.

"A sold-out holiday collection was a heck of a good start."

Cole shrugged off the praise with a grunt. His first order of business as CEO of Espresso's cosmetics division had been to sit down with the company's chief financial officer, Malcolm Doyle, to find out exactly where years of stagnant sales had left them financially.

The second had been to untie the hands of the creative and product-development teams and allow them to do their jobs. For too long their ideas had languished due to Victor's insistence on remaining loyal to what he believed Cole's mother would have wanted for her company.

"You've done more for Espresso in five months than I accomplished after years of being in charge." Victor's chin dropped to his chest, his gaze cast toward the carpet. "It's just I thought…"

"The success of the holiday collection was just a drop in the bucket." Cole cut him off, refusing to play the blame game.

All he cared about was making Espresso relevant in the cosmetics industry again. It was too late to take back the harsh words he'd exchanged with his mother the very last time he'd seen her. Now the only way he could make it up to her was to save her legacy.

He swallowed hard. "We'd need a tsunami to erase the red ink from the company books and our old-lady image from women's minds." Rounding his desk, Cole tapped at his computer keyboard until the survey he'd commissioned appeared on the screen. "I was going to email you a copy of this later, but you might as well take a look at it now."

Victor sat in Cole's leather executive chair, once again retrieving his reading glasses from his pocket.

"This is a survey taken over the holidays of customers shopping at various department-store cosmetics counters," Cole explained. He leaned over Victor's shoulder, right-clicking the mouse to expand a page. "Here are just a few of the comments female shoppers made when asked about Espresso."

The older man read aloud. "'My great-aunt uses their foundation. We call her Auntie Cake behind her back because her face always looks like it's been dipped in batter.'" Victor winced. "Ouch."

"It gets worse."

"You're kidding."

"Nope. Keep reading."

"'Their makeup counters are deader than a morgue.'"

Victor read another one. "'I didn't know they were still around.'"

Cole pointed out a remark made by a twenty-two-year-old woman actually making a purchase at an Espresso counter. This time he read it aloud. "'I'm only here because my grandmother ran out of her favorite pink lipstick. No way I'd wear this old-lady stuff. I'm a Stiletto girl all the way.'"

His stepfather exhaled a long drawn-out breath. "This is why you're so peeved about that article."

Cole nodded. "The more I think about it, the more I believe it's too late to change people's minds about us. Our senior-citizen image is too entrenched."

"But…" Victor started to protest, but Cole held up a hand to stop him.

"Hear me out," Cole said. "Why keep banging our heads against a brick wall? Stiletto already has the hip, edgy vibe and is gaining popularity with the young demographic we're chasing."

"I'm not following you, son."

Cole smiled for the first time in what felt like weeks. Why hadn't he thought of it before?

"It's the acquire-to-grow strategy—something I was in charge of implementing during my tenure at Force Cosmetics. Simply put, if we can't beat them, *we'll just have to buy them.*"

He paused to give Victor a chance to let the idea sink in. "We would keep Stiletto's name and packaging the same, meanwhile continue to revamp Espresso and rebrand it as makeup for the classic or mature beauty or something along those lines."

The older man pressed his lips together a few moments, before he finally spoke. "Couldn't we just develop our own offshoot brand?"

Cole shrugged. "We could, but that would take a long

time. Even then, consumers can be fickle. There's no guarantee it would catch on and turn into a winner for us."

"But how?" Victor frowned, deepening the creases in his forehead. "You heard what Doyle said. The cosmetics division is buried in red ink. Your sister's Espresso Sanctuary spas propped us up until you came back and threw us a lifeline."

Cole crossed his arms over his chest. While Espresso's finances had dwindled in his absence, his personal wealth had grown tremendously. "Don't worry. I've got it covered," he said. "I'm about to make Ms. Matthews an offer too good to refuse."

Chapter 2

Sage Matthews pulled the phone away from her ear long enough to give it, and the woman on the other end of the line, the side eye.

"Your makeup brand would be a perfect addition to our store lineup."

The buyer for the trendy boutique chain droned on, but the silent alarms on Sage's bullshit detector drowned out the rest of her spiel. It sounded identical to the ones she'd heard all morning.

"Strange—that isn't what you said a few weeks ago." Sage kicked off her shoes under her desk and wiggled her toes. High heels were the worst form of torture, but when you owned a company called Stiletto, you had to dress the part.

She glanced at the notation she'd scribbled on a message slip next to the buyer's name. "I believe you said Stiletto's branding was too provocative. Your exact words were *downright raunchy*."

"Um…well," the woman stammered. "You must have misheard me. I said it was *delightfully racy* as in sexy. Clearly, there's been a misunderstanding."

Misunderstanding, huh? Sage stifled the harrumph on the tip of her tongue. "Hard to tell," she said, "considering the way your secretary tossed me out of your office afterward like she was a nightclub bouncer."

"Oh, dear. Please accept my apologies if my staff was a touch overzealous. Again, I assure you it was all a big mistake. One I hope we can…"

"Just stop." Sage had heard enough.

"P-pardon?"

"Before you continue, you should know I refuse to do business with anyone who lies to me."

Silence.

Figuring the buyer was weighing her options, Sage waited, making no attempt to fill the dead air. Long awkward moments passed, before a sigh emitted over the line. "Okay, the truth is I didn't want to risk offending my more conservative clientele by selling lipsticks and eyes shadows with names like Spank Me and Missionary Position."

There was another sigh, this one deeper and more drawn out. "Next thing I know, the hottest female singer on the planet is telling a national television audience she adores your lipsticks. Suddenly the same customers I was worried about offending are clamoring for Stiletto products, and I couldn't be more sorry for turning you down."

Finally, Sage thought, *the truth*.

She'd returned nearly a dozen calls that morning from eager buyers, the same people who had practically slammed the door in her face previously, criticizing everything from Stiletto's faux black leather packing to the titillating names of their products. Of course, they'd changed their tunes in the weeks since pop star Crave had whipped out a tube of Stiletto lipstick and called it her secret weapon.

Sage knew it was just foolish pride. Still, she couldn't help feel irked that instead of owning up to their blunder, they'd tried to gloss over it. Insulting her intelligence with meaningless flattery.

"My assistant will contact you later today to schedule a meeting to discuss adding Stiletto to your boutique's lineup," she said, satisfied. "However, you should know that as circumstances have changed, so has my first offer. Any deal we strike now will definitely have terms more favorable to Stiletto."

"Eh…uh…of course," the boutique's buyer said. "I look forward to our meeting."

Sage ended the call just as her assistant, Amelia, bounded into her office clutching a pink message slip. A huge grin deepened the dimples in the cheeks of her smooth brown skin. "I thought it would take forever for you to finally get off the phone."

"What's up?" Leaning forward in her office chair, Sage propped her elbows on her desktop. She dropped her chin to her chest and began rubbing out the kinks that had developed in her neck from talking on the phone all morning.

"You'll never guess who called for you." The nineteen-year-old shifted from one leg to the other, practically bouncing with excitement. "Not in a million years."

"Well, don't keep me…" Sage stopped midsentence and glanced up at her assistant. "Hold on. What are you still doing here?" She glanced at her watch. "Your accounting class starts in five minutes."

Amelia huffed and rolled her eyes toward the ceiling. "I know. I know."

The teen had started working for Stiletto a few hours a week after school during her last year of high school.

Sage thought she was doing the girl a favor, but quickly discovered that in the efficient and organized Amelia, she'd struck employee gold.

A year later, when graduation and her eighteenth birthday aged her out of the foster-care system, the job became full-time with the stipulation that Amelia would enroll in college. Having grown up in the foster-care system, Sage knew the importance of having an education to fall back on when you had no one to depend on but yourself.

"Well?" Sage raised a brow.

"But I couldn't leave. Not just yet. Not until I tell you who..."

"I don't care who called. There isn't anything or anyone more important than you being at school right now," Sage said.

The same brusque tone that sent her other employees, and most people, scurrying for cover rarely intimidated Amelia. Nor did it dampen her bubbly enthusiasm over the caller she was dying to tell her about.

"Stand down, General. I'm going to class, but first you have to hear who called you before I explode."

"For goodness' sake. Spit it out so you can haul your fanny over to the community college." Sage sighed. "And if you're going to call me General, can't you do it behind my back like everyone else around here?"

"Cole Sinclair!" The name popped out of her assistant's mouth like the cork on a bottle of champagne.

Sage studied the message slip Amelia handed her and tried to place the familiar name. Then it hit her. "As in Espresso Cosmetics?" He and his family's company had been a footnote in a feature article on Stiletto that had run a few days ago in *America Today*.

"Well, yeah, but Cole Sinclair is worth way more than that granny makeup company he runs." Amelia dismissed the connection with a flick of her hand. "Remember the puzzle game we deleted from our phones and you banned from our office computers because it was too addictive?"

Sage nodded, recalling getting so caught up in the colorful game she'd spent an entire evening matching trios of circus clowns in an attempt to beat enough levels to earn the elusive title of ultimate ringmaster.

"Well, Cole Sinclair invested in the gaming studio that developed it years ago, back when it was just two college kids in their parents' basement. His meager investment turned him into a millionaire twenty times over when the business eventually sold to a major corporation," Amelia said. "It was one of the topics in my entrepreneurship class last semester."

While the background information on Sinclair was mildly interesting, Sage's concern was her own business and turning it into a multimillion-dollar endeavor. She stared at the name on the message slip. "Did he say what he wanted?"

"Only that it was important," Amelia said. "What do you think?"

Sage shrugged. "Maybe he's miffed about that article in *America Today*. The mention of Espresso wasn't exactly flattering. Nor was that photo of the young, chic woman symbolizing us versus the old one that was supposedly Espresso."

"Or maybe—" Amelia paused dramatically "—maybe he took one look at the photo of you with that article and fell head over heels for you. And he wants to ask you out on a date. Just think about it." The young woman let out a squeal. "A tall, good-looking millionaire is smitten by your photo, falls hopelessly in love and is determined to sweep you off your feet."

Sage stared at the dreamy look on the teen's face, unable

to believe the crap coming out of her mouth. How could a girl so smart about most things be so dumb about this one? Sage waited a beat, reaching for diplomatic words to set her assistant straight without hurting her feelings.

There were none.

"That is the stupidest thing I've ever heard," she said.

"It could happen," Amelia protested.

"Yeah, and maybe he'll charge into my office on a white horse wearing a suit of armor or bare chested like the men on the covers of those ridiculous romance novels you've always got your nose stuck in."

This time it was her assistant who frowned. "There's nothing wrong with being a romantic. In fact, the more I think about it, a date is just what you need. It would loosen you up, and maybe folks around here might stop calling you General behind your back."

They could call her Godzilla for all she cared, as long as they did their jobs—and did them well. "You need to spend more time with your textbooks and less reading those silly romances." Sage checked her watch.

"I'm going, but first I need to schedule your meeting with Mr. Sinclair."

Amelia pulled the smartphone she used for work from her pants pocket. "He wants to see you at your earliest convenience." She tapped on the screen with a stylus she'd retrieved from behind her ear. "Your schedule is packed, but I could bump one of your other appointments so you can see him later this afternoon or perhaps first thing tomorrow."

Sage held up a finger. "I haven't decided if I'm meeting with him at all."

The younger woman looked up from the phone. "You're joking, right?"

"You, better than anyone, know I rarely joke."

"Aren't you curious? I can hardly wait to find out what he wants."

Sage fixed her assistant with her most intimidating, no-nonsense glare. "You'll have to wait because you're leaving for your accounting class *right now*."

Grumbling, the young woman reluctantly did as she was told.

Sage had no idea why Cole Sinclair had called. But unlike Amelia, she didn't indulge in far-fetched fantasies. Sage lived in the real world.

And in the real world, when rich people wanted to talk business, they wanted to trick poor people out of something valuable.

Chapter 3

Money might not buy happiness, but Cole knew enough of it would buy just about everything else.

It was the reason he walked the short blocks from the Espresso building to the downtown restaurant he'd selected for his meeting with Sage Matthews, confident he'd be the new owner of Stiletto Cosmetics when he returned.

Cole was also intrigued.

The woman had actually put him off for over a week. A humorless chuckle pushed through his lips, leaving a vapor trail as his warm breath hit the January air.

No one put him on the back burner. *Not anymore*, Cole thought. When he snapped his fingers, people jumped. Especially women.

Another side effect of deep pockets.

So either Ms. Matthews had somehow missed the articles written about him by reporters obsessed with his bank balance, or she was one of the few people who simply didn't care.

A blast of heat hit him as he pulled open the restaurant door and strode inside. Immediately, he saw a woman with her back to him talking to the hostess.

Her big, bold hair and long, shapely legs left no doubt about her identity. Shiny, patent leather boots hugged her calves, and she wore a red wool coat with a thigh-grazing hemline just shy of indecent.

Cole felt the corner of his mouth tic upward into a reluctant smile as his stepfather's words popped into his head: *not a thing here that would put a frown on a man's face.*

He overheard the hostess, who hadn't seen him come in. "Mr. Sinclair hasn't arrived yet, but let me take your coat, and I'll show you to the table he reserved in our private dining room."

"No, thanks." Cole watched Sage Matthews consult a plain wristwatch with a worn, black strap, a feminine version of his own. "We're supposed to meet here in five minutes. If he's not on time, I'm leaving."

"Mr. Sinclair is always punctual," the hostess offered.

The woman in the short coat and high-heeled boots bobbed her head in a curt nod. "If he wants to see me, he'd better be."

Cole cleared his throat, the gesture commanding the attention of both women. "I'm here—" he glanced at his own Timex and then pointedly at Ms. Matthews "—with four minutes to spare."

She met his gaze, not a trace of sheepishness at being overheard in her expression. If anything, challenge flickered in her chocolate-brown eyes. "Good. Time is money, Mr. Sinclair. Mine is valuable."

Cole blinked. The statement was something he'd usually say, and she'd delivered it just like he would have— blunt and to the point. "Well, let's not waste either of ours standing here," he said.

Within minutes, the hostess had taken their coats, and escorted them through the bustling dining room to a staircase leading to the private room he liked to use when conducting business outside the Espresso building. As they walked Cole couldn't help notice the statuesque woman with the riot of kinky curls move through the upscale restaurant as if she owned it, garnering appreciative glances from every man in the room.

Including him.

However, this lunch had an agenda and nothing would distract him from it. Not even a sweet pair of legs, showcased by a minidress and fantasy-inducing shiny stiletto boots.

A waiter appeared with menus immediately after they were seated. He took their drink orders and disappeared to retrieve them.

"Thank you for agreeing to meet with me, Ms. Matthews." Cole didn't bother opening the menu. The entrées were the standard fare of most upscale restaurants. A minuscule serving of meat or fish smothered in creams and vegetables pureed beyond recognition and served on a plate that appeared destined for an art museum rather than someone's stomach.

However, this restaurant was currently the hot ticket in town for fine dining, and it made the right impression at lunch and dinner business meetings in an industry where image was everything.

Cole's personal preference would have been to conduct business over real food—a burger, barbecue sandwich or a slice of pizza. One of which he'd probably grab afterward to celebrate his having reached a verbal agreement with Ms. Matthews.

He glanced across the table at his lunch companion, who was perusing the menu. Again, she surprised him.

Most people would have rushed to fill the silence with small talk by now.

His gaze dropped to her lips, painted the same bold, sassy red as her dress. The firm line she held them in didn't distract from their fullness.

She looked up, and her eyes locked with his. Caught staring, Cole didn't divert his bold appraisal.

"I was checking out your lipstick shade," he said, making it clear both to her, and to himself, that any interest in her mouth was purely professional.

"It's one of Stiletto's bestsellers." She lifted a perfectly arched brow. "It's called Badass."

Cole licked his own lips, his mouth suddenly dry. *I'll just bet you are.*

The errant thought popped into his head so quickly, he feared he'd said it aloud. Her impassive expression assured him he hadn't, and he exhaled in relief.

The waiter reappeared with their drinks. Cole used the moments it took for them to order two of the chef's specialties to give himself a mental knock upside the head.

Stay on task, man, he silently warned. *This is a business meeting, not a date.* He reached for his water glass and took a long sip. No more getting sidetracked by shiny stiletto boots or impossibly red lips.

"Now how about you tell me what's on your mind, Mr. Sinclair?"

Cole swallowed, the question immediately shutting down illicit images of her full red lips pressed against his and those badass boot-encased legs wrapped firmly around his waist.

"Excuse me?" The words came out like a frog's croak.

"Since we've established neither of us likes to waste time," she said. "I assumed we could skip the preliminaries and get right to the reason for my being here."

An odd sense of déjà vu passed over him. How many times had he said the exact same thing? *Plenty*, Cole silently answered his own question.

If he didn't know better, he'd think he was sitting across the table from a female version of himself.

Nah, couldn't be, he thought.

Leaning forward, Cole crossed his arms on the table. "I want to buy Stiletto."

Her eyes widened, his only clue he'd caught her off guard. She recovered quickly, and then she, too, leaned forward in her chair and crossed her arms on the table.

"Then this meeting truly was a waste of time for both of us, Mr. Sinclair, because my company isn't for sale."

That's what you think, Cole thought. "Don't be too hasty, Ms. Matthews," he said aloud. The easy Southern drawl he'd thought he'd lost in Europe permeated his warning. "After all, you don't know what I'm offering."

"Doesn't matter."

"Oh, I think it will."

"Well, let's hear it."

Her tone taunted him with an unspoken challenge. Cole could hardly wait to see her expression when he not only met her expectations, but surpassed them.

Eye to eye, neither of their stares wavered. Nor did Cole's confidence that he'd leave here with what he wanted. Reaching into the inside pocket of his suit jacket, he pulled out a folded scrap of paper and slid it across the white linen tablecloth.

Her fingertips grazed his as she took it, sending an almost audible crackle of electricity through him. He scoured her expression for an indication she'd felt it, too. For the first time since they'd met, she diverted her eyes.

She'd felt it all right.

Abruptly snatching her hand back, she took the slip of

paper. His own hand still tingling in the spot where they'd inadvertently touched, Cole watched her square her shoulders. Her back stiffened as she straightened in her chair.

"It doesn't matter what amount you've written. I've already told you, Stiletto isn't for sale."

Cole simply inclined his head toward the slip of paper. He stared at her fingernails, painted the same bold red as her lips, while she opened it.

This time, Sage Matthews couldn't disguise her reaction. The paper fell from her hands on the table, and that delectable red mouth dropped open. A stuttering sound came out of it.

"O-oh, my God." She covered a gasp with her hand and stared up him. "You're joking, right?"

"I never joke about business, Ms. Matthews." Satisfaction and a sense of imminent victory flooded him. The taste was so sweet, he'd probably forgo dessert.

Cole picked up the paper bearing his offer and placed it back in her hand. She was still examining it when the waiter returned with their entrées.

"Why don't you just let that figure sink in while we enjoy lunch?" Cole did his best not to sound smug. "We can discuss it after we eat."

The woman recovered quickly, her surprise replaced with a mask of indifference. But Cole knew better.

"Fine by me." She refolded the paper and put it aside.

Cole switched focus to his food. He'd originally planned to go out for a simpler meal later; however, his impending triumph had given him quite an appetite. He'd just have to make do with the chef's specialty, an overdressed piece of fish so fancy it deserved its own art exhibit.

He reached for his fork, but the frown on his dining companion's face as she looked at her food stopped him. "Everything all right?"

She wrinkled her nose, and for the first time he noticed the faint smattering of freckles dotting it. "Honestly?" she asked.

Cole chuckled. "Somehow I don't think you know how to be any other way."

"I realize you're accustomed to sitting down to a so-called gastronomical experience at every meal, but I'm a simple country girl with simple tastes. I'd have been fine with a pulled pork sandwich or burger."

"Unbelievable," Cole murmured. *More like amazing.*

She held up a hand. "Don't go getting offended on me. It's just a personal preference." She picked up her fork and poked what appeared to be pureed spinach. "I'm sure whatever is under all this froufrou garnishing tastes just fine."

Cole threw his head back and laughed. Too bad this wasn't a date because Sage Matthews was almost too good to be true. If he wasn't careful, he could end up liking her...*a lot*. "First of all, from what I see there's nothing simple about you," he said. "Second, you and I have the exact same opinion when it comes to food."

"Really?" She brightened and a smile touched her lips.

He nodded, and then scanned the surroundings. "Write-ups in *Bon Appétit* and *Saveur* magazines have made this place a hot ticket. It impresses the people I do business with who love both its exclusivity and the cuisine." Cole shrugged. "But me? I'll take cheeseburger with a side of onion rings over froufrou every time."

"My absolute favorite meal," she said. "Thanks to an electronic billboard I pass on the way to work advertising a new burger place in town, I've been giving in to a craving for it every day for the past week for both lunch and dinner."

"Burger Tower?"

She nodded. "Have you eaten there yet?"

"I haven't had the opportunity; however, I can see the very same billboard from my office window. It leaves me practically drooling."

She leaned in conspiratorially, her brown eyes sparkling with mischief. "Well, Mr. Sinclair, from one burger lover to another, they're positively addictive."

Cole rarely acted on impulse, but Sage Matthews was such a refreshing change of pace. She didn't pander to him with her eyes on his wallet for what she could get. She impressed him as a woman who spoke her mind and didn't give a damn what he or anyone else thought about it.

He was well aware he'd asked her here for purely professional reasons. Still, he found himself wanting to see her again.

"Call me Cole," he said. "Because once we conclude our business, I'd like to take you out for one of those burgers. Feed both you and your addiction."

She blinked. "As in a date?"

His common sense told him this wasn't the time or place. Intermingling the personal and professional broke the most basic rule of business. A rule he'd never been tempted to bend until now.

He knew better.

Cole couldn't defend his actions. Nor could he stop himself from telling her exactly what was on his mind.

"You couldn't have missed it. I'm not even sure what to call it—an air of familiarity?" He searched for the right words to describe the coincidences, but came up empty and hoped he didn't sound like a fool.

"It's almost like looking in a mirror," she said, softly.

Cole exhaled, and then nodded.

"Not physically, of course," she quickly added. "But we do appear to have an awful lot in common."

"More than that…" Again, he found himself reaching

for just the right words, not wanting to make presumptions or come on too strong.

Her gaze dropped to his hand. The same one her touch had left tingling. "I felt it, too."

"It's the reason why I'm asking you on a date in the middle of a business lunch. I'd like an opportunity to get to know you better."

The sparkle in her eyes dimmed. "As much as I'd enjoy that, I don't think it's going happen."

"Why not? Are you involved with someone?" Of course, she was, Cole thought. He hadn't seen a ring on her finger, but that didn't mean anything."

"No, I'm not seeing anyone. Honestly, you're the first man I've met in a long time who's piqued my interest."

"Then what's the problem?"

"Oh, I'm not the one with the problem," she said. "You'll be, once I turn down your offer to buy Stiletto."

"Are you sure you want to do that?"

His voice was velvet smooth. Its deep, melodic cadence threw Sage off her game. She didn't think she'd had it in her to act like Amelia. Yet, for a while she'd let herself be lured into entertaining the ludicrous notions of instant attraction and serendipity.

Get a grip, she silently scolded. It was just one touch and a few coincidences.

Her guard firmly back into place, Sage needed to make her position clear. Before Cole Sinclair talked her out of her company and her panties.

"I've made my decision," she said. "No sale."

Cole raised a brow. "Maybe I haven't explained that the figure I gave you is merely a starting point," he said. "One I'm willing to sweeten with a few more zeros."

Sage swallowed, hard. The offer was already beyond

generous, and at this point, much more than her company was worth. *If* money was the only measuring stick.

The massive figure didn't take the intangibles into account. She didn't have family and had sacrificed the few friends and relationships she'd had by putting all her time and effort into her small company.

While Stiletto was simply a commodity to a man like Cole Sinclair, something easily bought or sold, it was her everything.

He leaned back in his seat and crossed his arms over his broad chest. "Think about it, Ms. Matthews," he continued. "We're talking about a lot of money here. You're a young woman. Wisely invested, it'll last a lifetime. You could travel the world worry- and responsibility-free."

"And how did that work for you?"

Sage caught the tic of a muscle beneath the shadow of beard along his strong jawline. The tiny telltale movement was the only indication her question made him uncomfortable. "You spent the past few years on your boat sailing around—where was it I read, again?—Italy? Greece?"

"Both."

"Yet, instead of continuing to enjoy the idyllic carefree life you described, you're back in Nashville running Espresso." She leaned back in her chair and crossed her arms over her chest. She noticed her unconscious movements mirrored his and abruptly unfolded her arms. "Not only that, you want my company, too."

"I came back home because my family needed me. The company my mother poured her lifeblood into needs me."

"Then you should understand why I won't sell Stiletto," she said. "I've spent years building this business. Now that it's finally showing some promise, you want me to just hand it over to you."

"Sell it to me, Ms. Matthews, for what we both know is triple what your small company is actually worth."

His statement brought up a question that had niggled at her since she'd seen his staggering starting offer.

"I'm curious. Why are you willing to pay big money for my 'small company'?"

Their waiter returned. A slight incline of Cole's head and he quickly removed the plates of barely touched food, then vanished as if he'd never entered the room.

Sage met the hard stare of that man across the table. She held it through a tension-filled silence, wondering if he'd give her the real answer to her question or some pat bullshit reply.

Part of her hoped he'd do the latter. It would make it easier to dismiss Cole Sinclair and snuff out any attraction she felt toward him.

"Our image problem is no secret. The article that ran in *America Today* certainly didn't help it," he said. "Acquiring Stiletto would give Espresso instant access to and credibility with a younger market, which we desperately need."

Sage shouldn't have been surprised. Everything about him so far had been straightforward. The stark honesty in his reply raised him in her esteem.

Despite her efforts to the contrary, she found herself actually liking Cole Sinclair, though not enough to sell him her company.

"While I understand your predicament, you'll have to find another solution to Espresso's problems. Stiletto isn't for sale. Not at any price."

"So you've said." He seemed nonplussed at her declaration.

However, Sage knew he wasn't ready to give up, because they seemed to be two of a kind, and in his shoes, she wouldn't.

"Be smart, Ms. Matthews. Not only is this a once-in-a-lifetime opportunity for you, it's one for your company, too," he said. "And while I applaud what you've been able to accomplish with Stiletto with such limited resources, I think you've hit a ceiling. You won't be able to take it to the next level."

And just like that, Sage didn't like him so much anymore.

"But you can?"

"Yes," he said, matter-of-factly. The lack of conceit in his tone irked her more than his words.

Sage snorted. "With what, money?"

"Money, along with two other things you don't have—infrastructure and experience."

Sage listened as he continued to build his case.

"Espresso may have an image problem, but it also has the distribution channels. We have the department store counter space and Espresso Sanctuary spas."

"Thanks to that mention from Crave, Stiletto is on a roll," Sage countered. "It's only a matter of time before I'll have those things, too."

Cole chuckled as if she'd told him a knock-knock joke. The deep, rich sound sent the same involuntary tingles through her body as his touch, and at the same time, ratcheted up her annoyance. "Perhaps in ten years or so," he said. "I can do it now."

Sage grudgingly acknowledged the man had a point, but only to herself. She'd never give him the satisfaction of saying it aloud.

"Like you said, I'm a young woman. Time is on my side." She spared a glance at the folded slip of paper with his offer, before leveling her gaze at him. "Besides, there's more to taking a business to the next level than deep pockets."

"Deep pockets and *experience*."

"Experience in what?" Sage muttered. "Lucky investments? Globetrotting?"

Annoyance flashed in his dark brown eyes as they bored into hers, but he extinguished the show of emotion as quickly as it sparked.

He exhaled a long drawn-out sigh. "I grew up in this industry at my mother's side." He spoke slowly as if he were correcting a naughty child. "During my hiatus from Espresso, I indeed made a shrewd investment that paid off royally, which gave me an opportunity to take off and see a bit of the world. However, I also spent seven of those nine years working my way up the ladder to vice president of acquisitions at Force Cosmetics."

Sage's mouth dropped open at his disclosure, and she promptly slammed it shut, hoping he hadn't noticed.

"The articles written about me tend to leave out that particular part of my bio, preferring to focus on my so-called lucky investment," he said.

Damn. An internet search on Cole Sinclair had pulled up at least a dozen articles. None of them had mentioned he'd had a top job at Force. They practically dominated the beauty industry.

Also, it seemed strange.

Why had he gone to work for an international giant like Force Cosmetics when he had blood ties to Espresso, she wondered. Sage shrugged off the question. It wasn't any of her business.

"Don't underestimate me, Ms. Matthews," he said. "There's a lot more to me than money."

"I'll keep that in mind." Sage conceded the round of verbal sparring to him. Still, it wouldn't get him what he wanted.

He rested his back against the chair. His easy smile

returned, oozing with Southern charm, but his dark eyes brimmed with an unspoken challenge.

"Also, don't let pride stand in the way of your common sense." Like his smile, the deep, melodic baritone belied the man's uncompromising words. "Let me take Stiletto off your hands because the bottom line is I can run your company better than you ever could."

Sage stood abruptly. The condescension and the kernel of truth in his hard-hitting statement stung as if he'd pelted her with a handful of rocks.

"This meeting is over, Mr. Sinclair," she said, walking toward the door of the private dining room.

Sage didn't intend to give him a backward glance but turned around at the sound of that arrogant, infuriating, *panty-melting* voice.

"Keep in mind, if you won't sell Stiletto to me, I'll be forced to go with my alternative plan. One I don't think you'll like."

Sage's eyes narrowed as she glared at him. Sitting there, surrounded by an air of confident cool, as though he didn't have a care in the world. "I have two words for you and your granny-makeup company, Mr. Sinclair. *Bring it.*"

"How about we get on a first name basis, Sage?" The smile never left his face. "Because I intend to bring it all right. I just hope you can handle it."

Chapter 4

Cole walked briskly through the streets leading back to the Espresso building.

Bring it!

The taunt echoed through his head, leaving him unable to determine if the vapor emitted by his body was generated by his breath colliding with the cold or the steam venting from his ears.

Not only did the stubborn woman dismiss his perfectly reasonable argument. She'd tossed an extremely generous offer back in his face.

Who turns their nose up at that kind of money?

"Sage Matthews, that's who," Cole grumbled aloud, oblivious to passersby making a wide berth around the man talking to himself.

Images of big hair, shiny black boots and tempting red-slicked lips bombarded him as he yanked open the lobby door of the Espresso building.

The once-modern concrete-and-steel structure, built by

his late uncle, had been a tremendous source of pride to his mother when it was erected thirty years ago. Now the eleven-story building stood half-empty, dwarfed by dozens of gleaming new towers dominating the Nashville skyline.

Cole sighed. Though they'd worked through most of their differences, the building continued to be a sticking point in his and Victor's relationship. Cole and his sisters had agreed selling it was their best option, but his stepfather wouldn't hear of it.

They could have easily outvoted him months ago. However, Cole thought the older man needed more time to accept the inevitable.

It was just as well, he thought. Right now he needed to focus on convincing the infuriatingly sexy Sage Matthews to give him what he wanted.

Her company.

Acknowledging both the security guard and reception desk with a nod, he strode across the lobby's marble floor to the elevators. Fortunately, two of the three elevators in the older building were working today.

This should have been a chip shot, he thought, as the elevator whisked him up to the executive floor. He'd expected to be talking with his lawyers by now, instructing them to prepare the paperwork sealing the deal. Only there was no deal.

And nothing had gone as he'd expected.

The elevator chimed and the doors opened on the eleventh floor. Cole pushed open the door to the outer office of the executive suite. He was relieved to see Victor's door closed. Cole wasn't looking forward to filling his stepfather in on the details of the disastrous meeting.

Or your totally unprofessional behavior.

Cole shook his head. He'd actually asked her out on a date. It was unlike him to be so impulsive or stupid.

Then again, he'd never felt so in sync with a woman. Sage Matthews had been right about one thing, when it came to their personalities and mannerisms, it was indeed like looking in the mirror.

"Is that frown tattooed on your face or do you wear it just for me?" The gravelly ex-smoker's voice of the secretary he shared with his stepfather broke into his thoughts.

Cole groaned inwardly, pausing at the large desk in the office bridging his and Victor's offices.

The way his day had been going today, it figured Loretta Walker would be faithfully manning her station instead of taking a long lunch when the boss was away like the secretaries and administrative assistants he'd had in the past. Cole fixed the silver-haired sexagenarian with a glare that would have sent any other Espresso employee fleeing to the opposite side of the building.

The woman didn't so much as flinch.

"This is my special face just for you," he said. "I laugh like the Tickle Me Elmo doll for everyone else."

"Lucky me. I get to spend my workdays looking at that sour mug." She handed him a few opened envelopes from the stack of the day's mail. "These require your attention. I'll handle the rest."

"You're welcome to retire anytime," Cole said as he sifted through them.

"No can do," Loretta said. "I've got a granddaughter to get through medical school, remember?"

"Then how about a paid vacation, somewhere far, far away?"

"Vacation?" Loretta threw her head back and laughed, the raspy sound filling the office that had been her domain for nearly three decades. "I can barely take a bathroom break without everything around here falling apart. Face it, I'm both indispensable and irreplaceable."

Despite his bluster, Cole couldn't refute it. Loretta was also smart, paid attention to detail and took no crap whatsoever from him, or the members of his family that bore the name Gray, including the late Selina Sinclair Gray.

As a kid, he'd once asked his mother why she let an employee get away with the kind of backtalk she'd never tolerate from her children or anyone else.

She'd told him Loretta was more than just a secretary. She explained Loretta kept the office operating with clockwork precision, which gave her the freedom to focus on running Espresso.

"More importantly, Loretta calls it like she sees it, and possesses the courage to speak her mind regardless of the consequences," his mother had said. "Everybody should have someone like her in their life."

At the time, Cole had believed his mother the wisest person he'd ever known. All her big decisions had been good ones, right up until her last one, which still confounded him.

He forced back the hard feelings that had separated him from his family for years. His thoughts drifted back to the woman he'd met this afternoon.

Sage Matthews hadn't had a problem speaking her mind, either.

Their short meeting had taken him through a gamut of emotions. He couldn't remember the last time he'd been so intrigued, irritated or challenged, and he had to admit, totally turned on.

"Is that a tic or did you actually just crack a smile?"

"Tic," Cole answered automatically, "brought on by a certain exasperating secretary." Although, he knew a smile brought on by the recent memory of a certain woman in red had indeed touched his lips.

Loretta grunted. "If you're all done twitching, mind

telling me what time you want your lawyers here to hammer out the details of the Stiletto deal?"

The next grunt that sounded in the outer office came from him. His lips tightened. Any hint of a smile connected to his lunchtime encounter vanished, replaced with the last emotion his lunch companion had left him with—annoyance.

"Well?" Loretta pressed.

"There is no Stiletto deal." Cole admitted, then quickly amended. "Yet."

The long-time secretary's hoarse cackle filled his ears. All she needed to complete the effect was a chalkboard to scratch her nails across. "Gave you hell, didn't she?"

Although he'd never admit it aloud, Sage Matthews certainly had.

"Good for her, bringing you down a peg or two," Loretta continued. Her gravelly voice trailed him into his office. "It's about time you met your match."

Cole closed the door firmly behind him. However, his secretary's parting shot lingered. He couldn't deny the similarities between them, but his *match*? Ms. Matthews had a long way to go before she possessed the capability to bring him down a peg.

Walking over to the window, he shoved his hands into his pants pockets. He stared blankly at the flashing billboard in the distance and plotted his next move.

"I can't believe you walked out on Cole Sinclair."

Sage rose from her chair, braced her palms on her desktop and leaned forward. Had Amelia lost her mind? "Did you not hear a word I just said? The man threatened to come after Stiletto."

"Well…" Her assistant hedged, tilting her head to one side.

"Well, what?" Sage snapped. She fisted her hands on

her hips waiting to hear what possible explanation the young woman could conjure up to justify the man's insufferable behavior.

"You did tell him to 'bring it,'" Amelia said. "And knowing you as I do, I'm sure it was more like a barked command."

"Me?" Sage asked incredulously. Her knuckles dug deeper into her sides. "All I did was show up for a lunch meeting, which I should add, *you* wouldn't give me a moment's peace about until I agreed to go."

Her assistant held her hands up. "Hold on, General," she said. "I certainly didn't mean for you to march downtown and purposely provoke him."

Sage plopped down in her office chair and crossed her arms over her chest. "He was the one provoking me."

"You aren't one of the richest people in town."

"Please, don't mention money." Sage rolled her eyes toward the beams and pipes stretching across the ceiling of the former factory that housed Stiletto's headquarters as well as several other businesses. "He was tossing out dollars like a freak in a strip club."

Amelia laughed and then stopped abruptly. She narrowed her eyes. "So exactly how much was his offer to buy Stiletto?"

"That would fall under the category of none of your business."

"How about a ballpark figure?" The teen shrugged. "You turned him down anyway. What difference does it make?"

Sage thought it over a moment. It wasn't as if Amelia would spread it around the office. She could be a loopy romantic, but she was as discreet as she was efficient.

"Let's just say it was a couple of ballparks."

"And you didn't take the deal?"

"Of course, not. Stiletto isn't for sale," Sage said. "And you weren't there. He was condescending and..." Her voice trailed off as the sound of his easy baritone came back to her. Deep, rich and melodic. It made her want him to eat dessert in bed with him, *naked*.

"And what?" Amelia raised a brow.

"H-he was just so smug," Sage stammered over the words.

A slow smile spread over her assistant's lips. "And what else?"

"O-overbearing, insufferable, overconfident..." Again, her reaction to him at lunch waylaid her train of thought, and she automatically rubbed the spot where their hands had accidentally brushed.

"Interesting." The young woman's eyes widened as if she'd just been told a secret, and the smile on her face morphed into a full-fledged grin. "He sounds an awful lot like someone else I know."

"What are you grinning at?" Sage snapped. "Stop it."

Instead, Amelia narrowed her gaze. She made a few *hmm* and *mmm* sounds as she looked her up and down.

Sage squirmed uncomfortably in her chair. "What on earth is the matter with you?"

The young woman ignored the question, continuing her examination. "Cheeks flushed. Eyes glazed over. You're practically glowing," she said, making Sage feel as though she was in a doctor's office instead of her own. "And notice how you were all breathless and stammering when you talked about Mr. Sinclair."

Amelia nodded her head knowingly as if she already had the answer to her own question. "Not in a million years did I think I'd be saying this to you, but you look exactly like a smitten heroine in one of my romance novels."

Although she was immune to them, Sage gave her assistant a laser-beam side eye. "I'm acting insulted and extremely annoyed…because I am."

However, Sage didn't know who she was more pissed at, the man with the bedroom voice who believed he could run her business better than she, or herself for even having considered a date with him.

"If you say so."

"I do say so," Sage insisted, remembering his last words to her and the excessive confidence with which he'd delivered them.

I intend to bring it all right. I just hope you can handle it.

His declaration had come off as a double entendre. She'd caught both the all-business challenge and the sensual promise. Sage only wished there was a way for her to show him he'd taunted the wrong woman and wipe the smug smile off his handsome face.

Oblivious, Amelia exhaled a dreamy sigh filled with youthful naïveté. "I think Mr. Sinclair made quite the impression on you."

Sage's stomach growled, reminding her she still hadn't had lunch. "He made me so mad, I didn't even eat…"

The words died on her lips as an idea hit her.

Not just an idea, a maneuver so outrageous it would make Cole Sinclair think twice about underestimating her again. *But you couldn't,* she thought. *You wouldn't dare go through with it.*

Oh, yes, I would.

Her assistant waved a hand in front of her face, and Sage blinked. "You haven't heard a word I've said. I was trying to tell you…" Amelia paused, then frowned. "Uh-oh. What's going on in that head of yours?"

Sage feigned cluelessness. "Whatever do you mean?"

"It looks like you just sprouted devil horns on your head. The only thing missing is the diabolical laugh."

Her decision made, Sage slapped her palms against her desk and stood. Time to rally the troops. "I want you to add fifty additional beauty bloggers to the invitation list for our Valentine's Day's event," she said. "We're going to make it even bigger and even better."

"Will do."

She watched her assistant make the notation. "Then send Joe Archer from advertising into my office. I've got a job for him," Sage said. "I'm about to teach Mr. Sinclair a lesson he won't soon forget."

Amelia shook her head. "Sounds like you've already made him angry. I really don't think you should provoke him any further."

"Never mind what you think. Just get Archer in here."

Her assistant heaved an exaggerated sigh. "All right, I'll do as you ordered, General. I just hope you don't start the battle of the Nashville cosmetic companies."

So what if she did? Sage thought. The man had made it clear he intended to bring it. She was simply firing the first salvo, because the best defense was a good offense.

Her only regret was that she wouldn't be there to see the look on Sinclair's face.

Chapter 5

A week after their disastrous lunch, Sage Matthews remained on Cole's mind. His thoughts bounced from those sexy, shapely legs to that sassy mouth of hers painted the hottest shade of red he'd ever seen.

"Mr. Sinclair?"

Cole blinked, the sound of his name dragging him back to reality. Damn, he'd done it again.

And again, he told himself he was only pondering his next step to persuade the woman to sell her business.

"Sorry, could you repeat that?" Cole glanced around the coffee- and croissant-laden conference-room table where Espresso's department heads had gathered that morning for their biweekly meeting. His uncharacteristic distracted behavior drew a quizzical stare from Victor and a smug, know-it-all one from Loretta, who had been needling him all week about Stiletto's owner rejecting his offer.

He looked past them to the company's special events coordinator.

Tammy Barnes adjusted her eyeglasses. "I was saying it appears the Valentine's Day minimakeover event at our department store counters will have some competition, at least locally," she said. "Stiletto Cosmetics is holding an event the same afternoon."

Preston Tate's buttons strained to keep his shirt closed as he hurriedly washed down his third croissant with a gulp of coffee. "So we anticipate a lower-than-expected turnout," Tate, who was the head of their marketing team, chimed in. "It'll also mean generating less buzz nationwide, when the bloggers take to social media with comments and photos all about Stiletto."

As Cole listened, he wondered if this event was Sage's idea of getting back at him. She'd been furious when she'd stormed out of the restaurant. Moreover, the woman had practically challenged him. *Just like you did to her.*

Seated at his right, Loretta glanced down at her tablet computer. She'd balked when he'd upgraded every Espresso employee to the latest technology upon his return. Now the tablet rarely left her hands.

"Next on the agenda is Lola," she said.

A collective groan echoed across the room at the mention of Cole's youngest sister, and a young man seated at the opposite end of the conference table cleared his throat. "A few days ago, she and some of her model friends held a wild party in London and totally trashed their hotel suite. Now the European tabloids are having a field day. I think we need to…"

"Nonsense." Victor cut him off. "You can't believe anything the media reports anyway."

"But they had photos, and considering Lola is the face of Espresso, it reflects badly on the company," the young man countered.

"Brat," Loretta grunted.

"Watch your mouths. That's my baby girl you're talking about," Victor warned. "Those damn tabloids are making a big deal out of nothing. End of story. Case closed."

The faces around the table turned to Cole, knowing he was the one with the final word on any subject concerning the company. "I agree with Victor," he said. "Lola's just high-spirited."

"Enabler." Loretta snorted.

Cole held up a silencing hand and then turned his attention back to their marketing head. "Tate, I want to hear more about this event of Stiletto's."

"I'll just bet you do," Loretta muttered under her breath.

Cole shot his secretary a censorious glare, which earned him another gravelly snort. If she were anyone else, she would have been looking for a new job.

"It's a meet and greet for social media beauty gurus," Preston said. "Light refreshments, swag bags, et cetera."

Cole tapped his fingertip against the table. "Do you happen to know if this was something they pulled together in the past week?"

"I don't think so." Preston shrugged. "Looks like they posted it on their website a month ago."

Cole nodded absently. He was just being paranoid, he reasoned. Sage might be bold. The name of her lip color crossed his mind. However, she wasn't badass enough to take him on...or was she?

A thump vibrated the conference table, jolting him out of his reverie.

"Dang it!" Victor stood abruptly, drawing concerned stares from the room. He stomped his foot. "Leg fell asleep."

The older man shook his leg. He walked over to the wall of windows, on the other side of the room to coax life back into his sluggish limb. Located two floors below Cole's office, the floor-to-ceiling windows offered the same panoramic view, but at a lower vantage point.

"Funny you should ask about last week, though." Preston swiped at his tablet. "It looks as though they expanded the event a week ago and reached out to more bloggers and YouTube vloggers."

Maybe he wasn't being paranoid after all, Cole thought. Was this Sage's way of taking him on? He dismissed the idea. The challenge she'd issued had simply been an angry rant. Nothing more.

Tammy raised her hand to get their attention before clearing her throat. "Does anyone know when Tia will be back? I need to talk to her about including the spas in an upcoming event."

Cole shrugged. His sister and brother-in-law, Ethan, hadn't had time for a honeymoon after their quickie Las Vegas nuptials six months ago. Last month they'd flown to Australia, where it was still summer, for an extended road-trip honeymoon.

"She gets back to Nashville on Valentine's Day but won't return to work until the week after," Loretta answered.

Tammy nodded. "Thank…"

"Holy Moley!" Victor bellowed from the other side of the room.

Again, his outburst attracted the attention of the department heads seated at the table.

"For goodness' sake," Loretta said. "The entire room doesn't have to be privy to your circulation problems. I'm no spring chicken, but you don't hear me squawking about every little twinge."

"It's not me. It's…" Victor turned away from the window. He wore a stunned expression on his face. "Cole, I think you should take a look at this."

Concerned, Cole rushed to her stepfather's side. The older man pointed out the window, and Cole looked in the direction of his finger.

"What the...?" Cole blinked.

He stared dumbfounded at the electronic billboard in the distance, unable to believe what he was seeing. The gasps of the employees who had followed him to the window filled Cole's ears.

No, the hell she didn't.

The ad for Burger Tower's mouthwatering burger was gone. In its place was an advertisement for Stiletto Cosmetics, featuring the man in drag from the newspaper article photo. Even though it was a mile away, the ad flashed boldly against the gray winter sky.

The faux old lady wore the same lopsided gray wig, a hideous paisley dress and a thick coating of outdated makeup. He was juxtaposed against a chic young woman in skintight leather pants and high heels.

Cole's molars ground against each other as he glared at the caption—Stiletto: Not Your Granny's Makeup. It was scrawled across the bottom of the ad, in the same shade of red as Sage's lipstick, as if she'd signed it personally.

The blasted woman knew he'd see it. He'd told her he could see this billboard from his office window.

He felt a nudge at his side, and Loretta handed him a pair of binoculars she'd somehow located in the minutes since everyone had gathered at the window. Her efficiency still amazed him. No wonder his mother, Victor and now Cole gave her insolence a pass.

Peering through the binoculars, Cole zeroed in on the billboard. Magnification only made the damn thing worse.

"Looks like you poked the wrong bear." Loretta's gravelly words went into his right ear.

"Stiletto's owner is not just good-looking, she's ballsy,

too." Victor snorted in his left ear as Cole stood between them, binoculars still trained on the offensive sign in the distance.

Bring it!

Sage's taunt and his own rising anger drowned out the voices of his secretary and stepfather. Anger mingled with the respect Cole grudgingly had to give her. This was something he would have done, if his attraction to her hadn't thrown him for a loop.

He continued to stare at the heavily made-up man on the billboard, silently ridiculing Espresso. The insult was just the kick in the behind he needed to make his next move.

"This meeting is adjourned," Cole said firmly as he turned away from the window.

His department heads started to file out of the room, still buzzing about the billboard. Cole glanced at Loretta, who was looking at Stiletto's website on her tablet computer. News of the Valentine's Day event dominated the page.

He smiled to himself and called out to two of the retreating department heads. "Tate, Barnes, I'll meet you both in my office in five minutes," he said. "You too, Vic."

"What are you up to?" Loretta asked.

"I'll fill you in when we get to my office," Cole said.

It was time he showed the bear the consequences of taunting a tiger.

Chapter 6

Sage slowed her run to a walk as the small, modest house came into view.

She had repaired the sagging porch, patched the roof and painted the faded exterior paint, and there was still more renovation to be done. But the wreath made of painted pinecones and blue grosgrain ribbons hanging on the front door gave her home a certain charm.

The sight of the tiny house never failed to make her smile. Only fifteen years of mortgage payments remained before it was all hers. Once she paid it off, she'd never have to worry about being displaced or shuffled between homes again.

Sage swiped at the sweat dripping down her face as she walked up and down the length of her driveway to cool down. The early-morning three-mile run was the price she paid for her junk food habit.

She yanked the iPod earbuds from her ears, and the

sound of her sneakers crunching against the driveway's crumbling asphalt replaced the thumping beat of her work-out playlist. Repaving the drive was another one of the items on the endless to-do list she'd amassed since becoming a homeowner last year.

She'd get to them all eventually. Right now her focus was on getting the house's interior up to par and building up the one thing she owned outright—her company.

Sage grinned. The thought of Stiletto brought to mind the new electronic billboard ad that had starting running yesterday. No doubt Cole Sinclair had seen it by now. Her grin morphed into a snicker as she imagined his reaction.

Damn, she wished she could have been the proverbial fly on the wall.

She stopped midstep as a second thought occurred to her. She'd better be on the lookout. The man would be out to get even. Sage was sure of it. In his shoes, she'd certainly be eager for some payback.

"Boo!"

Startled, Sage nearly jumped out of her sneakers.

A giggle sounded from the hedge she'd planted to replace the dilapidated picket fence separating her and her neighbor's properties.

Sage sighed and shook her head. So much for being on her guard. "I heard you laughing, so you might as well show yourself," she called out.

The bushes rustled, and a kid dressed in a fleece robe that covered superhero pajamas emerged. "Did I scare you?"

"Of course not," Sage said. "You hide in the bushes and shout boo at me every morning. No shock factor."

The kindergartener's hopeful face drooped, but a moment later his eyes narrowed with suspicion. "Then why'd you jump?"

"I didn't jump," Sage fibbed. If the little monster knew he'd actually gotten her this time, there would be no stopping him.

"Yes, you did. I saw you." He flashed her a triumphant snaggletoothed grin. "Got any Skittles?"

Sage reached for the zipper on the pocket of her jacket to pull out the packet of candy she put there every morning before she set out on her run.

"Kenny!" A voice bellowed over the hedge. "Kenny Hinton if you sneaked away from the breakfast table to pester our neighbor again, you're going to be in big trouble, Mister. Big trouble."

The front door of the house next door slammed.

"Uh-oh." The boy looked over his shoulder and then back at Sage.

Yanking the candy from her pocket, she tossed it to him. Kenny caught it and quickly hid it behind his back.

"I'm not bothering her, promise," the boy said moments later.

Evie Hinton peered over the hedge at her wayward son, two mugs of coffee in her hand. "March yourself right back into the house and finish your cereal. Don't get up from the table until you've eaten every bite."

The petite redhead passed one of the steaming mugs over the shrubbery to Sage as they both watched the little boy trudge back into his own yard and into the house. "Jeez, it's like living the movie *Groundhog Day*. Same thing every morning," Evie said.

"He's not bothering me." Sage wrapped both hands around the mug to warm them.

"You say that every morning, too."

It was true. She didn't consider herself much of a kid person, but Kenny had been the first person to welcome her to the neighborhood. Both he and his morning visits had grown on Sage. They made the child in her who had been shuffled between homes feel at home.

"And the two of you aren't fooling anyone, you know." Evie sipped her coffee. "I'm going to send you the dental bills when all that candy you slip him rots his teeth."

"What teeth? He's barely got any."

Evie laughed. "You got me there. Seems like the tooth fairy stops by our house every week."

Sage took a sip of coffee. She closed her eyes, briefly absorbing its warmth and caffeine. The notes of chocolate and coconut in her neighbor's coffee beans made everyday mornings feel like an occasion.

"Oh, do you think you'll be able to help me out with his birthday party in a few weeks?" Evie asked. "Kenneth will be on the road, and when it comes to kids' parties, most of the other parents tend to dump and run."

"Dump and run?" Sage wasn't familiar with the term.

"Dump their brats off and run like hell."

Sage laughed and readily agreed to help supervise the pizza party. Evie was always doing things for her, and she rarely got an opportunity to reciprocate.

"Kenneth due back tonight?" Evie's truck driver husband had been hauling a load of appliances to Miami.

The redhead shook her head. "Tomorrow," she said. "I'll be busy with your order tonight."

Sage had discovered she lived next door to a crafter extraordinaire shortly after moving in. Evie had stopped by to welcome her to the neighborhood, bearing a handmade door wreath fashioned from twigs, burlap and artificial sunflowers.

The wreath was stunning, as were the others the stay-at-home mom fashioned and hung on both their doors every month.

Evie had insisted her craft projects were just a hobby.

However, as the idea for Stiletto's first-ever event began to take shape, Sage knew she wanted her neighbor to make the centerpieces that would adorn the tables at the Valentine's Day morning affair.

"Keep in mind, I'm not complaining. Certainly not about the check," Evie said. "I'm still thrilled you even asked me."

It had been a good decision, Sage thought. Her neighbor had suggested adding a chocolate candy buffet, so in addition to making the centerpieces, Evie was also handcrafting chocolates shaped like lipsticks, compacts and stiletto pumps.

"I'm the one who's thrilled. Our guests will be, too, when they see those centerpieces and gorge themselves on your chocolates." Sage drained the last of her coffee and stared almost mournfully into the bottom of her mug.

"Why don't you come inside for a refill?" Evie asked. "I've got a batch of cooling chocolates earmarked for Stiletto. They'll be ready to sample soon."

Sage was tempted and not just by the offer of more coffee and chocolate. It was still early, and she enjoyed chatting with Evie. They'd become friends over the months, and the Hinton home was one of the few places she allowed herself to relax. She opened her mouth to accept the invitation, but then remembered the salvo she'd fired at Cole Sinclair.

Kenny wasn't the only one who'd be lying in wait for her. She'd have to keep her guard up for the foreseeable future.

"Not today." Sage handed the empty mug back to her neighbor. "I'm going in to work early. I want to make extra sure everything goes smoothly."

Evie smiled over her mug. "That's probably a good idea." Her eyes brightened. "I saw the billboard."

Sage had told her friend what she was planning a few mornings ago. Unlike Amelia, Evie didn't try to warn her off teaching the big, bad millionaire a lesson. Instead, she'd practically doubled over laughing and wished her luck.

"I didn't know you drove all the way downtown to look at it," Sage said. "Well, what did you think?"

Evie shook her head. "I thought it was even more hilarious than the mock-up of the ad you showed me the other morning, but I didn't go downtown. It was on the news."

"The news?"

"Yeah, I was watching the story on it until Kenny caught my back turned and escaped the breakfast table." Evie tapped one of the now-empty mugs against her forehead. "Oh, no," she groaned. "Tell me I didn't send my kindergartener into a kitchen filled with cooling candy?"

Sage winced. "You did."

"Kenny!" Evie shouted as she sprinted through her yard toward her house.

A small figure came to the Hinton's door in response, and Sage could see from her driveway that his face was covered in chocolate.

"Oh, Kenny." Evie said.

Sage turned to her own house, leaving her exasperated friend to her charge. It was time for her to get dressed and get to work. She had her own baby to keep a watchful eye on while trying to anticipate Cole Sinclair's next move.

An hour later, Sage sat at her desk reviewing the list of RSVPs from social media beauty influencers across the country.

It was a task Amelia had assigned to another member of the Stiletto staff and personally overseen, but this billboard thing had Sage jumpy. She continued to scroll through the names, excited to see it read like a who's who of beauty bloggers and YouTube makeup gurus—all with huge followings.

The phone rang, and Sage jerked so hard she nearly fell off her office chair. She'd gone from jumpy to down-right paranoid.

"For goodness' sake, Cole Sinclair isn't the boogey-man," she muttered aloud. "The only person waiting to ambush you is Kenny." And she wouldn't let the kid get the drop on her again.

The office phone stopped ringing, but immediately started up again. Sage was the only one there. With the exception of the security guard stationed in the foyer of the factory-turned-office-building, she was probably the only person around. It would be at least a half hour before Stiletto's staff and the workers for the various other businesses filed into work.

Sage debated letting it go to voice mail so Amelia could deal with whoever it was later. However, she saw the word *international* flash across the caller ID screen and curiosity drove her to answer.

A heavily-accented male voice greeted her. *"Buon giorno. Sage Matthews, per favore."*

"You're speaking to her."

"Hold for Signora Bertelli."

Her grip on the phone tightened. *Bertelli?* As in the Italian designer?

Slow down. Sage snorted. As if Signora Bertelli would ever call her. It was either wishful thinking on her part or some kind of prank.

Any doubts about the caller's identity were cleared up the moment a woman's voice came over the line. Sage recognized it instantly from a documentary feature film on the designer she'd watched dozens of times on DVD.

"Ms. Matthews, this is Marie Bertelli," she said. The

clipped tones of Boston's North End permeated her words as she apologized for the early hour. "I told my assistant to try anyway. Like most successful businesswomen, I suspected your workday began early."

Sage's hand began to tremble, and she clutched the phone with both hands. She'd never been starstruck or intimidated by anyone. Her motto being that everyone, including celebrities, put their underwear on the same way—one leg at a time.

Yet, she couldn't help the feeling of total awe that washed over her at receiving a call from someone whose work, especially her business acumen, she'd admired for years.

"What can I do for you, Ms. Bertelli?" Sage asked. Despite her excitement, her voice never lost its carefully honed cool.

"I read an article about you and your company in the international edition of *America Today* a few weeks ago," she said. "I was intrigued, so I asked my sisters to bring me a selection of your lipsticks when they came to visit."

An Italian-American born and raised in Boston, Bertelli had earned her undergraduate degree in fashion design from the Fashion Institute of Technology and an MBA from the prestigious Wharton School of the University of Pennsylvania.

The oldest daughter of an African-American mother and Italian father, she had relocated to Milan to work for the fashion house founded by her paternal grandparents.

"I loved the lipsticks," Bertelli said. "Especially the deep vampy purple one. I've had it on all day and received nothing but compliments. Darn it. I left the tube in my purse, and the name escapes me."

"One-Night Stand." Sage supplied and made a mental

note to have Amelia ship an entire case of the shade to her first thing this morning.

"Well, Ms. Matthews, it's definitely made a Stiletto fan out of me," she said. "Speaking of which, I had another reason for contacting you. I want to personally extend an invitation to you to attend the Bertelli runway show this month during Fashion Week here in Milan."

Sage froze as the invitation sunk in and then pressed her lips together to keep from screaming an excited yes in the woman's ear. She exhaled slowly in an effort to quell her excitement.

"Thank you, but I'll have to check my February calendar," Sage began, knowing full well she'd do whatever was necessary to make this trip happen.

"Of course," Bertelli said. "My secretary will be in touch. I really hope you can attend."

The two women spent a few moments exchanging pleasantries before ending the call. Sage was returning the cordless phone to its base when she heard the front door to Stiletto's main entrance open.

"Amelia," she called out from her desk, knowing the young woman was always the first of her employees to arrive. Her assistant would be ecstatic when she heard.

Sage opened her mouth to call out again just as the last person she expected to see filled the doorway of her office.

Cole Sinclair.

She blinked, her mouth still hanging open, and then Sage snapped it shut before she started to drool. He looked different today. His expensive designer suit was replaced with casual attire, the effect coaxing her long-dormant hormones out of retirement.

Sage ignored how his height left scant inches between the top of his head and the door frame, and the way his jeans hugged the muscles of his lean thighs. Then she convinced herself his sweater, which appeared to be milled from the softest cashmere, didn't tempt her to make a pillow out of his broad chest.

Cole wore a leather bomber jacket in a shade of deep olive that was more stylish than the classic black, yet didn't detract from its bad-boy appeal.

Sage licked her suddenly dry lips. He looked good.

"No. It's not Amelia," he said, the melodic baritone threatening to lure her into a trance. An almost imperceptible spark flared in his dark-eyed gaze. It said without words that the blasted man knew she'd been admiring the view.

Straightening in her chair, Sage fixed her face with her most intimidating glare. "What are you doing here?"

"Good morning to you, too." He rested a shoulder against the doorjamb, and for the first time she noticed he hadn't come empty-handed. He held a green-and-white box in one hand. Its aroma wafted from the doorway, smelling as good as he looked.

"How'd you get past the security guard?" The question was nearly drowned out by the racket coming from her rumbling stomach. Sage narrowed her eyes. "You bribe him?"

A hint of a smile lifted the corners of mouth as he nodded. "It cost me two Krispy Kreme doughnuts." He inclined his head toward the box. "The rest are for you."

"But you of all people should know I can't be bought."

His smile deepened, revealing a dimple she hadn't seen before. "They're hot."

Me, too, thanks to you. Sage crossed her legs under her desk. She intended to keep them that way until this surprise visit of his was over.

"Are you sure I can't tempt you?"

Her stomach growled again as the smell of doughnuts

filled the office. Sage huffed out a sigh and gave into it. "Well, since you're already here."

He pulled away from the door frame and strode toward her with the ease of a man comfortable in his own skin. Bringing his free hand from behind his back, he produced a bouquet of brilliant yellow flowers.

"Also for you."

Sage eyed his offering. The cheerful mix of sunflowers, yellow Gerber daisies and alstroemeria blooms instantly brightened her office. They'd be a sweet gesture coming from anyone else. However, Cole Sinclair had an agenda. One that conflicted directly with hers, and she'd best not forget it.

Finally, she rose from her chair and took the flowers from her nemesis's outstretched hand. She hesitated before bringing them to her nose to inhale their sweet scent. "These aren't laced with hemlock, are they, Mr. Sinclair?"

"It's Cole, remember?"

"Well, Cole." Sage continued to inspect the sunny bouquet. "Did you hide a listening device in these posies that would make you privy to my office secrets?"

He chuckled. The deep, rich rumble made her toes curl inside her five-inch heels. One brow lifted as his brown eyes bored into hers. "Have you done something that would make you feel paranoid around me?"

"I take it you've seen the billboard." Sage acknowledged the obvious.

He nodded. "Oh, I saw it all right."

Rounding her desk, she crossed the room and stepped out into her outer office. She retrieved paper plates and a vase from a cabinet. When she returned, Cole was lifting the lid on the box of doughnuts, which he'd deposited on her desk. Sage passed him the paper plates and stuffed the flowers into the vase. Cole topped one of the paper plates with a warm glazed doughnut and handed it to her, along with a napkin imprinted with the doughnut chain's logo.

"I brought you coffee, too, but your security guard appropriated it as part of the bribe," he said.

"Would you like some?" Sage told herself it was the least she could do since he'd come bearing gifts. "It'll only take a second. My assistant insisted on one of those fancy single-serving brewers for our offices."

"No, thanks. I'm an earlier riser. I've already had coffee this morning, plus I ran three miles."

Sage told herself it wasn't another one of the similarities they shared. Plenty of people ran three miles and drank coffee in the morning.

He plucked a glazed doughnut from the box. "But I'll take one of these off your hands."

Leaning shoulder-to-shoulder against the front of her desk, they chewed simultaneously as they each polished off a doughnut. Sage broke the brief silence. "While I'm not entirely shocked to hear from you today, this isn't at all what I expected."

"Let me guess, you were waiting for me to call or storm in here ranting, ready to take your head off."

"Something like that."

He helped himself to another doughnut and placed a second one on her plate. "I'd be lying if I said it wasn't my visceral reaction. I was furious."

"I'll bet," Sage said. "But you seem pretty chill now." *Suspiciously so*, she thought.

"You can't think when you're angry." Cole bit into his doughnut and slowly chewed.

"And I take it you've been thinking."

"Oh, yeah." He sounded casual and friendly, but there was no mistaking the unspoken promise in his seemingly innocuous words. Sage heard it loud and clear: *watch your back.*

"So is this all part of your strategy?" She glanced over her shoulder at the flowers and half-empty box of doughnuts on her desk.

"Actually, the flowers are my way of acknowledging that the billboard was a brilliant move on your part. I foolishly underestimated you," he said, "and you found a way to make me pay for it and at the same time advertise your brand."

Sage scanned his face, unable to believe what she was hearing. This time he'd genuinely shocked her, and she had to do a double take.

Not many men, or people for that matter, were able to openly admit to a mistake or being bested. Yet Cole had done so with no reservations. Once again, he'd raised himself in her esteem.

Too bad he was after her company.

"Bravo." Cole inclined his head in a slight nod. "In your shoes, I might have done the same thing. After all, the best defense is a good offense."

Sage blinked. Those had been her exact thoughts when she'd hatched the idea for the billboard. It was becoming increasingly harder to brush off their similarities as mere coincidences.

"I don't suppose this makes us even," she said finally. Deciding to stop at one doughnut, she placed the plate bearing the uneaten one on her desk.

Having already demolished his second pastry, Cole wiped his hands with a napkin and tossed it in the wastebasket. "Not by a long shot."

He turned and focused his attention on her, leaning in until his face was scant inches from hers. "Besides, you have something I want." Sage shivered as the deep voice dropped to a husky whisper. His warm, sweet breath fanned across her face. "Now I want it even more."

Sage slammed her eyes shut and swallowed hard, silently willing the parts of her body shifting into Overdrive back to into Neutral. She should have stayed behind her desk with her legs tightly crossed, because this man was on the verge of talking the panties right off her.

When she opened her eyes, his gaze was locked on her lips.

"Is this your idea of keeping friends close and enemies closer?" The mocking tone she'd hoped for fell flat, her question echoed in her ears like a breathless pant.

"You're not my enemy, Sage," Cole murmured. "You're a challenge." He raised his hand and brushed his knuckles down the side of her cheek. "And I do love a challenge."

Clearheaded, a snappy comeback would have been on the tip of Sage's tongue. However, her brain had taken the backseat in her headspace, allowing a wave of longing so powerful it drew her to him like he was magnetized, to take the wheel.

"That lip shade is beautiful on you." His eyes never leaving her lips, Cole swiped the pad of his thumb across a sticky spot near the corner of her mouth. Sage stood mesmerized as he slowly licked the sugary glaze from his thumb, while her imagination conjured up illicit images of him licking her *everywhere*.

"What's it called?" He asked.

"Taste Me."

"You just read my mind." Cupping her chin in his hand, Cole leaned in and his brushed his lips against hers.

Sage steeled herself against the pleasure of the brief contact. The protective wall guarding her emotions cautioned her to put an end to this, before she lost control. She lifted her hands to his chest with every intention of pushing him away.

Before she could, Cole withdrew and stared into her

eyes. "Kiss me, Sage," he said, the deep melodic tone both a plea and a demand. "And *bring it*. Don't hold back."

Sage shivered at the sexy command. She was a woman accustomed to giving orders, but right now she wanted to follow his...just this once.

Fisting the sweater in her hands, she tugged him to her and kissed him hard. Sage felt his arm around her waist as he pulled her flush against him.

She gasped and Cole deepened the kiss. His tongue swept inside her mouth and slowly stroked hers. He tasted of doughnuts, sinfully sweet, and if her body's reaction to him was any indication, the man was just as addictive.

Encircling her arms around his neck, Sage melted into his hard body. She savored the languid movements of his mouth that were somehow reminiscent of the cadence of his easy Southern drawl. Absorbed in the sensual demands of his tongue and the bulge pressing against her belly, she lost track of time and place.

Cole wrapped his free arm around her. His hand gripped her ass, and she moaned as he ground against her. It was all too much, and at the same time, not enough.

"Morning! What are you doing here so..."

Sage jumped at the sound of the all-too-familiar voice. Cocooned in Cole's powerful embrace, she turned to find Amelia standing in her office doorway, mouth wide open.

Damn, Sage thought at the exact same moment Cole muttered the expletive aloud. She extricated herself from his arms and watched as he ran a hand over his short-cropped hair. The expression on his face mirrored her thoughts. A few moments more, and they would have both been naked, tasting more than each other's mouths.

Sage exhaled. By now her assistant had recovered enough for her initial surprise to have morphed into a grin too wide for her face.

"Cole Sinclair, this is my assistant, Amelia Brown," Sage said, regaining her composure.

Amelia looked pointedly from Cole and back to her, still grinning like a loon.

Sage shot her a glare, and the young woman quickly excused herself. "Carry on, General," she said, as she exited. "I'll be at my desk if you need me, reading one of my *far-fetched* romance novels."

Chapter 7

Cole grasped Sage's hand, wishing the contact would whisk them back to the moment before her assistant had interrupted. When her body heat had seeped through his clothes, and he could taste her sweet surrender as she sighed into his mouth.

"I appreciate both breakfast and the company," Sage said matter-of-factly.

He raised a brow to indicate her casual tone wasn't fooling him. Not after the kiss they'd just shared.

She met his gaze head-on. "Anything more would be a bad idea."

"Why? We're both adults, and neither of us has felt this attracted to anyone in a very long time." He ran his thumb along the back of her hand. It trembled in his before she pulled away. "Don't bother denying it," he continued. "You want me just as much as I want you."

"We both know it's more complicated than that."

"It doesn't have to be," Cole countered.

Sage shook her head slowly, defeating any hopes he had of picking up where they'd left off. "You want more than I'm willing to give."

"Are we talking about your company *or you*?"

"Both."

She rounded her desk, and he turned to watch her slide into the chair behind it. Taking the hint, he prepared to go.

"You're making a mistake," he said. "On both counts."

The cold morning air greeted him as he walked back to his black Dodge Challenger. Too bad it wasn't a kick in the behind, Cole thought.

What was the matter with him?

The same man who'd shown no mercy when going after companies to add to the Force Cosmetics portfolio turned into an amnesiac in this woman's presence.

One look at that pink-painted frown on her angelic face, and he'd promptly forgotten his reason for showing up at her office. A glimpse of her legs in those heels and pencil skirt, and Cole had barely recalled his own name.

He started up the car, and briefly debated whether to return to his town house on the other side of town to change or wear one of the suits he kept at work. Sage Matthews still had his mind, making the simplest of decisions difficult.

Her throaty whisper echoed in his head as he automatically drove in the direction of the Espresso building.

Taste Me.

Cole had come within seconds of clearing her desk with a single swipe of his arm, shoving that skintight skirt up to her waist and tasting her until his name fell from those pink-slicked lips over and over again.

Cole licked his own lips at thought.

"Shake it off, man."

He merged the muscle car onto the expressway. Good

thing his next move to convince Sage to sell him Stiletto was already in place, and like her in-your-face tactic, he'd designed it to do double duty.

Cole waited for the smug sense of satisfaction he'd gotten every time he'd thought about what he had in store. The feeling eluded him. That damned kiss remained on his mind along with the quick glimpse of vulnerability he'd seen in her eyes.

He shifted lanes as the downtown skyline came into view, speculating on whether to follow through with his plan. He'd never let the personal creep into business before.

You've never encountered a woman like her, either.

He was still debating if he should call it off when he exited the expressway. The morning rush hour had yet to start, and the streets leading to Espresso's headquarters were clear.

A traffic light switched from yellow to red, and Cole braked. Perhaps he should try a more low-key tactic to convince Sage to sell Stiletto. Maybe…

Then he caught it out of the corner of his eye—that blasted billboard. He studied the insult to his family business, which could be seen for miles. It hadn't changed since yesterday. The same man in drag stared back at him mocking his mother's life's work.

Fortunately, the flashing reminder made Cole's goal crystal clear. Time he started thinking with the head on his shoulders instead of the one below his waist. He'd show Sage Matthews the lengths he'd go to in order to get his hands on Stiletto.

In the long run, it was the best thing for him, Sage and their companies.

Seconds later, the light turned green, and Cole made a left and parked in the garage across the street from the Espresso building. His mobile phone rang as he crossed the street. Retrieving it from his jacket pocket, he saw the international caller on the small screen.

Cole answered and a woman's voice came through the line.

"*Ciao*, Cole. It's Marie Bertelli."

Marie? This was a surprise. He hadn't talked to her in years. Not since he was still with Force Cosmetics, working out of their European headquarters in Milan. He briefly wondered what she wanted, but figured he'd find out soon enough.

Automatically switching to Italian, Cole greeted her and inquired about her grandparents, who had always been gracious to him when he lived in Italy.

Marie stopped him. "Oh, Cole." She tut-tutted. "I speak Italian all day long. Talk to me in English, so I can hear my native tongue tinged with your exquisite Southern drawl."

"What can I do for you?" Her casual tone and pleasantries didn't fool him. Marie Bertelli wasn't one for idle chitchat. Neither was he.

Her soft sigh sounded through the phone as he nodded at the security guard, who held the door open for him. "A few weeks ago, I read the most interesting article about you in the international edition of *America Today*," she said.

Cole frowned. He didn't bother mentioning the article wasn't actually about him. Stiletto had been the subject of the story, while the cheap shot at Espresso had only been a paragraph and, of course, that damned photo. Similar to the one Sage had used for Stiletto's billboard ad.

"As someone who also runs their family's business, I can appreciate how busy you are nowadays," Marie said.

Cole walked to the bank of elevators and frowned at the signs on the doors. Two of the three were out of order, *again*. With an old building, it was always something. He hoped they'd be repaired by the time the workday started, and that the working one remained operable.

He'd have to make some decisions concerning the Espresso building soon. Hopefully, one they could all live with, including Victor.

Marie said his name on the other end of the phone, and he returned his attention to the call.

"I wanted to personally invite you to the Bertelli runway show later this month during Milan's Fashion Week," she said. "A new designer is making his debut for our men's line, and I think some of his pieces would be a perfect addition to your wardrobe."

Cole pulled the phone away from his ear briefly and gave it the side eye. He stifled the grunt threatening to escape his mouth. "Now, Marie, you know as well as I do that men's fashion week was *last month*. Besides, I'm sure the status of my closet isn't the real reason you're calling," he paused to calculate the time difference, "at three in the afternoon on a workday."

"Well, now that you mention it…" She hedged.

Here it comes, Cole thought. Marie Bertelli had a talent for finding an angle and twisting it around to benefit her family's business. A company she probably loved more than her husband and children.

"As you know, Italy has had its share of economic troubles in recent years. That combined with the long recession in America has taken a toll on our entire industry and Bertelli's profits," she said. "I need important people in the audience at our next show to attract the cameras and generate interest. I was hoping you could help me out. Also, Lola is on the list of models in the show."

He started to tell her there was no way he could go to Italy but hesitated. Fashion Week wasn't until the week after Valentine's Day. On the plus side, he could check on the condo he still had in Milan and see his baby sister.

"I'll be there," he said finally.

"Great," she said. *"Arrivederci. A presto."*

Cole swiped a finger across the small screen and shoved the phone back into his pocket. He knew Marie liked to stir the pot and couldn't help speculating what kind of drama she was cooking up now. Regardless, a few days an ocean away would be good for him. He could forget all about kissing Sage Matthews, and then his only interest in her would be acquiring Stiletto.

If his next move hadn't already convinced her it was her best option.

The remainder of the morning was a bust.

Sage spent half of it trying to ignore smug, knowing looks from Amelia. The rest of the time, she sneaked peeks at the buttery-yellow blooms on her desk and relived her early-morning visit from Cole Sinclair.

Some general she made. One brush of his hand against her cheek and her common sense had made a hasty retreat. She'd transformed from a savvy businessperson to a woman whose only ambition was getting in his pants.

Sage sucked her teeth in disgust as she pulled her red Dodge Challenger into her driveway and shut off the muscle car's engine. By noon, she'd given up on getting anything done in her office and decided to spend the remainder of the day working from home.

She lifted the huge bouquet from the passenger's seat. It had been a distraction at the office, and she didn't want to waste another workday staring at it. Or thinking about how she'd practically thrown herself at Cole Sinclair.

"Wow! Somebody really likes you."

Sage looked next door to see Evie hanging a new handmade wreath on the front door to usher in the month of February. Shaped like a heart, it was fashioned from a fluttery mix of red, white and pink ribbons.

"I'll be over with the wreath I made for your door in a few minutes." Evie winked. "Then you can tell me why you're home so early and all about that beautiful bouquet you're holding."

Dang flowers. Sage rolled her eyes skyward. They were destined to be today's topic of conversation whether she liked it or not. "We can have lunch," she said, resigned to her fate. "I ordered a pizza on the way home. The delivery guy should be here soon."

"Sounds good to me. Only we'd better not let it slip to Kenny. Pizza and visiting you are two of his favorite things. I'll have the first-ever kindergarten dropout on my hands if he hears he missed out on both."

A half hour later, Sage sat at her kitchen table with her neighbor, remnants of the pepperoni pizza they'd demolished between them.

Evie picked up one of the chocolates she'd made for the chocolate buffet at Stiletto's upcoming event and passed one shaped like a high-heeled pump to Sage.

"Now that you can't stuff your mouth with pizza every time I ask a question about your early-morning visitor, how about an answer?" Evie bit into a white-chocolate compact.

"What? I already told you everything. He brought doughnuts. We kissed. He left. End of story," she said. "Oh, I picked up the bags I ordered for the blogger event, pink with black lettering. They're in the trunk of my car. Did you want to see them?"

"Later." Her friend looked pointedly at the flowers and back to her. Ignoring Sage's attempt to change the subject, she continued, "I still don't get how you went from teaching a man from one of the city's most prominent families a lesson to this morning's lip-lock."

Sage bit the spiked heel off the piece of chocolate. She'd left out the detail about how, if Amelia hadn't walked in when she had, they would have done more than kiss. *A lot more.* She popped the rest of the candy into her mouth.

"It's hard to explain. Everything got twisted around. I'd expected arrogance and outrage on his part. I'd prepared myself for confrontation. Instead he was real."

"Real?"

Sage reached for another chocolate, this one shaped like a lipstick. "Real charming, real honest and completely genuine," she said. "He even admitted he'd made a mistake in underestimating me."

"Whoa." Evie paused, holding the chocolate she'd been about to pop into her mouth in midair. She leaned forward in her chair. "Did I hear you right? A man who can admit to being wrong."

She nodded, but her neighbor looked skeptical.

"I've been married ten years and I can count on one finger the number of times Kenneth has admitted to a mistake," she said. "He won't even acknowledge making a wrong turn."

While her physical attraction to the man was undeniable, it was in that honest, genuine moment that she found Cole Sinclair most appealing, Sage thought. When he let his guard down and gave her a glimpse into the real man beneath the money and power.

"I guess this means you two are square now," Evie said. "No more worries about retribution."

Sage resisted the urge to reach for more candy. "I wouldn't say that. He made it clear that he wants Stiletto."

Her neighbor shrugged. "But it's not for sale. End of story."

Sage wished it were that simple. This morning, she'd done a more specific internet search of Cole's tenure with beauty behemoth Force Cosmetics. Not only had he acquired a half dozen smaller companies for them, he'd also helped turn them from moderately successful ventures into household names.

"He has a lot of friends in the industry. A few well-placed phone calls on his part could shut a lot of doors in my face, which would put me in the position of having to reconsider his offer." The thought made her anxious, and she automatically made a grab for more chocolate.

"But he obviously likes you." Evie looked at the flowers. "You also mentioned you two having a lot in common."

Actually, what she'd said was they were a lot alike.

"He wouldn't do that to you, would he?"

Sage shrugged. "He might."

She and Cole were indeed a lot alike, and in his shoes, Sage couldn't be sure of the lengths she'd go to in order to acquire something she really wanted.

"But I can't work scared. It's just not the way I operate," she said.

"So what are you going to do?"

"The same thing I've done since I started my company—work hard." Sage made the decision as she spoke. "Right now that means doing everything in my power to make sure Stiletto's upcoming Valentine's Day event is a huge success."

It also meant getting her reaction to Cole under control. That meant no more melting at the sound of his hypnotic baritone. No more falling into his powerful arms. And his addictive kisses were definitely off-limits.

Sage thought about her upcoming trip to Milan. Marie Bertelli's invitation had come up at the perfect time. It would give her the time and space she needed to get her head together and shut down the part of her she feared was falling for Cole Sinclair.

Chapter 8

*S*tupid Valentine's Day!

Snatching a bouquet of cellophane-wrapped roses from her customer service manager's arms, Sage shoved them back at the woman's boyfriend.

"Give her this on your time." She glanced pointedly at the Timex on her wrist. "Right now, she's on Stiletto's time."

Hustling the third uninvited boyfriend of the morning out the door, Sage rolled her eyes toward the pale pink tulle they'd attached to the ceiling earlier. It was like dealing with a bunch of love-struck teenagers.

The very day she needed her team to be at their best, their brains had simultaneously turned to mush. All anyone cared about was sending or receiving roses, chocolates and, of course, those idiotic glassy-eyed teddy bears.

Sage scanned the smallest ballroom of Nashville's premier downtown hotel. Shortly, it would host a hundred of the most influential women in the beauty blogosphere, all with huge makeup-junkie followings.

Everything had to be perfect.

She double-checked the checklist in her head. The champagne rested in silver ice buckets. The pink swag bags, brimming with Stiletto goodies, including a mini-collection exclusive for event attendees, were lined up on two massive tables. Evie was putting the finishing touches on the chocolate buffet.

Sage groaned at the sight of her advertising manager, Joe Archer, yapping on his cell phone, a big sloppy grin plastered on his face.

What had possessed her to schedule this event for the morning of Valentine's Day? she asked herself for what seemed like the millionth time. She blew out a heavy sigh.

Not bothering with preliminaries, Sage walked over to the advertising manager, snatched the phone from his hand and ended the call. "Hold the personal calls until *after* the event, lover boy," she said firmly.

"It wasn't a personal call," Joe said through clenched teeth. "You just hung up on Freddy Finch."

Sage lifted her hands in a questioning gesture. The name meant absolutely nothing to her.

"The guy who dressed up like the old lady for the newspaper and then we hired for our billboard ad." The frown on her employee's face deepened. "He was in the middle of thanking us, because the billboard has led to more people in the seats at his drag queen show."

Sage winced. "Oh."

"Yeah, 'oh.'" Joe held out his hand. "So may I please have my phone back?"

Sage placed the phone back in his palm, just as she felt a hand at her elbow. Amelia was at her side. The young woman's lips were pressed into a firm line.

"What's wrong?" Sage looked around.

"You."

Still holding on to her elbow, her assistant steered her toward the closed door at the entrance of the ballroom. Sage yanked her arm away.

"What's gotten into you, Amelia?"

"I'm doing an emergency intervention because you're driving everyone absolutely bonkers."

Sage bit her lip, but not wanting to let her assistant have it in front of the other employees, she shoved the double doors open and walked out of the ballroom. Amelia followed.

Her assistant raised her hands. "Before you blast me, I was just trying to get you out of there before you had a revolt on your hands."

Sage opened her mouth to tell the young woman she was being ridiculous, but Amelia then rested her hands on her arms.

"You pay me and the people in that ballroom generous salaries," her assistant continued. "Now stop micromanaging and let us do the jobs you hired us to do."

Sage's first impulse was to argue. Instead, she clamped her mouth shut and nodded once. The young woman was right. If the strained looks on her team's faces were any indication, Sage's close supervision wasn't being taken as the help she'd intended.

Besides, she'd worked for enough jerks before starting her own company. She didn't want to become one. It was time for her to back off.

Satisfied, Amelia's arms fell to her sides.

Sage exhaled and leaned against a wall outside the ballroom.

"You coming back in?" Amelia asked.

"I'm going to wait out here a while. Get my event jitters under control." Sage crossed her arms.

"I'll come back for you in a few minutes, so you can

give everything the once-over before we open the doors for our guests."

Sage nodded her agreement. After Amelia disappeared into the ballroom, she closed her eyes and pressed the back of her head against the wall.

"Relax, everything is going to turn out fine." She whispered the mantra aloud, and then took a few deep breaths.

When she opened them she could hear the faint din of hammers, drills and machinery coming from the direction of the hotel's Grand Ballroom. The racket had died down considerably since she and her team had come in to set up at dawn this morning. Sage had spoken to the hotel manager, who assured her the workers would be done before Stiletto's event started.

Pushing off the wall, Sage walked around the corner to the larger ballroom to investigate. Approximately triple the size of the smaller Petite Ballroom she'd rented for Stiletto, the hotel's premier ballroom took up over half this floor of the hotel. Orange construction cones sat at both entrances, and strips of yellow-and-black tape stretched across the closed doors.

As Sage looked at it, she couldn't help hoping Stiletto's next event would be bigger, better and held in the hotel's premiere ballroom.

First, she had to make sure today was a success.

Sage glanced at her watch, and then looked up to see a woman she recognized from her YouTube videos, standing at the escalators. She was talking to a hotel worker, who was pointing the way to Stiletto's venue.

It was almost showtime.

Sage exhaled. She'd make a quick pit stop to the ladies' room to check her makeup before returning to the Petite Ballroom. The construction racket in the Grand Ballroom seemed to have slowed to just the occasional hammer or drill, so she didn't have to worry about it drowning out Stiletto's party.

She lifted her hand to push open the bathroom door. The sound of her name coming from the other side of it stopped her.

"Y'all are out of line." It was Amelia. "Sage is a good boss."

Sage knew she should either make her presence known or walk away. Nothing good ever came from eavesdropping. However, hearing her assistant use her real name threw her.

"Well, she certainly isn't this morning. Did you see the way she treated my fiancé? He brought me a giant stuffed panda, and she wouldn't even let him in the ballroom to give it to me."

Sage heard her assistant's voice. "Come on, Shelia— this is a big day for Stiletto. How would you have gotten anything done with a four-foot stuffed bear in your arms?"

A third voice chimed in. It belonged to Stiletto's customer service manager. "Maybe if she had her own man, she wouldn't be hating so hard on those of us who do."

"How do you know she doesn't have someone special?" her assistant asked.

Sage's stomach did a free fall as she recalled the scene her assistant had walked in on when she'd practically glued her mouth to Cole's. She touched her fingertips to her lips at the memory.

While she trusted Amelia not to gossip, Sage silently prayed the young woman wouldn't inadvertently reveal what she'd seen trying to defend her.

"You're joking, right?" Shelia's laughter came through the door. "What man could handle the general's hard ass?"

"One who likes seeing her wear his balls as earrings,"

the customer service manager quipped before joining in the laughter.

If her eyes had been laser beams, Sage was sure they would have seared two perfectly round holes through the bathroom door by now. However, a small part of her couldn't help feeling stung by the kernel of truth in their words. Sage knew she could be both tough and intimidating, and if her track record in the romance department was any indication, most men couldn't handle it.

A brief flash of the kiss she had shared with Cole popped into her head. No doubt the man could handle anything she threw at him, including herself.

Sage heard Amelia clear her throat, propelling her to force the wayward images of Cole from her head.

"If Sage wasn't such a hard-ass and a perfectionist, Stiletto would have failed like most start-up businesses do in this tough economy," she said. "And Shelia, you'd still be using that master's degree in medieval literature to take breakfast orders at the Waffle House."

You tell her, Amelia, Sage thought. She decided against walking in on them. It would only make them uncomfortable when she needed them focused on today's event. Besides, she didn't hire the other women to be her best friends. They were there to do their jobs, and they both did them well.

After retouching her lipstick in another bathroom, Sage started to make her way back to the Petite Ballroom. She heard the clamor of women chatting excitedly as she rounded the corner and was delighted to see a throng of amateur makeup mavens waiting for the doors to open.

Sage spotting a waving arm and then saw Amelia pushing through the crowd. "I've been looking all over for you," she said. "We're ready for inspection, General. As soon as you give your seal of approval, we can open the doors."

Sage noted the irony as she walked through the ballroom, taking in even the smallest details. While the rest of her employees used her name to her face and sneakily called her General behind her back, Amelia did just the opposite. There was never any subterfuge with her assistant. She remained honest and loyal, and said what needed to be said, even when Sage didn't make it easy.

Elevating the young woman to basically her second in command at Stiletto had been one of her wisest decisions.

Sage picked up one of the attendee name tags to double-check that it included Twitter and Instagram handles. She placed it back on the table and contemplated another run through her checklist.

"Stop stressing," Amelia said. "You made sure everything is perfect. What could possibly go wrong?"

"You're right. Let's open the doors for our guests and enjoy some of our hard work.

Ten minutes later, Sage stood on the dais at the front of the room filled with women wild for makeup. Their energy fueled her excitement and boosted her confidence.

"Welcome to Stiletto's first annual blogger appreciation social." She spoke into the microphone.

Applause erupted in the ballroom, and she paused before continuing the short speech she'd prepared. Her assistant had been right.

This was Stiletto's moment, and absolutely nothing could go wrong.

Cole took mental inventory as he stood in the middle of the hotel's Grand Ballroom. It had taken two crews working around the clock to transform it. Now all that was left were a few finishing touches.

"Looks like we just might pull this off," he said.

Loretta grunted and looked down at her ever-present

tablet computer. "I don't see why I had to leave the office to come down here to supervise. Your aunt sent her best workers."

"People tend to work faster and better with you watching them," Cole said. "It's your gift."

Fortunately, his father's side of the family was in the construction business, and they were able to take on the last-minute job. Cole didn't remember his father, but he remained close to the Sinclairs. One short conference call with his aunt and cousins explaining the situation and what he needed, and they were eager to help.

"Speaking of gifts." Loretta lifted her arm and shook the shiny gold bracelet around her wrist. "Tia brought me this from Hawaii last year. With all the crap I put up with, I'm expecting an even better gift when you return from Milan."

Cole snorted. "When it comes to selecting a present for you, crap is exactly what I had in mind."

Loretta frowned, but his cousin approached them before she could respond.

"We're all done here, cuz." Riley Sinclair returned the screwdriver she'd been holding to the tool belt hanging from her waist. "Just wanted to make sure you were satisfied with everything before the boys and I took off."

Cole looked briefly at Loretta, who nodded her approval.

"We're good," he told his cousin.

He checked his watch. "Loretta, would you go upstairs to the hospitality suite to check on our guests? I don't want any snafus this morning"

"Yes, sir," she said dutifully.

Cole's eyes widened…then realization dawned. It appeared his cantankerous secretary might be on her best behavior until he returned from Milan, gift in hand.

"I appreciate y'all taking this on at the last minute," he said, returning his attention to his cousin.

Riley shrugged and pushed away a dreadlock that had escaped the ponytail holder. "No problem. We're family." She frowned. "Although I haven't seen much of my favorite cousin since you've been back in town."

Cole felt a twinge of guilt. Riley was indeed his favorite cousin, too. Her easy, one-of-the-guys demeanor had made her one of his best friends, as well.

Before he'd left Nashville, they used to meet after work at Jake's sports bar the first Friday of every month. They would eat dinner, have a beer and catch whatever game was on the television.

"Mom misses you. I do, too." Riley punched his arm.

Cole winced. He was no lightweight, but years of wielding power tools meant even a playful punch from his cousin packed a wallop.

"I didn't hurt you, did I?" Riley grinned. "Don't tell me you've gone soft from having your backside parked behind a desk all day?"

Cole rubbed his arm. "Nah, it just tickled, that's all."

His cousin's laughter filled his ears.

"I miss you all, too," he said. "I've just been up to my eyeballs trying to straighten out the mess at Espresso…" He stopped talking, hating the way his reasoning sounded like excuses.

"I'm under strict instructions from Mom not to leave here until I have your word you'll come to Sunday dinner," Riley said.

His aunt had issued him a standing invitation to the weekly dinner with the family, however he'd only managed to make it once in the months since he'd returned.

"I will, soon. Promise," Cole said.

"Nope." Riley shook her head. "That's not going to cut it. Mom said dinner will be served at six o'clock tomorrow evening, and she expects you to be at the table. No excuses."

Cole could tell by his cousin's tone that if he didn't show up to dinner tomorrow, his aunt would send her three daughters out like a posse to round him up.

"I'll be there." His family had made his request their top priority. It was time he reciprocated and made them a priority. Besides, seeing his cousin had reminded him just how much he truly had missed them.

Riley beamed up at him as if he'd given her a gift.

"We can talk about reinstating our standing monthly date for a beer at Jake's," he said. Then he remembered he'd been gone a long time. More than likely, Riley had a better way to spend a Friday night than watching sports with a cousin. "Unless your boyfriend has you on lock down."

Riley snorted. *"Boyfriend,"* she said incredulously. "Things haven't changed that much since you left. The men in this town still prefer their women to be like petite, delicate flower blossoms, which leaves a gal like me strictly in the buddy category."

"Their loss," Cole said.

His cousin shrugged, but he could see a flicker of sadness in her eyes.

"Now, if there isn't anything else you need, my men and I are going to take off," she said. "I promised them a late breakfast at the Pancake Pantry if we got this job done on time."

Cole reached for his wallet. "Since it's my job, I'll cover it."

"Don't worry, I've already added it to your bill." Riley stuck two fingers in her mouth and blew out an earsplitting whistle that commanded the attention of every workman in the room. "Let's get out of here and get some pancakes, fellas." She turned to Cole. "We'll be back to take everything apart this evening."

Loretta returned to the temporarily renovated ballroom

as Riley's crew gathered up their equipment and began filing out of it.

"Oh, good luck." Riley stopped at the door and looked over her shoulder. "Hopefully, when that Matthews woman discovers what you've been up to, she won't take *you* apart."

Cole glanced at Loretta, waiting for her to take advantage of the opportunity to deliver one of her smart-aleck zingers based on his cousin's warning. She didn't. However, he didn't miss that the older woman's lips were clamped together so hard the color had drained from them.

"After needling me all week, no wisecracks about there being hell to pay when Sage finds out?"

"Nope." Loretta shrugged. "When she comes storming through those doors, as I expect she will at some point this morning, I intend to grab some popcorn and enjoy the show."

Images of Sage bursting into the ballroom popped into Cole's head. Big Afro, a defiant pout on her pretty painted mouth and walking on impossibly high heels.

He'd told himself repeatedly that this was business, not personal, but the thought of seeing her again excited him—in a very personal way.

A trio of Espresso employees surrounded him, breaking into his reverie with a series of updates. Preston was telling him about the computer station, and another employee was rattling on about extra cases of blush and mascara.

Their voices faded into the background as his thoughts once again centered on the impending explosion when Sage found out.

A smile tugged at the corners of his mouth. Oh, she'd bring it all right, and he could hardly wait.

Chapter 9

Sage's apprehension diminished as she mingled with the room full of internet beauty mavens. It had been silly to think Cole was lurking in the darkness plotting payback for the billboard episode.

He'd come at her eventually, she thought. Fortunately, it didn't appear he'd do it today.

Sage grabbed a bottle of water and twisted off the cap. Talking nonstop to Stiletto's guests had left her throat parched. She looked around the small ballroom at the clusters of young women gabbing excitedly. They were gushing over the items in the exclusive resort makeup collection, included in their swag bags, many of which would probably be up for sale on eBay by tomorrow.

More importantly, photos were being snapped and fingers were typing away on mobile phones. Their fervor was spilling over into social media time lines under the hashtags #StilettoValentine and #IHeartStiletto, and the

news was being spread like gossip by their fanatical followings.

Sage took a long swig from the bottle. So far, her company's first event appeared to be a success. She thought
briefly of Cole and his proclamation that he'd do a better
job running Stiletto.

Too bad he wasn't here now. He'd see exactly what she
could accomplish.

Maybe you just want to see him again?

She tried to dismiss the notion, but images of the kiss
they'd shared in her office flitted though her head. Images
so vivid she could almost taste his sugar-tinged mouth,
feel his large hands on her ass and the sizeable bulge in
his pants pressed against her belly.

Sage took another gulp of the cold water to cool off.
Maybe the employees she'd annoyed earlier were right
and she did need to find herself a man, preferably one that
wasn't after her company.

Or didn't make her lose control like Cole Sinclair.

A young woman wearing smoky eye shadow and a nude
lip gloss walked up to her. "Ms. Matthews, I'm…"

"You're Liptastic," Sage said, grateful for the distraction. "I recognize you from your blog. I also follow you
on Instagram."

The women's eyes widened. "Really?"

Sage nodded. "I adored the photo you posted of your
holiday favorites that had a tube of Santa, I've Been
Naughty positioned next to a red, high-heeled marabou
feather slipper, mug of cocoa and a peppermint stick."

Liptastic nudged Sage's side with her elbow. "I won't
even mention what my fiancé did with that peppermint
stick after he saw me in that lipstick."

Sage's eyes widened. "Oh, my."

"The name of that lip shade explains it better than I ever

could." Liptastic giggled and then winked. "Let's just say I had a smile on my face for days."

Sage laughed along with her, wishing there was a way to press this moment between the pages of a scrapbook. Then she could revisit it after a long, frustrating workday and remind herself why she'd chosen this business.

As her mother used to say when Sage was a little girl, "A little bit of makeup can change a woman's life."

Moving through the crowd Sage chatted up a half dozen more beauty gurus including @MakeupandMojitos, who had amassed a fanatical following from simply uploading a daily photo of her lip print on a cocktail glass, @BudgetGlam, known for creating million-dollar looks with dollar-store cosmetics and @PrettyEverything, whose YouTube channel had over a million subscribers.

She made her way over to the chocolate buffet, where Evie was restocking the candy. She grabbed a piece of milk chocolate shaped like a lipstick tube.

"I hope you have some stashed away for us at home," Sage said.

"Nope." Evie smiled. "It looks like your guests love chocolate as much as they do cosmetics. They're going to clean me out."

Sage looked around the room. A feeling of unease crept over her, and she turned to her neighbor.

"Is it just me, or does the crowd seem to have thinned out?" Sage looked at her watch. "We only started thirty minutes ago, and the event doesn't end for another hour and a half."

Evie glanced up from the candy compacts she was arranging on a silver tray and surveyed their surroundings. "Looks the same to me."

"I dunno…" Sage looked toward the doors. Three women were walking out of them.

Her neighbor followed her gaze. "You're being paranoid," she said. "Maybe they're just visiting the ladies' room."

Sage nodded. "You're probably right."

Still, she couldn't seem to shake the feeling something wasn't quite right.

"Stop worrying about nothing," Evie said. "This event is a smashing success. You're a success. This is your moment, hon. Try to enjoy it."

Sage nodded. She was just being silly. Then she glanced at the door. Two more of her guests were leaving. Maybe they had Valentine's Day dates, she speculated. However, they'd scheduled the event for the morning to avoid potential conflicts with lunch and dinner dates.

She glanced back at the door and saw another woman walk out of it. The chatter had also begun to shift. Hushed whispers intermingled with the bubbly conversations.

No, Sage thought. She wasn't being paranoid or imagining it. The crowd had definitely thinned out since her welcome speech.

Both her eyes and her gut told her something was amiss—neither had ever let her down.

Making her way through the diminishing crowd, Sage was at the door when she felt a tap on her shoulder. She turned to see a petite pixie of a woman she recognized instantly from YouTube.

"I was beginning to think I wasn't going to get to meet you today," she said. "I'm…"

"The Wicked Glam Mother," Sage finished.

"Oh, so you've heard of me." The woman's brown eyes twinkled with mischief.

Who hadn't heard of her? Sage thought. Known for her hilarious and brutally honest reviews of both prestige and drugstore makeup brands, the Wicked Glam Mother was an internet sensation. She'd uploaded over three hundred videos, many of which had gone viral.

"Well, what did you think of the colors in our exclusive resort collection?" Sage asked.

So far the woman's reviews of Stiletto products had been overwhelmingly positive, but makeup lovers could be fickle, and a brand was only as good as the last collection.

The woman flashed an impish grin. "Wouldn't you like to know," she said.

"Yes, I would." Sage said. "But I don't suppose you're going to tell me."

The popular vlogger wagged a finger as she shook her head. "You'll find out later this afternoon, along with the rest of the world, when I upload my video."

Sage didn't bother trying to cajole it out of her, like the woman had obviously hoped she would. It wasn't her style. Besides, she recognized the deep berry shade on the Wicked Glam Mother's mouth. It was a lipstick from the resort collection the Stiletto team had dubbed A Good Lay.

As their conversation continued, Sage surreptitiously glanced at the door. Four of their guests had left, followed by another two.

What in the world was going on?

Finally, she was able to break free from the YouTube guru to investigate. However, Amelia and Stiletto's director of social media stopped her before she got to the door.

"I think we have a problem," her assistant said.

No kidding. "What's wrong?" Sage asked.

"People are walking out, and we're not even halfway through the event. Meanwhile, there are two new hashtags overtaking ours on social media time lines." Amelia inclined her head toward the social media director. "Show Sage what you just showed me."

Exhaling, Sage took the tablet and scanned the time line.

The hashtags #EspressoTakeover and #EspressoCosmetics jumped out at her as she read.

Free Valentine's Day makeovers with celebrity makeup artists. #EspressoTakeover #EspressoCosmetics

Get your Valentine's Day pretty on with the artists who create makeup looks for Rihanna and Beyoncé—for FREE! #EspressoTakeover #EspressoCosmetics

Cole, Sage thought. But he wouldn't…

She continued to glare at the tablet's screen as more messages appeared on the time line. An image of Cole in her office came back to her. Not the one of them kissing that had dominated her days and nights, but the expression accompanying his reply to her question about them being even after the billboard ad.

Not by a long shot. His words echoed in her head.

Cole Sinclair definitely would, Sage thought. Anger began a slow simmer in her gut, eclipsing the dread she'd felt just moments ago.

It kicked up a notch when she spotted a cell phone snapshot Liptastic had posted to social media showing off the results of her makeover with one of the celebrity makeup artists using Espresso cosmetics. She'd just talked to the woman, Sage thought. So much for brand loyalty.

"I'm not sure where Espresso has set up, but it has to be near the hotel for them to steal our guests," Amelia said.

Realization dawned and Sage closed her eyes briefly. "I have a hunch where they may be set up." A strong hunch, she thought.

Her assistant at her side, Sage walked out of Stiletto's event. They followed two beauty bloggers down a corridor and around the corner in the direction of the larger ballroom.

The thumping beat of music vibrated the carpeted floor beneath their feet as the Grand Ballroom came into view. Sage immediately noticed the doors were wide-open, and a banner with the words *Espresso Cosmetics Pop-Up Shop* hung above them. Her eyes zeroed in on the sign that had replaced the orange construction cones she'd seen earlier. It boasted free Valentine's Day makeovers by a list of ten celebrity makeup artists flown in from New York and Los Angeles.

"Damn." Sage muttered the word through clenched teeth.

She should have checked this room the moment she'd seen the workmen, instead of assuming the hotel was doing renovations. How could she have been so stupid? She should have known something was up—and who was at the bottom of it.

Sage stalked through the doors. She glanced around the huge room, which had been transformed into a temporary studio. Rows of tables were covered with lighted mirrors and stocked high with makeup, *Espresso makeup*.

Lines had formed by each table as defecting beauty gurus waited to have their faces transformed by the same artists who worked on the world's most beautiful faces.

Sage continued to scan the room until she spotted Cole standing in the midst of it all. He appeared to be having a conversation, but stopped and turned in her direction as if he'd felt her gaze boring into his back.

Their gazes connected, and even at a distance, Sage could see his brow raise and the slight incline of his head. He had been waiting on her.

"Mutha…" Sage swore, but the pounding beat of the music and accompanying rapper cautioning someone not

to mess with his money drowned out the rest of the word, and the string of curses that followed it.

"General!" Amelia, who was within earshot, admonished her.

Sage took a step forward, already anticipating giving Cole an earful. Her assistant caught her by the arm.

"You're not going to confront him, are you?" she asked.

"You bet I am." Sage practically salivated as she mentally calculated the steps between her and that infuriating man."

"Are you sure that's a good idea?"

"Do you not see what's happening? He sabotaged our event."

"Well, you did provoke him," the young woman pointed out. "If we're being completely honest, you started it."

Sage rolled her eyes so hard they nearly bounced off the ceiling. "I—I did no such thing." Fury made her stammer the words.

Amelia shook her head. "I'd assumed when I walked in on the two of you a few weeks ago going at it like the characters in my favorite romance novel, *Corporate Temptation*, that you and Mr. Sinclair had worked out your differences," she said. "What did you do to mess it up?"

"Me?" Sage ground out the question.

"Let's be real here—you can be abrupt." Her assistant narrowed her eyes. "And something happened to make him go from bringing you flowers and breakfast to purposely upstaging our event."

"Just whose side are you on?" Sage fumed.

Amelia sighed. "All I'm trying to do is get you to calm down before you go storming over to Mr. Sinclair and make things worse."

Calm down? Sage bit her lip to keep from unleashing on

her a tirade of words meant only for the ears of Espresso Cosmetics' CEO.

You can't think when you're angry.

Cole's words came back, and Sage inhaled a deep breath. As she exhaled an idea for extracting a little payback of her own began to form. Sage turned to her assistant. "Repeat what you just said."

"I was trying to get you to calm down."

"No, before that," Sage said.

"Oh, I was reminding you that I'd said the billboard, using a man in drag as a backhanded insult at Espresso, was a bad idea from the very beginning. *But noooo.*"

"Amelia, you're a genius." Sage threw her arms around the young woman in an uncharacteristic hug.

"Uh-oh." Her assistant stiffened. "You're making me nervous here."

Releasing her, Sage grinned in response.

Amelia's eyes widened before her lips firmed into a disapproving frown. "You're sprouting horns out of your head again, and that never bodes well."

"Never mind my head. I need to talk to Joe Archer." Sage cast a look in Cole's direction. He stared back at her, a half smile on his smug, handsome face. She noted again that he appeared to be waiting for her to pounce.

Turning back to her assistant, Sage suppressed a grin of her own. "Let's get out of here."

As they walked out the door, she heard Amelia sigh and grumble something about all hell breaking loose.

Chapter 10

Disappointment mingled with disbelief, as Cole watched Sage leave the ballroom. The polar opposite of the elation he'd experienced the moment he'd realized she'd arrived in all of her red-minidress and stiletto-booted glory.

He'd told himself all morning it didn't matter, yet he had found himself taking furtive glances at the door. Watching. Waiting.

Damn.

Cole continued to stare at the door. He'd seen the outraged expression on Sage's heart-shaped face and felt the heat of her temper from across the room.

"So she didn't take the bait, eh?" Loretta sided up to him.

Unfortunately, no, he thought, shaking off unwarranted dismay. He'd bargained on Sage's reaction. Expected her to march straight to him and treat him to a closer look of those spectacular legs showcased by what had become his absolute favorite dress.

"Doesn't matter," Cole said aloud. "This isn't about Sage Matthews."

"Isn't it?" His secretary's dark eyes looked right through him.

Cole averted his gaze and shoved his hands in his pants pockets. "This is about showing the owner of Stiletto Cosmetics the power Espresso still wields, despite our current image problems," he said. "We can take her company to heights she can't reach on her own."

"If you say so." Loretta glanced down at her tablet computer.

"I do," Cole reiterated. "And contrary to popular belief, I'm *your* boss."

"Well, if you want my advice…"

"I don't." Cole cut off the older woman, knowing it wouldn't stop her from having her say.

"All I'm saying is I'd grow eyes in the back of my head if I were you. If the look on her face when she left here is any indication, that young lady isn't done with you."

His mind rewound to kissing Sage in her office, and the warmth of her taut body penetrating his clothes as she melted into to him. He recalled the brief glimpse of vulnerability he'd detected in the depths of her soft brown eyes, when she momentarily dropped her guard and her need to be in control.

Cole hoped Loretta was right, because he certainly wasn't done with Sage, *not yet*.

He switched focus to the here and now. Sage was gone. He'd seen the last of her for today.

Cole tapped the top of Loretta's tablet. "So what have you done to earn your salary today besides give me unsolicited advice?"

His secretary grunted and inclined her head toward the makeup artists, who were still busy creating new looks for the beauty gurus they'd lured from Stiletto. "Spent a good chunk of it catering to the demands of these prima donnas you imported from New York and LA."

"Come on, they can't be that bad."

Loretta frowned. "This one can't work without a green smoothie made with coconut milk. That one needs an aromatherapy candle to clear the air of bad vibes," she said. "I swear they almost had me reaching for a cigarette."

"Delegate their requests to someone else." Cole didn't want the older woman to relapse and slip back into smoking. "Those cigarettes have left your voice gravelly enough. Every time you open your mouth, I look around for Darth Vader."

"Humph. No need for that now. I got fed up when the last one told me to find him a bendy straw to sip his coffee through," Loretta said. "I told him to do the job we contracted him to do, or else."

He wrinkled his face in confusion. "Bendy straw?"

"So the coffee won't stain his teeth," Loretta explained.

Cole lingered in the ballroom for another half hour. The room remained abuzz with excited bloggers, every makeup artist was busy and the lines for free makeovers had grown. By the looks of it, he'd succeeded in turning Stiletto's Valentine's Day event into an Espresso Cosmetics party.

There was nothing here his employees couldn't handle. Besides, without the underlying anticipation of seeing Sage again today, there was no reason for him to stick around.

Cole considered swinging by Burger Tower for an early lunch and pulled out his phone to place a to-go order. The red battery light flashed up at him, and he shoved it in back into his pocket. He'd call from his car, once he connected it to the charger.

A shriek of laughter reverberated throughout the room.

Cole, along with everyone else, turned toward it, and then his mouth gaped open.

The guy in drag, from the newspaper article and Stiletto's billboard, paraded through the ballroom in full old-crone regalia. He wore a huge sandwich board over an outdated floral print dress that read Ditch Granny's Makeup!

Sage.

She wouldn't. Anger seeped into Cole's bloodstream as the man began to work the room as though he was the guest of honor. Oh, but she definitely had.

"Look, it's the Espresso Granny!" A blogger yelled out over the music.

More outbursts of laughter joined the chorus.

The Espresso Granny?

"Oh, hell no." Cole's hands clenched into fists at his sides.

Crossing the room in three long strides, he effortlessly lifted "granny" by the collar until *her* white orthopedic shoes dangled above the floor.

"H-hey! What's going?" The goateed man cowered inside the oversize dress.

"Get. Out. Now." Cole growled.

"Stop picking on Granny." A blogger called out.

"Yeah, give the old girl a break. It's Valentine's Day," a second voice shouted, causing yet another round of raucous laughter to erupt throughout the ballroom.

Cole released the interloper's collar and watched him stagger to his feet.

The man held up his hands in surrender, a straw purse dangling from the crook of his hairy arm. "Look, I don't want any trouble." His lips, coated in chalky pink lipstick, trembled as spoke. "I'm just doing my job."

"What job?"

"The one I hired him to do." A familiar voice said from behind them.

Cole whirled around and came face-to-face with the woman he'd spent the better part of the morning pining for like a complete idiot.

"Cole Sinclair, meet Freddy Finch." A humorless chuckle fell from Sage's lips. "Better known to you as Espresso Granny."

Struggling to keep a lid on the fury in danger of consuming his entire body, Cole spoke slowly. "Do you realize the damage you've just done?"

"Kind of like you sabotaging my event with this little shindig?" Sage matched his hard glare.

"It's hardly the same thing," Cole said. "In five minutes, you've managed to cement in people's minds the very image I've been battling. Months of hard work down the drain."

"Miss me with the sob story." She swiped at an imaginary tear. "You were pretty good at dishing out the payback, how does it feel to be on the receiving end?"

Freddy cleared his throat. "Um, excuse me. Have you decided what you want me—"

"What are you still doing here?" Cole barked.

Freddy flinched and turned to leave, but Sage caught him by the arm.

"He has every right to stay," she countered. "Like the sign outside the door says, this event is open to the public."

Freddy glanced from Cole to Sage. A fine sheen of perspiration covered his forehead, sending the thick coating of makeup sliding down his face.

Cole shoved his hands back into his pockets to keep from doing something that would make the onlookers accuse him of elder abuse. He kept his voice low. "If I have to tell you again, my foot is going to do the talking when I put it dead in your…"

Freddy hightailed it out the door before he could finish his statement, and Cole pivoted back to Sage. "You've gone too far this time."

"Unlike Freddy, I don't scare easily."

Cole opened his mouth to argue, but he spied a television news reporter and cameraman entering the ballroom. He inclined his head toward them, and Sage followed his gaze.

"I'm not finished with you, but the last thing either of us wants to do is plaster fake smiles on our faces and answer questions right now."

She grunted. "Two things we can agree on."

"Let's continue this elsewhere."

They ducked out of the ballroom's side door but found the space outside it teeming with beauty gurus spilling over from both their events. Their conversation was bound to get ugly, and Cole was sure Sage didn't want to have it out in the open any more than he did. Besides, between all the chatter and loud music, he could barely hear himself think.

She walked a few feet ahead of him as they looked for somewhere they wouldn't be overheard. Cole caught the sweet sway of her ass in that minidress and the needle heels of her thigh-high boots as she walked.

Remembering the stunt this woman had just pulled, he tried to look away. However, his traitorous eyes stubbornly refused and continued to enjoy the view.

Get a grip, man, he silently admonished when the sight of her made him want to slide his hands along her toned thighs until they gripped her hips as he drove into her over and over again.

Cole blew out a breath and reached deep for willpower

he hadn't known he possessed. He forced himself to think of the faux crone who, thanks to the woman in front of him, would be associated with Espresso in the minds of some of the internet's most influential beauty gurus.

It did the trick and put an abrupt end to his unwanted hard-on. With the blood flowing back to the head on his shoulders, he could think clearly.

"In here." Cole yanked opened the door to one of the hotel's utility rooms around the corner from the ballroom.

Sage stopped, turned on her heels and followed him inside, closing the door behind them. She switched on the light, and he glanced around what turned out to be a linen closet. It was a tight space, but it would do for the serious conversation they needed to have—*now*. The tablecloths, sheets and towels stacked on the surrounding shelves would also muffle the inevitable yelling.

She crossed her arms as she lifted her chin to glare up at him. There was a mulish set to her jaw. Cole tried to process how Sage Matthews made red-hot fury look, well, *hot*.

Again, he forced himself to think of the newly dubbed Espresso Granny crashing his event and making a damn spectacle.

"Just what kind of game do you think you're playing?" he asked.

"Me?" Sage's outraged eyes continued to blaze into his.

"Yes, you! This was business, pure and simple. You and that Freddy character made it personal."

"Don't you dare try to put the blame on me. You took it there when you insinuated I didn't have the know-how to grow the company I started at my kitchen table." She raised her voice to match his as she pointed a finger at her chest. "*My* company, Mr. Sinclair, and you'd best believe it's going to stay that way."

"I wouldn't bet on…"

A loud thump sounded against the door. Cole stopped midsentence, and they both turned toward it.

"Are you sure the general's in there?" A muffled voice asked on the other side of the door.

"I saw her go in a few minutes ago," A woman replied.

"Why would she be in a utility closet?"

"I don't know. Probably looking for a broom to ride on." A couple of guffaws followed their so-called joke.

Cole looked at Sage, and they both turned back to the door.

"Make sure you jam it in there tight."

"What the...?" Sage lunged for the door and twisted the knob.

Cole heard smothered giggles over the music blasting from the Grand Ballroom as the covert conversation continued.

"That ought to hold her awhile," a third voice chimed in. "Now the rest of us can enjoy the remainder of Valentine's Day, General-free."

Sage raised her fist and pounded against the door. "If you know what's good for you, you'll open this door right now," she shouted, and then tried the doorknob again.

Nothing.

Cole watched her hit the door harder and then kick it. "Did you hear me?" She yelled. "Let me out!"

She glared over her shoulder at him. "I could use some help here," she said. "In case it's escaped your notice, we've been locked in here."

Cole folded his arms across his chest and leaned against the shelves behind him. "What exactly do you want me to do?"

"Break the door down." She kicked it and winced. "Or use a credit card to pop the lock like the burglars do on television."

"In case it's escaped *your* notice, that door is made of steel, and unfortunately, my undergrad major was in chemistry not breaking and entering."

Sage blinked. "Chemistry?"

"You, too?"

She nodded once. It shouldn't have surprised either of them. Every time they were together, another similarity came to light. He held her gaze a moment, before she diverted her eyes and returned her attention to the door.

"Help!" She pounded on it again. "Help! Open the door! Let us out of here!"

"You're wasting your time yelling," Cole said. "Sounds like someone cranked up the volume on the music. Nobody can hear. Call the front desk on your mobile. They'll send someone up to open the door."

Sage held up her hands up. "I left it in my purse—we'll have to use yours."

"Battery died. I'd planned to charge it in my car but got sidetracked by that dumb stunt you pulled back in the ballroom."

"Dumb stunt?" She harrumphed, folded her arms and leaned her back against the door. "You had no business in that ballroom or this hotel in the first place."

Cole tilted his head to one side. "Speaking of stunts, do you have any idea who locked us in here? I didn't recognize the voices," he said. "I also don't remember seeing any military personnel around here, and I certainly would have noticed someone with the rank of general."

A flush of pink tinged her light brown face. She looked down at the floor as she mumbled an answer to the question.

"Speak up, I couldn't make out what you said over the racket of the music."

"It's me, all right?" She exhaled. "Some of my employees call me General behind my back, and they're the culprits."

Cole snorted, shaking his head. "Which puts us right back to this entire mess of a morning being all your fault. I hope you're satisfied." He shrugged off his jacket and tossed it on top of a stack of clean towels. "Who knows when we'll get the hell out of here now, *General*?"

He watched her mouth open, close and open again like a beached fish gasping for air. Red overtook the flush of pink staining her cheeks. The fire of their tempers sucked the oxygen from the tiny space, making it feel even smaller.

"How dare you?" Her teeth were clenched as she ground out the words. "Today was supposed to be all about Stiletto. You're the one who made a mess of it."

Cole glowered across the small space at her. "So what did you expect me to do after that billboard? Roll over and play dead?" He was sure anger had left him just as red in the face. "You told me to bring it. All I did was honor your request."

A noise that sounded like a growl emitted from her, before she advanced on him, all high heels and big hair. Again, Cole couldn't help notice, even pissed off, that Sage Matthews was the sexiest woman he'd ever seen.

Sage jabbed a finger at his chest. "Y-you have got to be the most arrogant, the most infuriating, the most…arghh!"

Cole's instincts took control. Wrapping an arm around her waist, he hauled her against him. The lightning-quick move caught her off guard, and he felt a whoosh of breath leave her body.

Huge brown eyes stared up at him. They softened as he examined their depths. God, she was beautiful, he thought. Her caramel-slicked lips beckoned, and while there was a part of him still annoyed with her, the rest of him wanted her, badly.

"We're probably trapped in here for at least another hour or two." He brushed his knuckles down the side of her cheek with his free hand. "Not Stiletto. Not Espresso. Me and you. The last thing I want to do is fight with you. *What do you want?*"

She swallowed hard. Cole could see the rise and fall of her breasts beneath her dress, feel her nipples bead against his chest as her breath came out in soft pants. Sage's body told him what she wanted. He just needed her to say it.

"If you won't tell me what you want, maybe the answer lies in that pretty lipstick you're wearing." Still holding her close, Cole leaned in and kissed her softly on the lips. She moaned, and his cock hardened instantly. "What's it called?"

Her eyes sparkled, and she bit her bottom lip before answering. "Lick Me."

Chapter 11

"My pleasure."

Cole's deep voice rumbled through her, and Sage melted. The velvety timbre slipped past her defenses, and she dropped her guard.

"I'm going to lick you until you're hoarse from screaming my name."

His promise made her drop her panties.

They hit the floor, and Sage quickly stepped out of them, kicking the scrap of black satin aside.

There were a myriad of reasons why this was a bad idea, but at this moment, with this man, she didn't give a damn about any of them. Cole had awakened a long-dormant desire only he could satisfy.

"Again, I have two words for you, Mr. Sinclair." Sage raised a brow. *"Bring it."*

With a swipe of his arm, Cole cleared a top shelf of sheets, sending them tumbling to the floor. Sage rested her hands on his biceps as he placed his hands on either side of her waist. He lifted her above his head as if she were weightless and gently deposited on the empty shelf's ledge.

His chin level with her knees, he lifted his gaze. "Oh, I intend to bring it, all right," he said, echoing their first conversation. "I just hope you can handle it."

Sage's bare ass shivered against the cool steel shelf, but the rest of her body was on fire, her core already wet with anticipation. "*Ooh.* That's mighty big talk. Let's hope your tongue can back it up.

Cole stuck a finger inside the scooped-neck collar of her dress. He pulled her forward until her face hovered inches from his, and then closed the distance between their mouths. He kissed her long and deep. His tongue owned her mouth as it teased and tantalized hers in a carnal preview of the coming attraction.

Sage moaned and squeezed her legs together, on the brink of climaxing from a single kiss. There was nothing lacking in this man's tongue game. *Nothing at all.*

Threading his fingers through her hair, Cole fisted a handful of the kinky curls. His grip tightened, and he tugged her head back to end the kiss. The primitive action sent a shiver from her scalp down to the tips of toes, which curled inside her thigh-high boots.

"Not yet," he said, reading her body's signals as if they were his favorite bedtime story.

Minutes ago, she'd banged on the door desperate to escape. Now Sage didn't care if it ever opened. The music coming from the ballroom further secluded them. Its pulsing beat drowned out the outside word.

She watched Cole take a single step backward. He grasped her calf in one hand as his other hand and his gaze traveled down the length of her boot-encased leg to her ankle.

"Damn." He closed his eyes briefly as if he were struggling for control and then he stared up her. The lust she saw in his dark eyes matched her own. "Later, I want to see you wearing nothing but these boots and me on top of you, but for now…"

He draped her leg over his shoulder until it dangled down his broad back. The motion raised the hem of her short dress to the tops of her thighs, and Cole pressed a kiss to the inside of the one resting on his shoulder.

Sage's teeth sank into her bottom lip when he placed his free hand on her other knee and gently pushed it aside, splaying her open for his perusal. The appreciative expression on Cole's handsome face made the discomfort of her last Brazilian wax worth it.

She leaned back, and braced her hands behind her as he buried his face between her thighs.

Cole licked her once, drawing out the movement as if he had nothing but time.

Then he did it again.

Oh, my God. Sage's eyes slammed shut, and she pressed her lips together to keep the scream reverberating in her head silent. She felt him pull back and opened her eyes to find him staring up at her.

"Unbelievable," he said. "You taste even better than you look."

He put his tongue back to work alternating long, languid laps with quick flicks, overwhelming her clit with a deluge of sensations. Bringing her to the brink, then holding back as she squirmed and begged for more of the exquisite torture.

"Don't stop, Cole. God, please don't stop." Her frantic pleas filled the room as he continued, licking and sucking until Sage thought she'd lose her freaking mind.

The first spasm hit, and she nearly bucked off the shelf.

Cole's strong hands slipped beneath her. He gripped her ass and pulled her even closer.

Sage arched her body toward him, calling his name as she rode his tongue to a shuddering orgasm that left her sweating and shaking like a junkie.

And like an addict, she was already craving another fix.

Cole lifted her off the shelf, and Sage slid down the length of his body. He kissed her hard and deep, his talented mouth still tasting of her.

"Wow." It was the only word Sage could manage. Even then it sounded like a hoarse croak.

Cole held her close, and Sage didn't miss the smug satisfaction in his smile or the rock-hard cock in his pants. She slid her hand between them and palmed his erection.

She raised a brow as she gently squeezed. "Impressive."

Cole hissed out a breath as his cock pulsed against her hand. "If you're impressed now, just wait until I get inside you."

Sage took a step back and tugged at his belt. "As you probably already know, Mr. Sinclair, I expect you to…"

"Bring it." He smiled down at her as they both uttered, what had unintentionally become their favorite catchphrase, simultaneously.

"I just hope I can handle it." Sage fanned herself with one hand and unbuckled his belt the other. She was reaching for his zipper when they heard a noise at the door.

Before they could register what was going on, it opened. A woman wearing a hotel uniform stood in the doorway. Concern creased her features.

For the first time, Sage noticed the music had stopped. Not only had this man made her lose control, she'd lost track of time and place.

"Someone said they thought they heard a woman screaming in here. Then there was a chair wedged against the doorknob." The hotel worker turned to Sage. "Are you okay, miss?"

Sage averted her eyes, trying to remember just how much screaming she'd done. "Uh…"

"She's good," Cole said, still holding her close. "Damn good," he whispered against her ear.

The hotel employee glanced from her to Cole, then pointedly at Sage's discarded underwear on the floor. "Sorry to disturb you."

The woman shot Sage another look, this one filled with pure envy. "Lucky heiffa," she muttered, as she walked away.

Yet, with the door open and them free to return to the real world, Sage didn't feel fortunate. Deep down, she wasn't ready for their interlude to end. Not yet.

Exhaling, she prepared herself to make and hear the awkward excuses that came in the aftermath of an unexpected sexual encounter. She knew, in this case, it was probably for the best. In this room, they were lovers. Once they stepped out of it, they were back to being adversaries.

"This has been…but…" she began. Still in Cole's arms, her gaze drifted toward the open door.

He placed his forefinger to her lips, before she could finish, and then used the same finger to lift her chin. "I'll understand if you feel differently, but I have to confess that I'm not ready for the real world to intrude on us just yet," he said.

Sage looked into his dark eyes as words continued to tumble out of his mouth. Again, she found herself drawn to Cole's honesty, sincerity and a vulnerability she suspected he rarely revealed.

He also had the courage to say aloud exactly how she felt, but couldn't bring herself to express. Sage didn't miss the irony of it. The same woman who faced her fears and took risks regularly in business shrank away from both in her personal life, especially in matters of the heart.

"There'll be plenty of time to focus on our respective businesses," Cole said. "Spend the afternoon with me."

There wasn't anything she wanted to do more. However, her sensible side, the part of her that wasn't light-headed from his kisses and still pulsing from the aftershocks of his making love to her with his tongue, made her hesitate.

"I'm not sure if it's a good…"

Still holding her firmly against him, Cole shook his head once. "Don't think."

"But…"

"You turned down the offer I made you the first day we met. Now I want to make you an altogether different one," he said. "Will you hear me out?"

Again, her sensible side attempted to intervene. *Get your panties off the floor, put them on and get out of here*, it implored. Sage knew she should heed the warning, but instead found herself nodding her head.

She'd simply listen to what he had to say, she reasoned. Then she'd make her excuses and leave. Just chalk up what had happened between them to a temporary lapse of judgment.

"Let's finish what we started upstairs in a big room with a huge bed."

Sage pressed her lips together to prevent an involuntary moan from escaping. She wasn't sure whether it was the persuasiveness of his deep voice or the concrete feel of him pressed against her, but she nodded her agreement.

Cole's smile lit up his entire face, mirroring how she felt inside.

"Great," he said. "Let's find the front desk and check in, so I can get busy making you my Valentine."

* * *

Cole plucked a chocolate-dipped strawberry from the silver tray on the bedside table. He held it up, just out of reach from the naked woman lying across the bed.

"You're not playing fair," Sage said. She was on her stomach, propped up by her elbows, her chin resting on her hands.

The position offered an enticing view of her cleavage and an even better one of the ass Cole couldn't keep his eyes or his hands off. "I thought you knew by now I don't play fair."

He took a big bite out of the juicy berry and slowly chewed. Sage's lips, puffy from an afternoon of his kisses, drew into a pout.

"Don't even try it with that face," he said. "You know it gets me hard."

"Everything I've done since we checked in to this suite gets you hard."

Leaning his back against the headboard, Cole polished off the strawberry. He couldn't argue. Everything about this woman turned him on. They'd made love against the door within seconds of walking through it. Mental snapshots of those stiletto boots wrapped around his waist as he drove into her again and again clicked through his mind.

Next they'd steamed up the glass-enclosed shower before finally tumbling into the king-size bed for round three.

"But I'm not complaining." Sage's faux scowl transformed into a satisfied grin.

"Stop flattering me and answer the question."

"What did you ask me, again?"

Cole selected another strawberry from the tray, this one covered in milk chocolate and candied pecans.

"Tell me." The sheet covering the lower half of his nude body shifted as he leaned forward. He brought the fruit within an inch of Sage's lips. "Was Lick Me actually the name of that lipstick?"

"What makes you doubt it?" She tried to take a bite out of the strawberry, but she didn't answer his question and he pulled it away.

"I familiarized myself with Stiletto's catalog before I made the offer to buy it," he said. "I don't remember a lipstick with that name."

"Maybe it's a new shade that we haven't officially added to the catalog yet."

"Is that the case?" Cole polished off the fruit.

Sage rose to all fours and crawled toward him. The tips of her breasts brushed his bare chest as she reached across him and grabbed a berry from the tray.

"Seeing as how you're the competition, that information is confidential." She took a bite of the juicy berry and chewed slowly. She rested her chin on his chest and pinned him with those big brown eyes.

In them, Cole saw the sweet vulnerable side he suspected she didn't often reveal. The woman could be as frustrating and challenging as she was smart and beautiful, but at this moment he found her incredibly endearing.

It was a moment he wanted to savor as he enjoyed their sexy banter.

"My question involves a yes or no, Sage. Answering it wouldn't involve spilling any of Stiletto's secrets," he said. "Besides, this afternoon is about me and you, remember?" Cole touched a finger to his chest and then to the tip of her nose. "Not Espresso. Not Stiletto."

As if on cue, a text chime sounded from Sage's purse in the other room of the suite. Her assistant had instructed the front desk to lock it in the hotel safe when she'd been unable to locate her boss. The desk clerk had returned it to Sage when they'd checked in.

The phone began to ring. Sage raised her chin from his chest and looked toward the other room.

"I meant to shut it off after I texted Amelia from the front desk," she said. "Then we came up here, and you've kept me distracted ever since."

Once they'd entered the suite, somewhere between stripping off each other's clothes and making love against the door, he and Sage had come to an unspoken agreement to leave the world outside. And there would be absolutely no discussions involving their respective businesses.

"It has to be work." She seemed torn as her eyes darted from him to the doorway separating the bedroom from the front room. "I'm just going to take a quick look and read the message. I'll be right back."

Cole instantly missed the soft warmth of her body as she left the bed and padded barefoot into the other room to retrieve her phone. The seductive sway of her round ass made him want to reach out and grab it, throw her over his shoulder and haul her back into bed.

He tempered the urge to go caveman. Where in the hell had it come from anyway? This was simply an afternoon of great sex with a woman he was wildly attracted to. *Nothing more.*

Cole told himself he was satisfied and had worked her out of his system, but the burgeoning erection on the verge of tenting the sheet was downright greedy when it came to Sage Matthews.

Sage returned to the bedroom, phone in hand. Her face wore a rare indecisive expression. "It was someone from my team wondering if…"

She began to pace as she explained the reason for the text.

Exhaling, Cole steeled himself for the disappointment of her leaving to put out some fire at Stiletto. He of all people should understand. In the past, he'd also broken it off with a woman or two who hadn't been willing to take a backseat to his job.

Yet, it niggled at him.

Not because he was hoping for another round of sex, although more of it had been on his afternoon agenda. Nor was it that he was having fun getting to know her beyond their attraction and characteristics they seemed to have in common, although, he now craved her sharp mind and quick wit as much as her body.

Then it occurred to Cole that their similarities were exactly what bothered him. During his first stint working for his mother at Espresso and then later as an executive at Force, he'd been exactly like her.

It had taken walking away from both to make him realize he couldn't do it all. Nor could he control everything. He had to trust others to help him.

Cole reached for Sage's hand. He looked pointedly at the phone in her other palm and then at her. "Just. Let. Go."

"Of my phone?" Sage's pretty face scrunched up in confusion.

Finding her naked curves a distraction, Cole rose from the bed and retrieved plush white robes from the bedroom closet. He donned the larger one, before wrapping her in the other.

"Let's talk for a moment," he said.

Cole could practically see the wheels of her brain spinning. Although they hadn't known each other long, a part of him knew her as well as he knew himself. Mentally, she was already leaping ahead to whatever work problem she presumed only she could resolve.

"But I just told you, I have to…"

"This will only take a few minutes," he said. "And who knows, I might just give you back your underwear."

The corner of her mouth quirked upward into a hint of a smile, and she nodded her agreement. Taking her by the hand, Cole led her to the sofa in the front room.

"I know it's none of my concern, but I don't think either of us can deny anymore that we're two of a kind," he said.

She looked down at their joined hands. "I tried to chalk it up to coincidence, but there have been too many now," she said. "We can both be cocky, pushy, dominating, insensitive and even a little ruthless when necessary."

"And those are probably our good points." Cole chuckled. His heart did a strange flip-flop when she squeezed his hand and laughed along.

He pressed on, although chances were she wouldn't be pleased to hear his unsolicited advice. "With that said, we're also confident, responsible, honest, hardworking and competitive. There's also no denying we're good at what we do."

Sage's brown eyes narrowed. "Those all sound like virtues to me, so why do I sense there's an impending *but*?"

"Because in excess virtues turn into liabilities."

"I'm not following you."

"Are you enjoying yourself this afternoon?" He asked.

She spared a glance at his crotch. "Immensely."

Forcing himself to remain focused on their conversation, Cole looked past her heated gaze to the phone in her free hand. "And exactly when was the last time you enjoyed yourself?" he asked, and then quickly amended. "I don't mean sex. Tell me the last time you took a couple of hours for yourself. Saw a movie? Had a massage? Read the latest bestseller? Or turned into a couch potato in front of the television?"

Cole had already known the answers to his questions, however her silence and the blank expression confirmed it.

"You're here now. Let's continue to enjoy the day and each other."

"But I have to…"

Cole saw her grip tighten around her phone. "No," he said, "*you* don't."

"I have a business to run."

He saw the spark of annoyance in her eyes and expounded before her temper ignited. "I realize that. I also realize this isn't my place, and I should stay in my lane. However, part of me feels like I know you as well as I know myself," he said. "You've got to learn you can't control everything."

Sage extricated her hand from his and huffed out a sigh. "Just what I need, another person insinuating I'm a control freak."

Cole raised a brow. "Well, aren't you, *General*?"

Sage abruptly stood. "How dare you?" she ground out, the temper he'd hoped to avoid now full-blown. "The only thing you're right about is the fact you should stay in your lane. Just who do you think you are?"

"The admiral."

"Huh?"

"The admiral," Cole repeated. "It's the name the employees who worked under me at Force Cosmetics called me behind my back."

He took advantage of Sage's surprise to continue. "Coming from my family's company, I felt like I had a lot to prove, and I went about it by being a workaholic, micromanaging control freak."

She sat back on the sofa, and once again, Cole took her hand in his.

"I earned that moniker and probably a lot worse. Along with the disgruntlement of the people who worked for me," he said. "I was never locked in a closet, but only because they never got the opportunity."

They shared a private smile, and Cole could feel the tension melt between them and her anger ebb away. Sage stared down at the phone in her hand.

"Stiletto's more than just a business to me, it's…" She started, paused, and then started again. "Even if I wanted to, I'm not sure I can stop being the general."

"Were all of Stiletto's hiring decisions made by you?" He asked.

Sage nodded.

"Are you confident in your judgment?"

Again, she nodded.

"Then trust your decision and the people you hired to do their jobs. Take the first step." Cole pulled his hand from hers and placed it over the one holding the phone. *"Delegate."*

Her watched her gnaw at her bottom lip as she stared at his hand covering the phone.

"I'm not sure if you can understand this, but I'm not talking about surrendering control of your business. I'm talking about freeing yourself of the minutiae so you can truly take control of it." Cole patted her hand and rose from the sofa. "Now I'm going back to the bedroom to enjoy those delicious strawberries while I persuade Burger Tower to deliver. I hope you'll decide to stay and join me."

Cole hoped like hell she would. Deep down he didn't expect her to. With every step back to the suite's bedroom and the sex-rumpled bed they'd shared, he prepared to watch her get dressed and leave.

Ten minutes later, Cole was sitting on the bed scrolling through Burger Town's menu on his phone's web browser. He looked up to find Sage standing in the doorway. She was holding her own phone to her ear.

"Yes, you heard right. I want you to do what I hired you to do and handle it," she said into the phone.

Their eyes connected across the room. When she smiled, Cole's chest tightened with an emotion he couldn't identify.

"If there's anything else, contact Amelia," Sage said, the phone still against her ear. "I'm unavailable for the rest of the day."

She shut off the phone and tossed it over her shoulder. He laughed as she made a running dive for the bed. Sage landed on top of him, and Cole finally pinpointed the emotion blooming inside of him. *Happiness.*

"By the way, the answer to your question is no," she said.

"Huh?" He was so relieved she'd decided to stay that he had no idea what she was talking about.

"Earlier, you asked if my lipstick shade was really called Lick Me." Her smile turned seductive as she slowly shook her head. "The answer is *no.*"

In an instant, Cole was harder than he'd ever been in his life. "Mind telling me the actual name?"

"Not at all." Sage rose to her knees on the bed and shed the hotel robe. She leaned in and whispered the name of the lipstick shade in his ear.

He faced her. "Really?"

"Really," she confirmed.

Cole flung his phone across the room in the vicinity of hers and pulled her into his arms. "Well, let's see if we're both flexible enough to make that happen."

Chapter 12

The next day, Sage stood in her bedroom staring at her reflection in the full-length mirror.

It was a good thing Amelia wasn't around. She would have noticed the flush in Sage's cheeks, the extra sparkle in her eyes and the fact she was practically glowing—and blown it totally out of proportion.

Her assistant would have immediately jumped to conclusions and likened her to a heroine in one of those sappy romance novels.

"It was just good sex," Sage told her reflection as she as she switched her hoop earrings for black pearl studs. "Nothing more."

Her explanation disregarded the fact that the afternoon she'd spent with Cole had extended into the evening and then overnight. It overlooked that she was expecting him to pick her up any minute now for dinner.

She shoved her feet into a pair of gray patent-leather

combat boots, grateful to have a respite from her usual heels. She wore a gray minidress with matching tights. Cole had said he was taking her somewhere casual and there was no need to dress up.

Cole.

Sage smiled at the thought of seeing him again. Catching sight of her face in the mirror, she wiped the grin off her face.

They were simply having dinner together. Tomorrow morning, they'd return to the real world, sit behind desks at their respective businesses and resume being competitors. However, for the remainder of the weekend they were friends and *lovers*.

The doorbell rang. Sage sucked in a big gulp of air and exhaled to quell her excitement at seeing him again.

Good Lord, she'd just seen the man an hour ago. If she didn't keep herself in check, she would indeed be as bad as Amelia.

Sage opened the door and the grin returned to her face. Cole stood in the doorway. He wore wool pants and a sweater topped by a black leather jacket. She looked from his gray slacks and sweater to her own gray attire and shuddered.

"We're so much alike it can be downright spooky," she said.

He wrapped an arm around her, pulled her against him and kissed her. "I'm a lot more interested in our differences." His hand slid down to her behind. "Namely this gorgeous ass and those endless legs of yours."

Sage kissed him again, and then inclined her head toward the inside of her house. "Come in, before the neighbors see me throwing myself at you."

Sage hadn't had many visitors, just the family next door or Amelia, who occasionally stopped by for something related to Stiletto. As she led Cole inside, it occurred to her how modest the small cottage she took so much pride in must look to someone of his wealth and background.

"Nice house." His tone was genuine as he looked around her living room with its repurposed furniture and kitschy decor. "When things settle down at Espresso, I'm thinking of buying in this part of town."

"Really?" Sage couldn't keep the note of surprise out of her voice. Although it was rapidly changing, the neighborhood was still considered rough by most.

"Sure. Not only is it a great investment in an up-and-coming area, it's walkable, has a sense of community, as well as great restaurants," he said. "I'm always coming here to eat anyway."

Sage nodded. Those reasons along with her budget were the same reasons she'd settled here.

"Right now, I live in a town house I bought a few years after college, but I never took time to really make it a home. Not like this."

Again, Sage found herself taken aback that he appeared to see her house the same way she did. She was also surprised at where he lived.

"By the look on your face, I'm guessing you thought I resided in some mega mansion south of the city," Cole said.

Sage nodded. It had been exactly what she'd thought. It was also one of the two areas people with substantial wealth put down roots.

"My town house has an entire floor I'm rarely in." He shrugged. "It seemed excessive for me to buy a huge house to live in alone."

Remembering her manners, she offered him a seat and a drink.

Cole glanced at his watch. "We'd better get going if we want to be on time for dinner."

Assuming he'd made reservations at a nearby restaurant, Sage shrugged on her red coat and grabbed her purse. She hadn't eaten since Cole had ordered breakfast in bed from hotel room service that morning, and it was now nearly six.

Locking her front door, she saw his car parked behind hers in the driveway and did a double take at the black Dodge Challenger, which, except for the color, was identical to her red one. Sage looked up at Cole. "Again, spooky."

"Or perhaps it's kismet," he said softly.

Sage brushed off his words and the little piece of her heart they touched with a casual shrug. As Cole drove, she wasn't sure if it was the familiarity of the car or the similarities they shared, but she felt close to the man. They'd only seen each other a few times, but in some ways it was as if she'd known him her entire life.

Now who's the one being ridiculous? the commonsense part of her that often mocked Amelia questioned.

Caught up in her thoughts, Sage hadn't paid attention to where they were going until the car slowed along the cul-de-sac of a residential street.

"I thought we were going to a restaurant," she said.

Cole turned into the driveway of a two-story, Craftsman-style home. "I said I wanted to have dinner with you, but if I miss another invite to my aunt's for Sunday dinner she'll kill me," he said. "I didn't want to disappoint her. Also, I want to make the most of this time with you before we both return to work in the morning."

He didn't say it, but they both knew their obligations to their businesses overshadowed any feelings they thought they had for each other.

"You should have told me dinner was with your family," she said.

"I was afraid you'd say no."

Cole was right, of course—she would have. His family was powerful and wealthy, and Sage didn't like putting herself in the position of feeling like the poor, orphaned girl.

He reached over the console and grasped her hand. "I apologize for not telling you," he said. "If it'll make you feel better, my cousins are all girls so I'll be outnumbered."

Sage softened to the idea. "Well…"

"You'll like them and my aunt Janet," Cole said.

Sage nodded her agreement. In college, she'd dated guys from rich backgrounds, one seriously. None of them were eager to bring a woman who lacked both money and connections around their relatives. Yet Cole, a man who could buy the lot of them ten times over, was practically pleading with her to meet his family.

"Still, I wish I'd known. I would have brought flowers or a bottle of wine," she said.

"All you need to bring is yourself." Cole squeezed her hand. "That's plenty." He leaned over the car's console and kissed her.

Sage sighed into his mouth, swept away by the slow dance of his tongue mingling with hers. The man's panty-melting kisses would be the first thing she missed when they resumed their lives tomorrow.

A knock on the driver's side window startled them, and they broke apart, ending the kiss.

"Put it on pause. The rest of us would like to eat sometime this evening."

Sage looked from Cole's wide smile through the window to a woman standing by the car. She had honey-hued skin and shoulder-length sandy-brown dreadlocks. Her hands were fisted on her hips, but her warm smile matched the one on Cole's face.

He rounded the car and held the door open for her.

"Sage Matthews meet my rude cousin, Riley Sinclair," he said. His fondness of his cousin permeated his voice.

The woman raised a brow. "*The* Sage Matthews?"

"The very one," Cole said.

"Nice to meet you," Riley said. "Although after yesterday, I expected all I'd see of you was your foot in my cousin's…"

"Riley!" Cole scolded.

Sage stifled a laugh at the interplay between the two.

"My crew and I were responsible for transforming the hotel's Grand Ballroom into Espresso's makeover central yesterday," Riley said. "Hope you won't hold that against me."

"I won't," Sage confirmed, taking an instant liking to Riley Sinclair. "However, I will take your card just in case I need you to help me construct a little payback."

Cole's cousin slapped her on the back. Sage stumbled and nearly saw stars, the woman's friendly gesture packing quite a wallop.

"We'd better get inside. Mom's about ready to put dinner on the table," Riley said.

Cole's hand rested lightly on her back as Sage followed his cousin up the porch stairs and into the house. The place had the same warm, inviting vibe as Riley. Its open floor plan provided unobstructed views of both the living room and the dining room table, which was already set for dinner.

A woman who appeared to be in her midsixties fussed over the table. Her entire face lit up the moment she spotted Cole. She put down the napkin she was folding, rushed over and enveloped him in a huge hug.

"Glad to see you could make it to dinner." The older woman beamed up at him. "I thought I was going to have to send Riley after you."

"I wouldn't miss having dinner with my favorite aunt."

His aunt swatted his arm, and then turned to Sage. "And I'm even more delighted to see you've brought your girlfriend," she said. "Maybe she'll keep you here in Nashville, and you won't take off again, gallivanting all over the world."

"Oh, I'm not his girlfriend," Sage said automatically.

The older woman dismissed her claim with a wave of her hand. "Of course you are, hon. Why else would you have spent the past fifteen minutes in the driveway, steaming up my nephew's car windows?" she asked sweetly. Then she added a mischievous wink that made her look like her daughter.

"Aunt Janet, I'd like you to meet my *friend*, Sage Matthews," he said. "She also runs a cosmetics company here in town."

"Riley's already filled me in on the particulars," the older woman said.

"Nice to meet you, Mrs. Sinclair." Sage extended her hand.

The woman bypassed Sage's outstretched hand. Instead, she wrapped her in a hug as warm as the one she'd bestowed on her nephew. Cole had been right. She liked both his aunt and his cousin, and Sage suspected she'd feel the same about his other cousins.

"So where are Nina and Hope?" Cole asked, looking around.

"Nina's on a job in Memphis, and Hope's home sick," Janet called over her shoulder on the way to the kitchen.

"It's just a cold," Riley said. "I took some chicken soup over to her place earlier."

Soon the four of them were seated at the dining room table. The conversation was minimal as they dug into a Sunday dinner consisting of a juicy rotisserie chicken, salad, macaroni and cheese, mashed potatoes, and warm cornbread muffins smothered in sweet honey butter.

Good food overwhelmed the rules of etiquette and Sage was the first to ask for seconds, soon joined by both Cole and Riley.

"I don't mean to be rude, but unless my next door neighbor takes pity on me I don't sit down to a home-cooked meal often," Sage said, heaping another scoop of mashed potatoes onto her plate.

Janet and her daughter exchanged glances.

"Actually, you aren't sitting down to one this evening, either," Cole's aunt said. "Like most of my meals, this one was picked up ready-made at the grocery store."

"Sage isn't the only one who thought this was home-made. I thought you'd spent all day in the kitchen," Cole said, reaching for more chicken.

Janet Sinclair took a sip from her water glass and placed it back on the table. "Like you two, I have a business to oversee. Sinclair Construction doesn't run itself." The older woman inclined her head toward the kitchen. "So that stove in there is for looking—not for cooking."

Both Cole and Sage smiled, while Riley snorted. "That's no great culinary loss," she said. "Even before Dad died and you took over Sinclair Construction, anything you *cooked* came frozen on a plastic tray and accompanied by the beep of the microwave."

Janet shot her daughter a faux dirty look, which collapsed into laughter. "True," she admitted.

The older woman turned her attention to Sage. "We already know how Cole ended up in the cosmetics game," she said. "How about you? What prompted you to get in the beauty business?"

"My mother," Sage answered.

In her peripheral vision she could see Cole put down his fork and turn to her.

"Mom worked at a department-store makeup counter," she continued. "As a single parent, she simply couldn't afford to get me the dolls, games and toys kids all want. So she'd bring home samples of gorgeous lipsticks, blushes and eye shadow for me to play with and somehow managed to turn makeup into my absolute favorite game."

Janet nodded approvingly. "Your mother must be very proud of your accomplishments."

"I'd like think she is," Sage said. "She died when I was eleven, and I grew up in foster care."

"Oh, dear," the older woman said. "I'm sorry."

Sage nodded. She was facing Janet and Riley; however, her next words were meant for Cole more so than his family. "I do what I do to honor her memory, which makes Stiletto more than just a business to me. It's more than just my dream. It was my mother's dream for me."

She turned to Cole. More than merely their gazes connected. It made her feel closer to him in that moment than they had been in bed.

"So what made you decide to set up a cosmetics company in Nashville of all places instead of New York?" Riley asked.

The connection broken, Sage blinked and focused on Cole's cousin's question. "The internet makes it possible for me to anchor my business wherever I want, so I decided to stay in my hometown. I like it here, plus I can plow more money into the business because I don't have the overhead of maintaining a pricey Manhattan address."

Cole chimed in. "My mother often said it gave her the first pick of Tennessee State's and Fisk's new graduates."

"That, too," Sage said. "My advertising manager, Joe

Archer, is a Fisk graduate, and I'm a Tennessee State alumnus."

"So is Mom," Riley said.

Janet nodded. "I earned my teaching degree at TSU, but that was way before your time."

"Sage's undergrad degree is in chemistry, and she also has an MBA," Cole said. Sage could hear the note of pride in his voice.

It made her feel good.

Janet and her daughter exchanged glances.

"Oh, I picked up dessert at the grocery store, too," Cole's aunt said. "Anyone up for apple pie?"

"Of course, you know it's my absolute favorite, Aunt Janet."

He touched Sage's hand under the table, a question in his eyes.

She nodded and smiled at him. "It's my absolute favorite dessert, too."

Sage wasn't sure how long they sat staring at each other, goofy grins pasted on their faces. Janet cleared her throat, and Sage abruptly snatched her hand back. The cutlery clanked against the plates as her hand hit the underside of the table.

"Sage, honey, I was wondering if you would help me clear the table and give me a hand in the kitchen with coffee and dessert," Janet said. "Riley, I believe you had something to talk over with Cole."

"Um, sure." Sage rose from the table and began gathering plates and silverware.

Cole's cousin launched into a conversation about blueprints and Espresso's building as Sage followed Janet into the kitchen. She figured the older woman wanted to get the competition out of earshot so the two cousins could talk business.

Once they were in the kitchen, Sage began the task of scraping the plates over the trash can so she could load them into the dishwasher. Janet stopped her. "Leave it—my housekeeper will take care of it when he arrives in the morning."

Cole's aunt gestured toward a padded bar stool in front of the huge granite-topped kitchen island. The apple pie was already atop the island along with four dessert plates "Have a seat." Janet retrieved a knife. "You can slice the pie while I make coffee."

It was now apparent to Sage that the older woman's underlying purpose hadn't been to get her out of the dining room so Cole and Riley could discuss the Espresso building. Sage slid off the bar stool, washed her hands at the double sink and dried them with a paper towel.

Returning to the kitchen island, she picked up the knife and cut into the pie. "So exactly what do you want to talk to me about, ma'am?"

"You're direct," Cole's aunt said.

"I try to be," Sage said.

"Good for you. I see why my nephew's so taken with you."

Sage sighed. The older woman was jumping to all the wrong conclusions, but after she'd seen her and Cole steaming up the car windows, it wouldn't be easy to dissuade her.

Janet filled a carafe with water and poured it into the coffeemaker. "Cole's always so serious. Ever since he was a boy," she said. "I don't think I've ever seen him smile as much as I have tonight, and you're the reason."

Sage kept her mouth shut. It wasn't as if she could explain that being sexed up for nearly twenty-four hours was the real reason behind her nephew's smile.

"I'm not one for interfering in my girls' or Cole's lives,

but the last time he was hurt, he took a job out of the country. Both he and his sisters were tight-lipped about it. He didn't even confide in Riley, but I do know he was heartbroken." Cole's aunt added a scoopful of coffee to the coffeemaker and switched it on. She pulled mugs from a cherrywood cabinet. "I love my nephew, and I like having him back in town."

"Look, Mrs. Sinclair, I'm not exactly sure where you're going with this, but you've got it all wrong. Cole and I are not a couple."

The older woman faced Sage, a skeptical expression on her face. "As a mother of three who's been in business for nearly twenty years, frankly, that doesn't pass my internal bullshit detector."

Cole's aunt took advantage of Sage's surprise at her language and continued.

"I'm not blind. I saw the way he looks at you. I also see the way you look at him. I don't care what you two are calling your relationship, all I'm asking is you keep that smile on my nephew's face. I like having Cole in town, and I like seeing him happy."

Sage knew it was futile trying to convince the woman there was no relationship. Whatever she and Cole had this weekend would end the moment they each arrived at work tomorrow morning.

"You okay?"

Seated in Cole's car, they asked the question simultaneously.

Their moods had shifted over dessert. While they both continued to nod, speak or laugh at the appropriate times, Cole had noticed Sage seemed distracted. So was he.

The short discussion with his cousin about the Espresso building had put a lot on his mind. He and his sisters had pretty much decided to sell it. Although the three of them could easily overrule Victor's vote in the matter, they'd been trying to give him time to adjust to the idea.

Now Cole wasn't so sure selling it was the answer. Riley's alternative plan had intrigued him.

Waving out the window at his aunt and cousin, Cole backed the Challenger out of his aunt's driveway. He spared a glance at the passenger seat as he pressed the button to close the window.

"I hope Aunt Janet didn't grill you too badly while you two were in the kitchen."

"Not at all," Sage said. "However, I did spend most of the time trying to convince her we aren't together. I don't think she believes me."

Because maybe we should be together, Cole thought. And this was the perfect opening to say so.

"She missed me while I was away and has been a touch overprotective since my return," he said aloud. Inwardly, he kicked himself for blowing an opportunity to tell her he wished this weekend could be more than just a one-time occurrence.

Cole wanted it to be a beginning.

"She says you left Nashville over a broken heart," Sage said.

Cole's grip on the steering wheel tightened as he steered the car through the quiet residential streets leading to the expressway. Sage was unwittingly inching toward a matter he didn't discuss, with anyone.

"I guess you could say that," he said finally. That much was true. He had been heartbroken. "However, it had nothing to do with a romantic relationship."

His body remained tense as he braced himself for her to press the issue. In his experience, women rarely took things at face value. They had to delve into and explore every emotion, instead of just letting it be.

"Anyway, I think both your aunt and your cousin are great."

Instead of relentless questions, Sage had changed the subject. It was all Cole could do not to pull the car to the side of the road and kiss her. Tension ebbed away from his shoulders as he merged onto the expressway.

"I envy you for having a family that cares so much about you," she continued.

Cole heard the hint of wistfulness in her tone. Without stopping to think about it, he reached across the console separating the car's bucket seats for her hand.

"I do consider myself fortunate to have them." He'd gleaned from interviews he'd read about Sage that she had spent the majority of her childhood in foster care. "However, it doesn't keep me from sometimes feeling like I'm on the outside looking in."

He could feel her gaze on him as he drove.

"But, why?" she asked.

"Riley and my cousins lost their father, but still have Aunt Janet. My sisters and I lost our mother, but they still have my stepfather, Victor," Cole said. He released her hand, so he could signal before changing lanes. "Being the one with no parents makes me feel like the odd orphan out at times. If that makes any sense."

Cole had never admitted it aloud before. At thirty-four years old, he probably shouldn't give it a thought. However, occasionally it made him feel incredibly alone. His mother was gone, and all he'd had to know his father ever existed were old photos and the worn Timex he'd worn on his wrist.

Cole felt Sage's hand on his thigh. Its warmth penetrated the fabric of his wool pants, the gesture touching him deeper than words.

It also made him sad the weekend was rapidly coming to an end.

All too soon, Cole turned into Sage's driveway and parked behind her red Challenger. He didn't shut off the car engine and was relieved when she didn't immediately jump out of the car.

Her sigh filled the car's silent cabin. "As badly as I want to invite you in for the night, I don't think it's a good idea," she said. "It'll only make it that much harder to put an end to this in the morning."

It was hard now, he thought. Cole couldn't explain it to her. Hell, he couldn't explain it to himself. All he knew was he wanted to see more of her—both in and out of the bedroom.

"I have something I want you to think over," Cole said.

"Another offer?" She stared out the windshield.

He chuckled lightly, feeling more nervous than he had the day he asked the homecoming queen to the prom. "Something like that," he said. "I have a trip scheduled and will be leaving later this week. However, while I'm gone, I'd like you to think about us going out on a date when I return."

"B-but…" she began.

However, Cole wasn't done. Reaching across the console, he used his finger to turn her head until she faced him. "Believe me, I know as well as you do all the reasons we shouldn't," he said. "Still, I want to take you on a real date. Hold your hand in a movie. Buy you a milkshake and the biggest burger in town. Or cook dinner for you at my place and afterward make love to you in my bed."

The dim light of the car's controls softly illuminated

her face. A face he hoped to see more of when he returned from Milan.

"All I need you to do tonight is promise you'll think about it," he said finally.

Sage nodded. "I promise."

A promise Cole hoped would lead to the opportunity for him to win her heart.

Chapter 13

After their sabotaged Valentine's Day event, Sage hadn't expected the positive updates coming from her team at Monday morning's staff meeting.

She should have been overjoyed. Instead, she stifled a yawn.

"So while Espresso's horning in on us might have ended our event sooner than we would have liked, social media–wise, it was a success."

While Stiletto's social media manager droned on in the background, Sage reached for one of the two thermal carafes on the conference room table. She poured herself a second mug of black coffee and took a generous gulp.

It wouldn't replace the sleep she'd missed the night before, tossing, turning and longing for Cole. However, Sage hoped a caffeine jolt would give her enough energy to get through the remainder of the morning along with a dose of much-needed focus.

"Our invitees had no idea our party was being upstaged by Espresso. From their social media posts, it appears everyone believed it was a joint event," the social media head said.

Sage forced herself to concentrate as the woman continued to fill everyone in on her findings, including complimentary videos and blog posts by the notorious Wicked Glam Mother and other attendees. Normally, Sage would have been riveted.

However, the only thing on her mind was the promise she'd made to Cole last night. The irony wasn't lost on her. He'd only asked her to think about going on a date with him. Now the man was *all* she could think about—his hands, his lips, his tongue all over her body.

"So what do you think?" Joe Archer asked.

The question roused Sage from her reverie to the expectant faces awaiting her answer.

"Sorry, I was thinking about an idea for our Christmas collection," Sage fibbed. "Could you repeat what you said?"

She stifled another yawn, drawing a curious look from Amelia. Sage avoided her assistant's assessing gaze. Taking another gulp from her coffee mug, she directed her attention to Stiletto's head of advertising.

"I think it's a fantastic opportunity for Stiletto, but I know you like to manage these things," he said. The subtle emphasis he put on the word *manage* made it sound like the word she suspected he wanted to use was *micromanage*.

Again, Cole popped into her head. Not the escalating battle of one-upmanship between their companies or the similarities they continued to discover about one another, but the man who respected her enough as a businesswoman to offer his advice.

I'm not talking about surrendering control of your busi-

ness. I'm talking about freeing yourself from the minutiae so you can truly take control of it.

Cole's melodic baritone slipped into her head as if he'd just taken a seat beside her. Sage fisted her hands against the resistance rising up in her. When her mother died, so much had been out of her control that she couldn't help trying to dominate every detail of the company she'd created.

It had been easier to loosen the reins a bit, back at the hotel on Saturday, with the delicious options of Burger Tower and a naked Cole as a reward.

Trust the people you hired to do their jobs. Delegate.

Deep down, she knew Cole was right. Sage had also observed that his aunt Janet farmed out routine tasks like cooking and cleaning. She'd said it gave her the time and energy to be more effective at work.

Sage closed her eyes briefly. *You can do this*, she thought. *Do it so you can make Stiletto even better.* She cleared her throat.

"I trust your judgment, Joe," she said. "If it has your seal of approval, then it has mine."

The conference room fell silent except for the ticking of the clock on the wall. Anyone walking in would think they'd stepped into the middle of a Saturday-morning cartoon where every character's eyes bulged out of their sockets in exaggerated amazement.

"P-pardon?" Joe stammered. "I don't think I heard you correctly."

"Yes, you did," Sage assured him.

She gave herself a mental pat on the back. She wasn't sure if it was because she was proud of herself or if it was the caffeine finally kicking in, but she suddenly felt more energetic than she had all morning.

"Okay, next up, Shelia." Sage looked pointedly at the

woman seated next to Joe. "What do you have to say for yourself after Saturday?"

The young woman's eyes darted uncomfortably around the conference table as she picked up her notes. Both her hands and her voice trembled as she read from them.

Sage drummed her fingertips lightly against the table and watched her squirm. While she hadn't been able to pinpoint the voices of the employees who'd locked her in the linen closet, she had a pretty good idea who had been involved.

"Um…I'm writing personalized thank-you notes to include with the mini–lipstick samplers we're sending out this week." A fine sheen of perspiration covered the woman's forehead as she continued to stammer through her update.

Sage had been sweating herself when she'd first arrived at the office. The general vibe of the office and lack of commentary from Amelia had assured her that while everyone had heard about her being locked in the hotel's linen closet—they hadn't an inkling of what had actually gone down in the closet.

Her captors hadn't seen Cole walk in before her, and fortunately both events had ended by the time the hotel employee freed them.

Sage suppressed a shiver at the memory of Cole in the closet as well as later in the hotel suite.

She returned her attention to Shelia, who had finally wrapped up her update. "Is that it?" Sage asked, narrowing her gaze. "Are you sure there isn't something else you'd like to tell me?"

"Uh…no. That was all I had." Shelia's voice was still shaky. It possessed none of the rancor it had back in the hotel ladies' room.

Sage hoped she was having flashbacks of scooping up hot buttered grits at the Waffle House.

"Okay, then." Sage addressed the entire staff as their weekly meeting drew to a close. "As you know, I leave for Milan midweek. Do good work while I'm away, and Amelia can contact me if needed."

Back in her office, Sage sank into the chair behind her desk. Her assistant followed her into the office and pushed the door closed.

"So are you planning to eventually let Shelia and her closet cohorts off the hook?" Amelia pulled her phone from her pocket prepared to type in a notation if necessary. "Or should I begin reviewing résumés to find their replacements?"

Sage opened her mouth to answer, and then another thought occurred to her. "Exactly when did you find out they'd locked me up?"

"Not until this morning, when I heard them talking about it. What seemed like a wonderful idea two days ago now has them shaking in their pumps, expecting pink slips." Her assistant shrugged. "Anyway, when I couldn't find you, I figured you and Freddy Finch were somewhere in the hotel torturing Cole Sinclair, because I didn't see the two of them around, either."

Again, Sage was grateful Amelia had no inkling where she'd been, what she'd been doing and whom she had been doing it with. The young woman had been insufferable enough after she'd walked in on her and Cole kissing.

"I was hoping to snag one of those gorgeous centerpieces your neighbor made for myself, but our guests took them as souvenirs," Amelia continued.

"Evie did a great job," Sage agreed. "I'm hoping this encourages her to start her own business."

Rolling her chair closer to her desk, Sage tapped a finger on her computer's keyboard to rouse it from sleep mode.

"You haven't said what your plans are for Shelia and her coconspirators." Amelia raised a hand. "I know what they did is insubordination and a firing offense by any boss's standard. However, in their defense, you were a bit of a pill on Saturday, General, even more than usual. It was like watching a Valentine's Day version of *How the Grinch Stole Christmas*." Her assistant rolled her eyes. "I was seconds away from locking you up and throwing away the key myself."

Sage checked her watch, and then drummed her fingertips against the desktop. "Are you nearly ready to rest your case, because I have a lot of work to do before I leave for Milan?"

Amelia sighed. "I'm guessing you've already made up your mind."

She'd decided their fate before she'd come to work this morning. "They're good at their jobs, and I have no intention of firing them over a momentary lapse in judgment."

Her assistant froze, and her phone slipped from her grasp. She bent over to retrieve it. "So you're going to let it go, just like that?"

"Yep, just like that." Sage confirmed, looking at her computer monitor. "It's minutia. I need to reserve my energy to remain focused on the big picture." She'd enjoyed watching Shelia squirm this morning, but it was time to get back to business.

"What's gotten into you?"

Wouldn't you like to know. Sage kept the thought to herself, and her eyes fixed on her computer screen.

Amelia snorted. "Whatever it was, I hope you get a lot more of it."

* * *

A knock sounded on Cole's closed office door, and Loretta walked through it.

"Your next appointment is here," she said.

Cole looked away from the mood board Espresso's creative department had prepared with proposed ideas and color swatches for next year's spring collection. He exhaled. "You can show her...I mean *him* in."

"Do you need me to stick around to referee?" A gravelly grunt accompanied his secretary's question.

"Is he dressed like the Espresso Granny?"

Damn. Cole ground his teeth together. How was he supposed to convince the makeup-buying public the man had no association with Espresso when, thanks to Sage, he was starting to buy into it himself?

Sage. The thought of her and the stunt she'd pulled at the hotel should have left him angry. However, spending the remainder of the weekend with her made it seem as though it had happened a lifetime ago. He hoped when he returned from Milan there would be more weekends together in their future.

"Looks like Mr. Finch left his granny getup at home today," Loretta said.

"Go ahead and send him in," Cole said. "I'll yell if I need you to pry my fingers from around his throat."

Seconds later, Freddy Finch stepped hesitantly into his office. "Um, you wanted to see me."

Without the dress, wig and makeup, Finch appeared to be in his early twenties, Cole observed. Tall and lanky, he bore little resemblance to the overweight old crone he portrayed.

Cole walked away from the mood board set up on an easel. He took in Finch's threadbare jeans, old sneakers and worn Tennessee Titans jersey bearing the number of a player who'd retired a decade ago.

"Thanks for coming, Mr. Finch." He gestured to the chair in front of his desk. "Have a seat."

Freddy eyed the chair suspiciously before sitting down. "Hey, man, I don't want any trouble."

"I'm sure you don't." Rounding his desk, Cole sat in his own chair. As usual, he got right to the point. "Here's my problem, you dressing up as the so-called Espresso Granny is negatively impacting my company."

The young man shrugged. "The newspaper photo shoot and gigs I did for Stiletto were just to help me keep a roof over my head until my drag queen show takes off. My folks kicked me out, when I dropped out of college to pursue it full-time," he said. "Things are picking up, but it's been rough."

Cole let the young man rattle on about his song-and-dance routine for a few minutes before he stopped him. "Let's get down to the reason I asked you here."

"If you're going to sue me, you should know up-front I don't have anything."

That much was obvious, Cole thought. However, he had an alternate idea. If Finch agreed to it, Cole believed it might be a solution to both of their problems.

"Mr. Finch. I want to offer you a job."

Sweat broke out on the man's shaved head. "I don't know," he said, nervously. "The last job I took from Ms. Matthews nearly got my behind kicked the other day."

Leaning back in his chair, Cole crossed his arms over his chest. "I assure you the only thing this job will get you is well paid," he said. "Oh, and it just might help get that drag queen career of yours off the ground. Interested?"

He was interested all right, Cole thought.

"I'll take it." Eagerness replaced the anxiety that had creased the young man's features just moments ago.

"But you haven't even heard what you'll be required to do."

"Doesn't matter." Finch shrugged. "If it'll keep me from having to crawl back to my folks and boost my career, too, count me in, Mr. Sinclair."

Cole quickly outlined the job with Freddy Finch nodding in agreement at every requirement. "So you'll have to don your Espresso Granny outfit one last time," he said. "Then that's the last I ever want to see of it."

Again, the young man readily agreed.

"Great. My lawyers will have the contracts to you later this afternoon." Cole knew the kid needed the money sooner rather than later and would instruct his attorney to expedite the funds. "You'll receive your first check the moment you sign them."

Finch extended his hand, and Cole shook it, sealing the verbal agreement. "I can't thank you enough, Mr. Sinclair. You idea might just turn me into a headliner."

The young man rose to leave, but Cole gestured for him to wait. He picked up the phone on his desk and punched in a number. "Hey, Max. Is Tia available?"

Seconds later, his sister's burly assistant had her on the line. After welcoming her home from her belated honeymoon and inquiring about his brother-in-law, Ethan, Cole filled Tia in on what he needed and then asked for her help.

"That's correct, a head-to-toe makeover," he confirmed. "I also need you to handle this one personally."

"I don't know." His sister hedged. "I've never done a makeover like this before. It would definitely be a challenge."

"I know I'm asking for a miracle here, sis," Cole said. "But if there's anyone who can pull this off, it's you."

When the brief call ended, Freddy left the office with an all-day appointment set for the next day at Espresso Sanctuary's flagship spa.

Cole couldn't help feeling pleased with himself as he leaned back in his chair and propped his feet on his desk. Not only had he diffused the Espresso Granny problem, he just might be able to use it to his advantage.

Chapter 14

Sage awoke with a start as the wheels of the plane bumped along the runway before skidding to a stop at Milan's Malpensa airport.

"Benvenuti a Milano," a flight attendant said over the loudspeaker.

Sage yawned and stretched her arms over her head, but the movement did little to relieve the kinks the cramped economy-class seat had left in her back and neck.

The flight attendant announced the local time, seven o'clock in the morning. Sage stifled a second yawn with her fist. It meant she'd netted exactly twenty minutes of sleep during the entire fourteen-hour journey.

Much like her life, her plan to doze the entire overnight flight had been upended by Cole Sinclair. Images and thoughts of him had greeted her each time she'd closed her eyes. Being drawn to him, being infuriated by him, being kissed by him and finally being held by him as he made love to her deep into the night.

Sage sighed and peered out of the tiny window as the plane taxied to the terminal. Only days had passed since she'd last seen Cole, but she missed him. He'd lived in Milan during his stint at Force Cosmetics. Sage couldn't help wishing she would be seeing this incredible city with him as her companion instead of a paperback travel guide.

Girl, please, her inner voice heckled as she quickly made her way through customs with only a carry-on bag for the short trip. *You want him, all right, but not for playing tour guide.*

Sage tried to force thoughts of Cole from her mind as she slid into the backseat of a white taxi. She was in Milan during fashion week, and this afternoon she had a front-row seat to view the runway show of one of Italy's most iconic fashion brands. It certainly wasn't the time or place to be moping over a man she'd only known a few weeks. They hadn't even been out on a real date.

She stared out the taxi window at the gray skies as the city came into view. Then why did it feel as if she'd known Cole for a lifetime? she wondered. Moreover, why was she starting to think Amelia's belief in romance and finding true love might not be so far-fetched after all?

Removing her city guide from her bag, Sage covered a yawn with her fist. She flipped through the pages she'd highlighted during the flight, determined to shift her focus off Cole and onto enjoying her trip and rare time away from Stiletto.

The guidebook had noted the northern Italian city was a hub for business and lacked the monuments, picturesque piazzas and stunning views of the Mediterranean offered by the country's tourist destinations. Still, Sage had a short list of things she'd hoped to do while she was in town. She wanted to see the gothic cathedral known as the Duomo di Milano, tour the museum at the Teatro alla Scala opera house and buy a pair of kick-ass designer boots along the fashion capital's real attraction, the world-renowned Golden Quadrilateral.

"Scusi, signorina. Signorina."

Startled, Sage blinked and looked out the window. The taxi was parked at her hotel. She glanced at the open guide-book on lap and concluded she'd drifted off.

Sage yawned again. Sleepiness and jet lag overwhelmed her excitement as she counted out the euros to pay the driver and checked into her hotel. She'd intended to take a shower and spend the remainder of the morning sight-seeing before Marie Bertelli's driver arrived to whisk her to this afternoon's runway show.

Instead, she spent her first hours in Italy snoring be-neath the duvet of her room's full-size bed.

Cole observed the crowd filing into the courtyard of Sforzesco Castle. Huge white tents, winding red carpets and endless media trucks had temporarily transformed the centuries-old fortress into the city's weeklong fashion hub as well as the venue for the Bertelli runway show.

He'd attended fashion shows during Milan's fashion week in the past and had expected to see the requisite gaggle of fashion magazine editors, bone thin and dressed head to toe in black. However, the rest of the crowd looked like a virtual who's who of headline makers from across the globe.

Cole inclined his head at the CEO of a German de-partment store chain he'd become acquainted with dur-ing his Force Cosmetics stint. He recognized a smattering of American television reality-show stars, all famous for being famous, as well as last year's best-actor Oscar winner, who had passed out on stage in the middle of a drunken acceptance speech.

An uneasy feeling came over Cole. Not for the first time, he wondered why Marie had issued him the personal invite.

The only news he'd generated lately was a footnote in that god-awful article in *America Today* where that so-called Espresso Granny had made her, rather *his*, debut.

Cole rarely second-guessed himself. The main reason he'd decided to help Marie out with his presence was his fondness for her grandparents. However, he was starting to regret having made this trip. His time would have been better spent back in Nashville overseeing his own family's business, he thought. Although deep down he knew it wasn't his office at the Espresso building he longed for right now.

Cole wanted to be at the front door of Sage's cottage doing everything in his power to convince her to see him again.

Sage.

Damn, he missed her, entirely too much for a woman he'd only slept with one night. He'd thought about her nearly every moment of the long flight, her business savvy, her sass, the all-consuming passion she displayed both in and out of the bedroom.

Cole exhaled. He'd only been here a day, and already, he was considering shaving a few days off the trip. He'd arrived in Milan yesterday morning, rented a car and driven directly to his condo. The cleaner who came in once a month to maintain his place, which occupied the top floor of the four-story building, had readied it for his short stay, including stocking the fridge.

So this morning Cole had awakened in his own bed refreshed and looking out a window with a view of the Duomo, but longing for a woman an ocean away.

Give her some space, he cautioned himself. Sage had

promised to consider going out with him when he returned. It seemed ridiculous to be awaiting her answer about a date when he wanted so much more.

Surrounded by a throng of photographers with continuously clicking cameras, and security barking out orders in rapid Italian, Cole continued to make his way toward the elaborate tent where the Bertelli show was being held.

Once inside he immediately heard his name. Marie shouldered her way through the crowd. A worried expression deepened the lines in her forehead and grooves around her mouth.

"Please tell me you brought that sister of yours with you." She hissed, without preliminary, her panicked eyes searching around him.

Cole shrugged. "No. I haven't seen or talked to Lola in a few weeks," he said. "I was expecting to see her here."

"Well, she's not here. Her agency can't reach her, and she's not answering her damn phone." Marie bellowed over the din of the crowd. Forgetting her affected Italian accent, her intonation was straight out of Boston's north end. "She's supposed to wear our showstopper gown, and she's nowhere to be found."

Marie ran a hand through her short bob. "I don't know what we're going to do. I'd heard she could be unreliable at times, but I didn't think she'd screw me over, too."

Cole pulled his phone from the pocket of his suit jacket. "Hold on, I'll try giving her a call."

Three rings later, his youngest sister picked up. "Lola," Cole shouted into the phone covering his other ear with his hand.

Marie pushed aside a flap on the large tent, which led to a section that appeared to be a makeshift break room. There were pastries and bottled drinks set up on a corner table with several people milling around them.

It was a bit quieter, allowing Cole to hear what sounded like a party on the other end of the phone line.

"Hey, baby girl, where are you?" he asked, hoping both the party and his sister were nearby.

"What is she saying? Where is she?" Marie asked frantically.

Cole held up his hand as he tried to make out what his sister was saying. He only caught a few words, but they were enough to surmise what was going on.

"Met some friends…fun party…Madrid…stuck on a yacht …talk later," Lola said.

Cole called his sister's name, but either they'd been disconnected or she'd hung up. He hit the redial button. No answer.

Marie shook her head. "She's not coming at all, is she?"

"It doesn't sound like it," Cole said.

Before Marie could respond, a harried young woman carrying a clipboard approached them. From what Cole could glean from her excited, rapid-fire Italian, they'd located a last-minute replacement for Lola.

"Meno male." Marie's clasped her hands together, and her shoulders sagged in relief. She turned to Cole. "Your sister has burned a big bridge here today. If she keeps it up, no one is going to want to work with her. There aren't many girls as beautiful as she is, but there are plenty who are more reliable."

Cole loved his sister, but this time he couldn't defend her behavior. Tia had tried to talk to both him and Victor about Lola, but they'd both dismissed her concerns. Maybe it was time for them to have a sit-down with the youngest member of their family about her conduct.

An American reporter from a tabloid television show snagged Marie's attention. A camera in her face, she immediately snapped back into character with her synthetic Italian accent intact.

Cole grabbed a bottle of sparkling mineral water from the corner table. Twisting off the cap, he decided to take a few minutes before returning to the fray outside the break area.

"Ms. Bertelli, tell me, do you have any fireworks in store for us this afternoon on or off the runway?" the reporter asked.

Cole watched as Marie feigned an exaggerated disbelief at the question as she faced the cameraman. "Who, me?"

Both she and the reporter burst into conspiratorial giggles. "You'll just have to wait and see, won't you?" Marie teased.

Having had enough of watching the media dog and pony show, Cole left the break area. The crush of people had lessened considerably. With the show scheduled to start in twenty minutes, he presumed most of them had already found their seats surrounding the runway stage.

He handed an attendant his ticket and was immediately escorted down an aisle to the row of chairs closest to the stage. Sitting in his seat, Cole inclined his head at the young star of the reality show *Sugar Daddy*. The octogenarian seated on the other side of her wrapped a possessive arm around his borderline jailbait girlfriend and shot Cole a murderous look.

What in the hell had he gotten himself into?

The chair on the other side of him was vacant, and Cole didn't even want to speculate who would eventually sit in it. He glanced at his watch. Hopefully, this freak show would start on time and wrap up quickly.

"Is this seat taken?"

Cole's body recognized her voice before his brain could kick into gear, and his heart thumped wildly against his rib cage. Slowly he turned toward the familiar sound, hoping it wasn't a product of wishful thinking.

"Sage." Standing, he smiled as he said her name.

She wore a red wrap dress, his favorite color on her, and ridiculously high heels. Her coat was draped over an arm, and her kinky curls were piled on top of her head in some kind of updo his fingers itched to set free.

"I thought I imagined you," she said, the grin on her face rivaled his. "I can't believe you're here. When? How?"

Cole pulled her into his arms and stifled her questions with a kiss. He didn't care about the how or the why. He was just thrilled to see her, to hold her, to kiss her.

Sage flung her arms around his neck. She moaned softly into his mouth as his tongue caressed hers. The tenderness of the kiss belied his all-consuming hunger for her.

A few moments later, Cole ended the kiss but only so he could look at her face again and reassure himself she was really in his arms.

"I missed you." They said the words simultaneously as they took their seats.

Cole reached for Sage's hand. He didn't ever want to let it go. He didn't ever want to let her go. Again, his body instinctively knew what his brain had yet to register.

He'd fallen hard for Sage Matthews.

She squeezed his hand, and Cole gripped hers even tighter. He would have thought his feelings would have him running scared in the opposite direction. Instead, his fear was the very real possibility she didn't feel the same way.

For now, he simply wanted to revel in the fact that for this moment they were together. Cole raised Sage's hand to his lips. As he kissed it, he caught sight of Marie from the other side on the wide runway stage. Even at a distance, he could make out the frown on her face.

Realization dawned and he nearly laughed aloud. It

looked as though Bertelli's showing of the upcoming fall and winter fashions was going to have to stand on its own because a ceasefire had been declared in the battle between Nashville's two cosmetics companies. From now on, he and Sage would be making love, not war.

"Oh, my God, I think I just spotted Marie Bertelli," Sage said. "If I didn't know better, I'd think she was scowling at us."

"You're imagining things," Cole said, not wanting to ruin the show for her.

Shortly afterward, the lights dimmed and music began to play as an announcer welcomed the audience, in both English and Italian, to the showing of the House of Bertelli's ready-to-wear collection for the fall and winter seasons.

The models soon began strutting down the catwalk dressed in sweaters, dresses and coats in the autumnal colors of orange, yellow and rich brown. The clothes were stunning, Cole thought. He could hear Sage's excited *oohs* and *aahs* at nearly every piece.

Too bad Marie didn't realize she wouldn't need controversy to grab a share of the spotlight for her talented team of designers.

A leggy model walked onto the stage wearing a short yellow dress and a pair of high-heeled black boots. Immediately, Cole imagined those studded boots on Sage.

He leaned over and put his lips against her ear. "I want to see you wearing those boots and red lipstick," he said. "Nothing else."

"I suppose you want me back in that linen closet, too." Sage spoke into his ear so only he could hear.

Cole was about to tell her exactly where he wanted her, when a disturbance broke out in the other front row on the opposite side of the runway. He recognized the faces instantly, a rapper-turned-actor yelling at a boxer.

Both the music playing in the background and the models onstage came to an abrupt halt.

"Stay the hell away from my wife," the irate former rapper yelled.

The boxer bellowed a string of curses in reply.

Some of the models fled the stage in their teetering heels while others turned to watch the rapidly escalating argument. Security guards were pushing toward the fracas, but not before the former rapper threw a punch that connected with the boxer's jaw.

It appeared Marie was getting too much of the controversy she'd wanted.

Cole turned to Sage. "Let's get out of here."

She nodded her agreement. With the crowds edging closer to the melee, the two of them were able to easily slip out of the giant tent.

Sage shook her head in amazement. "Who's dumb idea was it to sit them next to each other?" she asked. "Their social media beef has been all over the news."

Cole shrugged. The same person who'd thought, after that article in *America Today*, that seating them next to each other would generate tabloid headlines, he thought. However, he'd explain all that to her later. Right now, he just wanted to enjoy her company.

"Have you eaten?" He asked as they navigated the tents, equipment and people in the castle's courtyard to the street.

"Not yet," she said.

"Then you're in for a treat," he said. "Walk with me." Cole held out his arm, and she linked hers through it.

He hesitated, glancing down at her shoes. "Can you handle a fifteen-minute walk in those?"

"I'll do my best," she said. "I've never seen more fashionably dressed people in my life than I've seen here. Not even in Paris."

Cole nodded as they walked along the narrow walkways leading to their destination. "What Milan lacks in Roman monuments and Renaissance splendor, it makes up for on the fashion front."

A long line snaking down the street signaled to him that they'd made it to their destination. Sage frowned as they stood at the end of it. "I have no idea what we're waiting for, but are you sure it's worth it?"

"Absolutely." Cole patted her arm, still looped through his "You will, too, once you taste a *panzerotti* from Luini's. It's a Milan institution."

Fortunately, the long line gave them a chance to talk, and Cole filled Sage in on the reason he suspected Marie Bertelli had personally invited them to her fashion show.

Sage snuggled into him. "I should probably be offended, but right now I couldn't care less why we're here. I'm just glad we're together."

Cole disentangled his arm from hers, and then wrapped both his arms around her waist. The heart this woman had managed to capture in such a short time expanded in his chest as he kissed the top of her head.

Finally, they made it through the doors of Luini's and were soon walking out again, their hands wrapped around the bakery's specialty.

Sage peeled the paper wrapper back on the half moon–shaped pocket of fried dough as they stood outside the bakery. Hers was stuffed with cheese and tomato sauce. "They look like fancy Hot Pockets." She inhaled. "But it smells heavenly."

"Try it," Cole encouraged.

He watched her take a tentative bite. A smile formed on her face as she chewed. "Oh, my God, the dough is sweet.

This is like having your meal and dessert in one." Immediately, she took another bite.

"So was it worth waiting in line?"

"I'd wait in a line ten times as long for one of these," she said enthusiastically.

Cole had pulled back the wrapper on his salami-and-mozzarella-stuffed panzerotti and was poised to dig in to it when a familiar figure approached.

The man slapped Cole on the back, a broad smile on his face. "So it is you," he said. "I thought I saw you at the Bertelli show earlier before that fight broke out. So when did you get to town, Admiral?"

"Oh, now that you're not working for me, you can call me that to my face." Cole laughed at Sean Cox, the man he'd hired to work at Force Cosmetics when was a kid fresh out of college.

Years later, when Cole left Force, he'd recommended the young man as his replacement.

Sean laughed. "Back then I was too busy quaking in my boots to even think it."

Cole remembered his manners. "Sean Cox, this is…"

"Sage Matthews of Stiletto Cosmetics," Sean finished, turning to Sage. "I've read about you and your company."

As the two shook hands, a mental red flag went up in Cole's head. More like his former protégé had been briefed on Sage's company.

Sean gave Cole a pointed look. "In fact, I was on a conference call the other day where *both of your companies* were mentioned."

Cole nodded, getting Sean's message loud and clear. Force Cosmetics wanted to add both Espresso and Stiletto to their brand portfolio. The only question was what lengths would the mammoth company go to in order to acquire them?

They talked a few more minutes and then Sean excused himself so he could stand in the growing line for his own panzerotti. "I'll be in touch," Sean said to Cole, as they parted.

Cole turned his attention back to Sage. He decided not to mention the impending offers for their companies that were almost sure to come from Force. Not yet. At this point, it was speculation on his part. Besides, there would be plenty of time for them to obsess over work.

For now, he wanted to continue to enjoy this time with her.

"So are you free for the rest of the afternoon?" Cole took a bite of his forgotten panzerotti.

"My schedule just happens to be clear for the next two days," Sage said.

"So what would like to do?" Cole asked. "We could take a walk along the rooftop of the Duomo or go shopping along the Quadrilatero d'Oro. Just say the word, and I'll take you anywhere you want to go."

She smiled up at him. Her brown eyes held their mischievous spark. "Take me to bed."

Chapter 15

Patience wasn't Sage's strong suit.

"Delayed gratification is for saints and suckers," she said, when they arrived at her hotel room. "I'm neither."

Housekeeping had turned down the bed, which beckoned a few feet from where they stood. Foil-wrapped chocolates adorned the plump pillows. However, there was only one sweet confection Sage was interested in unwrapping, and it was rock hard and pressed against her belly.

Sage ground against him as he held her. Cole's sharp intake of breath indicated she was one step closer to getting the satisfaction they both wanted.

"You're killing me," Cole whispered.

"Good," Sage said, continuing the slow grind. "Think of it as payback."

"Payback? After spending last weekend together, I assumed we were both out of the retaliation business."

Sage slid her index finger down the soft cashmere of

his sweater to the center of his chest. "That was before my sleepless journey across the Atlantic, where all I did was yearn for your touch, ache for your kiss and dream of having you naked and inside me."

Cole gulped. Sage watched his Adam's apple bob in his throat as he struggled with his resolve. He dropped his arms from around her waist, and then took a step back.

"It's obvious I want you." He glanced down at the bulge in his pants. *"Badly."*

Sage raised a brow and inclined her head toward the bed.

Shaking his head, Cole grasped her hands. "But I don't want a romp on a hotel bed." He raised her hands to his lips and pressed a kiss to them. "Not with you."

The intensity of Cole's gaze startled her. His dark brown eyes brimmed with an emotion Sage had never seen in them before. Or perhaps it was a reflection of her own feelings and the emotion she'd been waylaid by this afternoon at the unexpected sight of him—*love*.

Sage froze, startled by the realization. It didn't make sense. They were competitors. It was too soon, she told herself, but her heart wasn't buying into it.

"I want to take you to my place," Cole continued. "To my bed, where I plan to take my time making love to every inch of you until we're both too exhausted to move."

Sage's legs wobbled slightly at the illicit images his words brought to mind. "I promise to make it worth the wait." His melodic baritone rumbled through her.

Pull yourself together, she silently admonished, struggling to maintain her outer cool. Her insides, like her panties, were already on meltdown.

"Okay, you've convinced me," Sage said, managing to keep her voice from quivering like the rest of her body. She eyed his erection, which appeared on the verge of breaking through the front of his pants. "As long as I get what I want."

Cole followed her gaze. "Oh, you'll get it all right."

The short time it took them to check out of her hotel and arrive at Cole's place felt like an eternity to Sage. She'd clung to his hand during the short walk, savoring the innocuous contact of his skin on hers as he made lazy circles against her palm. She'd barely registered walking hurriedly along the unremarkable streets of the metropolitan city center, past the famed Duomo and ducking down narrow cobblestone side streets to avoid the chaotic temporary fashion hub set up around the Sforzesco Castle.

There was only one attraction Sage was interested in right now, and although it wasn't in her guidebook, she was positive it was the best this city would have to offer her this afternoon.

Cole stuck his key in the door of a charming older building that age and decades of summers had bleached into a muted shade of gold. Red shutters and window boxes surrounded its windows. Inside, he cast a glance at the ancient elevator, which, like the building, appeared to be a nineteenth-century throwback.

"I'm on the fourth floor, but you can't always trust the elevator," he said, then looked at her shoes. "I'll carry you if you'd like."

Sage eyed the steep flight of stairs. "I'll walk now, but save your energy." She shot him a look she hoped conveyed her meaning. "I anticipate climbing aboard and riding later."

Before she could register what was happening, Cole scooped her up in one swift motion. The air came out of her lungs with a whoosh as he tossed her over his shoulder caveman-style.

"Then it's *your* energy we'd better conserve," he said. "It's going to be a wild ride."

"That's mighty big talk," Sage called out from over his shoulder. "Hope you can…"

A sudden smack on her ass silenced her.

"Save that brash, sassy mouth of yours for when I get you upstairs," Cole said.

Sage pressed her lips together and did as he ordered. The general was fully prepared to let the admiral take charge.

With one hand lifting her suitcase and the other holding her firmly by the backside, Cole effortlessly climbed the flights of stairs. He set her suitcase down long enough to unlock the door, before carrying her and it inside and kicking the door closed with his foot.

Sage lifted her head off his back and glanced around at her surroundings. The gleam of the hardwood floors, the beauty of the art on the walls and the sumptuous furnishings were lost on her. Sage didn't care where they were, as long as she was with him.

"I think you can put me down now," she said, finally.

Ignoring her suggestion, Cole marched through the living and dining rooms with her still draped over his shoulder and his hand still splayed on her backside. As his sure stride ate up a long corridor off the dining room, Sage couldn't help noticing that, while he'd said his condo was on the fourth floor of the building, he'd failed to mention it was the entire fourth floor.

Sage felt her excitement build with every step he took. The brief tour ended in a bedroom large enough to fit her entire house into with room to spare.

Windows took up one wall, and although the draperies were drawn Sage was sure they offered a spectacular view of the city. She raised her head to see a sitting area on one side of the huge bedroom, with a large flat-screen television, sofa and plush armchairs. However, it was the half of the room behind her, which she'd caught a glimpse of as he carried her inside, that Sage found most appealing.

A king-size bed dominated it, rich mahogany wood as masculine as the man who slept in it. Sage's breath caught in her throat at a vision of their nude bodies transforming the pristine silver-gray bedding into a tangled mess of sweaty sheets.

Cole's hands moved to her waist and lifted her from his shoulders. He held her close enough for her body to slowly slide down the length of his until they were standing toe-to-toe.

Their gazes connected, and again his eyes radiated more than lust. He brushed a kiss across her mouth.

"Turn around," he said. "I want to show you something."

Sage faced the bed. Cole wrapped his arms around her and nuzzled her neck. His thick, impossibly hard erection pressed against her buttocks, and she bit her bottom lip to suppress a shiver.

"You're not the only one who couldn't sleep a wink last night." He whispered near her ear. "I lay awake in that very bed reliving all the things we did this past weekend. Then I fantasized about what I'd do to you and then beg you to do to me when I saw you again."

Staring at the bed, Sage released a shaky breath and licked her suddenly dry lips. "You should know by now that you don't have to beg." She turned in his embrace and raised her chin until her eyes met his. "Just tell me your fantasy."

Then an even better idea occurred to her. She grasped the collar of his jacket and slid it down over his broad shoulders until it fell off him onto the floor. Shredding her own coat, she tossed it on top of his. "On second thought, don't tell me. Let me guess."

"Guess?" Cole asked, his expression a mix of confusion and intrigue.

Sage nodded. Touching her palm to the center of his chest, she walked him backward to one of the armchairs across the room.

"I'm going to guess what you wanted to do to me last night and every little thing you wanted me to do to you." She pushed against his chest until he dropped into the chair, and then she leaned in until the tips of their noses met. "You tell me if I'm hot or cold."

"I can tell you now, you're hot as hell." Cole traced her bottom lip with his tongue, but she pulled back before she instinctively opened her mouth to him.

"Uh-uh." Sage wagged an admonishing finger. "Get comfortable, Mr. Sinclair, because this game is just getting started."

He eased back in the armchair. His dark eyes were glued to her every move as she slowly backed away. She made the mistake of stealing a glance at his crotch, and his cock twitched in response as if she'd called it by name.

Sage's mouth went dry and her panties dampened. The sight of it straining against his pants, hard and ready, nearly made her forget about the sexy game.

She closed her eyes to temporarily block it from her mind. Later, she intended to give it the attention it deserved. Sage dropped her chin to her chest, and raised her arms to her head to remove the bobby pins anchoring her updo. Relaxing her neck, she shook her head and fluffed her coils back into full-on Afro status.

Sage opened her eyes and looked at him sitting in the chair. "Fantasy-wise, am I hot or cold?"

"Hot," Cole said. "How did you know the first thing I

wanted to do when I saw you at the fashion show was set that wild hair free?"

"Because it's like we're two of a kind." Sage skimmed her hands downward over her breasts and the sensitive peaks of her nipples to the sash of her wrap dress at her waist. "And despite what some may view as a short acquaintance, we know each other almost as well as we know ourselves."

She yanked at the sash, and her dress fell open, revealing the lacy bra and matching panties underneath. Both were a soft shade of cotton-candy pink.

Sage shrugged off the dress, and let it drop to the floor. Clad in only her underwear and her heels, she posed the same question. "Am I hot or cold?"

"Damn, girl." Cole's reply was more of a groan, and his hands gripped the sides of the armchair.

Sage smiled, reveling in her feminine power, the game turning her on as much as it did him. "Sorry, but that's not one of the options," she said. "Again, hot or cold?"

"Hot." Cole shifted in the chair. Sage guessed it was to accommodate his growing cock, which looked as though it would break right through his zipper. "But I have to confess, those sweet and innocent pink undies aren't what I expected to see on a woman so deliciously naughty."

Sage pivoted to provide him with a backside view of her barely-there thong. She heard his sharp intake of breath as she looked back at him over her shoulder. "I assure you, I'm naughty to the bone."

"I wouldn't have it any other way," Cole said, his eyes riveted to her bare ass cheeks. "So far, you're my fantasy come to life."

Next, Sage moved to kick off one of her high heel pumps.

"Whoa. Cold," his deep voice called out without being prompted. "*Brrr!* Ice-cold."

She turned her head and smiled at him as she undid the front clasp on her bra. She let the straps slip from her shoulders, before letting it fall to the floor.

"Maybe this will help thaw the chill." Sage slowly spun around, now naked except for her heels and panties. There was no need for her to ask the question that had ruled their game. Cole's eyes darkened. She could feel the fire in his hungry gaze as it traveled from her breasts down to her heels and back up again.

"Very, very hot." He patted his lap. "Now, bring it here."

Gooseflesh erupted on Sage's skin at the husky command. Every cell in her body wanted to obey, but she steeled herself against the overwhelming urge. Instead, she allowed her eyes the pleasure of roaming from his strong jaw, covered in a shadow of beard she could hardly wait to feel against her mouth and between her thighs, to his broad chest and then downward to the tented slacks he'd had on entirely too long.

"Your turn," she said. "Take off your clothes."

Sage watched the corner of his mouth quirk upward into a lazy half smile. "Is that an order, General?"

"Please." Her dulcet tone belied the fact she was seconds away from marching over to that chair and tearing the clothes off him.

His grin widened. "Well, since you asked so nicely."

Standing, Cole grabbed the bottom of his sweater, and pulled it up and over his head. Sage sank her teeth into her bottom lip to suppress a gasp. Her fingertips tingled in anticipation of touching his solid wall of a chest, then clinging to those broad shoulders. She could hardly wait to feel those strong arms surround her within the confines of his embrace.

Sage looked on, mesmerized as Cole eased his zipper over his erection. Pants and underwear hit the floor, and his cock sprang free. Every bit as long, thick and hard as she remembered and, *oh*, the things he could do with it.

She opened her mouth to speak as he kicked away his shoes and socks, but her mind went blank. The gift for the snappy comeback eluded her. So did the ability of speech. All she could do was stare, stammer and drool.

Cole didn't miss her reaction. "You speechless?"

Sage assumed he raised a brow, but she wasn't looking at his face. Her nipples tightened, and her minuscule thong panties barely contained the moisture pooling between her legs.

He sat back in the chair and stroked his length once, then again. "Come, ride me," he said. Then he added in that rich melodic baritone that never failed to send shivers down her spine. *"Pretty please."*

"Well, since you asked so nicely." Her speech restored, Sage echoed his words of just minutes before as she did a slow strut toward the armchair.

She stopped short. "Condom?"

"My wallet." Cole inclined his head at his pants, which were currently beneath the spike heel of her shoe.

Sage retrieved the foil packet, then flung both his wallet and pants aside. She leaned over the chair and brushed aside the hand gripping the base of his cock, replacing it with hers.

"I'll take it from here." She allowed herself to stroke the magnificent length of the shaft, from base to the smooth, velvet tip.

"Don't." Cole gasped loudly. "Do that again and this will be over before it even starts."

Cole pulled her onto the chair, and Sage straddled him, her heated core hovering inches above his hardness.

He threaded his fingers through her hair. Fisting a clump of the tight coils in his hand, he crushed his mouth to hers. Sage moaned, and he plunged his tongue inside her mouth, deepening the kiss. The taste of him, his cologne, a heady mix of spice tinged with rum, nearly driving her out of her mind.

Close to getting what she'd been craving ever since their weekend together had ended, Sage ripped open the condom wrapper. She wrenched her mouth away from his and quickly sheathed him.

"I have never wanted anyone as much as I want you," she said.

Their gazes connected. "You own me, Sage Matthews, heart, body and soul." Even in the heat of passion, his words rang with sincerity, and Sage knew without a doubt, this man loved her as much as she loved him. "Now come get what's yours."

Sage moved to slip her thong panties aside, but he released her hair and clutched the scant fabric in his hand. She heard the lace rip as he tore them from her body and tossed them to the floor.

His forcefulness sent an erotic thrill coursing through her, and Sage couldn't wait any longer. Slowly, she lowered herself onto his cock inch by delectable inch.

Their simultaneous moans echoed throughout the room as he stretched and filled her. A rush of sensations bombarded her core, and her walls contracted around him. The overwhelming power of their connection, both physical and emotional, took her by surprise.

"Ah," Cole rasped. His body froze, and he touched his forehead to hers, as if he, too, needed a moment to regain control. "You're so tight. And so damn hot."

Sage rose and slid down his steely length. Then she did it again and again. The next time, Cole thrust upward to meet her in one stroke, followed by another and another easing her into a slow, steady ride.

He trailed kisses from her throat to her breasts, which he cupped in his large hands. She groaned when his thumbs brushed over the sensitive peaks. The feel of his hands, of him inside her, threatened to send her over the edge.

He flicked his tongue over a nipple and then covered it with his mouth.

"Cole." Sage threw her head back and called his name as he alternated sucking and teasing. Moving from one breast to the other, the man's tongue, lips and teeth were as relentless as the upward thrusts that continued to fill her over and over.

She called his name again, and he raised his head, capturing her lips in a kiss. He swallowed her moan of delight as his tongue delved into her mouth.

Driven by excitement and ravenous need, Sage's thighs squeezed against his and her slick walls clamped around him. Her body acted of its own accord. She could barely handle what he dished out, yet everything in her begged for more.

Cole's hands slid from her breasts over her belly button down to her hips. His fingers gripped her roughly, breaking both their kiss and the rhythm of their ride.

"You feel so good. I want to make this last forever." He stilled, his tone both harsh and pleading.

Catching her breath, Sage stared into the depths of his eyes. "You own me, Cole Sinclair, heart, body and soul," she whispered, her voice cracked with emotion. "Now take what's yours, because it only gets better."

Cole's fingers dug into her hips. His gaze didn't waver as he surged upward. Sage gasped at the force of the powerful thrust and the ones that followed it. Her hands moved from his chest to his broad shoulders, and she held on tight.

Rising and falling on his cock, she met each of his deep strokes. Harder and faster. The more he gave her, the more she craved until spasms of pure pleasure ripped through her. Wave after wave, the orgasm overpowered her very being.

With one last violent stroke, Cole yelled her name. He followed her over the edge, his hands clutching her hips as his cock pulsated inside her.

She sagged against him, and he encircled her in his embrace. As their hearts slammed against their chests, Sage wasn't surprised to feel them throb to the exact same beat.

Then the words weighing on her heart unintentionally escaped her lips. *"I love you."*

Chapter 16

"Do you always hold a Q&A session after sex?"

If Sage thought her question would dissuade him, she was mistaken, Cole thought. "It's a simple question," he said. "I even made it multiple choice so it would be easy for you to answer."

The woman cradled in his arms sighed contentedly and snuggled deeper into his chest. Their marathon had come full circle, starting in the armchair, moving on to his bed, next beneath the shower spray and now finally back to the chair again.

Cole adjusted the flannel throw he'd yanked off the sofa over their naked bodies. He'd finally relented and let her take off those sexy shoes. Now her bare feet were tucked under her as she leaned against him.

"Well?" he persisted.

"Could you repeat the question?" Sage hedged.

He shifted in the chair until they were face-to-face.

"When you said you loved me earlier, did you mean it, or did I put it on you so good, I had you talking out of your head?"

Sage snorted. "Nothing wrong with your ego."

Her tone was filled with the playful banter that had become a hallmark of their relationship. Yet, the straightforward woman who never backed down from him, or anyone else, averted her eyes. The drapes were open, and she stared out the window, which offered a picturesque view of the starlit night sky and the city in the distance.

Cole let his question sink in. Despite her facade of bravado, she was scared. Her hesitance wasn't in deciding on an answer, but rather whether to trust him with it.

Pushing Sage probably wasn't his best idea. Yet, he needed to hear it. He needed to know if she was as caught up in the whirlwind of a romance that could be as challenging and infuriating as it was heartfelt and sexy. The more layers he pulled back from the complicated, smart and beautiful woman in his arms, the more he found to admire, respect and, yes, love.

Everything in the way she'd responded as he made love to her told him she felt the exact same way. However, he had to know for sure.

Cole smoothed his knuckles down the side of her cheek. She sighed softly as she met finally met his gaze. Her body trembled against him.

"I probably shouldn't feed that massive ego of yours." She tapped her forefinger against his bare chest. "But I can't deny the fact that you indeed put it on me, and that thing you did with your tongue in the shower made me forget my own name."

Though he should probably be flattered, Cole felt his hopes deflate. It hadn't been the answer he'd wanted or expected. He kept his expression impassive to hide his disappointment as she continued.

"I also can't deny the fact that I love you," she said. "I meant everything I told you when we made love."

Cole exhaled, his disappointment replaced by pure delight. He knew he was grinning like an idiot, but he didn't care. "Now was that so hard to say?"

"No, but it does make things complicated."

"It doesn't have to be," he said. "I love you. You love me. I can't think of anything simpler."

Sage rested her head on his chest. "Right here. Right now, that's true. But eventually we have to get back to the real world. Our real lives. Loving you doesn't change the fact that we're competitors, or that you want my company."

Cole did want Stiletto Cosmetics. However, real life had indeed intruded, and now he wanted Sage more. Enough to find an alternative solution to solving Espresso's problems.

She craned her neck to look up at him. "I'm sorry. I shouldn't have brought up work," she said. "As important as Stiletto is to me, I'm enjoying this time with you too much to think about it right now."

He dropped a kiss on her forehead. "But since you did bring it up, I think we need to talk about it. Returning to Nashville and our real lives is only a problem if we make it one."

Sage sighed. "That sounds good when we're together and naked, but eventually we'll have to put our clothes on and go to work."

"I'm rescinding my offer to buy Stiletto," Cole said. He didn't add that he had a strong suspicion she'd soon get one from Force Cosmetics. At this point, it was still speculation and would further complicate a situation he was trying to make easier for both of them.

Sage sat up and looked at him. A surprised expression blanketed her pretty features.

"There are other ways to put the brakes on Espresso's downhill slide, ones that don't include acquiring your company," he said.

Sage continued to stare at him. "I don't understand," she began. Then a corner of her mouth quirked up into a half smile. "Or did I put it on you so good, it made your forget about coming after my company."

"Touché." Cole threw his head back and laughed. "But to be honest, I think I actually made the decision to back off when we were at my aunt's house for dinner."

"I don't get it. Did your aunt say something to change your mind? Or was that what you and Riley were talking about when I was out of earshot?"

"No, on both counts," he said, his tone growing serious. "It was what you said about your mother." Cole's shrug belied how much that part of the dinner conversation had gotten under his skin. "Before Victor and then my younger sisters came along, my mother was also a single parent. My father died in a construction accident a few months after I was born, so I have no memory of him. However, I do remember the struggle and the sacrifices my mom made to start Espresso."

It wasn't something Cole talked about often, if ever, especially after the last angry conversation he'd had with his mother. He'd been young, brash and stupid. If he'd only known it was to be their last conversation, he would have handled things so differently.

Unfortunately, there was no way to turn back the hands of time, or for the older and wiser man he was now to shake some sense into the hotheaded kid he'd been then.

Sage rested her head back on his chest, and he smoothed

a hand through her hair, which felt like soft puffs of cotton beneath his fingertips.

"I guess I always thought of you as coming from money, and then being savvy enough to make more of it," she said. "I didn't see the struggle."

"Mom took the insurance check she got after my father died to start Espresso, so I grew up with it, just me and her. In fact, my earliest memories are of stuffing lipstick and compacts into boxes to help her fill mail orders. I felt like it was our business."

It was why one of his mother's last decisions had cut him to the core. The dull pang he carried around like a piece of luggage surfaced in his chest.

Again, she lifted her head and faced him. "Then why did you leave Espresso to work for Force?" She asked. "I wondered about it when you mentioned it during that first lunch downtown. Listening to you now has made me even more curious. You and your mom started a cosmetics empire, what on earth would make you walk away from it?"

Ordinarily, Cole would shut down at this point. Find a way to change the subject or ignore the question altogether. While Sage probably wouldn't press him for an answer, he found himself wanting to share things with her he didn't tell anyone else. He wanted her to know it all, the good, the bad, even the ugly.

"It's a long story, and some of it's not very pretty," he said finally.

She squirmed against him in the chair and readjusted the throw. "I'm a captive audience," she said. "Besides, the fact we're similar in so many ways means I already know so much about you. I want to hear all the things I don't know."

Exhaling, Cole began to explain, starting with the good. "My mom was a lot like us—confident, hardworking, competitive and stubborn as hell." He smoothed Sage's hair off her face and dropped a kiss on her forehead. "As a young widow with an infant, she received a lot of advice from well-meaning people who thought she should find a part-time job, put the insurance check from my father's death in the bank and live off the profits from the construction company my father owned with his brother."

"Riley's dad?" Sage asked.

"Yes. My late uncle Simon," Cole said. "He also built the Espresso building. Anyway, my mom obviously didn't follow their advice. She sold my father's interest in Sinclair Construction to my uncle, and she used the money from it, along with the insurance check, to start Espresso."

Sage craned her neck to look up at him. "Gutsy move. Especially nearly thirty-five years ago when it was more difficult being a woman in business."

"Mom said she did it for me. Because I'd lost a father I wouldn't remember having. She wanted to give me more than just a decent childhood. She wanted to give me a legacy, something that could be passed down from generation to generation."

The woman in his arms was quiet. She placed her hand over his, and Cole could feel the warmth and understanding in her touch.

"She worked hard for it, and she pushed me hard, too. Mom never let up on me, even after she married Victor and my sisters were born. She was constantly grooming me to one day take over Espresso," Cole said. "I followed her blueprint, working at Espresso part-time through high school and college and, of course, every summer. After graduation, I became one of the company's two vice presidents, my stepfather was the other one."

"Was that a problem for you?" Sage asked.

"Not initially," Cole said. "We were responsible for different departments, but we both reported to my mother, who always had the final word. The three of us worked well together. Besides, Victor's been in my life since I was eight. He's the one who helped me with my homework as a kid and showed up at my Little League games, even more often than my mom."

"What changed the dynamic?" Sage asked.

Sharing the good had been easier than Cole had expected. He'd genuinely enjoyed working with his parents. Even after he'd bought his town house, he frequently ate dinner at their house where, in spite of Tia and Lola's protests, they often talked business.

"New companies came on the scene. They began offering women of color, our core customers, new product lines and trendier colors. Also, mainstream brands like Force began to step up their game in catering to the growing multiethinic market," Cole explained. "Every time I brought it up with Mom or Victor, along with ideas to keep Espresso competitive, they shut me down. My mom didn't take it or me seriously. She believed those companies were flashes in the pan that wouldn't last long and that the best course of action for Espresso was to continue what we were doing. Do what we do and do it well, she'd say."

Cole summed up the two years he'd spent warning his parents the business was rapidly changing and imploring with them to make changes. Each time they'd rejected his suggestions and dismissed his concerns. "The more I tried to talk to them about it, the more my mom dug her heels in."

"Stubborn." They said the word simultaneously, knowing the same could be said of them.

"Then she got sick and, despite the treatments, we all knew she wouldn't get better." Cole told her in as few words as possible about his mother's breast cancer battle and felt Sage hold his hand a bit tighter.

It reinforced his decision to confide in her. Cole exhaled a shaky breath. "When she was advised to get her affairs in order, she met with her lawyers at her bedside."

Time hadn't faded the smell of prolonged sickness and impending death that came back to him when he thought about his mother's final days. It was then that the memory of the cancer-ravaged version of her overshadowed the vibrant, demanding, beautiful force to be reckoned with that Selina Sinclair Gray had been the majority of her life.

"Afterward she informed me Victor was the new president of Espresso. She said my ideas were too radical, and at twenty-six, I was simply too young to leave in charge of the company I'd always believed we'd built together."

Sage kept a firm grip on his hand. He wasn't proud of how he'd reacted to his mother's decision. Unfortunately, life didn't offer do overs.

"We were both hotheads. I said some harsh things out of anger. So did she," he said. "She told me to get out of her sight, to which I replied, 'Gladly, I don't want to look at you right now, either.'"

Cole sighed. He'd never before shared his last conversation with his mother with anyone. The most he'd said to his family was that they'd had words.

"I had driven halfway back to my place—then I turned the car around to go back and apologize, but it was too late. She was dead."

The toughest part of the story already told, Cole pushed through to the end. "After she died, Victor and I continued to butt heads at work over the same issues. Only he was even more resistant to making changes and had the final say," he said. "I didn't want to continue arguing with the only parent I had left, so I handed in my resignation and left both Espresso and Nashville. A few months later, I went to work at Force."

Cole was relieved when Sage didn't offer up meaningless platitudes, which only tended to make the person saying them feel better. Nor did she try telling him that despite their horrible argument, his mother loved him. He already knew she did.

Instead, Sage released his hand and then she wrapped her arms around his neck and hugged him tighter than he'd ever been hugged in his life.

"It's why you try to think first instead of acting out of anger, isn't it?" she asked.

Cole nodded. "It was a lesson I learned the hard way," he said. "If I could do it all again, instead of lashing out I would have simply told my mother how much her decision hurt. I'd ask her why, after years of making Espresso my number one priority, she didn't have enough faith in me to know I would do whatever was best for our company. The bottom line is, in the end, she didn't trust me."

"Yet, you're back at Espresso now, trying to stage its comeback," Sage said.

Cole nodded. Despite, his bank balance and business experience, he still was a man with something to prove, if only to himself. "That angry exchange with my mother is a weight I'll carry with me forever," he said. "But knowing I put the company she poured her entire life into back on top will help ease the burden."

Tears brimmed in Sage's eyes when she met his gaze. "The woman in me who loves you wants to do everything in her power to help you achieve that goal." Her voice cracked with emotion. "But to my business side, we're still competitors."

Cole swiped away one of the tears with the pad of his thumb before it could roll down her cheek.

"I didn't tell you all this to further complicate things between us. But when you told us about your mother at dinner, it helped me understand why Stiletto is more than a company to you," he said. "The more important you became to me, the more I needed you to know why I have to save Espresso."

"I do understand." She snuggled back into him. "I also think Nashville just might be big enough for two cosmetic companies."

Cole shifted in the chair, so he could see her face. "Does this mean our temporary cease-fire is permanent?"

"I'm ready to wave the white flag if you agree." She laughed.

"Agreed." Cole extended his hand, and she shook it.

Sage resumed her position, resting her head on his chest. "Great. Now that we've brokered the peace, I can finally stop worrying what you have up your sleeve and get a good night's sleep."

"Oh, you'll have a good night." He caressed her bare bottom with his hand. "But I doubt you'll get much sleep."

Sage rose, hands clapping enthusiastically with the rest of the audience as the cast of *Aida* took their final bows to thunderous applause.

The house lights came up, and the throng of opera patrons slowly began to exit the lavish auditorium of the Teatro alla Scala opera house. Exuberant conversations in several languages broke out all around her. She didn't have to understand what they were saying to know they were all buzzing about the performance they'd obviously enjoyed as much as she had.

"I'm not sure what was more beautiful, those powerful voices or this place." Sage soaked in the gilded wood and red velvet interior of the world-renowned venue.

She felt Cole's hand at the small of her back as they walked through the majestic mirror-lined foyer and out into the night. Even through the layers of her coat and dress, the gesture sent a warm shiver down her spine. Moreover, it made a woman who'd always taken care of herself feel protected, cherished and very much loved.

"Neither. You are the most beautiful thing about this entire evening," Cole said.

Sage snorted to hide her delight at the compliment. "You don't have to sweet-talk me," she said. "You're definitely getting lucky tonight."

"Already?" Cole joked. "Technically this is only our first date."

Sage linked her arm through his as they continued the short walk back to his place. "When it comes to you, I'm easy."

"And I meant what I said—you look stunning tonight. When I saw you in that dress, my eyes nearly popped out of my head."

"I'm glad you like it."

After taking in a view of the city from the rooftop of the Duomo cathedral and viewing Leonardo da Vinci's masterpiece *The Last Supper* at the Santa Maria delle Grazie church that morning, they'd spent the afternoon in the up-scale shopping area know as the Quadrilatero d'Oro, home to the country's top designer logos.

"There nothing I love more than seeing you in a sexy red dress," Cole said. "What I didn't like was your adamantly refusing to let me buy it for you."

Sage grunted in response. Just as she had when he'd attempted to pull out his credit card at the counter of the chic designer store.

"I can pay for my own clothes." The dress had indeed been pricey, but it had been her one and only splurge.

"That's not the point."

The wide city streets narrowed into side streets as they got closer to Cole's condo. Sage's heels clicked against the cobblestones. They'd already discussed it, and she refused to rise to his bait.

"You wouldn't let me buy you anything," He continued to rant. "Not the other dresses or the shoes and boots you were practically drooling over. I could see in your eyes that you wanted all of them."

"It's called window shopping, Cole," Sage said, patiently.

"What good is having money if you can't spend it on the people you care about?" he countered.

Sage halted midstep, a few feet from the entrance to his building. She extricated her arm from his. He stopped walking and faced her. Their gazes locked. "I don't want anything from you…but you," she said.

Cole pushed out a defeated sigh. "Stubborn."

"Right back at ya." Sage looped her arm back through his, and they resumed walking.

"Life with you is never going to be easy, is it?" Humor permeated his deep voice.

"Nothing worth having ever is."

Later that night, after they'd given both Cole's bed and their favorite chair a long, hard workout, Sage stood at the window wearing one of his T-shirts, staring out at the city. She'd arrived here excited to attend her first international runway show. Now it was a forgettable footnote.

She felt Cole's arms encircle her as he came up from behind. The shadow of beard clinging to his jaw tickled her neck as he bestowed it with a series of kisses.

"I was thinking we could spend the next few days at Lake Como," he said. "I sold my villa there when I left my job at Force, but we can stay…"

Sage stopped him. "I leave for home tomorrow evening."

"Can't your staff hold down the fort at Stiletto for another day or two?"

She shook her head. "It's not work. I have a previous engagement."

Cole raised a brow. "Then cancel or reschedule it."

"I can't," she said. "It's with another man."

Chapter 17

"You might have mentioned earlier that this other man of yours was six years old."

Cole looked on as Sage wrapped an old-fashioned candy dispenser reminiscent of a grocery-store gumball machine in festive birthday paper.

"Then I might not have had the pleasure of your company on the trip back to Nashville," she said.

When Sage said she had a previous engagement with another man back in Milan, Cole had done two things. First, he'd taken her back to bed and made love to her until the only man's name falling from her lips was his, over and over again. Next he'd booked the seats next to hers on her flights to Nashville.

They'd arrived late yesterday evening and spent the night at his town house sleeping off jet lag. This morning, they'd celebrated their return to the dirty South with breakfast at the Waffle House, and now they were at Sage's house, preparing to head to her neighbor's birthday party.

Cole slapped a red bow on top of the toy truck he'd wrapped for her. "You know, that lipstick you're wearing today suits you perfectly." He'd recognized it the moment she'd smoothed the bold red shade over her lips. "You are a badass."

She topped the wrapped candy dispenser with a huge blue bow and then rounded her kitchen table to plant a lingering kiss on his mouth. "I warned you back in Milan—I'm naughty to the bone."

At the word *bone*, Cole leaned over and whispered an equally naughty joke in her ear.

Pursing her lips into a prudish frown, Sage smacked at the arm he'd wrapped around her waist. Cole caught the mischievous spark in her eyes, just before she winked. "Later." She laughed. "We've got a party to attend."

A short while later, Cole came face-to-face with Sage's other man. Wearing a red sweatshirt emblazoned with the words *It's My Birthday*, the little boy dashed toward them the moment he spotted Sage at his front door.

"Whatcha bring me?" He blurted out in lieu of a greeting.

"Kenny!" A harried redhead admonished the kid. "Manners!"

"Whatcha bring me, *please*?" The kid added a snaggletoothed grin to his second attempt, and Cole stifled a laugh.

Shaking her head at the little boy, the woman ushered them inside her house, and Sage quickly introduced them.

"Nice to meet you, Mr. Sinclair." Evie put a restraining arm around her kid to keep him from snatching the gifts from their hands. "And this etiquette-school dropout is my son, Kenny."

"Cole," he corrected. Then he addressed the woman's son. "Happy Birthday, Kenny."

"Well, Cole, like I told Sage earlier when she said you didn't mind lending us a hand, it's much appreciated. I've got two-dozen kindergarteners and ten pizzas descending on this house in two hours and definitely need reinforcements."

"Glad to help out," Cole replied, genuinely meaning it. If being here was important to Sage. It was important to him, too.

Taking their coats and hanging them in a closet near the front door, the woman turned to look at Sage. "Thanks, again. Not many friends would leave one of the most glamorous cities in one of the most glamorous countries in the world to help out with a kiddie party."

Cole silently agreed. He wished they could have stayed longer and enjoyed some time together at Lake Como; however, Sage's loyalty to her friend impressed him. Every day he was with her, Cole found something else to love and admire about this woman.

"There was no way I was going to miss Kenny's sixth birthday," Sage said.

On cue, the birthday boy stood on tiptoe and attempted to put his ear against the wrapped box in Sage's arms. His eyes were pleading when he stared up at her. "Is there a puppy in here?"

Evie put her fists on her hips and narrowed her eyes at Sage. "There had better not be."

"Not this time," Sage said. "But it's something I think you'll like almost as much."

Kenny looked to his mother. "Can't I open just this one before the party?" he asked, quickly adding an exaggerated *please*.

"Yeah, *please*." Sage mimicked her small friend.

Evie sighed. "Oh, all right."

As she led them through to the living and dining rooms,

Cole noticed the house was laid out exactly like Sage's. It had a lived-in look about it, which, despite being a stranger, made him feel welcome.

The furniture had been pushed into corners. Three folding banquet tables covered with red paper tablecloths and surrounded by chairs occupied the dining room. The living room was filled with children's games.

Sage placed her present on one of the tables then hoisted Kenny until he was standing on one of the chairs. "Happy Birthday," she said.

Without preliminaries, Kenny ripped the wrapping paper off the box as the adults stood by and watched.

"Hey! It's a candy machine," he yelled excitedly, "full of Skittles!"

Kenny threw his arms around Sage and hugged her. "Thanks!" He didn't waste time in turning the knob on the machine, which dispensed him a handful of the candy. He shoved it into his mouth and happily chewed. Almost immediately he turned the knob for another handful of candy, this one he held out to share with Sage.

"Thanks, kiddo." Sage accepted the candy. She looked like a kid herself, Cole thought, as she also shoved the small pieces into her mouth.

Kenny helped himself to another handful of Skittles, and then announced he was headed his room to watch his favorite cartoon.

"A candy machine." Evie frowned at both Sage and Cole once her son was out of earshot. "I'm going to send you two the dental bills when all that candy rots his teeth."

Cole thought about the kid's mouth. "What teeth? He's barely got any."

He watched the woman's eyes go wide and chin drop to her chest. Thinking the offhanded comment offended her, Cole considered apologizing.

"Oh, my God," Evie said, looking from him to Sage and back at him again. Then she pointed a finger at both them and laughed. "You two are exactly alike."

"I told her the same thing about her son's lack of teeth just a few weeks ago," Sage explained.

"No doubt about it." Evie smiled. "You're absolutely perfect for each other."

Cole wrapped an arm around Sage's waist and pulled her to his side. The adoring look she gave him made his heart turn a backflip in his chest.

Sage's neighbor was right. They were perfect for each other. He'd finally convinced Sage of it in Italy, and that their companies could peacefully coexist.

Now all he had left to do was persuade her to be his wife.

A knock sounded on Sage's office door, and she looked up to see Amelia wearing her smug *I-told-you-so* expression on her face, which only meant one thing.

"Prince Charming's here," the young woman teased.

Sage narrowed her eyes. "You would think you'd be sick of needling me by now."

After all, her and Cole's relationship was old news. They had returned from Italy six weeks ago, and while their days were dedicated to running their respective businesses, nights and weekends were devoted to each other. In fact they hadn't spent a night apart since reuniting in Milan, dividing their time between her home and his town house.

Sage couldn't remember ever being happier. Neither could Amelia, who reminded her daily that she'd predicted a romance between them before they'd even met.

"Nope. Never gets old," Amelia confirmed. "What was it I told you again the day Cole first called?"

The man in question strode through the door of Sage's office door. "A tall, good-looking millionaire will be smit-

ten by her photo, fall hopelessly in love and then proceed
to sweep her off her feet," Cole answered the question.

Amelia crossed her arms. "You know the rules, Mr.
Sinclair," she scolded. "You're aren't supposed to come
in this office until we make sure there aren't any Stiletto
secrets on Sage's desk."

Cole raised a brow at the use of her actual name.
"Sage?"

Sage watched the smug look return to her assistant's
face. "Nobody calls her general anymore," the young
woman said. "Ever since you two got together, she's gone
from grizzly bear to teddy bear." Amelia inclined her head
in a short bow. "The entire Stiletto team is in your debt."

Sage stood and rounded her desk. In an instant, she was
in Cole's arms. He captured her lips in a kiss that didn't end
until she heard Amelia's dreamy sigh in the background.

"Is your boss free for lunch today?" As always, Cole
directed his question at Amelia, who knew her schedule
better than she did.

"No. She has three appointments this afternoon," the
young woman said. "And your *nooners*…uh, I mean
lunches always turn into three-hour affairs."

Sage glanced at her watch and then at her assistant.
There was one subject she'd retained her grizzly-bear attitude toward.

"I'm headed to class now," Amelia said.

"Good," Sage said. "Shut the door behind you."

With the door closed, Sage gave Cole a real kiss. One
filled with the soul-deep passion she felt for him.

"What if I promise to be good, and have you back at
work in an hour?"

Sage felt his growing hardness pressed against her. Her
entire body wanted to believe him, but she knew better.
Plus, during work hours, Stiletto business took precedence

over sexy business. "You're always good, but we've never been back in an hour."

Cole sighed and released her. Sage retreated behind her desk, using it as a physical barrier between herself and temptation.

"I had a surprise for you, but I guess it'll just have to wait until tonight," he said.

Sage's eyes narrowed. "I hope you didn't go out and buy me anything. If you did, you'll just have to take it back to whatever pricey store you got it from," she said. "I don't want anything from you, but you."

Cole's face creased with the familiar frown that crossed his face whenever the subject came up. It was the only thing they disagreed on. "You've told me enough times," he said.

Then he leaned over her desk and kissed her forehead. "I said I have a surprise for you, I didn't say I bought you anything."

Sage opened her mouth to tell him he had better not have, but he pressed his forefinger to her lips to silence her.

"My place. Tonight," he said.

She nodded mutely.

Cole looked down at a report on her desk, and she swiftly swept it into her top drawer.

"You know the rules," she said. "We don't discuss business."

"Then I guess you don't want to tell me who your appointments are with this afternoon," he said.

Sage wasn't even sure herself. As she continued her efforts to stop micromanaging and free her employees up to do their jobs, Amelia had a more active role in determining who and what was worth Sage's time.

She leaned forward and crossed her arms on her desktop. "I'll tell you right after you tell me all about the Espresso business you handled this morning."

"Touché, Ms. Matthews," Cole said. "I'll see you tonight."

"Want me to bring Chinese or pizza?"

"Pizza," he said. "And those sexy heels you're wearing."

Sage watched his retreating back and began counting the minutes until she'd see him again tonight.

Two appointments later, she glanced at her watch, eager to get her third and last one of the day behind her. Right on cue, Amelia walked through her door followed by a man Sage recognized.

"Your next appointment is here," her assistant said. "Sean Cox of Force Cosmetics."

Chapter 18

Cole heard Sage's key in the lock of his front door that evening and looked up from the furniture he'd spent the past half hour rearranging.

"Upstairs," he called out to her from the master bedroom.

"Want me to bring the pizza up?"

"Just yourself."

Her footsteps sounded on the staircase leading to the second floor of his three-story town house, and Cole exhaled. He hoped Sage would be pleased with the surprise as well as other things he had in store for her tonight.

He met her at the threshold of the bedroom.

"Sorry I'm late." She chewed at her bottom lip.

"Everything, okay?" Cole asked, his protective instincts on full alert.

She shrugged off the question, but worry lingered in her eyes. "Just work stuff."

They'd agree on the flight home from Milan that if they were going to pursue a relationship, conversations about their respective businesses were off-limits. They were lovers, but they were still competitors.

"Well, let's see if I can't take your mind off Stiletto," Cole said. "Close your eyes."

She did as he asked. He grasped her hand and led her into the bedroom.

"Okay, you can open them now," he said, and then held his breath waiting on her reaction.

Sage gasped and a delighted expression replaced the worry he'd seen on her face. "Oh, my God. It's exactly like the one…"

"No," he interrupted. "It's the same one."

Cole looked from the grin on her pretty face to the armchair he'd had shipped here from his Milan condo.

"I'm assuming the bottle of champagne and two glasses on the table next to it are for us to celebrate being reunited with our favorite piece of furniture," she said.

The mischievous spark Cole had grown to love as much as he loved her gleamed in her brown eyes. He sat down in the chair and patted his lap. "Come sit with me," he said. "I have something to talk to you about."

Sage shed her coat and tossed it on the bed. She raised a brow. "Will I need my underwear for this *talk*?"

"For now," he said.

Sage sat in the space next to him on the large chair. "What's wrong?"

"Our living situation," Cole said. "I don't want to do this anymore."

"I don't understand," she said.

"Two nights at your place, another night at mine." He cupped her cheek with his palm, and their gazes locked. "I want us to have one place. Our place. With our kitchen, our television with our remote control to fight over and most of all, our bed to share every night."

Sage blinked. A hesitant smile touched her lips. "You want us to move in together?"

"I do. We've proved over these past weeks that we can keep our business lives from interfering with what we have together," Cole said. "But I want to share more than just housekeeping, Sage. I'm asking for forever. I'm asking you to be my bride."

The moments it took for her to absorb his proposal seemed endless as Cole waited on a response. Tears brimmed in her eyes, before a single one splashed onto the hand holding her cheek.

She kissed his hand and nodded. "Yes." Her voice cracked with emotion.

Cole reached into his shirt pocket and retrieved the ring resting against his heart. He saw Sage's eyes light up, and he knew he'd selected the right one.

Taking her hand, he slid the pear-shaped ruby, which was flanked by two diamonds, onto her finger. "I chose a ruby ring because you made red my favorite color."

"It's beautiful." She held her hand up. "I love it, and I love you." She continued to stare at the ring as the stones glittered under the bedroom lights.

"Now that I'm officially your fiancé, there's something we need to get straight from the start," Cole said.

Sage looked past her ring at his face. "You put this ring on my finger, not through my nose." She arched a brow. "You're not the boss of me."

He leaned over and kissed her sassy, red-slicked mouth. "We're partners in this life, Sage. There are no bosses," he said. "However, I am going to find you the biggest, the glitziest, the most luxurious house in Nashville."

She opened her mouth to protest, but he continued. "I'm

buying it outright and handing you the deed. It'll be yours free and clear." Cole grasped her hand and gently squeezed it. "So you will always have a home of your own that you'll never be displaced from."

She opened her mouth again.

Cole cut her off before she could protest. "This is the one thing I won't compromise on," he said. "Nor will I take no for an answer."

"I wasn't going to say no." She squeezed his hand back. "All I wanted to say was thank you, and that I love you."

Cole patted his lap. "Why don't you climb aboard and tell me just how much."

Sage's dress gathered around her parted thighs as she sat astride him. She wrapped her arms around his neck. "Will I need my underwear for this part of our discussion?"

Cole grinned. "Absolutely, not."

Chapter 19

Sage stared at the clock, watching the glowing digital numbers change in the darkness.

She was in the bed beside the man she loved and could feel the weight of his ring on her finger. They'd been engaged three days now, yet the joy she'd found in her personal life didn't keep her work worries at bay.

Force Cosmetics can be your best friend or your worst enemy. Sean Cox's words crept into her dreams and stole any chance of sleeping.

She'd been a fighter her entire life, and she'd fight this, too. She just had to figure out how. Sage lifted Cole's arm and gently extricated herself from his embrace. It was three in the morning, and she didn't want to wake him. After all, this wasn't his problem.

"I'm awake." Cole's deep voice pierced the silent night.

"Go back to sleep," Sage said. "I'm just headed downstairs to make some chamomile tea." They were staying at his town house tonight. Over the weeks, she'd become as comfortable here as she felt at her house.

Before she could get out of bed, Cole threw back the covers and switched on the bedside lamp. "I'll make you a cup of tea," he said. "And when I come back with it, I want to know exactly what's kept you awake the past three nights."

Sage sighed wearily and rested her back against the headboard. Stiletto wasn't Cole's concern. When he returned with her tea, she'd simply tell him so.

Minutes later, Sage took a tentative sip of the hot brew. Cole sat down beside her. He wore pajama bottoms and his hard, muscled chest was bare.

"What going on, Sage?" he asked. When she didn't immediately answer, he continued. "I noticed you were distracted before I proposed, but I thought it was simply a rough day at work and let it go. Now you've barely slept in three nights. Talk to me."

She swallowed another sip of tea. "It's Stiletto business."

"When you're picking at your dinner and not sleeping nights, it becomes my business," he said.

"I'm the CEO of Stiletto. It's *my* company, and *I'll* handle the problem," she insisted.

Cole took the mug and sat it on the bedside table. "You see these shoulders?"

Sage took in the breadth of his broad, strong shoulders and nodded. He patted one with his hand. "Right here is where you lay your troubles. *All of them*."

She started to refuse again.

"Trust me, Sage," he said.

Sage closed her eyes briefly and blew out a breath. "Sean Cox came to my office three days ago. Force wants to buy Stiletto."

Cole nodded, his lips pressed into a firm line.

"You don't seem surprised." It had been the first reaction Sage had expected from him.

He rubbed at the back of his neck. "I'm not. After we saw Sean in Milan, I suspected they'd were looking to acquire both Stiletto and Espresso."

"Has Cox contacted you yet?"

Cole shook his head. "But if he's in town, I'm sure it won't be long."

Sage hadn't wanted to talk about this with him, but now that they were, there was no reason not to tell him the rest. "They're offering a quarter of the amount of money you did for it."

Cole nodded. Again he didn't appear taken aback. "First, Sean made you a lowball offer, then he also offered you the 'opportunity' to continue to run your company as their employee for a six-figure salary," he said. "However Force, as the new owner, would have the final approval over any major decisions."

"That's exactly what he said." Sage reached for the mug on the bedside table and took another sip from it. "But how did you know?"

"Because I trained him. He's doing my old job," Cole said. "What came next was a warning about Force either being your friend or your enemy."

She wrapped her hands around the mug, absorbing its warmth. Maybe she should have confided in Cole earlier. He was certainly familiar with Force's playbook. Perhaps he could have told her days ago that Sean's warning was just an idle threat and put her mind at ease.

"So he's just trying to scare me, right?"

"It wasn't a threat, Sage," he said. "It's a promise."

"I turned down the offer. Force can't make me sell my company to them."

"But they can make you wish you had," Cole said. "For example, do you remember the organic brand Naturally Glamorous Cosmetics?"

"You mean, Nature's Glam, don't you?"

"Exactly," Cole said. "Years ago, I made the owners of Naturally Glamorous Cosmetics an offer similar to the one Sean made you, which they turned down. Force started up Nature's Glam, with branding and packaging similar to Naturally Glamorous, and they threw tons of money into it. A small company, Naturally Glamorous ended up going out of business."

"B-but they should have taken them to court." Sage was outraged on the smaller company's behalf, and at the same time, terrified about Force doing the same thing to her company. "I would have sued their asses off."

"They tried that," Cole said. "Force's legal department overwhelmed their lawyers with delays, hearings and other very expensive red tape. The company went belly-up fighting them while Force's version of them is still going strong."

"It's not fair," Sage said, already knowing life wasn't fair. However, Stiletto was the only thing in the world she could call hers. She couldn't hand it over without a fight.

She sighed. "You don't think I can survive a battle with them, do you?"

She searched Cole's face for signs of hope. Instead, he gave her facts.

"Force Cosmetics has twenty-five cosmetic and skincare brands, including their own, and forty-two thousand employees worldwide. Last year, they had eleven billion dollars in sales," he said.

Sage hands trembled as the facts sank in, and Cole took the nearly empty mug from her hands and sat it on the night table. "Whether I sell to them or not, I'm screwed."

Then she recalled Cole was expecting a similar offer for his family's business. She also remembered why his mother had started Espresso, and why it was so important for him to restore it to its former glory.

She touched a hand to his shoulder, the one he'd told her she could rest her troubles upon. "What about Espresso?"

He covered the hand she placed on his shoulder with his own. "My personal resources and familiarity with Force's tactics puts Espresso in a better position to fend them off than Stiletto." He shrugged. "But I don't know for how long."

"Stiletto's mine. I won't let anyone take it from me. I won't let them win," Sage said, the words for herself as much as Cole.

He took her hand in his. "The bottom line is I don't think either of our companies going it alone can survive this."

"I'm not following you."

Cole looked down at their joined hands, before his gaze locked with hers. "I'm suggesting we merge Espresso and Stiletto."

Sage blinked, unable to believe what she was hearing. "I thought you understood that I don't want to turn my company over to anyone."

"That's not what I'm saying at all."

"Aren't you?"

"Hear me out," Cole said.

She nodded once, fighting off the trickle of ugly suspicion creeping into head.

"I'm talking about bringing in Stiletto as a division of Espresso, like our Sanctuary spas. You'd continue to run it as you do now."

"Sounds a lot like Force's offer," Sage grunted. "Stiletto wouldn't be mine anymore, and I'd be your employee."

"It's nothing like Force's offer. I'm not talking about bringing you in as an employee. I want you to be a partner in the Espresso empire with equal interest and voting power as my family and me. I'd have to get the approval of Victor and my sisters, but I'm positive they'd agree."

Sage's journey to get her company where it was today unfolded in her head.

The sacrifice.

The struggle.

Most of all, the fact that Stiletto Cosmetics was the only thing in the world that belonged to her and her alone.

"But I'd have to give up Stiletto," she whispered.

"You'd have to *share* Stiletto, just like we'd be sharing Espresso with you." Cole's face looked hopeful as he squeezed her hand. "Share the responsibilities, share the problems as well as the successes because that's what families do. The combined companies would be a family business. You'll be family, Sage."

She listened as he continued.

"Maybe it's unrealistic to think we can take on Force," he said. "But I think you're the savviest, smartest, most innovative businesswomen I've ever met, and I believe together, there isn't anything we can't accomplish."

Realization dawned as he spoke, and Sage's trickle of doubt became a flood, overwhelming even the heartfelt sincerity she heard in his voice. She didn't like what she was thinking, but she couldn't help suspecting him all the same. "You said earlier you'd been expecting something like this to happen since Milan. Is that why you asked me to marry you? So you could finally get your hands on Stiletto?"

Cole flinched as if she'd slapped him across the face, and he dropped her hand. "Is that what you really believe?"

She saw the pain in his eyes and averted hers.

"Look at me." His deep voice lacked the warmth it had held just seconds ago. "I asked you to marry me because I love you, and I thought you loved me, too."

"I do love you."

"Trust is a component of love, Sage. You can't truly have one without the other. I trust you enough to offer you my heart, my last name and a piece of the only thing I have left of my parents, their legacy."

Cole placed his hands lightly on her arms. "Before we can take this relationship any further, I need the answer to this question," he said. *"Do you trust me?"*

The intensity in his dark brown eyes told her exactly what was at stake. However, he wanted something from her she couldn't give up. *To anyone.*

"I can't," Sage whispered.

Cole dropped his hands from her arms. The raw hurt in his eyes made her turn away as he rose from the bed.

"Then we don't have anything."

Chapter 20

Cole stared at the phone on his desk. Everything in him wanted to pick it up and call Sage, if only to hear her voice.

A week had passed since she'd placed her engagement ring on the bedside table, left his town house and his life. A week of days he'd crammed with as much work as he could and nights he couldn't sleep for thinking of her. Longing for her.

He snatched up the cordless phone and got as far as punching in the first two numbers before replacing it on its base. She'd made herself clear during their last conversation. There was nothing left to say.

She doesn't trust you.

The realization cut deep, even deeper than when he'd discovered his mother hadn't trusted him. The two women who had meant the most to him, to whom he had only given his best, had both regarded him the same way.

Untrustworthy.

A brief knock sounded on his door, and Loretta walked in. The sparkle of the earrings and necklace, he'd selected for her at the Buccellati boutique in Milan, caught his eye. She'd worn them every day since she'd opened the box.

"Sean Cox is here," she said.

"Send him in," Cole said.

The older woman hesitated. "Can I get you anything?" Her gravelly voice was filled with concern.

Cole wanted to tell her to go back to being her annoying, cantankerous self. With everything else in his life turned upside down, he needed something to remain steady.

"I'm good," he said aloud.

After an awkward greeting, Sean sat in the chair across from his desk. His former protégé was nervous.

He was about to launch into his spiel, but Cole held up a hand to stop him. "I know what you're going to say, because I taught you every word."

"Then I'll get right down to the terms of our offer for Espresso," Sean said.

"Save it. Espresso Cosmetics isn't for sale at any price, under any circumstances."

Sean eyed him across the desk. "You trained me, Cole, so I don't have to tell you what comes next, but I will anyway as a reminder. If we can't buy you, we'll break you."

Cole had used the same line himself, while working at Force. However, he'd never had it turned on him.

A phrase of Sage's popped into his head. It felt like the perfect reply. Cole leaned back in his chair and crossed his arms over his chest. "Bring it," he said.

His chest tightened at the memories the phrase brought rushing to his head.

Sean blinked. "That's exactly what Sage Matthews told me when I was in her office." He shook his head. "Wow, you two really are well matched."

Cole had thought so, too. Turned out he was wrong.

"But even with your vast resources and wealth, Force is bigger and worth even more," Sean said. "You can't win."

Their conversation gave him a momentary flashback of another one. The one between him and Sage when he'd initially offered to buy Stiletto. He'd been even more condescending than Sean.

First he and now Force had come after Stiletto. No wonder Sage was so defensive and protective of the company she'd built...*and wary.*

For the first time since their breakup, Cole wondered if he'd misjudged her. He'd gone on and on about trust, but hadn't given her the benefit of the doubt.

The man Cole had mentored cleared his throat. "I guess that concludes our business." He started to stand but hesitated and sat back down. "You know, I'm just doing my job here. It's not personal—just business."

"I get that," Cole said. "Still, I need you and Force to back off Sage and Stiletto."

"I can't do that," Sean said.

Cole found himself issuing his own warning. One he didn't know exactly how he'd back up, but he would. Even if it took every nickel he had in the bank.

"Then expect a hell of a battle on your hands in Nashville."

Sage watched Shelia retreat from her office and suppressed a twinge of guilt.

Shaking if off, she returned her attention to her computer monitor. What did she have to feel guilty about anyway? Stiletto was her company, and she would run it the way she saw fit.

Over a week had passed since her breakup with Cole and misery, along with her fears over Force Cosmetics, had resurrected her tendency to micromanage and control every aspect of her business. It had intensified to the point her employees were probably calling her worse names than General behind her back.

Sage sighed. What choice did she have? Now that Stiletto was in Force Cosmetics' crosshairs, she had to make sure everything was perfect, and the only way to ensure that was to handle it on her own.

It didn't have to be this way, a voice inside her whispered. *You had the perfect partner, and you chose to go it alone.*

She glanced down at her hand. She'd only worn Cole's ring for three blissful days. Still, she missed the solid weight of it on her finger. She missed having him in her life.

Sage's office door opened and Amelia stormed through it. "You've gone too far this time, General." She planted her fists on her nonexistent hips. "I just got back from class to find Shelia in the bathroom in tears."

"You mean the Shelia who called me names behind my back and locked me in a closet?" Sage replied.

"I thought that was ancient history, and you and I both know she's a hard worker who cares about this company. We all do, despite your making it extremely difficult lately. Ever since you and Cole broke up, you've been acting like a big…"

Sage held up a warning hand. "Watch it, Amelia," she said in the firmest tone she'd ever used with the young woman. "This has nothing to do with Cole. You know better than anyone the kind of pressure I'm under now that Force Cosmetics is looking to come after this company."

Her assistant sighed heavily. Her hands dropped to her sides. She walked over to Sage's desk. "You can't do this alone. You don't have to do this alone," she said. "That's why we're all here."

"But ultimately this company is my responsibility," Sage said.

"When you began learning to trust the team you put together to do their jobs, did they ever once let you down?"

Sage didn't have to answer. They both knew they hadn't.

"Also, did you know there was an error made last week on a packaging order from China?" Amelia asked. "We nearly ended up with a million eye shadow pans instead of a hundred thousand. I don't have to tell you how much that would have cost Stiletto."

A small fortune, Sage thought.

She was on the verge of demanding to see the employee responsible when she remembered handling that particular order herself. She'd stayed at the office until midnight that night because she hadn't wanted to go home and face an empty house without Cole.

The look on her assistant's face confirmed that Amelia was well aware who had made the error.

"But how…"

"Shelia discovered it," Amelia said. "She noticed how exhausted you were from the long hours you've been putting in here and took the initiative to double-check the order. She didn't want me to mention it to you because she knew you were going through a rough time."

Sage closed her eyes briefly. When she opened them she couldn't quite meet her assistant's gaze. Shelia had not only done her own job, she'd stepped in and done hers, too. "And I just took her head off over something insignificant," she said to herself more than Amelia.

Sage thought briefly of Cole and how much she respected him for making a special trip to her office that day to admit he was wrong. That was the day she'd fallen for him.

She rounded her desk and walked past Amelia.

"Where are you going?" her assistant asked.

"To apologize to Shelia for underestimating her and to try to make amends," Sage called over her shoulder as she left her office for the ladies' room.

Shelia wasn't the only one Sage had treated badly and needed to make amends to. She just hoped it wasn't too late.

Chapter 21

"You look like hell, son."

Cole didn't doubt Victor's word when he ran into him in the lobby of the Espresso building the next morning. After tossing and turning most of the night, he'd finally fallen into a fitful sleep only to be awakened by his alarm clock an hour later.

He'd been dreaming of Sage, all decked out in red with sky-high heels and hair as wild and untamable as the woman herself.

"Why don't you come stay at the house for a while to get your mind off things," Victor suggested. By things, Cole knew he meant his broken engagement. "There's plenty of room, and it would be good to have you at home again."

Cole appreciated the offer, but he was too old to go running home to his stepdad. "I'll be okay, Vic," he said. "How about I come out there for dinner one day his week."

His stepfather's eyes lit up. "I'd like that. It's been pretty lonely rattling around in that big house all these years without your mother and you kids." The older man shrugged. "I've even been thinking about dating again, which I know sounds ridiculous at my age."

At the bank of elevators, Cole jabbed the button with the arrow pointing up. Again, only one of the three was working. With Force Cosmetics targeting Espresso, the building issue would have to remain on the back burner for now.

"So what do you think?" Victor asked.

"About what?" Cole said absently as they boarded the elevator car.

"Your old man dating again."

"I think it's way overdue. You should have gotten back into circulation years ago."

His stepfather shrugged. "But I don't even know where to start."

With his own love life in a shambles and the woman he loved no longer sharing his bed, Cole was in no position to offer advice. However, all the older man was really looking for was encouragement.

The elevator dinged and the doors opened on the eleventh floor.

"Next time you see a woman you're attracted to, ask her out," Cole said. "It's that simple."

"Thanks. I'm going to do just that."

Cole nodded as he pushed open the door to the executive level's outer office. Victor's problem was easy to solve. Now he had to figure out a solution to his own relationship, not that he even had one anymore.

"Morning." Loretta was already at her post. She inclined her head toward the waiting area. "Someone here to see you."

A tall, honey-skinned blonde, reminiscent of Beyoncé,

sat in a chair flipping through a magazine. Familiar eyes lit up as she spotted them, but Cole couldn't place them.

Victor cleared his throat. "Well, well, well. I think it's time your old dad got himself back into circulation."

"Hold up a sec, Vic," Cole said. He couldn't put his finger on it, but something about this woman didn't sit right.

"Step aside, son," his stepfather said. "She may be a little young for me, but I've waited long enough."

Ignoring him, Victor went into waiting area. The Beyoncé doppelganger stood, towering over his stepfather. Cole continued to stare as the two talked, trying to work out in his head where he'd seen the woman before. She wore a leather pencil skirt and pumps. *Very large pumps on very big feet.*

Loretta snorted. Cole turned to find an uncharacteristic grin on her face, and then looked back at the woman his stepfather was practically fawning over.

Good Lord, that was no woman, Cole realized. It was Freddy Finch!

"You'd better stop Victor before he tries to 'put a ring on it.'" Loretta's gravelly laugh filled the office.

"Freddy," Cole called out, eating up the space between his secretary's desk and the waiting area in two long strides.

"Mr. Sinclair," Freddy slipped from the falsetto he'd been using with Victor into his masculine voice. "They're shooting my first YouTube video for Espresso today, and I thought I'd stop by and show off your sister's handiwork."

Freddy spun around, and Cole watched his stepfather's jaw slacken.

"You look great, man," Cole said. "Tia outdid herself."

"Freddy isn't short for Fredricka, is it?" Victor asked.

"I'm afraid not." Cole shook his head, his own bruised heart going out to the older man.

"Well, I'm off." Freddy leaned over and kissed Victor on top of his graying head. "Thanks for the offer. If I were a woman I'd definitely take you up on it."

Still wearing a stricken expression, Victor headed for his office, only pausing at Loretta's desk. "Not. One. Word." He growled at the secretary and went into his office, closing the door behind him.

Frowning at a grinning Loretta, Cole went into his own office. He clicked the mouse to rouse his computer and slid behind his desk. At least the Espresso Granny problem would soon be resolved.

Cole felt confident that, once Granny's makeover videos hit YouTube, Freddy and Espresso would be an internet sensation.

Loretta's gravelly cackle sounded from the outer office. Cole exhaled. She'd enjoyed a good laugh at Victor's expense, but enough was enough. He marched out of his office to tell her to knock it off, but stopped short in the doorway.

Sage.

Clad in a red minidress with indecently high heels, she stood at his secretary's desk, holding an open green-and-white box bearing the logo of his favorite doughnut shop. Cole struggled to maintain his cool while his pulse skyrocketed.

Loretta plucked a glazed donut out of the box. "He's in there," she said, so focused on the doughnut, she didn't see him standing in the doorway. "Go on in."

Sage turned toward the door. She blinked at the sight of him and began gnawing at her bottom lip. Cole watched her incline her head toward the box. "I brought you breakfast," she said, tentatively. "But I had to bribe your secretary with one of the doughnuts to see you."

"Come in," Cole said.

Sage picked up a bouquet of yellow flowers from Loretta's desk. They looked exactly like the ones he'd brought her. "These are for you," she said, as she walked through the door of his office.

Cole took the flowers and closed the door behind her. "Thanks," he said, looking at the bouquet in his hand. "It's good to see you."

"Have a doughnut?" she asked.

Cole shook his head and an awkward silence that had never existed between them before ensued. They just stood and stared at each other.

"Sage."

"Cole."

They both spoke at the same time.

"You go first," Cole conceded.

Sage looked down at the box in her hand. "I'm here to ask for a do over. I want to turn back time to the last night we were together so I can say the words I should have said, if I hadn't allowed fear and insecurity to steal my voice. My heart has been paying the price for it ever since."

Cole took the box from her hand and placed it and the flowers on his desk. He faced her. "I want that do over, too," he said. "So I can rephrase the question."

He rested his hands lightly on her arms and their gazes connected. "Do you trust *us*, Sage? Do you trust how much I love you?"

"With everything in me," she replied. "And with everything I have."

Pulling her into his arms, Cole kissed her. A soul-deep kiss that was both a healing balm for the heartache they'd caused each other, and a promise to face whatever came at them in the future *together*. When they finally came up for air, Cole reached into his shirt pocket and retrieved her engagement ring.

"How did you know I'd come here today?" Sage asked.

"I didn't. I've carried it with me every day since we broke up, praying I'd be able to put it back where it belonged." He slid the ring onto her finger and then kissed her hand.

"The only time I want that ring to move on your finger is when it's time for me to add your wedding band," he said. "Is that clear, General?"

Sage stared at the ring a few moments, then back at him. "Whatever you say, Admiral," she said.

Epilogue

"I still don't believe it." Cole said.

Sage leaned back on her new husband's naked chest after spending their first few hours as man and wife in the bedroom of his town house, enjoying their absolute favorite chair.

"That we're married?" Sage held her hand up to look at her engagement ring, to which Cole had added a diamond-and-ruby-encrusted wedding band this afternoon.

"No, that I would have given you the biggest, most extravagant wedding this town has ever seen, and you chose the judge's chambers at the courthouse."

Sage shook her head. "I told you, all I want is you," she said. "Besides, after we get the Espresso-Stiletto merger underway, we'll be spending an entire month in Italy for our honeymoon."

Cole nuzzled her neck. "I can hardly wait."

Sage tilted her head back and looked up at him. "Do you regret not making our wedding day a big splashy affair?"

"Maybe just a little."

"Really?" Sage asked.

Cole shrugged. "Then I'd have a video of the expression on the judge's face after you promised to love, cherish and *bring it* for as long as we both shall live."

"A vow I intend to keep," Sage promised again. "I just hope you can handle it."

* * * * *

TAMING HER BILLIONAIRE

YAHRAH ST. JOHN

To my husband Freddie Blackman,
you light up my life.

Chapter 1

Maximus Xavier Knight stared at the beautiful woman who'd just entered the library of his family's estate for the reading of his father Arthur Knight's will. Had she really just said she was his partner? Was he in some alternative universe? Surely his father's attorney, Robert Kellogg, hadn't just informed him that his father had bestowed 49 percent equally to him and his illegitimate older brother, Lucius Knight, and given this random yet stunning woman the remaining 2 percent?

One thing was for sure, she was a knockout. His eyes skimmed over her. The wrap dress she wore clung to her shapely curves, showing him she had generous breasts and hips he could grab on to and legs that went on for miles. Long, flowing black hair hung down her back in soft luxurious waves. Her smooth tapioca-colored skin looked soft to the touch. He drank in every detail, her high cheekbones, finely arched eyebrows and full kissable lips, which held a hint of pink lipstick. Her expressive large brown eyes were mascara-coated and looking at him intently.

"Maximus, I presume." She held out her hand. "Tahlia, Tahlia Armstrong."

Maximus extended his hand, cupping her small, soft one in his, and shook it. The brief contact sent an arc of desire shooting straight through him. They stared at one another for several beats before she lowered her hand, making Maximus wonder if he'd imagined the electric connection.

"Ms. Armstrong, welcome," Robert said. "I was hoping you would have come earlier."

"Sorry." Tahlia blushed. "Promptness isn't my strong suit." She found an empty chair beside his half brother, Lucius, and took a seat. She was clearly embarrassed by her tardiness but seemed to have known more than any of them did.

"Omigod!" Maximus's mother, Charlotte, cried into her handkerchief by his side. He knew she must be in shock just as he was by his father's bequest, but he was determined not to show weakness.

"Robert." Maximus remained standing and walked over to his father's longtime friend. "Is this will ironclad?"

The attorney frowned. "Meaning was your father of sound mind when he wrote it?"

"Of course he was," Lucius's mother, Jocelyn Turner, burst aloud, jumping out of her seat. "This was his way of finally acknowledging Lucius." She pointed to her son, who was still seated next to his fiancée, Naomi Brooks.

"You have no say here." Charlotte Knight stopped sniffing long enough to speak and rise from her seat to face her nemesis. "Arthur was my husband, not yours. You were nothing more than his low-rate mistress, one he couldn't bother to be seen with."

"Mother! That's enough." Maximus didn't want an all-out brawl to break out. Lucius had stood as well and stepped in front of his mother in full protective mode.

"Everyone, please," Robert spoke loudly, interrupting the crowd. "I need you all to take your seats."

Reluctantly, both mothers sat down while Maximus and Lucius remained standing. Maximus didn't know what to make of his older brother, but he knew he'd be a formidable opponent. He was six foot two with a square jaw and an athletic physique. Even though he worked out often, Maximus wasn't sure he could take him down physically, but there were other ways.

"Why would he do this?" Lucius asked, turning to Robert. "I know nothing about the shipping business, and I want no part of any inheritance Arthur Knight may have left for me."

"Good." Max smiled. He was glad to see that he and his brother were on the same page. He didn't need or want Lucius around, and apparently he felt the same way. "It's settled. You can sign over your shares and we can be done with this business."

"No!" Tahlia's voice rang out. "It's not what your father wanted."

Maximus spun around on his heel. The withering look he gave her may have frightened many an employee in his office, but not Tahlia. He guessed she was somewhere in the neighborhood of five foot nine or ten, and wasn't backing down from him even though he stood several inches taller. "And how would you know what my father wanted?"

"I'd like to know the answer to that question, as well," his mother said. Fury was etched across her face. How was it that she was in the dark about yet another woman in his father's life?

"Because he talked to me about his failure to do the right thing by his sons," Tahlia responded.

So she knew about Lucius? How long? Was she another one of his father's mistresses? She was young and incredibly beautiful. How had she gotten herself mixed up with an older married man when she could have her pick of men? A million questions scrambled Maximus's brain, but before he could fire them at her, Robert interjected.

"Everyone, I know Arthur's wishes must come as a shock to all of you," Robert stated, "but I can assure you he was of sound mind and body when he wrote this will. Further, as Ms. Armstrong has stated, it was Arthur's hope that you both could work together side by side and truly become brothers."

"Robert, you act like this is some kind of family reunion," Maximus returned, "when that's far from the case. We—" he motioned around the room "—are here because my father was a liar, a cheat and a coward. It sickens me. And only now in his death does he have the courage to speak up? This is nothing short of Shakespearean."

"Please, take some time to let all of this sink in, give it time to settle," Robert replied softly. "You'll see he was *finally* trying to be fair."

"While ripping the ground right out from underneath me? He's given a complete stranger—" Maximus responded with contempt as he pointed to Tahlia "—two percent of his company, and I want to know why."

"I don't know why," Tahlia replied, squaring her shoulders. "I certainly didn't ask him for it. I was just a friend. An ear to listen when he needed it. And vice versa. I know that may be hard or strange to believe given our age difference, but nothing untoward happened between me and Arthur. He was like a father to me, giving me advice about life, work…and I—I miss him, too…" Her voice broke, and she turned away from him, clutching her hand to her mouth.

It made Maximus feel like a heel because he'd clearly upset her when he hadn't meant to. He just wanted answers. He had a right to know why half of the company he'd devoted his life to had been given to a son his father never claimed and someone who wasn't even a member of the Knight family. He was boiling with rage, but venting at a woman wasn't his style. Nor would he give Lucius the satisfaction of seeing him falter, but one thing was for certain: he wasn't about to give up the battle for Tahlia's 2 percent, which was rightfully his.

Maximus bent down to speak to his mother, who was still reeling at the news. He whispered in her ear, trying to soothe her frayed nerves. "There's nothing we can do at this moment. Give me some time to figure this out, okay?"

She nodded.

Maximus glanced up and watched Robert pack up his briefcase and then come over to him. "Max, I'm sorry how this all turned out for you," he said. "I warned Arthur that this wasn't the best approach, and he should have discussed his choices with you sooner rather than blindsiding you."

Maximus shrugged. "Why should I be surprised, Robert? I've never been able to do enough or achieve enough to gain my father's respect, and now this? He didn't even think I could run his company."

Robert patted his shoulder reassuringly and quietly walked away.

What was he supposed to do now? Maximus's mind was jumbled as to what his next move should be. He glanced across the room and saw Lucius, Jocelyn and Naomi speaking quietly while Tahlia stood in the background, watching the entire scene. She was clearly uncomfortable to be in the middle of a family squabble. And it surprised him that he felt protective over a woman he'd just met and wanted to comfort her, but he did.

So he strolled toward her.

She smiled when he approached, and Maximus's stomach flipped. Something that never happened with other women. Usually his time spent with the fairer sex was either as a companion for an event or his bedmate. Nothing more.

Tahlia Armstrong fit neither of those categories.

"Are you all right?" he inquired.

"Shouldn't I be asking you that question?" she responded with a half smile. "I mean, I didn't have my entire life turned upside down today with no warning."

"Very true, but you also became an instant millionaire today," he said smoothly, regarding her intently. "Two percent in Knight Shipping is nothing to laugh at."

"No, I don't suppose it is," she said demurely.

And then there it was again, a hint of a blush on her rosy cheeks. She looked downward, not quite looking at him, and that was when he realized Tahlia Armstrong was flustered by him. Maximus had to figure out how to use that to his advantage.

"You should stay for dinner," he stated quietly, surprising even himself with the offer.

"D-dinner?"

He grinned. "Yes, you do eat, don't you?"

She chuckled, and Maximus had to admit he liked the sound of it. "I do."

"Then join me. I mean, me and my mother that is."

Tahlia glanced over to his brother. "Is Lucius and his family welcome to join us?"

Max bristled inwardly. He hated being backed into a corner, but in order to figure out his next move where Tahlia was concerned, he might have to tolerate a meal with his older brother and harlot of a mother. Though he had no ill will against Naomi.

"If that means you'll agree, then yes."

Tahlia smiled. She'd won a small victory in getting Maximus to agree to dinner with his brother, Lucius. When Robert had first telephoned her a couple of days ago, she'd been unprepared for the bombshell he was about to drop on her. One day she was a lowly assistant at an art gallery in Los Angeles, the next she was the owner of the gallery as well as a 2 percent partner in Knight Shipping, one of the largest shipping companies in the United States. Talk about a change in circumstances overnight! Not to mention she was finally going to get close enough to Maximus to actually have a conversation after seeing him only from afar!

Tahlia had been so shocked by the turn of events, she'd kept the news to herself and hadn't even told her mother, Sophia, or sister, Kaitlynn. How could she tell them she was tied indefinitely to the Knights and Maximus, the man she'd secretly crushed on the last year? Ever since she'd first seen him from across the room at one of the gallery's exhibit openings, he'd been on her mind. Not that he had noticed her that night. When she'd asked Robert why he was telling her in advance of Arthur's bequest, Robert indicated he thought there might trouble between the two brothers when they learned their fate and was hoping she'd play peacemaker.

It was a tall order, one which she knew wouldn't be

achieved overnight, but it was a start. They were family after all. And for some reason, Arthur, her dear friend, had chosen her to lead the effort, and Tahlia was determined not to let him down.

Tahlia tried not to show nerves as she and Maximus walked over toward Lucius and his family, but instantly a chill spiked in the air.

"Lucius." Maximus nodded in his direction.

"Max." Lucius used his youngest brother's nickname, and Tahlia felt Maximus immediately tense beside her. She was sure it was used only by family and close friends, certainly not a brother he'd known nothing about until a couple of weeks ago.

Tahlia had been horrified when she'd heard that Arthur had been caught in flagrante with Lucius's mother, Jocelyn, in a hotel room and had a heart attack. The news media had been unforgiving in their portrayal of the shipping magnate and his womanizing ways. And when the press had realized that Lucius was the product of their decades-long affair, they'd been brutal. It was no wonder both men were angry. They had a right to be. Arthur should have been honest with them much sooner.

"I've invited Ms. Armstrong," Maximus began, but she interrupted him.

"Tahlia."

Maximus nodded. "I've invited Tahlia to dinner this evening. And she thought you and your lovely fiancée might like to join us."

Tahlia frowned. She was sure she'd said Lucius's family, including his mother, but was that asking too much under the circumstances?

"That's quite generous of you, Max," Lucius replied with a wide grin. "And I'll stay if my mother is welcome."

Lucius was purposely baiting him, and Tahlia hated that she was the cause, but Maximus didn't seem fazed—or at least not that he was showing outwardly. In Tahlia's opinion, he plastered a fake smile on his face before saying, "I suppose, but it might be best to keep both our mothers on opposite sides of the table."

"That would be prudent," Lucius responded.

Soon they were all headed in the direction of the dining room. Tahlia was shocked when Maximus returned to her side after briefly speaking with his mother. She could see Charlotte Knight recoil with the turn of events as evidenced by the glare she threw in Tahlia's direction, but she remained silent and did as Maximus instructed.

Once they made it to the beautifully appointed dining area, Charlotte immediately sat at the head of the table, making it clear this was her home and they were all just visitors in it. Maximus flanked his mother to the left, leaving the seat to her right open, which Tahlia reluctantly took. Meanwhile, Lucius and his mother sat beside Tahlia while his fiancée sat next to Maximus.

A uniformed man Tahlia could only assume was the butler came to speak with Mrs. Knight. Several seconds later waitstaff entered to fill their water glasses as well as offer them wine with their meal. Other than everyone selecting their choice of red or white, the silence in the room was deafening.

"Th-thank you for having us," Tahlia offered, glancing at Charlotte. "It's really quite generous."

"Did we have much choice?" Mrs. Knight queried under her breath.

"If you don't want us here, we can leave," Lucius responded tightly from across the table, and Tahlia could feel the tension ratchet up a notch, but Maximus intervened.

"We've invited you and you're our guest," Maximus stated wanly. He turned to the company on his side. "Naomi Brooks—" he offered her his hand "—it's a pleasure to finally meet you. I've heard quite a lot about Brooks & Johnson. I believe you use their products don't you, Mother?"

He turned to Charlotte.

She gave the first sincere smile Tahlia had seen since she'd arrived. "Yes, I do. They are the only products my salon carries where I get my facials." She lightly touched her cheek. "They're really quite remarkable products."

"Thank you." Naomi smiled.

"You started the company with your best friend, yes?" Maximus inquired, sipping his wine and leaning back in his chair to regard her.

"Yes, in our apartment in college," Naomi replied.

"And turned it into a billion-dollar business," Maximus added. "You've got yourself quite a find here, big brother."

Tahlia gave Lucius a sideward glance. The love in his eyes was evident as he grinned across the table at his fiancée.

"And you?" Charlotte turned her attention to Tahlia. "What is it that you do, dear?"

"Mother," Maximus cautioned. The tone in his voice told her to tread lightly.

"I'm just being cordial," she replied, reaching for her wineglass.

"Up until recently, I worked as an assistant at Art Gallery Twenty-One."

"That was one of Father's favorite galleries," Maximus said, offering Tahlia a warm smile.

"Have circumstances changed?" Charlotte asked.

"As a matter of fact they have," Tahlia answered. "Robert informed me that Arthur was owner of the gallery and has bequeathed it to me."

A loud gasp escaped from Charlotte, but she soon recovered. "So now you own it? You must have made quite the impression on my husband." She took another sip of her red wine. "Very much like other people I know."

Her implication was clear that Arthur and Tahlia had an intimate relationship, a seedy one. Fury boiled inside Tahlia, but she needn't have worried because Jocelyn rose to the bait.

"If you're insinuating something, Charlotte," Jocelyn spoke after being silent since they were seated, "just say it. Maybe then we can all end this whole charade."

Tahlia suspected it must be very difficult for Jocelyn to sit in her former lover's home with his wife and son, knowing she'd had an affair with the man for years and produced a child. A child who was sitting beside her but had never been acknowledged, until now.

"Au contraire, contraire," Charlotte replied with a snort. "It gives me great pleasure to sit with the mistress of my lying, cheating excuse for a husband and her illegitimate offspring after you've in essence ripped *my* child's inheritance right out of his hands."

"I did no such thing!" Lucius roared from beside her. His dark eyes blazed with indignation. "I didn't ask for any of this. Neither did he." He flung his hands in Maximus's direction. "Did you know Arthur was cheating on your mother?"

Maximus glared at him, and at first Tahlia thought

he wouldn't respond, but then he shook his head. "Of course I didn't," he finally replied. His dark brown eyes were very much like Lucius's. "Do you think if I did I would have let Arthur continue to humiliate my mother with yours?"

Tahlia tried to speak. "Everyone, why don't we calm down. I think dinner is coming." Or at least the salads were. Several waitstaff entered the room carrying plates filled with mixed greens, cranberries and walnuts and what appeared to be some sort of vinaigrette. As they set a plate in front of her, Tahlia couldn't wait to dig in.

Maximus gave her a small smile from across the table, but it was pointless because Jocelyn rose to her feet. "I'm sorry, Lucius." She turned to her son. "I can't sit here and break bread with these people in A-Arthur's home. It's just too much." Seconds later, she pushed her chair back and rushed out of the dining room.

"Good riddance!" Charlotte said with a smile.

"That was uncalled for, Mother," Maximus hissed. "Apologize."

"For what? For speaking the truth in my *own* home?" she replied bitterly.

Lucius rose from his chair beside Tahlia, and she watched in horror as Naomi did the same. Despite her best efforts to bridge the gap between the brothers, it was all in vain.

"We're leaving," Lucius stated, throwing his napkin onto the table.

"You don't have to go." Tahlia attempted to save the day.

Lucius patted her on the shoulder, preventing her from getting up. Then he bent down and whispered in her ear. "Good try, ole girl, but you're going to have to do a lot better than this to get us to become a family.

C'mon, Naomi." He extended his hand to his fiancée and headed for the door.

Maximus stood as well, buttoning his suit jacket that looked sexy as hell on him, and strode confidently to the dining room door and met his brother at the exit.

"Lucius." He inclined his head. "I'm sure we'll be speaking soon."

"No doubt," Lucius replied. Seconds later he and Naomi were gone.

"Did you really have to be so gauche?" Maximus asked, turning to his mother after Lucius and his family had gone. It was only the three of them remaining.

"Quite frankly I did." She stood. "You should be happy I was willing to get through salad, given everything that woman—" she pointed to the door Jocelyn Turner had just vacated "—did to me."

"That you *let* them do to you," Maximus corrected. "Don't try to rewrite history."

"I—I'm not going to talk about this right now," Charlotte huffed. She reached for her wineglass and without another word took it along with her as she stormed out of the room.

"Was it something I said?" Tahlia asked when it was just her and Maximus alone in the dining room.

He let out a loud rumble of laughter that was so infectious Tahlia couldn't resist and joined in on the fun. Soon, they were both howling, unable to control themselves. After several moments, the chuckles finally subsided and Maximus came beside her, pulling out the chair next to her that Lucius had vacated.

"That was a complete and utter disaster," he stated unequivocally, leaning back in his chair and staring openly at her.

She nodded her agreement. "It was."

"I applaud you for trying to calm the waters, but considering the circumstances, you must know that this is an untenable situation. We are never going to be a family."

"Who says? There are all sorts of families."

"You're not really that naive are you?" Maximus inquired, peering at Tahlia. Where the hell had she come from anyway? He knew his father liked to frequent the art gallery. And now he knew she was the cause. And could he really blame his father? Tahlia Armstrong was a bombshell.

Had she, too, been carrying on an affair with his father right under their noses? Or at least under his mother's since she'd known for years about his father's affair with Jocelyn Turner. How could she stomach staying in the marriage knowing he was unfaithful?

Maximus would never have tolerated such a betrayal. When he married, *if he married*, his wife would be his and only his. He'd kill the man who dared look at her, let alone touch her. It was why he couldn't understand how his mother allowed the adultery to continue for *decades*.

"I'm not naive," Tahlia responded. "I just choose to be positive and was trying to make the best of the situation."

"Very noble, but wasted on us," Maximus replied, rising to his feet. "Can I walk you out?"

She blinked several times. Perhaps she thought they were still going to continue with dinner. Not tonight. He needed time to think and strategize his next move.

"Uh, yeah, sure," she said.

Maximus pulled her chair out and followed Tahlia as they walked down the corridor. He purposely walked behind her so he could enjoy the view of her backside.

His groin tightened as she swayed, and God help him, he wanted her.

Suddenly she stopped short and turned to him. "In the spirit of keeping the peace, I want to make it clear to you that nothing happened between your father and me."

"And you expect me to believe that?"

Her eyes narrowed. "Yes, I do, because it's the truth. When your father visited the gallery, all we did was sit and talk during his lunch hour. He was a father figure to me, Maximus. Nothing more."

"What on earth would he have to discuss with you?" As soon as he said the words, he knew they sounded harsh. "Listen, I'm sorry, all right? But even you have to see where I'm coming from. A woman I've never met had a relationship with my father that not only did no one know about, but apparently he was more caring with you than he'd ever been with me."

When they made it to the large oak door with a stained glass insert, he held it open for her, and she stepped outside. "I'm sorry. Truly sorry that Arthur wasn't more open with you and that you didn't get to know the man I knew. And th-thank you for dinner." She smiled up at him with her big brown eyes, and Max felt his manhood swell. He'd only just met Tahlia, but she was having a profound effect on him.

"It wasn't much of one, I'm afraid."

"You tried."

"Have a good night." He watched her walk to her car and shut the door. Then he headed directly for the library. He usually loved the room because it was surrounded on three sides by bookshelves up to the crown molding at the ceiling. The furniture was upholstered in rich chocolate-brown leather to match the solid oak desk his father had once used. But Maximus didn't care for any of that tonight and went straight for the wet bar. He poured himself a bourbon straight up. He walked over to the French doors across the room and opened them, staring out over the manicured great lawn. He sipped his drink and thought about his next move.

He hadn't felt such a strong physical pull toward a female in a long time, if ever. Wanting Tahlia Armstrong was irrational and not advisable. He needed to figure out how he could control her and the situation. She now owned the *two* most important percent of shares at Knight Shipping because hers was the deciding vote, thanks to his father's machinations. Had his father done this to spite him because Maximus had suggested taking Knight Shipping public when Arthur was adamantly opposed to it? Had he given Tahlia those shares to ensure it never happened? If so, she was no match for him. Expansion was inevitable, and the board now composed of Lucius and Tahlia would have to vote on it. Maximus would do *whatever* was necessary to ensure he was successful.

He'd seen the way she looked at him today. She wasn't unaffected by him either. He'd noticed earlier that she stammered whenever he came within close proximity to her. Perhaps their mutual attraction could work to his advantage. Sexing her was an intriguing possibility.

Maximus heard a noise behind him and turned to find his mother standing in the doorway. "Care to pour me one of those?" she asked, inclining her head to the drink in his hand. The red wine she'd had earlier was nowhere to be seen.

"Sure." He stepped back into the library and took care of making her a drink. Then he walked over to where she'd made herself comfortable on his father's favorite easy chair and handed her the bourbon.

"Thank you." He settled across from her in another chair, and they were both quiet for a long moment before she finally spoke. "I'm still in shock, Max. I can't believe your father did this to us."

"You mean to me," he responded. "I'm the one he pushed and pushed to be the best at everything. I'm the one he said would run Knight Shipping one day, but instead, he gives half the company to my illegitimate brother? A son he couldn't even acknowledge while he lived? A son who knows nothing about the shipping business? You have no idea what it feels like to be in my shoes, Mother." Maximus threw back the remaining bourbon in his glass and then jumped up and went to the bar for another one.

Maybe, just maybe, he could drown out the hurt and betrayal he felt at a father who'd never loved Maximus as much as he'd loved him.

"I'm so sorry, Max," his mother cried. "I thought I was doing what was best for you."

He spun around on his heel. "By staying with a man who didn't love you and pined for another woman? For what? So I could inherit the keys to the kingdom?" He chuckled wryly. "Well, you can see what good that did you. He screwed you over yet again."

"He screwed us both, Max," his mother responded tightly. "He's given half your birthright over to that no-good playboy brother of yours."

Maximus eyed her warily. "Be careful, Mother. Be very careful."

"Why? Don't tell me you're feeling sentimental about a brother you never knew you had and who's trying to take what's rightfully yours."

Maximus didn't believe for a second that was the case. Lucius had been as shocked as he was by the bequest. He hadn't known he was Arthur's son until that moment in the hospital a couple of weeks ago, when his mother had railed at him. Maximus had seen the horror that had crossed his older brother's face when the realization had sunk in that not only had his mother been carrying on an affair for decades with their father, but that he'd been the result of it. Lucius had been devastated.

Despite that, however, Maximus wasn't about to let an interloper, an outsider, walk in and take what was his. He'd been groomed his entire life to run Knight Shipping, and *no one*, brother or no brother, or their sexy partner, Tahlia Armstrong, would get in his way. He would see to it.

"Of course I'm not sentimental, Mother," Maximus responded. "But haven't you heard the old phrase 'you catch more flies with honey'? Don't worry."

Her brown eyes stared at him incredulously. "How can I not be worried when half your inheritance is being stolen?"

"We have to play it cool, Mother. Because if there's one thing I've learned in business, it's that we mustn't show our hand. I promise you, I'll get what's mine. I promise you. All in due time."

"How?"

"I have a plan."

Chapter 2

"You own Art Gallery Twenty-One?" Kaitlynn Armstrong, Tahlia's sister, stared back openmouthed as they sat at Tahlia's breakfast bar the next morning. Tahlia had stopped by Kaitlynn's apartment to tell her about the dinner at the Knights' estate and to share her amazing news and good fortune.

"Sure do," Tahlia replied with a self-satisfied smile. "Arthur Knight transferred the title to me. So now that witch Bailey will be coming to me for approval."

Tahlia was referring to her boss, Bailey Smith, who was into traditional art. Tahlia had been trying unsuccessfully to get her to branch out to show unconventional pieces. It was only when Arthur had liked a piece from an up-and-coming artist that Bailey had relented for a small showing. It was at that opening that Tahlia had first laid eyes on Maximus Knight.

She'd been setting out canapés when he'd walked into Art Gallery Twenty-One just as confident as he pleased in a designer suit, skinny tie and expensive loafers. He looked every bit the wealthy shipping magnate. From her vantage point, he'd looked serious and intent when he'd spoken to his father. Tahlia had watched him from afar, soaking in every bit of his aura, from the curly fro on his head that she would love to run her fingers through to the bushy eyebrows above sexy eyes to those sinful lips.

Unfortunately, Maximus Knight hadn't stayed long at the gallery. She'd been pulled away to help a customer, and when she'd finally looked for him, he'd been gone. But now everything had changed. Arthur's death had set her on a new path that Tahlia could only hope she could prove worthy of.

"I still can't believe it," Kaitlynn said. "Did you have any idea that Arthur Knight put you in his will?"

Tahlia shook her head. "None."

"Have you told Mom yet?"

"No, not yet. She's at work now," Tahlia responded. Their mother, Sophia, was an RN at UCLA Medical Center and had just started her evening shift. And Tahlia couldn't possibly tell her this news over the phone. *This news* had to be delivered in person.

Kaitlynn glanced down at her Apple watch. "Oh, yeah, right. I'd forgotten. She'll just die when she hears the news."

"Just like I did," Tahlia responded. "It's so surreal."

"Why do you think Arthur did it?"

Tahlia shrugged. "All I can think of is that I was kind to him. Sometimes he'd come in on his lunch break to just stare at the paintings. He'd be so wistful that I'd come over and chat with him. I could tell something weighed on his mind heavily at times, but he never shared with me the full details."

"So you had no idea he was carrying on an affair?"

"Of course not. But I did know he had another son whom he had treated unfairly. I suspect Arthur regretted his actions, which is why he's taken such drastic actions now in his will."

"But to make *you* the deciding vote?" Kaitlynn said. "That's heady stuff. He clearly thought very highly of you, sis."

"I feel honored," Tahlia said, lightly touching her chest. "And scared out of my wits. I mean, Kaitlynn, I know nothing about the shipping business."

"Perhaps Maximus will teach you." She grinned with a wink. "I think you'd like that, wouldn't you?"

Tahlia jumped up from her stool to cover the blush she could feel creeping up her cheeks. "Why would you say that?"

"C'mon," Kaitlynn teased. "I've seen how you react whenever Maximus is mentioned in the news or on social media. You've got a crush on him," she said in a singsongy tone.

"Do not," Tahlia said, spinning around to face her.

"Preach to the choir because I'm not listening." She covered her ears with her hands.

"Even if I did," Tahlia responded with her hands on her hips, "I doubt Maximus would be interested in a peon like me."

"I beg to differ. You're in a position of power now, and Maximus will have no choice but to stand up and take notice of you."

"Because of the shares I have?"

"You're the deciding vote," Kaitlynn responded. "He'll want to keep you close. The question is how close will you let him get?"

Tahlia smiled at Kaitlynn's teasing tone. She'd wanted Maximus to see her, but she would rather it was because he genuinely found her interesting, not because he thought she was a pawn he could use. But perhaps if they spent some time together he'd see her as something more than a vote in his favor. Only time would tell just what her relationship with Maximus would be.

"This is stunning news, Max," his best friend, Griffin Cooper, stated when they met up on Sunday at the Los Angeles Country Club. Now seated in the main dining room, they were sharing breakfast over a cup of coffee. They'd forgone their weekly racquetball session to just sit and talk.

"You're telling me," Maximus replied. "I knew my father was a cunning liar, but I never in my wildest dreams imagined he would cut me out of what's rightfully mine."

"You've worked your butt off for Knight Shipping," Griffin concurred. "It's not fair."

"No, it isn't." Maximus seethed in his seat. He'd been awake for nearly half the night mulling the situation over, remembering everything he'd ever done to win his father's favor. The countless times he'd made sure to excel in school, to be the best in sports, to get into Harvard Business School, and still it was never quite enough. His father always pushed and pushed him. And for what? So in the end he could share running Knight Shipping with Lucius? And Tahlia Armstrong? Where in the heck had she come from?

"Why do you think he did it?"

"At first, I was so sucker punched, I couldn't think of a single reason why. And then it came to me."

"What came to you? Don't leave me in suspense."

"Tahlia may think my father's motives were altruistic in giving her those shares. And maybe they were." Maximus's lips twisted in a cynical smile. "But I suspect the old man wanted to ensure that I never took Knight Shipping public."

Griffin's expression grew still, and he became serious. "Do you really think he went that far?"

Maximus shrugged.

"What are you going to do?" Griffin inquired. "Contest it? I would imagine your father made the will iron-clad." Griffin was an attorney at a well-known law firm in Los Angeles.

Maximus nodded. "Robert said as much."

"So? Do you think Lucius will sign over his shares?"

"It's doubtful," Maximus responded. Despite the fact that Lucius hadn't asked for or even wanted the inheritance, Maximus doubted he'd walk away from it. His older brother struck him as the proud type. He'd keep the shares, just to show Maximus that he could and to prove to himself that he could run it. He'd done his research, and Lucius hadn't become a corporate raider by chance. Lucius had obtained an MBA before investing in his first business venture, an up-and-coming technology firm. The gamble paid off, and he'd made his first million before he was thirty.

Unlike Maximus, who'd been groomed since he was young that one day he'd take over the company Arthur had started with his mother Charlotte's help. Oh, yes, Maximus had learned years ago that his father had married into money and had used her family's money to start Knight Shipping. No doubt, that was why he'd stayed married to her because he didn't want to lose his empire. Yet, he continued his affair with Jocelyn Turner, the woman he'd truly loved.

It burned in Maximus's craw.

"Max?" Griffin interrupted his thoughts. "What are you thinking? I can see your mind spinning a mile a minute. Are you thinking about the overseas deal and how you're going to salvage it?"

Knight Shipping had been offered lucrative contracts to transport electrical machinery and luxury vehicles, but they needed capital to expand, especially if Knight Shipping wanted to compete with the other cargo and shipping companies in the Port of Los Angeles marketplace.

"I am thinking about it. But there's no getting around Lucius," Maximus responded, "at least for the moment. I'll have to choose a different route."

Griffin studied him, trying to read his next move. "The girl?"

"Bingo." Maximus smiled devilishly.

"How?"

"Get her on my side. Convince her to see things my way."

"And how do you plan to do that?" Griffin inquired, sipping his coffee.

Maximus shrugged. "It's quite easy. Seduce her."

Griffin choked on his beverage. "Excuse me?"

"You heard me. Tahlia Armstrong likes me," Maximus replied. "I sensed it yesterday when she stayed behind for dinner."

"Your mother dined with the woman who'd been carrying on an affair with her husband for years?" Griffin was aghast.

"Trust me, it didn't last long. But it was Tahlia's idea. From what I gather, my father intended her to be the peacekeeper between Lucius and me. Last night was her first attempt, which although a bust gave me just the ammunition I need to get out of this quagmire my father has left us in. I mean really, Griff, he gave both of us forty-nine percent? What was he thinking?"

"He wasn't. He felt guilty for keeping Lucius in the dark about his true identity. This was his way of making amends."

"At my expense," Max said hotly. "He could have given Lucius money, baubles, anything—even a smaller percentage of the company. Why did he have to give him an equal share in Knight Shipping? He knew how much the company meant to me. The only thing I can think of is he did this to spite me, get back at me in some way because I was never the son he really wanted."

Griffin frowned. "What do you mean?"

"Isn't it obvious? He wanted Jocelyn. He wanted their son, Lucius, but he could never have them because he was bound to my mother because her money was used to build his company."

"C'mon, Maximus. That sounds twisted. I'm sure that's not it."

"Isn't it?" Maximus had never truly felt loved by his father. Arthur had been happy to see him go away to boarding school and college. And when he'd come home, Maximus would be so happy to see him and eager to show his father the reports of how well he'd done, but Arthur could never be bothered. He was always working. For what? A company he told Max would be his, only to give half of it away to Lucius, the son he really wanted?

"Max, bro." Griffin grabbed his shoulder from across the table. "Don't. Don't do this to yourself. Don't second-guess everything that ever happened between you and your father. It'll drive you crazy."

"No crazier than learning my entire life was built on a lie," Maximus stated harshly, shrugging Griffin's hand away. "Finding out my father married my mother for her money and only stayed with her because of it.

He never loved her *or* me. We were both just a means to an end."

"Max…"

Maximus rose to his feet and buttoned his suit jacket. "Anyway, thanks for hearing out me, Griff. I guess I just needed to get some things off my chest."

Griffin stood, as well. "Of course. Anytime you need an ear, I'm here to listen."

Maximus turned to leave, but Griffin stopped him.

"What about Tahlia Armstrong? Were you serious about your intentions toward her?"

Maximus hesitated in his footsteps. No, he wasn't sure this was the right move. He didn't relish hurting anyone, least of all an unsuspecting, sweet and beautiful woman like Tahlia Armstrong, but his hands were tied. "It's the only way."

Tahlia stood outside Art Gallery Twenty-One in the Arts District on Monday morning and looked up at the white stucco two-story building. She still couldn't believe she *owned* it, lock, stock and barrel. Arthur Knight had purchased the art gallery on her behalf and bequeathed it to her in his will.

A smile formed on Tahlia's full lips. He'd done this for her. When all she'd ever done was listen to the older gentleman when he came to look at artwork. She'd had no idea that small act of kindness would lend itself to Arthur being so generous.

"How long are you going to stand outside?" asked Faith Richardson, a petite blonde with a luscious mane of hair that Tahlia would kill for. Faith was one of the main reasons she'd stayed at the gallery. In addition to sharing a love of art, they were also friends as well as coworkers. Of course, she wouldn't be a coworker for too much longer once Tahlia shared her news.

Tahlia couldn't wait for the opportunity to tell Bailey Smith who was boss now.

"Oh, I'm coming in," Tahlia said as Faith swung open the double glass doors into the gallery.

Every time she did, Tahlia loved how wide, open and airy the gallery was. With its white walls, covered with paintings and other works of art, it was her dream come true to exhibit at a place like this. She'd never imagined that one day she'd own it.

"There you are," Bailey Smith, Tahlia's boss, stated as they arrived. "You're late."

The slender brunette was wearing a scowl as Tahlia and Faith approached her, though Tahlia had to admit she was looking ever the fashionista in a navy pantsuit and cream silk top and was no doubt wearing designer heels. Meanwhile, Tahlia was her usual self in a twisted-drape pencil skirt and an off-the-shoulder sweater with a slew of dangling necklaces.

Bailey flashed a disapproving look at her ensemble before starting in on her. "How many times must I remind you about promptness, Tahlia?"

Tahlia sighed. "I've lost count." It was only a few minutes after 9:00 a.m., and there were no patrons in the gallery. Most didn't arrive until just before noon. She didn't understand why Bailey insisted on riding her. It wasn't like she didn't stay late when needed.

"Then I would think you'd remember to be on time," Bailey reminded, "but that's inconsequential. I've just been told that our new owner will be arriving to this morning's staff meeting. Come, the attorney is here."

She ushered them toward the back of the house where

Bailey's office, Tahlia and Faith's even smaller office and the small kitchenette were housed.

When she arrived, Tahlia found Robert Kellogg, Arthur's attorney, already seated. She smiled and he returned it with one of his own. Only the two of them knew what she was privy to but would soon be revealed to the group.

Tahlia took a seat at the six-seater table while Bailey sat at the head of the table with Robert and Faith flanking her to her left.

"Mr. Kellogg, we're very eager to hear news of the new owner," Bailey began. "Please fill us in."

"And I am eager to share with you," Robert returned.

"I'm just so sorry to hear of Mr. Knight's passing. He was a lover of the arts. Of course, I had no idea he actually owned the gallery." Bailey chuckled nervously.

"He preferred to keep his interests private," Robert said, looking in Tahlia's direction.

Bailey glanced at Tahlia with a raised brow. Could she tell that the gauntlet was about to drop on her? Tahlia was just happy that Robert was here to give the news.

"As I mentioned to you a couple of days ago, Ms. Smith," Robert began, "the reading of Arthur Knight's will occurred yesterday and Arthur Knight was named as owner of Art Gallery Twenty-One, and he bequeathed it...."

"Will his son Maximus be taking over the gallery?" Bailey asked, interrupting him.

"No, Arthur had someone else in mind."

Bailey's eyes lit up with anticipation. "Who, then?"

Robert turned to face Tahlia. "Ms. Smith, meet the new owner of Art Gallery Twenty-One."

"W-what?" Bailey's eyes grew wide with disbelief. "I—I don't understand."

"Omigod!" Faith's hand flew to her mouth.

"All right, then let me be clear. Arthur Knight bequeathed the gallery to Ms. Armstrong. She is the gallery's new owner." He slid the deed of ownership over to Tahlia.

"That simply can't be," Bailey said. "Why would he do such a thing? She—" Bailey motioned toward Tahlia "—is a lowly gallery assistant, while I have been running this gallery for over three years."

Robert shrugged and closed his briefcase. "I don't know what to tell you, but the will is a fait accompli. Ms. Armstrong." He glanced at Tahlia, who couldn't resist sporting a huge grin at Bailey's disbelief that *she* actually owned the gallery. "If you need anything, please—" he handed her his business card "—give me a call. Arthur asked me to be at your disposal for whatever questions you might have as you take on your new ventures."

"Ventures? As in plural?" Bailey inquired incredulously. "What else did he give you?"

"Good day." Robert nodded at Tahlia and left the room, leaving the three women sitting at the table.

"This is such great news," Faith said and rushed from around the table to give Tahlia a warm hug. "I can't believe it. You own the gallery. But why don't you seem surprised? Did you know already?"

Tahlia nodded. "I received a letter from Mr. Kellogg that Arthur requested the gallery be given to me upon his death, but I didn't have the actual paperwork until now." She held up the deed in her hand.

"You!" The one word from Bailey that came across

the table was bitter and caused Tahlia and Faith to both look up in alarm.

Bailey's normally porcelain skin was red with fury. "You own the gallery! What did you do? Sleep with the old man?" She laughed. "You must have. How else to explain why a wealthy man like Arthur Knight would give a gallery to you, a peon, a nobody."

Anger boiled in Tahlia's veins. She wouldn't be put down by this woman a second longer. She'd been Bailey's whipping boy—or girl, for that matter—for two years, but no more. "Watch yourself, Bailey. Be very, very careful before you utter another word."

"Why? Because you'll fire me?" Bailey laughed, throwing her head back. "Well, don't bother. I quit!"

"Good, you've made my life easy," Tahlia responded, facing the angry-faced woman. "I don't have to fire you. Please pack your belongings and don't let the door hit you on the way out."

Bailey took a step toward Tahlia. "You've no idea how to run this gallery. Mark my words, you'll be out of business within the year because you're a flighty ditz."

"Get out!"

"Gladly." Bailey stormed from the conference room.

Tahlia followed Bailey to her office. She watched her open and close drawers and bang items around as she packed a box. She was keeping an eye on the woman because she wouldn't put it past Bailey to try to sabotage her. Her former boss was packed in five minutes flat and stalking toward the front door, her stilettos hitting the wood floor like spikes. When the door finally slammed behind her, Tahlia let out a long sigh of relief and leaned against one of the walls.

"Wow! That was dramatic," Faith commented from behind her.

Tahlia breathed in deeply before she spoke. "Yes, it was. I just hope she wasn't right."

"Right about what?" Faith asked, folding her arms across her chest. "About you failing? That's a lot of hogwash. Bailey just had sour grapes because Arthur Knight didn't leave her the gallery. Though I shouldn't be surprised it was you. You and he always did have a special bond."

"Yeah, we did." Tahlia became wistful as she glanced at one of the benches where they used to sit. With her father gone, Arthur had been like a father figure to her, filling a void she hadn't known she'd needed filled until she had someone to confide in about her hopes, her dreams and her fears. She remembered sitting with Arthur during his lunch hour and talking at length. He hadn't wanted to go back to the office. Instead, he wished he was in the Louvre in Paris. With Lucius's mother, perhaps?

"Don't worry." Faith reached across and patted Tahlia's arm. "You'll do great. You've always had tons of great ideas that Bailey would never listen to. But this place—" she spread her arms wide "—is yours now. And you can do with it as you please. Invite whatever artists you want to exhibit."

Tahlia beamed as she stood up from the wall. "You're right. We're—" she pointed to Faith "—going to do great things here. And Bailey Smith will rue the day she ever underestimated me."

And so would Maximus Xavier Knight. If Kaitlynn was right in her assumption that he would try to charm her, then Tahlia was going to have to have her wits about her.

Chapter 3

Maximus pulled his blue Bugatti sports car in front of Art Gallery Twenty-One later that evening. He'd tried unsuccessfully to make it earlier so he could invite Tahlia out for lunch. His schedule had been an endless array of meetings as he tried to keep Knight Shipping clients calm. They were all worried with Arthur's death about the status of the company. And quite frankly, so was Maximus. How was he supposed to run a company with only half the power? He needed to be free and clear to make decisions unilaterally. But those days were gone. He'd have to consult big brother Lucius as well as Tahlia on every major decision that he made. The machinery deal had stalled, but the luxury vehicle opportunity was still on the horizon. They had to strike while the iron was hot.

Damn his father for putting him in this position!

He'd always done everything that was asked of him and more. And this was how he was repaid, with a knife in the back? Or at least that was how it felt to Maximus. While Lucius and Tahlia were laughing all the way to the bank. Speaking of Tahlia…

Maximus glanced at the whitewashed stucco building. Inside was the woman who held the key to whether his running of Knight Shipping would go smoothly or whether it would be hell on earth. He needed Tahlia on his side. He could offer to buy her shares outright, but if she said no then that would cloud anything that transpired between them after that. No, better to wait. Maximus hoped that with a little schmoozing Tahlia would vote to effectively neutralize Lucius. Just how far he would go to make that happen remained to be seen.

He'd told Griffin he intended to seduce Tahlia, but Maximus was hoping it wouldn't come to that. Maybe Tahlia would see things his way and need very little convincing. Exiting his vehicle, he strode purposefully toward the door.

The gallery was well lit with vibrant paintings adorning the walls and several sculptures strategically placed throughout the open floor plan on pedestals or suspended from the ceiling. It was nearly closing time, so there were less than a handful of people milling about the room. Maximus strolled through the gallery, peering at several pieces of artwork. He'd come once before for an artist's exhibition, but he'd hardly seen any of it. He'd come here that night to talk to his father because he'd left the office early before they'd closed a deal. He'd found Arthur hadn't been interested in discussing business. So Maximus had stayed on his phone until the deal was finalized. But now he had time to look around to see what his father had seen in this place.

He stopped in front of a particularly intriguing painting.

"It's quite complex, yes?" a soft feminine voice said from his side.

Maximus glanced sideways and saw that Tahlia had joined him and was looking at the painting. "Yes, it is."

"I've told the artist that he should dig deeper like he did with this piece. I think he's very talented."

"Is there more of his work here?"

Tahlia shook her head. "At the time, I could only convince my boss to exhibit one."

"Shouldn't be a problem for you now," Maximus stated, moving from the painting to walk toward another, "now that you own the gallery." He noticed that Tahlia followed behind him.

"No, it won't be," she responded, "but why does that sound like an accusation?"

He turned to face her and offered an apologetic smile. "I'm sorry. I didn't intend it that way. I was merely stating the obvious, which is you're a wealthy woman now and the gallery is yours to run as you see fit."

She eyed him suspiciously, as if she didn't believe him. "Yes, it does, and I have some ideas."

"Care to share them over dinner?" Maximus inquired. He glanced down at his watch. "It's about closing time, isn't it?"

"Yes, it is, but I would need a few minutes to shut down."

"That's no problem," he responded. "I can wait."

"Why would you?"

"I thought it might be a good idea to get to know my business partner since we'll be working together."

She nodded. "Yes, I suppose that makes sense."

"Then join me." He trained his dark brown eyes on hers.

"All right," she replied. "Give me a few minutes, okay?"

"Sure thing. I'll just mosey around."

He stared at her retreating figure. He shouldn't want Tahlia, but he did on some elemental, visceral level. Every time he looked into her eyes, they sizzled with fire, blasting through every reserve in his arsenal. He had not felt anything with his previous lovers other than the physical release his body craved, but there was something about Tahlia that triggered an untapped need in him to care for her, guard her. He had to figure out what it was. He couldn't afford any distractions, not if he wanted to keep what was his.

From the loft above, Tahlia stared down at Maximus as he moved through the gallery like a sleek panther hunting his next game. And was that her? Was that why he was here?

He'd said it was because they were going to be partners at Knight Shipping, but Tahlia didn't believe him—at least not entirely. The way he'd looked at her told her it might be something more personal. She wouldn't mind if it were. Maximus Knight was a gorgeous man. And tonight she'd been made increasingly aware of that fact.

She'd been stunned when after finishing up with a customer, she'd noticed him in *her* gallery staring at one of her favorite paintings. Since he hadn't noticed her, she'd been able to soak him in. Power radiated from the man—along with a killer instinct, which she was sure served him well in the business world. But there was a sophistication and polish to Maximus that came from being born into money. And his looks—he was well-groomed with a boldly handsome face that appealed to her. The tiny curling tendrils encircling his head made Tahlia want to reach out and finger them. He stood proud and strong in an arresting dark suit that outlined his shoulders and towering presence.

He was, however, deep in thought, and she'd wondered what could have him so perplexed. And so she'd stepped toward him, eager to find out. His compelling gaze made Tahlia nearly lose her breath, but she'd put up a good front. She knew he wasn't happy about her new role in his company.

If she'd had her pick, it wasn't the role Tahlia would have chosen, either. She'd have wanted Maximus to notice *her* because he'd found her attractive. And maybe he did, but she suspected he was spending time with her now only to try to figure out where she stood. And exactly where was that?

Tahlia wasn't sure, but maybe she'd figure it out tonight.

Maximus watched Tahlia saunter toward him. His eyes roved over her figure, and he missed nothing. Not the way the drape of the skirt hugged her curves or how the sleek sweater showed off her naked shoulders. His tongue flicked out to moisten his parched lips. Tahlia was mighty fine. And Maximus had to admit, he would enjoy his dinner companion for the evening.

"Ready to go?" he asked when she made it to him. Her large expressive eyes were alive and glowing, and Maximus liked what he saw there. She was most certainly interested in him, which could play into his game if he decided to go there.

"Yes, let's do it." She headed through the doors. He stayed close behind her as she locked up, so when she turned around her face was mere inches from his.

"Oh." She stepped back for a moment and nearly

stumbled, so Maximus reached out and circled his arm around her waist.

"Careful."

They stayed that way for several seconds, both of them staring at each other. Maximus looked her over seductively, and when his gaze went to her full lips, he felt her tense almost immediately and she stepped away.

"Where to?" she asked, moving toward the sidewalk. "I'll follow behind you."

"We should take my car," Maximus said. "I don't mind driving."

"That isn't necessary."

"I insist."

In the end, Maximus won out and he opened the passenger door for Tahlia to his Bugatti, and she slid inside. He came around to the driver's side, hopped in and started the engine. Tahlia seemed uneasy beside him as he drove to dinner despite the fact that she looked damn good in the red leather bucket seat. After several long, excruciating silent minutes, Maximus patted her thigh. "Relax, Tahlia. I don't bite."

"Are you sure about that?"

He grinned. "What have you heard? Or should I say read?"

"You have a reputation for being determined."

It seemed like she'd thought that word through very carefully. "You mean ruthless?"

"That word has been used."

"And you're wondering how it applies to you?"

"Shouldn't I?" Tahlia asked. "I know I stand in the way of something you want."

"Who's to say you're not what I want?" Maximus said as he pulled into the valet area of a well-known French bistro. He glanced at Tahlia and saw the stunned look on her face, just as he exited the vehicle and handed his keys to the valet.

He was at her door in no time, grasping her hand and pulling her from the vehicle. He liked touching her and that when he did, her reaction to him was purely physically. He planned to keep on touching her. With his hand at the small of her back, he led her inside the bistro.

"Jean George," Maximus greeted the maître d'.

"Mr. Knight," Jean George replied. "It's a pleasure to have you dining with us again. Your same table, I presume?"

"If it's available."

"For you, of course. Please allow me." He led Tahlia and Maximus to a quiet booth away from the bustling interior.

Tahlia slid inside the booth, and Maximus eased in beside her. When their thighs began to touch, Maximus felt his skin prickle and heat up in awareness. Or was it the playful scent of her peony fragrance that permeated the small space they shared? They both peered at their menus for several moments, but Maximus didn't need to look; he knew what he wanted.

When Tahlia glanced up, she found his gaze was riveted on her. "What are you doing, Maximus?"

"Call me Max. All my friends do."

"And is that what we are, friends?"

"We don't have to be enemies," he stated firmly.

"I guess that depends on you," Tahlia stated, and his eyebrow rose. Tahlia wasn't as naive as he imagined her to be.

A waiter came over and took their drink orders, a scotch for Maximus and a club soda for Tahlia. Once he'd gone, Maximus responded to Tahlia's comment.

"All right, I'll bite. I didn't anticipate having you or Lucius to answer to when running my company."

"Don't you mean *our company*?" she responded quickly.

He was about to correct her when he saw the smile in her eyes. She was teasing him. "All my life I've been groomed to run Knight Shipping, so imagine how you would feel if the shoe was on the other foot and interlopers came in to tell you how to run it."

"I can only imagine that you feel slighted, as would I," Tahlia said. "But this doesn't have to be a battle between you and your brother, Lucius."

"And how do you foresee this going, Tahlia?"

He liked how her name rolled off his lips.

Tahlia shrugged. "I'm not sure. We'll have to make it up as we go along."

At her words, he frowned. Maximus didn't leave anything to chance. He was all about facts and figures and making a well-thought-out educated decision before proceeding in life as well as in business. It was why he'd been so successful.

"Listen, no one said this was going to be easy. I think your father put me in the middle to help negotiate a peaceful truce between the two of you."

"You don't resent that he's put you in the middle of an untenable position?"

"At first, I did," she answered honestly, "but then I began to see it as an honor and that I could make a difference."

"Are you always this positive?" Maximus inquired, steepling his fingers and staring at her. "Because that's sort of a Pollyanna way of thinking."

"That might be so, but I'm here and I'm not going away."

There was never a truer statement, Maximus thought. "No, you're not, so we might as well get to know each other if we're going to be spending so much time together."

"At the office, I presume."

The waiter returned and set both their drinks on the table.

After they'd ordered dinner, Maximus immediately reached for his drink and took a sip. "As a shareholder in Knight shipping, your presence, although not required, is expected at functions in town or around the globe if needed."

"I only own two percent. You and Lucius have the lion's share. You don't need me there." Tahlia reached for her beverage and drank liberally from her club soda.

"What if I want you there?" Maximus countered.

Tahlia looked up at him through thick lashes, and Maximus's stomach lurched. He did want her around and not just for business. He wanted her for himself. He wanted to get to know her story and how she'd become this beacon of positivity.

"I—I'll be there, if I'm needed."

She didn't rise to his bait, but that was okay. Maximus wasn't sure where this was going, but there was an attraction between them. He felt it because his heartbeat was thumping at a rapid pace and he couldn't take his eyes off her and vice versa. She was looking at him like she wanted to jump his bones. And if she did, Maximus wouldn't mind at all.

"So, Tahlia, tell me your story." He drank a bit more of his scotch and regarded her with interest.

"You mean you haven't researched the interloper who just burst into your life?"

He stared at her long and hard until she looked downward. "No, I haven't. I was hoping to do that *person-ally*."

"All right," she said. "What do you want to know?"

"Everything."

"That's very vague. Hmm…" She paused. "I guess I can tell you that I was raised by my mother, Sophia Armstrong. It's always been Mama, Kaitlynn—that's my baby sister—and me. My mother is an RN at UCLA Medical Center, and my sister is an accountant."

"And your father? You didn't mention him. Where's he in the picture?"

"He was mugged and shot one night coming home from work. He—he didn't survive his injuries."

Maximus noted how formal she sounded about losing her father so young. It had to have been devastating for her. "How old were you?"

"Ten years old," Tahlia said. "Kaitlynn was only six. She barely remembers him, but I do. He was such a good dad. He taught me how to ride a bike, he helped me with my homework. He tucked me into bed at night and read us stories…" Her voice trailed off, and he could see the toll talking about it was having on her. Her eyes had become misty and wet with tears.

Maximus reached across the table, placed his hand over hers and squeezed. She didn't move away. Instead, she let him comfort her, and he used his other hand to wipe away an errant tear that slid down her cheek. When she looked up at him, so soft and tender, all Maximus wanted was to wrap her in his arms and kiss her until the hurt went way. Instead, he just slid closer and wrapped his arm around her, and they sat silently for several minutes.

"I'm sorry," he finally said.

"No, I'm sorry. I didn't mean to get emotional. I

just get choked up talking about my dad sometimes."
Tahlia sniffed.

Maximus turned to her, offering her his handkerchief. "Don't be, you loved him. And it shows. I don't
think I've even cried over my father since his death."

She glanced up at him through lashes damp with
tears as she dabbed at her eyes with the hanky. "You
haven't?"

"We didn't have the sort of relationship that you and
your father did." He finished off the rest of his scotch
and placed the empty glass on the table.

"You didn't?" She sounded incredulous as she moved
out of his embrace to look inquiringly at him.

"That surprises you?"

"If I'm honest?" she asked. "It does. Arthur was always so caring toward me. And I suppose losing my
dad so young that having Arthur in my life was a god-
send. We had a special relationship that went beyond a
love of art, but was genuine."

"Then I envy you," Maximus said. "Because my father was never affectionate with me. In fact, it was quite
the opposite. Whenever I seemed to be around, he was
cold, distant and indifferent. Which is why I'm still
boggled over why he stayed with my mother. And the
only thing I've come up with is money. He stayed with
her for money and the power that came with it.

"No." Tahlia shook her head. "That can't be. I can't
reconcile that with the Arthur I knew."

"Then you didn't know him at all. He was a master of lies."

"But he loved you. He loved both his sons."

"He did?" Now it was Maximus's turn to be in disbelief. He'd shared so much with a stranger, but yet he
hadn't been able to tell his own sons those words? It

didn't make any sense. He was understanding Arthur Knight less and less with each passing day.

At the stunned look on Maximus's face, Tahlia knew she'd said the wrong thing. She'd thought her words would give him comfort, but they were having the opposite effect. "I'm so sorry, Maximus. I don't know why Arthur wasn't honest with both his sons about his true feelings. I only know he wanted to claim his other son. But he never revealed it was Lucius. Just that it was his wish that both of you would run the business together one day."

Maximus snorted. "For an outsider, you sure do know a lot about my family. Or should I say my father? It appears as if maybe you did know him better than any of us." He signaled the waiter over.

"I'll have another scotch." He turned to Tahlia. "What would you like?"

"Nothing for me."

The waiter departed, leaving them alone again. Tahlia noticed Maximus was silent as he pondered her words. Arthur Knight was a mix of contradictions. He was outwardly cold to Maximus and his mother, Charlotte, passionate with Jocelyn Turner and a father figure to her. And now Maximus would never know the answer to the burning questions he must have.

"Max," Tahlia began. "What can I do?"

He frowned. "I'm not sure you can do anything, Tahlia. You're in the middle of this mess, and we'll have to navigate our way through it."

Tahlia didn't like his answer, and she wished she'd never told him just how much Arthur had shared with her. She hadn't meant to hurt Maximus, but it was clear she had. His father had been open with her and not him. That had to sting.

She tried to change the subject. "I never got to finish my story," she said. "You asked me about myself."

"Hmm… I did, didn't I?" Maximus sipped his scotch. "Why don't you tell me how you got involved with the gallery?"

His question brought a smile to Tahlia's face. "Actually, I'm an artist."

He peered at her with intensity. "You are? Then why are you *working* at the gallery and not exhibiting?"

Tahlia shrugged. "I wasn't very successful at getting my own art displayed, so I thought what better way to stay in the field than to help other struggling artists?"

"And your own art? What became of it?"

"I still dabble."

"Would you show me your work sometime?" he inquired.

A smile of enchantment crossed Tahlia's lips at the request. "Yes, I would like that."

"It's a date," Maximus said. His look was so galvanizing it sent a tremor through Tahlia, and her heart began hammering loudly in her ears. She wanted to respond and tell him she'd love to go out with him again, but a knot rose in her throat and all Tahlia could do was nod.

The waiter brought their entrées and they both dug into their French meals. The food was rich and decadent, but delicious. Tahlia had no qualms about finishing the meal, and Maximus commented on it.

"You enjoyed your meal?" He inclined his head to her empty plate.

She blushed. "I'd think that was obvious." She wiped the corners of her mouth with a napkin.

"I love this place and come here often," Maximus said. "It might be small and quaint, but I believe in quality over quantity, and the food is best—thus why I have a special table."

"Thank you for the invite."

"You're welcome. Would you care for dessert? Coffee?"

She patted her stomach. "Oh, no, I couldn't eat another thing."

"All right, I'll get the bill." He motioned the waiter over.

Once the bill was settled, Maximus and Tahlia made their way back to the valet station. And once his Bugatti was procured, they were on their way back to the gallery, where Tahlia's car was parked. Conversation continued until they arrived at the deserted parking lot. Maximus pulled up alongside her VW Bug. Next to his Bugatti, her car looked like a relic, but because she'd been a struggling artist, it was all she could afford at the time. Though now, she could afford much more. But Tahlia was determined not to be frivolous. Robert had offered to help her, and she suspected she'd need all the help she could get, starting with an accountant and a financial adviser.

"I enjoyed tonight," Tahlia said, once Maximus had opened the passenger door and walked her to her car. She stood at the door ready to glide in, but something in the way he was looking at her held Tahlia back.

Was he going to kiss her?

If he were, she wouldn't stop him. She'd welcome it after the wonderful night she'd spent in his company. Last year, when she'd seen him from across the room looking so deliciously handsome, she'd secretly wondered what it would be like to *be* with Maximus, but for now she'd settle for a kiss.

"So did I. And I'd like to see you again." He leaned forward toward her, pressing Tahlia backward into the driver's door. "Perhaps you can come to Knight Shipping? I could give you a tour of the facilities. You can see for yourself what you've inherited."

"You'd do that?" Tahlia asked softly, looking at his sinful lips. She ached for them to brush hers.

"For you, yes." His mouth was so very near hers.

"But not for Lucius?" she inquired. The ire on Maximus's face at the mention of his older brother's name had Tahlia immediately regretting her choice to bring him into the conversation.

Maximus straightened and took a step backward. "I extended the invitation to you, but I suppose I might as well get it over with, so fine, invite him. Have a good night, Tahlia."

He turned on his heel to leave, which meant he wasn't going to kiss her tonight. She'd put her foot in her mouth because of her do-gooder ways.

"I will," Tahlia said to his retreating figure as she watched him get into his sports car and drive off. She clicked opened her car and slid in. Then she slammed her fists on the steering wheel. Why hadn't she kept her mouth shut? Her hands flew up to her lips. If she had, she was certain Maximus would have kissed her, and now she wouldn't know the feel of his mouth on hers. Would she ever?

As he drove away, Maximus realized he had Tahlia exactly where he wanted her. Or did he? Tonight hadn't gone exactly as he anticipated it would. The impending deals that would lead to expansion and going public had been far from his mind. Instead, his purpose had been to find out more about Tahlia, and he had. She'd grown up fatherless, a struggling artist needing someone to look after her. There was a certain naïveté and innocence about her that intrigued Maximus and apparently his father, too.

Arthur Knight had been the father Tahlia no longer had, but then their relationship had changed and she'd become his confidante. He'd shared secrets with Tahlia about his wishes that he could never share with his own family until his death. But she didn't appear to be using that knowledge with malice or avarice. Or at least none that Maximus could see. She also seemed steadfast in her intent to ensure that he and Lucius formed a brotherhood, as if that were possible.

It wasn't.

Maximus may not fault Lucius for his existence, but he didn't share. Knight Shipping was his and his alone because he'd earned it. Lucius and Tahlia stood in the way of that. Maximus had to neutralize Lucius's power. The only way to do that was to get to Tahlia. And tonight he had.

She'd wanted him to kiss her as much as he'd wanted to. And he might have, if she'd had the good sense to leave Lucius out of the conversation. Instead, she would have to wait, wait until Maximus decided it was time. He didn't relish seducing Tahlia and the potential of ruining the positive bubble she lived in, but there was no way around it.

He would have to be smart about it, though. Slowly court Tahlia until she didn't notice that he had her under his thumb. But at the same time Maximus would have to keep his heart locked up tight because something told him if he wasn't careful, he'd fall under Tahlia's spell.

Chapter 4

"You own this place?" Tahlia's mother, Sophia, said when she and Kaitlynn returned from taking Tahlia out for lunch several days later. It was her mother's day off from the hospital, and she'd finally had the time to come by and see Tahlia's new venture.

"I do," Tahlia said with a wide grin. She'd already made some small changes by rearranging the artwork throughout the rooms and reaching out to several artists she'd recommended to Bailey, who'd dismissed them without ever reviewing their work. Tahlia was looking forward to showcasing their talent at a future exhibition.

"Will you show your own work, too?" Kaitlynn asked, turning around to face her sister.

"Max asked me the same thing."

"Max?" Kaitlynn's brow furrowed at her use of his nickname.

"Maximus," Tahlia repeated.

"As in Maximus Knight of Knight Shipping?" her mother stated. Apparently, even her mother had heard of him.

Tahlia nodded. "Yes, that's the other part of the surprise I have in store for you."

Her mother folded her arms across her bosom. "Tahlia Ann Armstrong, you better start talking."

"Come to my office." Tahlia led them toward the back offices. They passed Faith on the way.

"Hello, Mrs. Armstrong."

"Hello, my dear." Sophia gave Faith a hug. "So great to see you again." Tahlia had had Faith over for dinner at her mother's, and the two women had hit it off famously.

"You, too," Faith replied.

When they were behind closed doors, her mother stared back at her in anticipation. "Well, I'm waiting, young lady."

Tahlia stared back at her mother. Even at forty-six, her mother was still a knockout in her book. Her brown skin was bright and clear with no signs of aging. Meanwhile, thanks to her schedule as a RN, her mother was constantly on the go, keeping her body fit and trim—although you couldn't tell from the baggy jeans and tunic she wore now.

Now that Tahlia had a little money, she and Kaitlynn would have to take their mama on a mommy makeover. In the meantime, she responded to her mother. "I didn't exactly tell you the whole truth a few days ago."

"What did you leave out?"

"Well… In addition to leaving me this place, Arthur Knight gave me two percent ownership in Knight Shipping."

Sophia jumped up from her seat. "He did what?"

"Mama, please sit down."

"How can I sit down? Do you have any idea what that stock is worth?"

"I've some idea, but listen, there's more," Tahlia continued, taking a seat. When she did, her mother did the same.

"So there's a catch?" asked her mother, reaching out for her hand. "What is it?"

"I'm the deciding vote between Maximus Knight and his illegitimate brother, Lucius Knight."

"Oh, dear," her mother exclaimed. "I've seen the news reports about their father. But how did you get involved? Why would he put you in the middle?"

Tahlia shrugged. "I don't know, Mama. I think Arthur thought I'd help bridge the gap between them. You know how much I believe in family. I mean, look at the three of us and how tight we are. I think Arthur thought I could do the same for his family."

"That's a tall order," her mother replied. "I've seen the news reports. Up until recently, Lucius Knight was a bachelor playboy, but I believe he's engaged now, yes?"

Tahlia nodded. "I met his fiancée, Naomi. She's amazing and so talented. She started Brooks & Johnson."

"I love their products." Her mother touched her cheek.

"Mama, that's not the point," Kaitlynn intervened. "I don't trust Maximus. I don't put him above using Tahlia to get his own agenda through."

"I disagree. If you got to know him, he's a really nice guy," Tahlia stated. "We had dinner the other night, and he invited me to tour Knight Shipping and he invited Lucius."

"And whose suggestion was that?" Kaitlynn raised a brow.

"His," Tahlia responded. "But listen, until he does something to make me think otherwise, I should give him the benefit of the doubt. Isn't that right, Mama? You've always taught me to see the good in people."

"That's right, sweetie," her mother said. "You should, but you also need to be cautious. You wear your heart on your sleeve."

"I'm surprised that's still possible after Paul," Kaitlynn replied.

Tahlia frowned at her sister's mention of her exboyfriend, Paul Archer. "Did you have to bring him up?" They'd dated on and off for the better part of five years. Paul was the only serious relationship Tahlia ever had and the only man she'd ever loved. It had been hard accepting that they weren't meant to be like her parents.

It had been love at first sight when Sophia and Darryl Armstrong had met in the hospital. Her father had been a promising surgical resident who could have gone on to do great things, but his life had been snuffed out way too soon. Tahlia had always wanted a love like that one day. She'd thought she and Paul were meant to be, but in the end she'd learned they didn't want the same things. She wanted to be a wife and mother, and Paul didn't even want kids. When she'd been late and thought she was pregnant, even though she hadn't been, it had cemented that their relationship was doomed, and they'd parted ways soon after.

"I'm sorry, sis," Kaitlynn apologized when Tahlia's expression became downcast. "I just don't want a repeat of Paul. You and Maximus, Max, whatever he calls himself, are on two different playing fields. It's best you don't get your hopes up for something more."

"Why shouldn't I shoot for the stars?" Tahlia asked. "Unlike Paul, I knew the moment I saw Maximus that we'd have a connection."

"Did he realize that?"

"No," Tahlia admitted with a frown, "but he may now. Last night at dinner, I could have sworn he was going to kiss me."

"Tahlia, really, must you always have your head in the clouds?" her mother asked. "I'm sure a man like Maximus is taken."

"You don't think I can catch his attention, either?" Tahlia inquired. "Thanks a lot, Mama."

"It's not that, sweetie. Sometimes, you're a little too optimistic."

"You're wrong," Tahlia replied. She hadn't imagined that Maximus wanted to kiss her. She'd just put her foot in her mouth by including Lucius. But it was Arthur's dying wish that his sons get along and run Knight Shipping. So Tahlia had to do everything in her power to see that happen. She owed it to Arthur.

And she was positive that Maximus Knight was interested in her, and she couldn't wait to see him again.

"Tahlia Armstrong and Lucius Knight are here to see you, Mr. Knight," his assistant, Elena Masters, advised him from the intercom on Friday afternoon.

Maximus pressed the speaker button. "Thank you, Elena. Tell them I'll be with them in a minute." Then he sat back in his executive chair and took several deep breaths.

He was happy to see Tahlia again. Unfortunately, the request came along with an annoyance: Lucius. He would have turned Tahlia down immediately when she'd asked, but if he did, he would have raised a red flag. He needed Tahlia to be pliable, and the only way to ensure her cooperation was to act like he was keeping an open mind when it came to Lucius, when that was far from the case.

Rising from his chair, Maximus walked to the double doors of his office and opened them. His gaze immediately went to Tahlia, who sat on the sofa looking delicious in a bohemian-style crinkle skirt and tank top covered by a black blazer rolled up to her elbows. He assumed this was her twist to make it professional.

Meanwhile, his brother, Lucius, who was at least two inches taller than him, stood in what Maximus knew was a designer suit because he had the exact same one, although thankfully he wasn't wearing it now. Lucius sported his signature crew cut, mustache and goatee. And he was talking to Elena and had the poor girl blushing several shades of red.

He and Lucius couldn't be more different. Lucius was all flash and liked to be the life of the party, or so he'd heard, while Maximus was much more reserved and liked to observe and view the lay of the land before engaging. Their only similarity was the fact that they shared the same taste in clothing.

"Lucius." Maximus came forward, extending his hand.

"Aw, here's my little bro," Lucius said when Maximus came forward, but instead of accepting his handshake, Lucius drew Maximus into an awkward and unwanted hug. Maximus glanced at Tahlia from the sofa, and she was beaming at the contact. He tried not to recoil as he lightly patted Lucius on the back and pulled away.

"That really wasn't necessary," Maximus whispered.

"Of course it was." A faint light of amusement twinkled in his dark eyes. "We're brothers."

"I'm so glad you could join us, Lucius." Tahlia stood to her feet. "Max." She inclined her head toward him.

"Max, is it?" Lucius glanced in her direction, and his

brow rose. "It's like that now? How long have you know him, Tahlia? All of a week? Did I miss something? Do I get to call you Max now, too?"

Maximus forced himself to be polite when he'd like nothing more than to wring his older brother's neck. He was purposely stirring the pot, trying to rile him up, but Maximus was used to loud, overbearing men like Lucius and knew how to handle them.

"That's right," Maximus responded. "Tahlia and I have been getting to know each other." He gave her a wink and watched her eyes brighten at the action. "But no, I'd prefer you call me Maximus. Unless you'd like me to call you Luke or maybe Lucifer."

At that comment, Lucius howled with laughter. "I like you, Max." He slapped Maximus's shoulder. "You've got a sense of humor. Why don't you lead the way and show us *our empire*."

Maximus seethed inwardly but started walking down the hall. He led them through the executive offices first and then showed them the different departments on several floors before eventually ending in the shipping yard. This had always been his favorite place as a child even though it could be dangerous with all the cranes and shipping containers on the move. Tahlia asked a lot of questions throughout, but Lucius was silent, taking it all in. Knight International, Lucius's company, specialized in technology, not shipping. Maximus hoped he could see that he was out of his element.

"Looks awfully tight," Lucius commented as he peered at the shipping yard filled with cargo containers.

"Yes, it is," Maximus replied, surprised at his insight. "Expansion is the next logical step if we want to compete in the Port of Los Angeles with the other major players. If you didn't know it already, it's the largest port in the US."

Lucius rolled his eyes. "And I assume you're already looking at the feasibility and finances on moving forward?"

"Of course.

"Good. I look forward to seeing it in the future."

When the tour was over and they were headed back to the main building, Lucius commented, "This is quite an operation you have on your hands, Maximus." Gone was his previous arrogance about *their empire*. If he wasn't mistaken, Maximus had gained his older brother's respect.

"Thank you."

"Are there any major decisions that have been tabled given Arthur's death that you need Tahlia and me for? I assume you can handle day-to-day operations."

"Yes, of course," Maximus stated testily. "I've been president for the last two years and am quite capable of running things."

"I know that," Lucius responded. "It's clear Knight Shipping is in excellent hands. I only meant that if we—" he glanced at Tahlia "—could be of any assistance, we're here."

"There's a board meeting next month and we'll be discussing expansion options," Maximus responded, "but until then, I've got it."

Lucius stared at him long and hard as if debating his next answer, but then he just said, "Of course you do." He turned to Tahlia. "Tahlia, it's been a pleasure. Thank you for the invitation." He glanced at Maximus when he spoke. Lucius knew there was no way in hell he would have ever purposely invited him to tour the facilities. He glanced again at Tahlia. "Be careful of this one, though. He's real smooth." Then he looked back at Maximus. "Max, I'm sure we'll be speaking soon. Take care, little bro." He ruffled Maximus's curls and walked toward his car.

Tahlia was silent beside Maximus as he patted his hair back into place. He didn't appreciate the constant reminders that Lucius was the oldest and, in fact, could have been the heir to Knight Shipping if he'd been acknowledged as Arthur's son. As much as he hated it, Maximus would always be Lucius's younger brother, but did he have to mess his hair up?

"Max, I'm sorry about Lucius," Tahlia replied. "He's been baiting you all day with the bro comments and calling you Max. I'm sorry I extended the invite."

"Don't be, it's not your fault he was being a complete and utter jerk." Maximus turned to face her. When he did, he saw concern was etched across her beautiful features. "Really." He touched her shoulders. "I'll live."

"I know." She gave him a half-hearted smile. "You didn't rise to the bait."

He shook his head. "I learned a long time ago to be coolheaded and to not react, because isn't that what he expected?"

"And where did you learn not to show your emotions?"

"Ah, Tahlia, we're not getting into this discussion now," Maximus responded.

"When, then?" she asked boldly.

Maximus walked up to her until he was so close he could smell the shampoo she'd used that day. It smelled of lemon and lavender. "When would you like?"

He heard the breath hitch in her throat, saw her pupils dilate at his nearness. "I would imagine you'd want to keep your distance, given Lucius's warning to be wary of me."

Her lips thinned. "I make my own judgments."

"And what have you decided about me?"

"That I can trust you," she said, and then she added, "For now."

He studied her. He was getting to her. "Join me for dinner tomorrow night. I have a charity function."

Tahlia shook her head. "I can't, but if you'd like to share a meal, I'm free on Monday night. And I know just the place. I'll text you the address."

Seconds later, she was gone, leaving Maximus to wonder who was playing whom.

Chapter 5

Maximus's weekend was super busy. He attended a charity dinner with his mother on Saturday night and was now meeting up with Griffin on Sunday for their weekly racquetball match. It had always been an outlet for him when he needed to relieve some stress, and today was no different.

After the tour on Friday ended with Lucius and Tahlia, Maximus was preoccupied. Since his father's death, many decisions had to be made to keep Knight Shipping running. Now that he knew Lucius and Tahlia wouldn't be looking over his shoulder every five minutes or expecting a report, Maximus was free to make them. Lucius had even been open to the idea of expansion, though he didn't yet understand what that might entail. So it was up to Maximus to put together the best prospectus he could to convince Lucius, the businessman, that going public was in the company's best interest. But even if Lucius wasn't on board, Tahlia's vote would give Maximus the majority vote he needed to take Knight Shipping public.

Business decisions came easily, but another, more

personal one stood heavy on his mind, and that was whether he should continue on this quest to seduce Tahlia. He'd come up with the idea after he'd been steaming mad after the reading of his father's will, but now that he had time to think about it, he was beginning to question its legitimacy. Tahlia was gorgeous and had an inherent kindness that didn't lend itself to his machinations. But Maximus couldn't figure out any way around getting her vote, except appealing directly to her sensibilities. If she was interested in him, cared for him, it could sway any potential vote his way.

"Max, get your head in the game," Griffin said when a ball flew past Maximus's ear.

"Sorry, Griff." Maximus returned his focus to the game and got in position. Within seconds, another ball was coming at him, and this time he hit it with such force that it went sailing across Griffin's head.

Griffin glared at him. "What the hell was that?"

"Playing ball. Now stop your whining and let's get on with it."

An hour later, they were in the locker room having just finished up their match. Griffin had beat him by a point, 5 to 4. It hadn't been Maximus's best game because deep down he'd been thinking about Tahlia. Her lustrous black hair that hung in soft waves past her shoulders. Her big brown eyes. Or maybe it was those kissable lips that he knew were aching for him to kiss them.

"You let me win," Griffin said as they dressed after showering.

Maximus frowned. "Why would you say that?"

"Because you're distracted."

"You should take the win, Griff. You know I don't like to lose, and you might not ever get another chance to gloat." He'd already donned a pair of khaki trousers and was buttoning up a casual shirt.

Griffin shrugged as he pulled on his jeans. "I want to beat you when you're at your best, not when you're preoccupied with your family business or your beautiful new partner."

"Lucius?" Maximus said with a smirk. "I certainly wouldn't call him beautiful. Arrogant would be more like it. The other day during our tour, the jerk tried to rile me by calling me little bro and Max."

His friend chuckled. "Oh, I bet that really got your goat," he said, pulling on his polo shirt. "But you know good and well who I'm talking about."

"Tahlia."

"Of course," Griffin replied as he slipped on his shoes. "Have you followed through on your intent to seduce the woman in the hopes she'll part with her shares or vote with you?"

"And? What if I were?"

"I would tell you I think it's a bad idea. I know you have a way with women, but say you do seduce her. Who's to say that the relationship won't go sour and Tahlia votes against you anyway for spite? There's no guarantees this will play out exactly how you envision. Surely, there must be another way," Griffin said. "Some legal maneuver you can use to get Lucius out of the company. Has it even been confirmed that he's Arthur's son? Force him into a paternity test. You could drag this out in court for years."

"Only in the end to have to share the power with him after I've royally pissed him off?" Maximus asked. "No." He shook his head. "My way is better. If I can get Tahlia on my side or convince her to sell me her shares, it's the better method."

"If you say so, but you're treading a very fine line, my friend," Griffin said.

"I know that," Maximus said. But Tahlia was also a grown woman who could make her own choices. He'd heard Lucius warn her about him. She could choose to ignore his advances and he'd be back to square one. Ultimately, it was her decision.

"All right. When the script is flipped, don't say I didn't warn you," Griffin said and finished tying up his shoes.

"Don't sound so ominous," Maximus responded. "I can handle this."

Tahlia paced the sidewalk as she pulled the collar of her wool peacoat around her neck. It was a chilly Monday evening, and she was freezing her bones off as she waited in front of the homeless shelter where she and Maximus would be serving dinner tonight. Thanks to her mother's altruistic spirit, she'd always made sure Tahlia and Kaitlynn understood just how lucky they were when others were less fortunate. And so, she'd made sure her girls volunteered in some capacity throughout much of their teens. Now, into adulthood, Tahlia had continued giving back to her community, and serving dinner each week was just a small way for her to do so.

She hadn't told Maximus exactly where they'd be going for dinner tonight. She'd only texted him the address. As vehicles passed her by on the street, she looked out for his Bugatti. It would be very conspicuous in this neighborhood. Tahlia wondered if he'd even get out of the car or whether he'd pull up to the curb and tell her to hop in before driving her someplace more upscale.

But Tahlia planned on digging in her heels. Tonight was a test if Maximus was truly serious about wanting to spend time with her and not using her as her sister Kaitlynn suggested, as did Lucius, who'd warned her to be careful. And Tahlia was curious whether Maximus would pass it.

Instead, he pulled up alongside the curb at 6:00 p.m. on the dot in a Mercedes-Benz rather than his blue Bugatti sports car. He was nothing else if not prompt as he exited the vehicle looking handsome in a wool coat and scarf wrapped around his neck.

He smiled at her as he approached, but it faded once he glanced at the building. Then he looked in her direction. "Interesting choice for dinner."

"You don't mind, do you?"

Maximus shrugged. "It's ladies' choice. So let's get out of this cold." He motioned for her to walk ahead of him.

Once inside, the shelter was a bustle of activity as the staff prepared for the dinner rush. While they removed their coats, Tahlia allowed herself a few moments to take in Maximus. He'd clearly just come from work because he'd removed his suit jacket and wore a dress shirt, slacks and a tie, and here she was having him serve dinner in his designer duds to the homeless. She was sure he probably wanted to wring her neck, but he was a good sport and quickly dispensed with his tie and slid it into his pants pocket.

Tahlia was still pulling off her coat when Maximus came over to help relieve her of it. "Thank you." She glanced behind her.

"You're welcome."

Then he took both their coats and followed her into

the large room. Patrons were already lining up in preparation for dinner service. "C'mon." Tahlia inclined her head. "I'll show you where we can put up our coats." She walked with purpose toward the center's director, who was in charge of volunteers. The older woman smiled on her approach.

"Tahlia." The director gave her a quick hug. "It's so good to have you with us again." She glanced behind Tahlia at Maximus. "And who did you bring with you today?"

Maximus stepped forward and extended his hand. "Maximus Knight."

"It's a pleasure, Mr. Knight." The director shook his hand. "It's so great to have someone with your reputation helping out today. Let me show you where to put your things, and then I'll put you to work. With tonight's cold temperatures, we'll have a full house tonight for dinner."

"Lead the way," Tahlia said.

Fifteen minutes later, Tahlia and Maximus were outfitted with aprons, gloves and large spoons to help serve the food that was spread across several rectangular tables. At least a dozen volunteers were milling about and either serving food or on cleanup detail. Tahlia had signed them up for meal service.

Once the lines opened, patrons came past their table, and she and Maximus added spoonfuls of mashed potatoes and green beans to go along with the meat loaf already on their plates. It didn't take long for them to find a rhythm and to keep the steady line moving. Tahlia was sure this was the first time Maximus Knight had ever served anyone, but he was taking it in stride.

"Enjoying yourself?" she asked, glancing in his direction.

He offered her what seemed like a genuine smile. "Actually, I am. I can't say I've ever served the homeless on a date before, but yes, I am enjoying myself."

"Is that what this is?" she asked, her pulse speeding up. "A date? I thought we were just two business partners having dinner."

His eyes swept over her face, surveying her, then he leaned down to whisper in her ear. "You know it's a date." Then he served the next patron, and all Tahlia could do was stare up at him. The implication sent waves of excitement surging through her. She'd hoped it was a date, but having the confirmation caused an invisible warmth to wrap around her insides, which already felt like mush whenever Maximus was near.

The next patron was standing in front of her, and Tahlia had to look away from Max and remember why she'd come: to help others. They continued serving meals until nearly 8:30 p.m., when the director came over and allowed several of the volunteers to take a break and have dinner themselves.

"You don't mind having dinner here?" Tahlia asked when she and Maximus moved from the other side of the table to stand in line with the patrons. She handed him a paper plate.

"Not at all," he responded, accepting the paper plate. "I enjoy helping others, and if I get to spend time with you in the process, it's a bonus."

He delivered the line so smoothly, Tahlia was so flustered one of the patrons had to gently remind her to keep the line moving. Once she and Maximus had filled their plates, they sat at one of the picnic-style tables in the main hall with their now-loaded plates of meat loaf with all the fixins. Tahlia wondered what

Maximus was thinking as he sat across from her with a faint glint of humor in his eyes. *Is this how he envisioned our first date?*

Maximus stared at Tahlia. His dark eyes pierced her brown ones, and they sparkled when she deduced his obvious interest in her. If he was honest, he'd been eager to see Tahlia again after the tour and was curious as to where she would select to have dinner for their first date. He'd never in his wildest dreams imagined she'd take him to a homeless shelter for a meal. He glanced down at the less-than-appealing entrée.

But he had to hand it to Tahlia. She had spunk.

Not many people could surprise him, and Tahlia had. She'd offered him a glimpse into a cause near and dear to her heart. Because of it, he intended to write a check later and give it to the shelter director. Maximus liked what he saw on the inside as well as the outside. Tonight, she was wearing a sweater dress that showed off her fine hips and shapely thighs along with boots that covered her calves. Despite the fact that she was covered from head to toe, Maximus was just as turned on as if she wore a minuscule bathing suit. He could only imagine how she'd fill out a bikini.

Tahlia was a breath of fresh air in his otherwise mundane life. Up until now, his life had been about achieving the lofty goals his father had set for him. But once he'd achieved one, it had never been enough and he'd set another one, a higher goal, until eventually his life had become so structured, he'd forgotten what it was like to just have fun.

Tahlia offered him that and so much more.

He wanted her.

And as he regarded her, he found a joyous satisfaction in knowing she was studying him just as much. She wanted him, too. He wanted this feeling to last, so he would take their relationship slow until she was finally in his bed.

"Why are you still single?" Maximus suddenly asked.

Tahlia frowned. "Where did that come from?"

"A woman as beautiful as you should be taken, so why are you on the market?"

"I could ask you the same thing," she responded, forking some meat loaf and plopping it in her mouth.

"Then I would answer and tell you that up until now I didn't really make time for activities outside of work."

"And now that's changed?" She quirked a brow.

"I'm not answering until you share your story," Maximus responded.

Tahlia shrugged. "All right, if you must know, there was someone once. Paul was his name, and I fell hard for him only to find out that he wanted a casual relationship and wasn't interested in a long-term commitment that came with marriage, kids and the white picket fence."

"His loss is my gain," Maximus responded. The man was a fool if he didn't realize what a gem Tahlia was. "And to answer your question, yes, circumstances have changed for me and I'm suddenly interested in extracurricular activities."

Tahlia blushed, and Maximus made a gallant effort to eat the meal in front of him and dug into the meat loaf. It wasn't the worst meal he'd ever had. And he'd do it for Tahlia to show her he wasn't some overprivileged rich kid who couldn't eat with those less fortunate.

"How's the meat loaf?" Tahlia asked with a smirk.

"Not bad."

"C'mon, Max," she said and laughed. "I know you'd

much rather be at some fancy restaurant having a chef-prepared entrée along with a bottle of expensive wine or something."

Maximus put his fork down. "Of course I would, but tonight was your pick. Next time, it'll be my choice."

"Next time?" She raised a brow and tried to hide a smile. "Who said there'd be a next time? I don't recall being asked."

"Then allow me to remedy that." Maximus reached across the table and laid his hand over Tahlia's. A surge of heat bloomed between them, and he could almost feel her skin heat up along with his. "Tahlia, will you go out with me on Saturday night?"

She gave him a genuine smile. "I'd love to."

"See, that wasn't so hard, was it?" he asked, not removing his hand. He noticed that she was shifting in her seat because he hadn't let her go.

"N-no, it wasn't." She tried unsuccessfully to slide her hand from his grasp, but instead, he linked his fingers with hers, without a thought to where they were or who was looking at them. He leaned across the table and did what he'd been wanting to do since she'd walked into the family estate for the reading of his father's will: he brushed his lips softly across hers and kissed her in the middle of the dining hall.

It was the lightest of kisses and it didn't last nearly as long as he would have liked, but eventually he sat back down across from her and looked at her. Her eyes were hooded with desire, making Maximus rethink his decision to take their relationship slow. But he didn't have time to think too long, because the room erupted with clapping.

Apparently, his little kiss had caught everyone's attention. Tahlia was embarrassed, and he watched her cheeks flush pink. There was a certain innocence to Tahlia that beguiled him. A woman of her age had to be experienced, but yet she appeared so sweet and genuine. Would his plan ruin that spark in her?

Tahlia had been unprepared for their first kiss. Sure, she'd wanted it from the moment she'd laid eyes on Maximus at the crowded gallery opening a year ago, but the reality was so much more than she could ever have imagined. She'd reacted strongly to his whisper of a kiss, and it hadn't even been a full-blown attempt. What would it feel like when Maximus lost control and kissed her with abandon?

Since she didn't like being the center of attention, Tahlia rose from the picnic table and reached for Maximus's plate. "You ready to go?" she asked. She didn't like that several people were openly staring at them. Perhaps ready for more of a show?

"Are we done?" he queried.

"I'll check with the director, and if we're no longer needed, we can scoot out."

It turned out they were needed and ended up staying another hour to finish up dinner service, and to her surprise, Maximus helped with some of the cleanup in the kitchen. It was well after 10:00 p.m. when they returned to the director's office, where she'd locked up their coats and her purse. Maximus helped Tahlia into her coat.

"This was really awesome," Maximus said. He spun her around and, to her surprise, began buttoning her coat.

"I can do it," Tahlia said, halting his hands with her own.

"I want to make sure you're warm," Maximus said, brushing her hands aside as he continued his task.

Tahlia looked down. Didn't he know she was not only warm, but she was also on fire from his touch? She hadn't recovered from his earlier kiss, and being in this confined space with Maximus was playing havoc on her senses. Her heart was already beating an erratic rhythm.

"Tahlia, look at me." Maximus's voice was husky with desire.

She met his eyes with hers, and they scanned her face slowly and seductively. And when his gaze slid downward to her lips and he lifted his thumb to caress them, her pulse quickened. Maximus tilted her chin upward with a finger to inch her closer to him. Tahlia knew what was coming next, and there was no hesitation on her part. She twined her fingers into his curly hair at the back of his head as she'd been longing to do. Sweet relief flooded her as he hauled her against him, bent his head and closed his mouth over hers.

This kiss was different from the one in the main hall. That had been a chaste peck in comparison with this one—his mouth claimed hers with skill and precision. His mouth possessed hers fully and deeply, so she kissed him back with all the passion she'd held inside her for this man. She didn't care that she was revealing her deep-seated need for him. Tahlia only knew that in the moment she had to give her desire free rein. She allowed him to push her against the office wall so he could have his way with her. She parted her lips, allowing his tongue to access the warm recesses of her mouth.

It was impossible to fathom the tumultuous emotions that he aroused in her. Maximus was an attractive and powerful man, and he easily swept away any barriers she had around herself as he intently discovered every sensual part of her mouth. His was a mission of discovery. But could he know that he'd been the man of her secret dreams and whom she'd fantasized about kissing?

She ran her hands over the bunched muscles of his upper arms that strained against the fabric of his shirt as he kissed her again and again, over and over. His lips were warm and firm in an unhurried exploration that drugged Tahlia's senses and apparently his, too, because she heard a groan from deep in his throat. She was no longer herself either, but a mass of needs wrapped around this one man.

When he lifted his head and stared down at her, his eyes were clouded. "Christ, Tahlia!" he whispered. "You're so darn eager. Do you know what a turn-on that is?"

Tahlia shook her head, and her cheeks flooded with color. She was equally as turned on. No other man had kissed her with quite the same intensity or fervor that Maximus had just now, not even Paul.

Slowly, he released her, and Tahlia had to right herself to keep from falling. She felt weak in the knees from his kisses. She watched him suck in a deep breath as he, too, tried to get a hold of his senses. After a few minutes, she dared to look at him and saw a look of blatant hunger lurking in those brown depths.

"I should walk you to your car."

She nodded. "All right."

They left the shelter and within a few moments were outside in the blistering cold. The chill would certainly help cool Tahlia down after Max's heated kisses. He grasped her hand, and they held hands all the way to her car. When they reached it, she turned to him. "I had a good time tonight."

"So did I." Maximus nodded. "And I'm looking for-

ward to Saturday night. But first I need something to
hold me until then."

And before she knew it their kiss had resumed, and
this time his mouth not only searched hers, he conquered it. His mouth crushed hers, holding her firmly
in place. The kiss was deep, raw and all-consuming.
When he finally let her go, he had to open the car door
and help her inside. She needed the assistance because
she trembled with blooming need inside her for more.
But Maximus didn't push. Instead, he seemed content
to take it slow. Tahlia just hoped she didn't go up in
flames in the meantime.

Chapter 6

Kisses. Sweet kisses. Tahlia. That, or should he say she, was all Maximus could think about last night. Thinking of her had kept him up half the night. How she'd tasted, how she responded, how much further he could have gone if…

"Maximus, darling, where have you been hiding yourself?" his mother inquired the next morning at the kitchen's breakfast nook. He had a place in town, but since his father's death he'd been spending time at his mother's mansion. She said it made her feel better.

"I've been busy, Mother." Why did she have to interrupt his most delicious daydream?

"I hope finding a way to overturn your father's will," she responded. "I mean, really? I can't believe he gave away half the company to Lucius. The rumors are already starting to get out, you know, that you're not solely in charge."

"And how would those rumors get out, Mother? Have you been talking to the gossipmonger friends of yours at the country club?"

"Don't speak ill of my friends, Maximus," Charlotte Knight said. "They've been nothing but support-ive of me throughout this entire mess. You've no idea what I've had to face—the press reporting your father's affair, the media constantly hounding me, my friends being harassed for details. All the while you get to go to work with no repercussions."

Maximus sighed. He had been in his own world and internalizing how his father's will affected him and his dreams of expanding Knight Shipping, so much so he'd been neglecting his mother. She'd been hurt by all this, too, and deeply embarrassed by the scandal. Though some of it was of her own making. "I'm sorry you feel you're facing this alone. I know this must be hard on you."

"It is." His mother sniffed, and he reached inside his suit jacket for a handkerchief and handed it to her. "I never thought this revelation would ever see the light of day, much less that your father would betray me, betray you in this fashion. He promised me."

"What do you mean?"

"I didn't know about Jocelyn until nearly five years into our marriage. I'd always thought Arthur married me for love, so imagine my surprise when I found out there was another woman, another son."

"How did you find out?"

"He'd gone away to Europe one summer, and when he returned, something was different. I could see he'd changed. He was happier and lighter somehow. I'd thought the time away had done him some good and he'd returned reinvigorated for our marriage, but he wanted a divorce."

"What?"

She nodded. "The thing is, I was already pregnant with you. Arthur was torn between doing the right thing for one son and the right thing by *me*, *his wife*. He chose me, us—" she pointed at Maximus "—but I suspect he stayed with me because my father had died and I'd inherited a large sum of money. Arthur's ambitions got in the way of his ultimate one true love, Jocelyn."

"So he hated you, *me*," Maximus stated, "because he was forced to stay with us."

"Maybe he did."

"So he punished me because I wasn't Lucius? Because he gave him up?" And his mother punished him by not sharing Lucius's very existence with him. She'd never told him he had an older brother. Who knew what relationship they could have had if the adults in their lives hadn't been so selfish.

"Maximus." His mother reached across the table. "You mustn't think that way. Your father loved you. If there was anyone he hated, it was me because I threatened to take it all away from him and leave him with nothing if he ever left me."

Maximus rose from the table. Now he was angry with both his parents. "Give it whatever spin you like, Mother. Arthur Knight was not only selfish, but he was a coward for choosing the easy way out and not going after the woman and son he loved. Maybe if he had, we all would have been better off." He strode toward the door. "I'm going to work. Thanks for the chat."

All it had done was remind him that he deserved Knight Shipping. After all Arthur had put him through, it strengthened his resolve to get what was due him: Tahlia's shares. Knight Shipping was rightfully his. He and his mother had paid their entire lives for the privilege. He just hated that the only way to that end was through Tahlia.

* * *

"Someone is on cloud nine. What gives?" Faith commented when Tahlia drifted through the gallery throughout the day as if she were walking on air. Even though there was a lot of work to be done for an up-coming exhibit Bailey already had in the works before her ownership, Tahlia was ecstatic.

She wasn't even the least bit put off when one of their top customers had railed at her for getting the framing wrong on an order. It hadn't been one Tahlia had taken, but she'd promised the woman they'd have it corrected and couriered to her home. Her resolution had brought a smile to the customer, and she'd finally left satisfied about her purchase.

"I am happy," Tahlia finally said. "Why do you ask?"

"I don't know." Faith shrugged. "Maybe it has some-thing to do with the enormous arrangement that came for you today."

Tahlia smiled, thinking about the large bouquet of roses and calla lilies that had arrived earlier that morn-ing from Maximus. The card had read Can't Wait for Saturday. Neither could Tahlia. She'd been so giddy last night after sharing not one, not two, but three kisses with Maximus at the shelter.

She'd been so sure he would hightail it and run once he realized their dinner date was at a homeless shelter, but he'd surprised her with his fortitude. She'd received a call from the shelter director that Maximus had a siz-able check delivered to the shelter just that morning. He also hadn't been as stuck-up as she'd thought and had been willing to lend a hand, including washing dishes. Just thinking about his large masculine hands in the hot bubbly soap, hands that roamed her body when he'd kissed her, caused Tahlia's skin to get heated.

"You're blushing," Faith said.

"Stop staring at me, then," Tahlia countered.

"Are you going to share details?" Faith asked. "You used to not mind sharing news about your dates." She followed Tahlia into the back office.

"This is different. Those men were merely warm-ups for the main attraction."

"Because it's Maximus Knight?"

Tahlia spun around. "How'd you know?"

"I saw the card. But you've never been this jumpy or secretive before."

Tahlia let out a sigh. "That's because I've never liked a guy as much as I like Maximus."

"The feeling is apparently mutual," Faith surmised. "Those flowers are gorgeous."

"Aren't they?" Tahlia couldn't help gushing. She felt like a teenage girl.

"When do you see him again?"

"Saturday night."

"I'm so excited for you, Tahlia," Faith said. "I know you've had a crush on him for a while now. I'm glad to see it's not one-sided anymore."

"No, it's not. It's definitely mutual."

"You're certain of this?" Maximus asked the highly recommended probate attorney he'd hired to go over his father's will. "There's no way I can contest its validity?"

The attorney shook his head. "Everything is in order here, Maximus. Robert Kellogg is a fine attorney. He would have made sure of it."

Maximus nodded. He knew it was a long shot, but he'd had to try to see if there was anything he could do before he continued taking drastic measures to get his rightful inheritance. His mind wandered to Tahlia and how happy she'd sounded when she'd called him a couple of days ago to thank him for the flowers he'd sent. He typically didn't do the flowers-and-candies thing with women he dated.

Usually, his female companions were on his arm for just one night to attend a function or an important dinner. But for Tahlia, he was willing to pull out all the stops and be her Prince Charming. Yet it had continued to niggle him that he had to use her for his own means, kind of like Arthur had used his own mother to start Knight Shipping. And as much as he hated his father's actions, in this instance the old adage applied. *Like father, like son.*

"Thank you again." Maximus stopped his pondering long enough to shake the attorney's hand and walk him to his office door. "I appreciate the effort."

"Wish I could have done something for you."

Maximus shrugged. There wasn't anything anyone could do, which was why he would continue his quest to seduce and ultimately bed Tahlia.

"I have great news," Tahlia said when she called Kaitlynn late Friday afternoon.

"Oh, yeah? What's that?" her sister asked from the other end of the line.

"I just scored VIP tickets to the Bruno Mars concert tonight."

"Get out. That show has been sold out for months!" Kaitlynn exclaimed. "So how did you… No, let me guess. The illustrious Maximus Knight got you tickets?"

"No." Tahlia shook her head even though Kaitlynn couldn't see her. "We're not scheduled to go out until tomorrow night."

"Well, how, then?"

"One of my clients was so happy with his pieces that he gave me tickets. Can you believe my luck?"

"I sure as heck can't. So I hope this call means you're taking me as your date."

"Even better," Tahlia replied. "I have four tickets. So *you* and *I* can bring a plus-one."

"Seriously? That's great, Tahlia. I'm just finishing up here and I need to call Jonathan to see if he'd like to come." Jonathan Baker was Kaitlynn's pseudo boyfriend, or in Tahlia's opinion her friend with benefits, but who was she to judge? "And you? I assume you're bringing Max."

"Maybe. I haven't asked him. What if he's too busy? It's short notice after all." They were just getting to know each other, and he could have other plans, even another date.

"How will you know if you don't ask him?"

"I don't know…"

"Don't be a wuss, Tahlia. You want the man to come don'tcha? So just call him up and see if he's free."

After Tahlia hung up with Kaitlynn, she placed her smartphone on the desk in her office and stared at it. She wanted to call Maximus, but it was spur-of-the-moment and she would be disappointed if he turned her down. In the end, she decided to take her sister's advice.

"What are you doing?" Tahlia asked when Maximus answered the phone several moments later.

"Working. Why?"

"Oh." She was crestfallen, especially by the short tone in his voice. It was near the end of the workweek, and she was hoping he'd tell her it was quitting time. Although they didn't have plans until tomorrow, she wanted to see him again and had just the excuse.

"Tahlia," he chided, "what is it? Did you have something in mind?"

"As a matter of fact, I do," she replied in a rush. "A client of mine was so happy with the pieces he purchased at the gallery that he offered me four tickets to the Bruno Mars concert tonight. My sister is coming with a date, and I know it's short notice and all, but I was wondering if you didn't have any plans for tonight if you might want to come?"

"So you're asking me out on a date?" This time there was a smile in his voice.

"And if I were?"

"The answer would be yes," Maximus responded. "What time shall I pick you up?"

"Since I'm the one taking you out," Tahlia said, "I'll be picking you up. And be ready at six." Since he didn't have time to go home and change, Tahlia arranged to pick him up at his office. Luckily for her, however, she had just enough time to close the gallery and run home for a quick shower.

"You don't mind closing up?" Tahlia asked Faith when she was heading for the door.

"Of course not. At least you have plans for Friday night other than sitting home with a movie and a bowl of microwave popcorn like me."

"That does sound divine."

"Not nearly as much as moving and grooving to Bruno Mars with Maximus Knight. Now go on." Faith shooed her out the office. "You'd better get a move on it. You don't have a whole lot of time."

An hour later, Faith was rushing out of her apartment and down the stairs to her VW Bug to pick up Max. She'd had just enough time to shower and slide on her favorite jeans, cropped tank top, denim jacket and boots. She'd decided to leave her hair down since Maximus seemed to enjoy running his hands through it the other night when he'd kissed her. After a touchup on her makeup and a quick spritz of perfume in all her secret spots, she was driving to Maximus's office.

She was sure it came as a surprise to him that *she* had offered to pick him up, but she didn't mind being the one in control for the evening. Maximus Knight was used to being in charge and having everyone fall in line. Tonight, he was on her turf and he would play by her rules.

Maximus exited his office bathroom after a quick change into khaki pants, a button-down shirt and a sports coat. He usually kept several changes of clothing at the office. He had to admit he was looking forward to the concert. It would be a change of scenery for him to do something other than work late on a Friday night. He actually had plans. A date. With Tahlia.

He smiled when he thought of her. The woman was sure full of surprises. Telling him that *she* would pick him up. If she wanted to be in charge tonight that was just fine with him. He would just take a back seat and let her do all the driving—literally.

He locked up his office and took the elevator to the lobby, arriving at 6:00 p.m. just as she'd instructed. He smiled when he exited the building and saw Tahlia leaning up against her old beat-up VW Bug. She looked like one of those pinup girls in the snug-fitting jeans she wore, crop top that revealed a hint of her belly button and a denim jacket.

It gave him all sorts of wicked ideas on what he'd like to do to her on top of it. But instead he said with a wry smile as he walked toward her, "Are you sure it's okay to get in that death mobile? You sure you don't want to ride in the luxury that is my Bugatti? It's just in the garage." He pointed toward the building.

"Ha, ha, ha," Tahlia feigned laughter. "No, we are taking my baby here." She leaned over to caress the hood of the car, and when she did, it gave Maximus a view of her generous backside, and without thinking about it, he smacked her on it.

"Max!" She popped upright. "What are you doing?"

He laughed. "I don't know. You just looked so good standing there… I—I couldn't resist." Maximus couldn't remember ever losing control and slapping a woman on her behind. It was completely out of character for him, but so was going to a pop concert.

"Well, in that case," Tahlia said, tossing her hair over her shoulder, "look all you want."

He watched her sashay to the driver's side of the car and give him a wink before hopping in. Tonight was going to be a fun evening.

Chapter 7

The tickets Tahlia procured came with a special parking pass, so when they arrived at the venue, they had a prime parking spot. "This is really nice," Maximus said, feeling somewhat awkward that he couldn't make it around to the driver's side to open her car door for her. But Tahlia didn't seem to mind. She'd already sidled up to him as they walked to the arena.

Maximus slid his hand in hers and they walked side by side to the box office, where her sister and beau were already waiting for them.

"Tahlia!" A beautiful albeit shorter version of Tahlia approached them with a tall gentleman sporting baggy jeans, sweater and a baseball cap. Her sister looked directly at him. "And you must be Maximus."

"Call me Max." But before he could finish the sentence she'd already hugged him and was turning to her companion. "Jonathan, I'd like you to meet…"

"Maximus Knight," Jonathan answered. "I've read a lot about you. You're considered the next big thing for black-owned businesses."

"I don't know about all that." Maximus laughed. "But I hold my own."

"Are you guys ready to go in?" Tahlia asked from his side, holding up the concert tickets. "Because I'm ready for some 'Uptown Funk'!"

They all laughed in unison, but Maximus completely missed the joke. What was "Uptown Funk"?

He soon learned after the foursome stopped at concessions for hot dogs, popcorn and beer and made their way through the throng of people to the front row on the floor. Maximus couldn't remember the last time he'd had a hot dog, much less a beer. Tahlia was getting him out of his comfort zone, and he liked it—he liked it a lot.

"So 'Uptown Funk' is a song," Tahlia told him once they were seated and munching on their dogs and swigging beer. "C'mon, don't tell me you've never heard of it."

Maximus shrugged.

"We really do need to get you of the house more," she said with a chuckle.

"I told you. I don't get out much," Maximus replied loudly over the roar of the prelude music. "Usually work, work, home and the occasional social function."

"That's no kind of life, Max," Tahlia yelled back. "I'm going to make it my mission in life to loosen you up."

"I'm open to ideas," Max said, eyeing her intently. He could think of a horizontal way that would loosen him up quite nicely, but it was still too soon to be thinking along those lines. If he came on too strong, Tahlia might think it was all about sex when it wasn't.

He was truly enjoying her company and everything she had to offer. When he'd first come up with the idea to seduce Tahlia, it had occurred to him that maybe their connection would merely be physical. But Maximus was learning that every minute he spent with Tahlia was one of his own self-discovery.

When the lights blinked, indicating the concert was about to start, Tahlia scooted closer to him, and Maximus used the guise of darkness to press a kiss on her soft lips.

Her eyes widened slightly, and she looked at him but didn't pull away. Instead, she allowed his mouth to cover hers hungrily as he explored hers more thoroughly.

When they finally parted, he heard someone yell, "Get a room!"

Tahlia laughed, blushing, and bumped her shoulder with his. Maximus couldn't recall a time when he'd felt this alive.

The night only continued to get better, and not just from the opening act and main attraction of Bruno Mars, but just by being with Tahlia. He fed off her intense energy. He wasn't much of a dancer other than the formal training he'd received to dance the waltz at social functions. But he loved the way Tahlia moved to the music, especially when a particularly good song came on. He liked it when she stood in front of him and he was able to wrap his arms around her. When her behind brushed his crotch as she swayed to the groove, Maximus felt his erection grow in his jeans.

He wasn't the only one who noticed. Tahlia turned behind her and gave him a wicked grin. Oh, she knew what she was doing to him. *The little minx!*

He would get her back real soon.

After the concert, the foursome filtered out of the arena. "That was a lot of fun," her sister, Kaitlynn, said. "But I'm not ready for the night to be over. Do you guys want to come out and hang?"

"Sure, what did you…" Tahlia began, but was interrupted by Maximus.

"No," Maximus stated, circling his arm around Tahlia. "We're going to call it a night."

"Okay, well, we're going to head out," Kaitlynn said. "I'll see you on Sunday at Mom's?"

"Absolutely." The sisters hugged while Maximus and Jonathan shook hands.

"It was great to meet you, Kaitlynn."

"You, too, Max. Don't do anything I wouldn't do." She winked at them as they walked away holding hands.

"So, did you enjoy yourself?" Tahlia asked, swinging their arms as if they were two small children to the lot where her car was parked in a reserved space.

"Yes, I did. I had a lot of fun, but I especially enjoyed watching you."

Tahlia paused midstep. "Me? Why?"

"I loved your inhibition and freedom as you danced and grooved, uncaring of what anyone else might think."

She shrugged. "Dancing is just a form of self-expression. You should try it sometime, Max, and not be so reserved. You have to be able to let yourself go."

"How about we start with this?" Maximus swung her in his arms, backing her up against the car so his entire body could cover hers and she could feel the erection she'd been teasing half the night. He ground the steel of his shaft against her, and she gasped. That was when his mouth moved over hers, smothering her lips, devouring their softness. She was shocked at Maximus's boldness, giving him the window he needed to break through the barrier of her lips and to invade her mouth with his tongue.

Tahlia groaned when he changed the pace from hungry, raw kisses to slow, gentle ones that were no less demanding as he cupped her breasts. Desire, hot and demanding, coursed through Maximus when she began rubbing against him, and he felt her breasts swell.

"Jesus, Tahlia!" He lifted his head as he nearly came undone. "You're killing me."

"You started it," she whispered, placing a feather-light kiss on his chin. "I think you wanted to show me you're not so reserved, right?"

He chuckled. "Mmm…I guess I did start it, but we can't finish it tonight, at least not here in this parking lot." Concertgoers and passersby were still walking to their cars, and they'd already given them quite a show.

"All right, I'll take you back to the office." Tahlia reluctantly disengaged from him. The car ride back to the Knight Shipping office crackled with sexual tension as memories of their sexual encounter in the parking lot stirred them. She was happy when the car came to a merciful stop in front of his building.

"I had a wonderful night," Max said, running his hand down the length of her arm. "And I can't wait for tomorrow night. Dress comfortably." He lightly caressed her cheek, and seconds later he was out of the car, leaving Tahlia feeling restless and oh so horny.

Tahlia excitedly waited for the doorbell to ring the following evening. She'd been ready for the last half hour and nervously pacing her one-bedroom apartment. She didn't know where they were going, only that Maximus had told her to dress comfortably.

She'd decided upon her favorite minidress that clung to her behind and teamed it with a black leather moto blazer and some ankle boots. Since it was a bit cool for a winter evening, she added a loose scarf to wrap around her neck.

Tahlia couldn't remember the last time she'd been this excited for a date, certainly not since Paul. She'd been cuckoo for Cocoa Puffs for him at the time, and he'd easily told her what she wanted to hear, but not Maximus. It surprised her just how different he was from what she'd expected. From afar, she would have thought him somewhat rigid, but so far he'd shown an amazing willingness to go with the flow. Tahlia had never been one to follow the crowd, and it was nice to know that Maximus could do the same.

When the doorbell rang, Tahlia didn't wait for him to come up. Instead, she rushed down the stairs and met Maximus on the first landing and threw herself in his arms. She buried her face in his throat and inhaled his magnificently masculine scent that was his alone.

"Hello, beautiful." When he brushed his lips across hers, it sent a shiver down Tahlia's spine. "Are you ready for a night of surprises?"

"Yes, I can't wait." She flashed him a grin.

On the drive to their mystery destination, Tahlia shared with Maximus her ideas and goals for the gallery. She wanted it to be a place for free expression and thought. A place where you could find the traditional and the unconventional. Maximus was all ears and gave her some sound advice on how best to achieve them. She was enjoying the conversation so much she didn't realize their destination until he stopped his Bugatti in the middle of a helipad.

"What are we doing here?" Tahlia exclaimed after Maximus had helped her out of his vehicle and she saw the helicopter with a pilot standing beside it.

"I'm taking you on a sunset tour of Hollywood. We're

riding in style, baby," Maximus said, grabbing her hand and leading her toward the helicopter. "C'mon."

In no time, Tahlia was strapped into one of two passenger seats and given headphones so she and Maximus could communicate, and then the pilot was taking off.

"Maximus, this is amazing," Tahlia said over the roar of the engine and wind as the helicopter soared in the air. She'd never done anything this thrilling in her entire life, and he was the reason for it. They took in all the sights Los Angeles had to offer, from the famous Hollywood sign to downtown Los Angeles to the Venice Beach boardwalk, celebrity homes, mountains of Malibu and the beautiful California coastline. Although it was dark, the lights of the city and Los Angeles skyline shone brightly.

When the exhilarating adventure was finally over, Tahlia and Maximus thanked the pilot. He'd given them a bit of history about each landmark they passed, making Tahlia want to do it all over again. She told Maximus so in the car on their drive to dinner.

"You outdid yourself," she gushed when they were on land. "I've never been in a helicopter before."

"No?" he asked with a smirk.

"I'm sure you have," she said, "no doubt to make important business meetings."

"But of course." He laughed. "That's how we moguls roll."

Tahlia playfully punched his arm. "You know, Maximus, I think I'm starting to like you." The moment she said the words aloud, she covered her mouth. Why did she always say whatever came to her mind?

Maximus took his eyes off the road long enough to say, "I'm starting to like you a lot, too."

Her heart took a perilous leap, and Tahlia swallowed

tightly, dropping her gaze to her trembling hands. With one hand on the wheel, Maximus grasped hers with his other and gave it a gentle squeeze. Tahlia could feel the blood surging through her fingertips from the simplest of actions, but it meant everything to her.

They ended up at Wolfgang Puck's restaurant at the Hotel Bel-Air. The food was delicious, the service impeccable and the company was everything Tahlia could hope for. Maximus was a lot funnier than she gave him credit for and regaled her with stories from his days at Harvard while Tahlia told him about growing up without a father.

"It must have been very hard for your single mother raising two girls on her own," Maximus said as they shared a dessert.

"It was. And at times we struggled," Tahlia admitted as she dug her spoon into the creamy mousse. "And it was in those moments that I missed having a father. But my mother gave me and Kaitlynn all the love we could ever need. I never for a moment doubted I was loved."

"I wish I could say the same," Maximus responded, "because all I've ever done is doubt my father. Did he love me? Did he not? He certainly wasn't one for showing it, so I guess I'll never really know."

Tahlia stared at him for several long beats. "I know he didn't show it, Max, but Arthur did love you. It may not seem like that now, but he told me how proud he was of you and your accomplishments. Everything that you've achieved. Please believe that."

Maximus's gaze darkened, and Tahlia could see how deeply her words were affecting him. "Thank you, Tahlia, and I know you mean well, but we're well past the point of my caring what my father thought of me."

Tahlia shook her head. "That's not true. I think you

need to hear it to believe it so you can make peace with him and with your older brother one day."

Maximus stared incredulously at Tahlia. He couldn't believe this was happening. That they were sitting here discussing his father as if he hadn't ripped his heart out of his chest when he'd given half the company to Lucius. It seemed so surreal.

"Tahlia, let's drop this topic of conversation, shall we?" Maximus said brightly. "Tonight was meant to be about you and me, not the ghosts of our past, present and future."

She smiled at his comment. "True, I just…"

She didn't get another word out because Maximus leaned toward her and brushed a featherlight kiss across her lips. He opened his eyes and glanced at her, and when she didn't resist him, he kissed her again, but this time he lingered, savoring the moment. When he finally pulled away, their breaths were both ragged.

"Maximus…"

"Do you have any idea how hard it is not to take you upstairs to one of these rooms and ravish you all night long?"

Tahlia inhaled sharply, and he could see that she, too, was struggling with what was the right move in this situation. They'd known each other only a couple of weeks, and although the attraction between them was strong, he wanted her to be sure before she went to bed with him. It had to be her choice. The fact that she didn't make a move or utter her consent made Maximus's decision easier. "I'll take you home," he said softly.

They were contemplative on the ride to her apartment, so much so that when they arrived, they both seemed equally shocked. "We've arrived," he said, turning off the engine.

"Yes, we have." But Tahlia made no move to go inside.

He twisted around, and his large hands grasped both sides of her face. "If you ask me in, you know what will happen."

She didn't speak. Instead, she wound her arms around his neck and brought his head down to her waiting lips. His entire body jolted at the contact, kicking him into high gear. Maximus pressed his lips to hers, and it was all over. In that moment, she was his, and he sealed it by sliding his tongue in her mouth and initiating a series of slow, drugging kisses, then deeper ones as he plundered her mouth.

Lust was jackknifing through him, and he couldn't resist pulling at her leather jacket so he could touch her. His hands roamed and his thumbs sought her nipples through the sparkling top. He squeezed them between his fingers and watched them bud for him. He so desperately wanted to taste them, taste her—he had an overwhelming need to be inside her.

Tahlia clutched at him, and a smothered sigh of longing escaped her lips. It caused Maximus to slow his passionate raid and to kiss a path from her lips to her throat, to her ears and back again to her lips. He didn't want their first time together to be a fevered coupling in a car. He wanted time to properly savor her.

"Tahlia, we have to stop," Maximus murmured. He pulled away from her and leaned his head against the headrest of his seat while he caught his breath. When he finally asserted enough willpower over his own wayward flesh, he looked at Tahlia. "Soon," he promised. "Soon you'll be mine."

Chapter 8

Maximus's words replayed in Tahlia's mind while she and her sister, Kaitlynn, took a yoga class midweek. Tahlia had hoped that the activity would ease some tension and allow her mind to rest, but all she could think about was how incredible it had been like to be with Max, how deliciously addictive he'd tasted, how thrilling it had felt to have his tongue mate with hers. She couldn't wait for the coming weekend because that was when they planned on seeing each other again.

It just seemed like the longest wait ever. Tahlia wasn't sure she could go the entire week without having him kiss her. Maximus had aroused her so much that his slightest move made her pulse quicken. She couldn't seem to control her reaction to him. He made her crave to be held in his arms, touched by him, such as when his fingers had skimmed her breasts and brought her nipples to peaks. She'd felt safe in his arms.

"Earth to Tahlia," Kaitlynn said, waving a hand in front of her as they wiped their sweaty faces from the workout in the locker room of their local fitness gym.

"Sorry, sis," Tahlia said and returned to the conversation.

"You've got it bad," Kaitlynn said. "I didn't think it was possible after Paul broke your heart, but Maximus Xavier Knight has you strung up tighter than the strings on a guitar."

"Does not."

"Does, too," her sister responded, "and I'm a bit worried. I saw you with him at the concert, and you seem awfully invested so soon into this relationship. Perhaps you should be taking this slower."

"We have been," Tahlia whispered, "so slow. We haven't even slept together."

Kaitlynn raised a brow. "You haven't? I would have thought that was a foregone conclusion, seeing how into him you are."

Tahlia spanked Kaitlynn's behind with her towel. "I'm very conservative, you know. I don't just sleep around. And, well, Maximus is being very patient. We're waiting for the right time."

"I sure hope that comes quick," Kaitlynn said with a laugh. "Otherwise, you're going to combust."

Tahlia rolled her eyes upward and then laughed herself. "You actually might be right. I didn't know it was possible to be this *horny*," she whispered so none of the other women could hear her.

"You—" her sister pointed to her "—need to take care of that, stat. When's your next date?"

"Saturday night."

"If I were you, I'd let him know in no uncertain terms that Saturday night is the night."

Oh, Tahlia intended to do just that. There was no way she could go through another night like last night. She'd actually ached between her thighs because she'd wanted him so much. It had taken every ounce of restraint not to drag him from the car and into her apartment building.

"And one thing, sis?"

"What's that?"

"Just be careful with your heart," Kaitlynn said. "I know you're an adult and everything. And you're feeling him all kind of ways, but remember at the end of the day, you're also business partners. There may come a time when you're on opposite sides of the fence and you'll have to decide where your loyalties lie."

Tahlia frowned. She hated that Kaitlynn was raining on her parade, but her sister had a point. Neither she nor Maximus had discussed exactly how a relationship between them would work, especially when it came to Knight Shipping. She'd been so caught up in the man that she hadn't given thought about the business since her tour with Lucius. And Maximus certainly hadn't brought it up during their dates together. He hadn't even mentioned the expansion he suggested during their tour. But surely, they wouldn't be put to the test that quickly. How bad could it really get?

Maximus was excited when Saturday finally arrived because he knew that tonight was the night. He would no longer push down his need to have Tahlia. Tonight he would unleash the passion he'd been restraining since they'd first met.

Since their date the previous Saturday, he'd made sure he had a steady diet of work, work and more work with an occasional stop for food, to work out and to enjoy his Sunday racquetball session with Griffin. When his friend had questioned him as to the status of his relationship with Tahlia, he'd remained mum and said it was progressing. He didn't need any recriminations at the moment.

Maximus figured if he kept busy, he'd keep his mind off Tahlia, but that lasted until only midweek. On Wednesday, he'd broken down and stopped by with lunch. He'd brought her and her assistant, Faith, salads to the gallery, and they ate in the conference room, all the while gazing at each other hungrily. His body was in tune to hers, eager to feed off her passion. Because when he touched her, her reaction was instant. Her responsiveness would only fuel his appetite in the bedroom, and there was no way he would be bored.

Oh, yes, tonight she would become his.

He'd planned a romantic evening ahead for them, ending with a stay at the bachelor pad he kept in downtown Los Angeles. It was his private retreat. He'd been staying at the estate since his father's death only because his mother had seemed so fragile without him. Though in his mind, she'd never really had his father's heart. It had gone to Jocelyn decades ago.

Maximus was dressed in his tuxedo and headed to the limousine parked outside the estate when his mother's voice stopped him on the steps leading to the foyer.

"Another evening out?" she inquired.

"Yes, and don't wait up. I'm spending the night at my place." He didn't wait to hear her response because he had somewhere to be.

Tahlia stared at herself in the mirror, impressed with the results she'd achieved. It was a miracle what makeup could do for you. She'd sprung for a treat and had her makeup and hair professionally done for her date with Maximus. Normally, she'd never have the money to spend on such an extravagance, but now that the gallery was hers, Tahlia figured she could splurge on a new look for tonight. When Maximus had told her to dress formally, she'd gone shopping. Now she was sporting a form-flattering gown and some strappy heels. She loved how the dress lifted her bosom and curved to her backside, giving her an hourglass figure.

He was right on time as usual, and her doorbell rang at 6:30 p.m. Tahlia reached for her small clutch and an overnight bag. She knew it was presumptuous as they'd not agreed that tonight they would take their relationship to the next level, but she suspected that Maximus was just as eager as she was to finally give in to the rampant lust that had colored their every encounter.

When she saw him, her heart did a somersault. He looked delectable in a black tuxedo with a silver bow tie. And he must have liked what he saw, because he whistled. He actually whistled when she came toward him.

"You look stunning!" He tucked her arm in his while his other grabbed her overnight bag. He didn't say anything about it. Instead, they walked to the limo, and once he'd helped her inside and given her bag to the driver, Max slid in beside her.

Tahlia was surprised at how nervous she felt given this wasn't their first date. She supposed it was because she'd made the decision to become intimate with him, and once sex entered the equation it changed everything.

"Relax." He reached for her hand and squeezed, but he didn't let go. He merely held it in his for the duration of the drive.

Tahlia began to suspect their destination as they climbed the hill and was pleased when the limo stopped and the driver helped her out of the car. They were at the Griffith Observatory.

"This place is spectacular."

"I know," Maximus said. "I've always loved the view, and since I know someone who works here, I've been able to arrange a little something special."

As they walked into the observatory, an older gentleman came toward Maximus. "Max, good to see you tonight."

"You, as well. Dennis Marshall, meet my girlfriend, Tahlia Armstrong."

Tahlia beamed inwardly. They'd never discussed titles, and although it was early on in the relationship, she was glad he felt that way. "Nice to meet you."

"As you know, I couldn't rent out the entire observatory to you, but we do have a terrace that's being refurbished thanks to your generous donation as a friend of the observatory. It's been set aside for you both. Follow me."

Dennis led them to one of the many terraces at the observatory. When they arrived, Tahlia was stunned to see a candlelit table for two set up along with a uniformed waiter and a harpist standing nearby.

She spun around to face Maximus. "You arranged all this?" No one had ever gone to this much trouble to impress her, and Tahlia had to admit she was blown away.

He shrugged. "For you, I'd do a lot more."

His breath was warm and moist against her face, and Tahlia's heart raced. She was truly touched that he would try to make this night memorable for the both of them. She didn't protest when he took her hand and led her to one of the seats. Instead, she settled back to enjoy the evening ahead, though it was hard to do because she couldn't tear her gaze from his face. He was so very good-looking and she was attracted to him.

Tahlia didn't know how she'd sit still without jumping his bones, but she did.

She enjoyed a delicious four-course meal that was one of the best she'd ever had as they talked about their week. Maximus shared with her bits and pieces about Knight Shipping and a new contract he'd landed. Not nearly as much as she would have liked, but they were taking baby steps. Meanwhile, Tahlia shared that she was working on her own art exhibit.

He grinned, clearly pleased with himself. "You're taking my advice."

She nodded. "I've always wanted to have one of my own, but after I got rejected by several galleries, I'd begun to wonder if I was any good."

"Don't let others' opinion sway you," Maximus said. "You're capable of great things, Tahlia. You just have to believe in yourself."

"I'm beginning to."

"Will you let me see what you're working on?"

His steady gaze bore into hers, and she nodded. "If you'd like me to."

"I would like that very much."

After dessert, Maximus pulled her into his arms and they danced to the strains coming from the harpist. Her arms moved of their own volition, clasping behind his neck as she melted into him. Because of it, she was conscious of where his warm flesh touched hers, and her skin tingled when his thighs brushed hers.

Eventually, she relaxed, sinking into his embrace. It was a magical night, and with the stars twinkling overhead, it was a night made for romance. More than that, Tahlia enjoyed being cradled in Maximus's arms as he rocked them back and forth. She could feel the evidence of his arousal pressed against her stomach. She could hardly believe that she was here in this moment with him, the man she'd dreamed about but never thought she'd ever meet. And now they would become lovers.

One of his hands stroked her cheek. "What are you thinking about?"

"Me. You. All of it," Tahlia answered honestly. She didn't know how else to be when she was around him. Whenever he was near, she was an open book, but Tahlia longed for the moment when Maximus wasn't so restrained. She wanted to see him completely lose control. Would he do so tonight when they made love for the first time? Would he allow himself to be vulnerable?

As if reading her mind, he cupped her face in his warm hands and kissed her deeply. Her tongue tangled with his, and Tahlia pressed herself against him, wanting every part of her body to be touched by him. When he lifted his head, his eyes were riveted on hers. She could hear his uneven breathing as he held her close. "Can I have you tonight? Will you be mine?"

"Yes."

Maximus's control was slipping. After Tahlia told him she would be his, it had taken every ounce within him to pull away from her so he could bring their evening at the observatory to a close. He thanked Dennis on his way out before they settled into the limousine so he could focus solely on her. All night he'd been mesmerized by her, from the soft peach color of her couture spaghetti-strap dress showing off the delicate slope of her shoulders to the sexy heels that added at least four inches to her height. She'd looked twice as sexy as she ever had.

As soon as the limo door closed, they reached for each other. Maximus had Tahlia underneath him in five seconds flat, and they began kissing, touching and caressing each other.

"You are so beautiful." He whispered a litany of praises as he tongued Tahlia's ear, and she responded by moaning and writhing on the limo seat. He could feel his erection swell in his tuxedo trousers. If she kept this up, it would be over with quickly.

"Tahlia, slow down, babe. We have all night."

And they did.

Tahlia had brought an overnight bag because she, too, had known that the time for waiting was over. Tonight, he wanted her hot and wet underneath him. If he could, he'd do it right now. He'd lift her dress up and skim his hands all the way to heaven, but he had to cool things down a bit. Slowly, he pulled them both upright until they were in the seated position.

Tahlia's hair was mussed and her lipstick barely visible because he'd kissed it clean off. By the end of the night, he intended to have her a lot more disheveled. In fact, he wanted her begging for him to come inside her.

As the limo came to a stop, Tahlia combed her fingers through her hair and he helped fix her dress back in place. He'd been desperate to taste her, so one shoulder strap had come down because he'd been kissing and nipping at the soft flesh. He exited the vehicle first and whispered to the driver to see that her bag was delivered to the penthouse. Then he helped Tahlia from the limo.

He curved her arm in his as they walked inside the building. He greeted the doorman with a terse nod and went for the penthouse elevator. He had his own private elevator that would take them to the top floor, where they would not be disturbed for the rest of the night.

Because that was exactly what it would take for him to satiate the desire he had for Tahlia.

All night.

* * *

Tahlia didn't notice much of Maximus's beautifully appointed penthouse when they arrived because they never turned on the lights. With the moonlight streaming through the windows, she spun around to face him. His gaze traveled over her face, searching her eyes. If he thought he'd find reticence, he wouldn't. Tahlia had never been surer of what she wanted. And she wanted Maximus.

He stepped forward, clasping her body tightly in his, and without a single word lifted her into his arms and walked straight to his bedroom.

She wanted this man. Oh, how she wanted him. And when he laid her down on the king-size bed, Tahlia reached up to draw him down to her.

Maximus tasted so good, so deliciously addictive, that Tahlia parted her lips and allowed his bold and daring tongue to do thrilling things to her mouth. It swirled and danced and played with hers, making her want more, much more of Maximus. Every part of her ached to be touched by this man, and she clung to him, wrapping her ankles around his, eager to be closer.

He lifted his head and looked down at her. His eyes were hazy with desire. "We should undress. I want to see you naked. Feel your skin on mine."

Tahlia didn't blush at his words. Instead, she untangled herself and began wiggling her way out of her dress.

"Here, let me help." Maximus's hands lightly brushed her skin as he lifted the silky fabric over her shoulders and head and dropped it to the floor. Tahlia wasn't wearing anything other than a strapless bra and bikini panties, and the look of unadulterated lust on Maximus's face made her feel desirable.

"God, you're beautiful…"

She smiled and reached behind her to unfasten her bra, but Maximus stopped her. "Let me…" He unclasped the unwanted garment and tossed it aside. His eyes feasted on her bare breasts.

Maximus reached out and cupped them in his palms. "I can't wait to taste you," he said, stroking her chocolate nipples. They puckered in response to his touch. "But you still have too many clothes on."

Tahlia leaned back on her forearms so Maximus could hook his fingers into the band of her panties and glide them down her trembling thighs. When she was completely naked, he peered down at her. His gaze riveted on her sex. Then he began stripping off his clothes.

Tahlia sucked in a deep breath as she watched him remove piece after piece of clothing. Maximus wasn't overly muscular like some men; his body was all lean muscle and sinew. And when he removed his pants and she got to see the most intimate part of him, she stared unabashedly at his big and powerful shaft. He was more beautiful than she could have ever imagined. She reveled in the knowledge that tonight he was *hers*. And vice versa.

When he joined her again on the bed, Tahlia couldn't wait to get her hands on him and began touching him everywhere she could, from the rippled muscles of his arms to his taut nipples to his flat, lean stomach, to his firm behind. She wanted all of it, all of him. He allowed her to explore him, barely touching her with only the slightest caress of his fingers. It didn't matter. He'd already lit a fire inside her from the moment they'd officially met.

And when his hands cupped her face and he kissed her slow and deep, Tahlia nearly whimpered with hunger. She was feeling so much. Having Maximus's lips, tongue and hands on her was *everything*. They were finally naked, their bodies touching, her breasts against his hard chest, hips and thighs tangled together. Tahlia laced her fingers through his curls, and as his kiss became more intense, her response became feverish to his searching tongue.

Maximus worked her mouth while his hands moved downward to tease her breasts with his fingertips. Her already sensitive nipples were aching for him, and he read her mind, his mouth leaving hers to find its way to where she needed him. He took her breasts in his hands, and his mouth closed over her nipple. He licked and teased her with featherlight flicks of his wet tongue before sucking on the hardened tip.

After leaving one breast, he moved to tease and coax a response from the other. His mouth continued its exploration as he made his way down her body, kissing and caressing her every nook and crevice. His hot mouth and searching fingers were blazing a trail of fire everywhere he went, striking a match to her need. All she could do was lie back, propped on her elbows, and watch him. Hunger was etched across his face as he skimmed his way down her entire body before stopping at her center.

"I can finally taste you properly," Maximus murmured as he hovered over her, and Tahlia held her breath in anticipation of what was to come. She was unprepared for the openmouthed kiss he placed there, and her hips jerked involuntary.

"Easy, baby," Maximus whispered, grasping her hips in his hands. "I've got you."

Tahlia was in disbelief that this handsome man's head was spread between her open thighs and was poised to give her more pleasure than she'd ever known. Tahlia arched her back, baring herself to him, so he could take all of her. But she wanted even more. "Please…"

He bent his head again, and the sensation of having his mouth on her caused Tahlia to tip her head back and moan. And when he slid a finger inside her to stroke her walls, she shuddered. His mouth and fingers didn't stop their exploration of her wet heat. It was such a delicious torment that Tahlia gave herself over to him.

"Oh, yes. Yes!" She let go, her hips rising to meet his searching tongue and fingers. And when she could take no more her, her muscles contracted, her body tensed and she climaxed.

Maximus slowed his actions as Tahlia's entire body felt sated. "I'm not done with you yet," he said as his hands slid up her torso to toy with her breasts again. "This was just the beginning."

As he looked down at her, Maximus had to admit he was enjoying every moment of Tahlia's first climax with him. He'd known she'd be this way, this responsive to him, his kisses, his touch, but she'd been completely uninhibited with him, and he wanted more. It surprised him that in a short amount of time, he'd come to care for her, want her. It had taken a supreme amount of patience for him not to beg her to let him come up last Saturday night, but he was glad he had. Because this was so much better. The buildup of their first time together had made him even more excited of what was to come.

He wasn't the only one ready for more. Now that she'd recovered, Tahlia was pushing his chest down until he was flat on the bed. She ran her hands across his chest. She bent her head and trailed a path of hot kisses all over his chest. He acknowledged her taking control by running his fingers through her hair. But when she came to his nipples and brushed her lips against one, he tensed.

He was going to be in trouble.

She teased his nipples with gentle flicks of her tongue, and every cell in his body came on fire. She stoked the flames. Her hot tongue moved from one nipple to the other, paying each equal homage. But she wasn't done with him yet. She continued worshipping his body, kissing his abdomen and stomach before going straight to the source of his inferno.

As she crouched on her knees, her long hair brushed his abdomen, and Maximus let out a long sigh of appreciation from deep within him. And when her small hands grasped his burgeoning shaft, Maximus nearly leaped off the bed. This fiery vixen had *him* quivering. His erection pulsed in her delicate hands, but she didn't shy away from him. Instead, she licked him.

Again and again, she licked the sides and bulbous head of his shaft, teasing him with light flicks of her tongue and then with bold strokes. His body responded, and he swelled even more in her hands, and that was when she took the crown into her mouth and sucked.

Sweet Jesus!

Maximus wasn't sure he could take it, but take it he did. In fact, he groaned, "More…"

And she gave him more, bobbing her head up and down his shaft, taking him even deeper into her mouth. Maximus was just a man, and she brought him to his knees as he came inside her mouth. Tahlia licked every bit of him up with her tongue, and when she raised her head and stared up at him, she asked, "Did you like that?"

Maximus's heart was pounding loudly in his chest

and his heartbeat had yet to return to normal. "You—you know I did."

She grinned mischievously. "Turnabout is fair play."

Maximus reached for her and pushed her back into the pillows. "Well, then, let's see who comes first next time."

Tahlia felt even more excited by Maximus's playful and provocative words. She'd taken charge, and he'd come undone just as he'd made her. It was powerful knowing the effect she could have on this man and that he was finally willing to be vulnerable with her, but she suspected they'd only just touched the surface on how deep their connection went. She watched as Maximus reached inside his nightstand for a foil packet and put on a condom.

Then he returned to her, and she parted her legs to make room for him so his mouth could plunder hers once more. He stilled and looked into her face, into her soul. Then he reached between them to ensure she was still wet and ready for the moment. She was and lifted her hips and felt him position himself, and then he kissed her just as he eased inside her.

Tahlia cried out, closing her eyes from the intensity—the feel of him. Her fingers caught in his hair at the unbearable pleasure of having him inside her. He paused while her body got used to his. She was trembling. So his arms encircled her, and he thrust in again, this time deeper, filling her.

Talia wanted him to lose control as he'd done a moment ago, so she began working her muscles around him. His eyes widened. So she worked them harder—it pleased her when he let out a hiss of air. She was getting to him. She grasped his butt cheeks, pressing him closer.

The move ratcheted up the level of passion inside him, and she could sense he was rallying to the challenge.

A low, husky laugh escaped his lips. And he began moving faster inside her, demanding she keep up the rhythm he was setting. He was in charge, his hands cupping her bottom as he surged in and out of her again with deliberate strokes. All thought of who was in control left Tahlia's mind. She could only feel the heat of his body, the heavy rasp of his breathing, the slapping of their bellies as he drove harder inside her. She wrapped her legs around his middle, sweeping her fingers down his back.

And when rapture finally hit her, she screamed, and he shouted a purely animalistic cry as their control broke and they came tumbling back down to earth.

Chapter 9

Bare-chested and wearing only his pajama bottoms, Maximus stared out at the Los Angeles skyline. He was bowled over by the lovemaking Tahlia and he shared last night. They'd transcended any other experience he'd ever had. He'd never felt so close, so in tune to another human being. Tahlia had fulfilled every one of his fantasies, and then some. She was so open and honest with her feelings and how much she enjoyed everything he'd done—they'd done. Maximus smiled because he had the scratches on his back to prove it.

And she'd been insatiable for him. They hadn't stopped at one time. They'd made love several times through the wee hours of the morning. He'd particularly enjoyed Tahlia on top as she'd straddled him, easing up and down his shaft. He'd encouraged her, holding her hips to find a rhythm. She'd ridden him until he'd flipped her over and taken her from behind. Images of them together throughout the night flooded his mind.

Maximus wasn't sure he could continue with his seduction scheme. He'd known it was wrong from the start to use another person. But more important, he liked Tahlia a lot, much more than he'd ever imagined he would. He liked her openness, her kindness and her giving spirit. She was a truly unique person, and he considered himself lucky to have met her.

Tahlia emerged from his bedroom sleepy-eyed and wearing the tuxedo shirt he'd carelessly thrown on the floor in his haste to be with her. She looked sexy as hell with her hair mussed and lips swollen and wearing his shirt.

"Good morning, beautiful." He held out his arms to her, but she shook her head and walked toward the overnight bag in the foyer that the driver had to have brought up last night.

"Let me brush my teeth first," she said. She grasped her bag and quickly headed back to his bedroom.

He smiled. He loved the air of innocence about Tahlia. It was appealing given the sophisticated women he'd been with in the past. They wouldn't have dared walk out of his bedroom without their hair in order and face fully made up. Tahlia, on the other hand, looked appropriately bedded. She was down-to-earth, and that was what he liked.

She reemerged five minutes later, and this time her hair had been brushed until it gleamed, and when she came toward him, she smelled clean and minty, like toothpaste and peppermint mouthwash. "Good morning." She kissed him full on the mouth.

He stroked her hair, and she glanced up at him with her big brown eyes, and Maximus's heart turned over in his chest. He couldn't describe the feeling that came over him, only that he didn't want to let her go. He patted his pajama bottoms, making sure he'd thrown in a condom. Then he hauled her closer to him and kissed her again.

She parted her lips and let him devour her mouth. He deepened the kiss, cupping her bottom against his erection because as soon as he'd seen her, he'd come to life. Maximus began walking Tahlia backward toward the couch. They fell on it a mass of limbs, but Maximus recovered long enough to start unbuttoning the shirt she wore. When her breasts were bare to him, he caught one in his mouth and teased it a little with his tongue and then moved to the other one.

Tahlia began writhing on the couch as he trailed hot kisses down her body. He was happy to find she hadn't put on any panties, and he wasted no time easing her thighs apart and burying his face in her womanhood. He dipped his head to taste her, and Tahlia cried out. "Ah…"

He knew how to please her, and she gave herself over to him as he slipped her legs over his shoulders and opened herself up to him. She trusted him now and closed her eyes, allowing him to bring her through the storm as he toyed with her clitoris. She cried out wildly as she rode the wave, allowing him enough time to push down his bottoms, put on a condom and slide inside her as little aftershocks tore through her. He loved how her body clenched around him and would do so again with him inside her.

"Please, Max, please…" She gripped at his shoulders, desperate for him to move.

He took her hands in his and lifted them over her head, then he fixed her with a penetrating gaze. She stared at him for several long moments as she took in the intense look on his face. Then he surged forward—thrusting in and out.

She gasped, working her hips underneath him in tandem with him, and his hold loosened and she laced her fingers with his. Their eyes remained locked as they moved as one flesh. Maximus couldn't break the gaze. As the intensity grew between them, she didn't look away, either. Instead he sank deeper and deeper until finally their bodies shook and her name passed from his lips again and again.

"Tahlia. Tahlia."

After running home to change, Tahlia made it over to her mother's for Sunday dinner with her sister, Kaitlynn. She'd stayed most of the day at Maximus's penthouse, laughing, talking and, of course, making love. The pleasure and satisfaction she'd found in his arms was immeasurable, and she could attest to it thanks to the soreness between her thighs.

Maximus was not only a skilled lover, but a voracious one. She'd never been made love to with such authority and intensity. It was as if he *owned* her body and she'd been powerless to do anything but be as honest as she could be and hide nothing from him. She'd shown him exactly how much she'd desired him when he'd asked if he was pleasing her or if she wanted more of whatever delicious activity they were engaged in at that moment.

She was in so deep with Maximus. She was falling for him, and it terrified her. The emotions she felt for him were much stronger than what she'd felt for Paul.

"Tahlia," her mother, Sophia, greeted her in the hall after Tahlia used her key to come inside.

"Hey, Mama," Tahlia said. Then she sniffed with her nose. "What are you cooking?"

Her mother shrugged. "Just your favorite homemade chicken potpie."

Tahlia smiled. "You spoil me."

"But she made my favorite dessert," Kaitlynn said, rising from the sofa in the living room where she was watching television.

"Hey, sis." Tahlia gave her sister a one-armed hug.

"I like spoiling both my girls," Sophia replied. Then she inclined her head to the bottle of wine in Tahlia's hand. "You want to open that up while the potpie finishes? Shouldn't be much longer now."

"Sure thing." They all filed into her mother's small kitchen, which had only enough room for a four-seater table.

Tahlia looked around. "Mama, we need to get you a bigger place."

"Why?" her mother asked as she fished a wine opener out of one of the drawers and began opening the bottle. "This is just fine for me. No need in spending money just because you have some."

"I know, but you've been here since we were little," Tahlia replied. "You deserve something nicer. Doesn't she, Kaitlynn?" She turned to her sister for confirmation.

"I agree with Tahlia, Mom. You could do better than this place."

"Why would I want to leave?" She pulled three wineglasses from above her head in the cabinet, poured the wine and handed both of them a glass. "This place has all my memories of you girls growing up." She went over to the doorway and lightly touched the markings that held their growth spurts through the years.

"I know," Tahlia said, sipping her wine. "I just want the best for you."

"And now that you're dating a wealthy boyfriend, it's probably hard to come back down to earth, huh?" Kaitlynn teased, eyeing her.

Tahlia glared at her. "Don't hate just because Max and I are in a relationship."

Kaitlynn's brow rose. "So you're admitting he's your boyfriend?"

"He called me his girlfriend the other day when he introduced me. So yes, I guess I am."

A smile formed on her sister's lips. "Then I'm glad to see I was wrong. The only reason I'd cautioned you to be careful around him was because I thought Maximus was using you for your vote."

"Her vote?" her mother inquired.

"Don't forget, Mama, Tahlia is the deciding vote at Knight Shipping if Maximus and his brother should butt heads."

Tahlia was silent. She hadn't yet been put to the test on what Max's expectation of her was where her vote was concerned. They'd never really discussed it. Did he see it as a foregone conclusion that she would automatically side with him?

"Can we not talk about business?" Tahlia inquired. She was so happy after spending last night in Maximus's arms that she wanted to bask in the moment. "And just have dinner?"

"Of course, sweetheart," her mother said, and Kaitlynn agreed, but Tahlia couldn't quite dismiss her sister's concerns. Maximus knew she was fair and honest. He wouldn't expect her to always agree with him. Would he?

"Good game," Maximus said after he and Griffin finished up their racquetball game at the country club and were now seated at the bar having an afternoon drink. "I am back in my stride now."

"Yeah, yeah," Griffin said, swigging a beer. "Don't gloat just because you won."

"You need to accept the natural order of things," Maximus said.

"Next week, I'll wipe the floor with that smug smile of yours."

"We'll see." Maximus chuckled. "And how is life at the firm?" Griffin was working long hours to become partner at his law firm.

"The usual, eighty-hour workweeks," Griffin replied.

"And is there any woman on the horizon?" Maximus inquired. "Are you holding out on me? I've told you about Tahlia."

"Only as much as you want me to know," Griffin responded. "Besides, there's no one special in my life. Unlike you, who's all Machiavellian."

"That's not true. I care for Tahlia," Maximus replied. "Actually, I like her a lot."

Griffin regarded him quizzically for a moment and then he said, "You're starting to fall for her, aren't you? Now it won't be so easy to go through with this ridiculous scheme you've concocted."

"I admit I've developed strong feelings for Tahlia."

"But have you told her why you started seeing her to begin with?"

Maximus frowned. "Of course not. That would hurt her." And he didn't want that. Tahlia was so sweet. Knowing that he'd been planning on using her to get his way would devastate her.

"Then you're in quite the predicament, my friend," Griffin replied. "Because mark my words, there will come a time when this scheme of yours and your developing relationship with Tahlia will all come to a head. And when it does, it won't be pretty."

Maximus looked at his friend. Was Griffin right? Was he walking into the eye of the storm? Should he retreat and let Tahlia go before either of them got hurt?

Tahlia glanced down at the canvas in front of her. She was working on a new piece that would go with her exhibit. The idea had come to her after the amazing weekend she'd had with Maximus a few weeks ago. Since then they'd been seeing a great deal of each other and not just on the weekends.

During the week, they would go out for a bite to eat, catch a movie or just stay at her place and watch Netflix. Tahlia took great pleasure in showing him how the other half lived as they shared a bowl of microwave popcorn and vegged out in front of the television. She'd even broached the subject of Knight Shipping when they were curled up together.

"Why are you bringing up work?" He'd pulled away to look at her strangely.

"Because…" She'd trailed off. "I want you to share with me what's going on in your world. I may not understand it all, but you could explain it to me. For instance, how's your work on the expansion coming?"

Initially, Maximus had been startled by her request, but eventually he'd started talking about his dream for expanding the company and all the jobs it would bring to the community. He had Tahlia so invested, she couldn't think of a single reason why she wouldn't vote his way.

He'd even introduced her to his friend Griffin, and they'd gone out on a double date with him and a new woman he was seeing. Tahlia had liked Griffin immediately. She could see Griffin could be a ladies' man just like Maximus with his dark chocolate skin, bald head and basketball player build. She also noticed that Griffin was the yin to Maximus's yang. Although he was an attorney, he was much more laid-back than Maximus, but Tahlia was doing her best to change that. She'd even corralled Maximus into going dancing. She was crazy about him, but he was terrible at freestyle dancing, although it didn't matter to Tahlia because she was happiest in his arms.

And the nights, well, Tahlia blushed when she thought about their active sex life. It was a rare night when they didn't make love. Maximus was an imaginative lover, making sure she was satisfied each and every time.

She hadn't realized just how important Maximus had become to her day-to-day routine until he went on an overnight trip during the middle of the week and she was alone in bed and unable to spoon with him. She also hadn't received a phone call from him during the day or a text to see how her day was going as she usually did. And so she had gone up to the gallery loft to paint and while away the hours. She was concentrating so hard on her work that she didn't notice it had become dark or that she had a guest.

Tahlia glanced up and found Maximus staring not just at her, but also at the canvass. "Hey," she said, smiling as he came forward to peer at her artwork.

He brushed the briefest of kisses across her lips and said, "This is good, really good, Tahlia."

She beamed with pride. "You think so?"

"Yes, of course I do. Will this piece go in your exhibit?"

She nodded. "When did you get back?" she asked over her shoulder as she walked over to the sink and washed her hands.

"A little while ago," he answered, still looking intently at her painting. "I came straight here. I missed you."

Tahlia turned around, and the lusty look on Maximus's face made her rush into his arms, wet hands and all. He flattened her against him, branding her lips with urgent, moist kisses, letting her know that he was as desperate as she was to be together.

She stilled. "The door..."

"Faith was leaving when I arrived. She locked up," Maximus said, planting kisses on her ear and neck. "We're alone."

Tahlia quickly began pulling at his overcoat, sliding it down his muscular arms. Then they were both tearing at each other's clothes until they were nude. She didn't think it was possible to get aroused this fast, but Maximus brought out this side to her, made her wanton and greedy.

"I want to see all of you," Maximus groaned as they slid to the floor on top of the sheet she'd used to ensure paint didn't get on the floor. But in this moment Tahlia could care less. She wanted Max. He climbed on top of her, covering her body with his. She opened her legs to cushion his hardness, but he withdrew from her.

"Hold on a second. Need a condom..." he groaned. He reached for the wallet in his trousers to sheath himself and returned to her. When he returned to her, he stared down at her as if he were seeing her for the first time.

She held out her arms, and he sank down, pressing his lips to hers. Then they were once again kissing, tasting and nibbling at each other's flesh. Tahlia's eyes glazed with passion when she felt his fingers at her entrance, sliding deep inside her, making sure she was stimulated, lubricated and ready for him. She whimpered, seeking more of him, and he delivered by removing his fingers, flexing his hips and plunging inside her.

Tahlia arched off the floor, going blind with unimaginable pleasure. "You feel...so good...inside me," she panted as her arousal heightened. "More... Max..."

Maximus wanted to drown in Tahlia and her rising passion. Her core was throbbing tightly around him, milking every last thread of control he had to make this last. So he thrust in again, stroking deeper, and her cries rose and she bunched her hands in his hair.

He withdrew, then plunged in again, burying himself to the hilt. Tahlia shattered around him, but he didn't stop. He couldn't. He was enraptured, and he surged into her again, reaching new heights, so much so that Tahlia's entire body began convulsing around him and his own orgasm tore through him, so hard that he roared out his release so loud he was sure everyone on the street had to have heard him. He fell forward on top of her, then carefully rose on his shins to look down at her.

Her eyes were slumberous, and her entire body relaxed beneath him as aftershocks continued to jolt through their bodies. Maximus didn't disengage from her. He was still hard and throbbing inside her. He wanted her again.

But not here.

They'd go back to her place or his. He didn't care, but he would spend all night making love to her until they both slept.

Later, when they made it back to her place and were cuddled in bed, Maximus knew he wanted to spend more time with Tahlia. He'd known it when he'd lain in his hotel room the night before and missed Tahlia's warm body beside him. He hadn't even stopped at the office, which was his usual MO after a business trip, and headed directly to her gallery. He'd known he'd find Tahlia there, and he had.

She was painting again. And he hoped in part that it was due to his encouragement that hers was as good as any other artist's work that she exhibited at the gallery.

"You awake?" he whispered in her ear when her backside was firmly planted in his crotch.

"Hmm…" she moaned sleepily.

"I was thinking we should go away this weekend, to Big Sur. There's a great place I know of with the best views."

Tahlia turned around in his arms to face him. "You want to go away together?"

He grinned down at her. "Yes, my dear, but only if you don't have any other plans."

"I was going to paint," Tahlia said, stifling a yawn, "but I can finish the piece when I get back."

He grinned. He'd thoroughly worn her out. "I don't want to stop your muse."

She laughed huskily. "You won't. Maybe you're my muse." Her voice was still thick with sleep.

He peered at her intently and wondered if she really meant that or she was just saying it in the heat of the moment. He stroked her cheek. "Go back to sleep, my love, and we'll talk details in the morning." He kissed her forehead and then held her until she fell asleep.

But he didn't go to sleep right away. In his wildest dreams, he couldn't have created a woman who fit him so perfectly. The result was electric, and her unguarded response to him stirred his soul. This furnace of mutual passion couldn't last forever, could it? Surely, they'd blaze out control, but somewhere deep in the recesses of his mind, Maximus wasn't sure that was true—and that scared him to death.

Chapter 10

My love. He'd called her his love. Tahlia could still hear his words as she packed for their Big Sur trip on Friday. She was probably putting too much emphasis on them, but surely they meant something. Or maybe she'd misheard. She had been drifting off to sleep when he broached the subject of a weekend getaway. And he hadn't repeated the endearment since. Not over the phone to say he was working late or again today when he'd asked if she was all packed for the trip.

Tahlia was certainly starting to feel the sentiment, but she was afraid to say it first. With Paul, she'd been quick to reveal her feelings, and look where that had gotten her. Looking at it logically, they'd only been seeing each other a month. So she would keep her feelings to herself until she was sure they were returned and it wouldn't blow up in her face.

She continued packing, putting in warm clothes as well as a swimsuit because Maximus had indicated the room they'd be staying in had a hot tub. Tahlia's face flamed when she thought about what they could do inside that tub. She was so deep in thought that she nearly missed hearing her cell phone ring. When she did, she found it was Maximus's assistant, Elena, calling to inform her of a board meeting next week.

"Will you be attending?" Elena inquired.

Tahlia hadn't given much thought to the running of Knight Shipping because she'd been so caught up with Maximus, taking over the gallery and preparing for her own exhibit. She supposed Maximus had made her and Lucius's life easy by handling the day-to-day operations, but now it was time for Tahlia to fulfill the duty Arthur had given her.

"Ms. Armstrong, are you there?" Elena asked after her prolonged silence.

"Yes, I'll be there," Tahlia replied swiftly. She ended the call and sat down on her bed. When they returned from their weekend getaway, their relationship would be tested for the first time. Tahlia's stomach lurched at the prospect. She could only hope that the foundation they'd made wouldn't crack under the pressure.

Maximus was excited to pick up Tahlia and take her to the Post Ranch Inn in Big Sur. It was known for its romantic rooms with a view, and he'd made sure to select the top-of-the-line room for them. Nestled on a cliff, the room was by far their best, in his opinion. He just hoped Tahlia would like his choice.

She was waiting for him on the sidewalk when he pulled to the curb to pick her up. He jumped out of the car and greeted her with a searing kiss. Then he stepped backward to drink in the cute outfit she was wearing, her usual fashion of skinny jeans and oversize sweater. Tahlia made it look like a fashion statement. She'd put her hair up in a chignon with loose tendrils framing her face and wore minimal makeup with the exception of lip gloss.

"Let's go," Maximus said, opening the passenger door for her. "I want to get on the road before traffic picks up."

"Of course." Tahlia slid inside while he dealt with her overnight bag.

The drive to Big Sur was uneventful, and they chatted conversationally about the week. But Maximus noticed that Tahlia didn't bring up the fact that Knight Shipping had a board meeting coming up when they returned next week. He'd forgotten it himself until Elena had reminded him this morning and begun contacting board members, including Lucius.

His brother had been sure to tell Elena that he wouldn't miss it. Maximus had no idea how the meeting would go. He suspected that Lucius would be as ornery as possible just to get under his skin as he had on the tour, but it was Tahlia he was most concerned about.

Maximus just wanted it over with as quickly as possible. He'd been running the company the last month quite well without either Lucius's or Tahlia's assistance or interference. Thankfully, they'd taken a back seat and let him do the job he'd been groomed for.

He looked over at Tahlia. She was staring out at the coast, and he wished he could be as carefree as she was in this moment. He would try his best not to think about next week and be in the moment with her. She must have sensed him watching because she glanced over at him and smiled. Maximus's heart swelled in his chest.

They arrived to the inn in a little under three hours and walked a short cobblestone path to the cliff room. When he opened the door, he let Tahlia precede him so he could see her enjoyment.

* * *

Tahlia glanced around and was shocked at just how stupendous the room was after they'd entered it from an enclosed garden courtyard. It was a freestanding structure and held a massive king-size bed. And directly in front of her was the breathtaking view through the glass-walled bedroom. She glanced at the wood-burning fireplace on her way to the deck. Once outside, she could see they were suspended on a cliff. They could watch the sunset and sit on the two loungers outside or in the stainless steel outdoor hot tub.

Tahlia turned to Maximus, who'd followed her. "You've outdone yourself, Max."

He smiled. "I'm glad you like it."

"What's not to like? This is every woman's romantic getaway."

"C'mon." He grasped her hand. "You didn't see the rest."

He led her back into the living area and past the bathroom's glass door so she could see the soaking tub. "How would you like a bath in that?"

She grinned mischievously as she pulled him closer. "Where do I sign up?"

They spent the rest of the afternoon touring the inn's amenities before retiring to their room to change for dinner. They both dressed casually, Maximus in slacks and a button-down shirt while Tahlia opted for knit slacks, an oversize sweater and some flat sandals. Being in the mountains, it was a bit colder than in Los Angeles, but Maximus told her he'd keep her warm. Tahlia had no doubt he would; it didn't take much to stoke the flames of their desire for one another.

The dinner at the inn's restaurant, Sierra Mar, overlooked the coast and offered a stunning view. Tahlia felt like she hadn't been living fully until she'd seen nature in all its splendor. After dessert, they retired to the room, where Maximus made gentle, sweet love to her, touching her in places that made her quiver and moan in pleasure. She called out his name more than once because he satisfied her every need. Eventually, they both drifted off into a peaceful sleep.

Maximus awoke on Saturday morning feeling better than he ever had. He felt rejuvenated even though he'd gotten very little sleep. He'd thought he had an insatiable appetite, but Tahlia more than matched him in sexual compatibility. The way she'd stroked him with her searching fingers, he'd been unable to resist her, and he'd succumbed willingly to her.

And now, as he drove them to the Esalen Institute, Tahlia talked animatedly about the institute and all of its offerings. When he'd thought of Big Sur, the nonprofit retreat center had come to mind because Tahlia always seemed so self-aware that he thought she'd appreciate its emphasis on the mind-body connection. Plus, there were tons of workshops on self-help, gardening and Tahlia's favorite: art. Max suspected they'd spend their entire Saturday there. He wondered if the weekend could get any better. Why had he never taken the time to get out and smell the roses? Because he'd always been trying to please his father. A wasted effort.

Tahlia's first activity choice was for them to take a meditation class. Maximus hadn't been interested, but Tahlia had talked him into it. He didn't see the purpose of sitting for an hour and focusing on his breathing, but afterward he had to admit he felt more relaxed and less stressed than he had in a decade.

"See? I told you you'd like it," Tahlia said as they

left the yoga studio and began to explore the farm and the institute's sustainability program before venturing to the art center.

Maximus knew that Tahlia would appreciate the painting workshop, so he left her there and took in a leadership workshop. He immersed himself for an hour in the transformation leadership session about how he could live his authentic self while nourishing the lives of others.

They ended their self-reflective day with hour-long massages followed by a dip in the hot springs. He and Tahlia opted to wear swim trunks and bathing suits while others went with the clothing-optional route. Maximus thought Tahlia would shy away from the experience, but then she'd surprised him by removing her bikini top and then her bottom and luxuriating in the water.

"Don't be afraid," she teased as she stood there completely nude.

Her abandon caused Maximus to lose his trunks and circle his arms around her. They basked in their freedom until the sun began to set and it was time to head back to the inn.

It was by far the most liberating experience Maximus had ever had. Tahlia brought out a different side of him, a more playful side. Instead of following a set, rigid path, she was opening him up to new experiences and allowing him to let go. He wasn't sure he'd fully be able to thank her for the joy she was bringing into his life. All he could do was show her.

After showering, they donned the thick terry cloth robes that came with the suite and chose to have room service outside on the deck facing the cliffs. Tahlia stepped outside first, giving Maximus just enough time to slide a condom into his robe pocket. When he joined her on the deck, the staff had already set up a candlelit table for two with silver domes covering their meal.

"I really enjoyed today," he said, staring at her from across the table after they were seated.

"Which part?" she asked, amused. "Your meditation workshop? No, wait, I bet it was that leadership talk. That had to be really gripping." She chuckled to herself.

"You know that wasn't it."

"Oh, no?" she asked, her eyes filled with glee.

"It was seeing you take off your bikini and bask in your nudity."

A blush crept up Tahlia's face, starting from her neck and moving to her cheeks. She looked downward and then up at him. "I've never done that before."

"Gone skinny-dipping?" He'd done it only once, at Harvard as part of a dare.

She nodded. "No, not ever. I was living in the moment."

"So am I." Maximus rose from his chair, and in two steps he had Tahlia in his arms. He would have loved to have made love to her in the hot springs, but they were not alone, so he'd had to temper his passion for her, but not now. He wanted her hot, naked and bucking underneath him. He reached between them and untied the knot, letting the robe slip from her shoulders and fall to the floor. Then he grasped both sides of her face and kissed her like he'd wanted to do earlier.

Tahlia wrapped her arms around Maximus's middle as he made love to her mouth. His tongue darting in and out was such sweet torture that she moaned. She arced her body to find contact with him, eager to relieve the friction between her thighs, but instead of giving her what he wanted, his lips left hers, sliding down her body to the swell of her breast. She was so sensitive that when he drew the first bud into his hot waiting mouth and laved it with his tongue, she moaned. When she swayed, Maximus kept a steady hold on her, keeping her upright. Then his mouth traveled slowly down her breasts to her belly until he was bending before her and cupping her swollen mound.

"Oh, yes," Tahlia moaned when he slid a finger inside her folds.

"Does that feel good?" He glanced up at her; his eyes were molten fire.

"Y-yes," she cried out softly, not sure she could survive the pleasure Maximus was inflicting on her most sensitive place.

"How about that?" he asked, adding yet another finger inside her and swirling it around.

"Oh, God, yes…" Tahlia threw her head back in abandon.

"Then you're going to love this." He replaced his fingers with his mouth, and she closed her eyes, leaning her head against the glass doors of the deck as he took her to ecstasy.

Maximus thought he would dictate the pace of the evening, but he'd been wrong. Tahlia was a force to be reckoned with, and she was showing him that she wanted him to possess her. He quickly pulled out a condom and barely had time to put it on before Tahlia threw her arms around his neck and wrapped her legs around his waist. Maximus knew what she wanted and what his body demanded, and he thrust upward, sinking into her with an animalistic shout.

"You're mine, Tahlia," he groaned when she began

moving her hips deliberately, letting him know that he was hers, too.

All he could do was stand firm, supporting her weight with his hands clasped under her buttocks as she ground her hips up and down on his shaft, driving them both to the peak of ecstasy and back again. He could feel her inner walls contracting all around him, and this time, Maximus was the first to cry out his release, with Tahlia following an instant later as she bucked against him.

Limp, her legs fell to the floor, so he moved swiftly, lifting her in his arms and carrying her to the bed. Then he lay down beside her, amazed at how perfectly they fit together. He'd never let go like that with a woman. He'd always been sure his lovers came first, but he'd been powerless to resist Tahlia's hold over him.

They'd come together like two forces of nature, but now he wanted to take his time and slow the pace of their lovemaking. They continued kissing, touching and teasing until they both fell into an exhausted yet blissful sleep.

Chapter 11

"I'm in love with Maximus," Tahlia told Kaitlynn after returning from her Big Sur getaway the next day. Her sister had stopped by the gallery to preview some of the selections Tahlia might put up for her exhibit. The words just slipped from her lips because she'd been dying to say them out loud and had almost said as much in Big Sur when Maximus had made love to her so gently, her eyes had filled with tears. But she'd kept the words to herself. Tahlia wasn't sure how Maximus would react or what he would say. She knew he was into her—that much was obvious. But how much? Did it transcend the physical like it had for her?

"Wow! Okay." Kaitlynn sat across from Tahlia in her office and leaned back in her chair. "I certainly wasn't expecting that revelation today. Do you feel better now that you've said it out loud?"

Tahlia nodded.

"Has Maximus said the words back? Has he told you he loves you, too?"

Tahlia shook her head. "No, because I've only told you."

"Me?" Kaitlynn's voice rose an octave. "I would think you'd be telling him. You know, shouting it from the rooftops and all that. You're the romantic one, while I'm the practical one."

"Well, I'm being practical here," Tahlia responded ruefully. "I'm not sure of Maximus's feelings for me—" she drew her brows together "—or at least not entirely, so I'm kind of playing it close to the vest."

"Because of Paul?"

"You know how open I was with him. How I just laid my heart bare only to find out we weren't compatible. I won't do that again, Kaitlynn. I have learned from my past mistakes."

"Of course you have. But don't you think you should try to see how Max does feel about you?"

Tahlia came from around her desk and sat beside Kaitlynn. "Yes, I do…"

"But…"

"I don't know, something's holding me back."

Kaitlynn stared at her. "You don't trust him entirely, do you?"

Tahlia bowed her head. She didn't want to admit that Kaitlynn's warnings had merit. Tahlia didn't really know what Maximus expected from their working relationship, and because of it, despite how much she'd fallen for him, she hesitated revealing her true feelings for him.

"Tahlia?"

When she finally glanced up, tears shone on her lashes. "I worry that you could be right about Max."

"That he could be using you for your vote?"

Tahlia nodded. "I don't want to have these doubts, Kaitlynn, and he's never asked me to vote for him, but at the same time I can't ignore that they're there and they're valid. We did get involved so quickly. Yet we've never really talked how my two percent share and vote would work, but I guess I'll find out soon."

"What's going to happen to help you decide?"

"We have a board meeting at Knight Shipping. It's the first one since Arthur's death. Both Lucius's and my attendance is recommended. I know I'll be there, and I'm sure Lucius will be, too. It amuses him to toy with Max."

"So you'll find out Maximus's true motives then," Kaitlynn said. "Surely that must give you some comfort that you'll know one way or another how he truly feels about you."

"Does it?" Tahlia inquired. "Or will it shatter all my hopes and dreams of a future with Max?"

"You could talk to him now before the meeting. See where his head is. And if he's honest with you, you'll know where you stand."

Tahlia nodded, but she was scared to face the truth. She didn't want to lose what she had with Maximus, but if they didn't have honesty and trust, the foundations of any good relationship, what did they have?

"Maximus." His mother beamed when he stopped to visit her at the estate on Tuesday evening. He hadn't seen her much in the last few weeks because he'd been spending much of his time with Tahlia or staying at his own place. Even though he'd spent the entire weekend with Tahlia at Big Sur, he'd still stayed at her place the last two evenings since their return.

"Mother." He kissed both of her cheeks.

"Where have you been hiding yourself? I've barely seen you."

"I've been staying at the penthouse."

"During my time of need?" she queried.

Guilt assailed Maximus. She was right. His father had been gone only a couple of months and she was still grieving, although in his opinion, Arthur Knight did not deserve her tears, or any emotion, for that part. Since the truth about Lucius had come out that night at the hospital, Maximus had found it hard to have any sort of compassion for him.

However, he'd been a good son and stood by his father's bedside as he'd tried to recover from the massive heart attack he'd had while in bed with Jocelyn, but that was as far as it went. It was as if the love he'd once had for his father had evaporated. Not that Maximus had shown his love easily. Why should he when Arthur had always rebuffed his overtures?

Maximus could remember a time when he was nine years old and he'd been so proud of a project showing the creation of Knight Shipping and all that his father had achieved. His father had scoffed at it and asked him if that was the best he could do. Maximus had immediately smashed the project until it lay in tiny pieces on the floor.

"Max, are you all right?" his mother asked when she noticed he was a million miles away, in the past with all the memories of a father who'd never truly loved him.

He blinked several times. "Yes, I'm fine. And I'm sorry I've stayed away too long. Come, let's have dinner together."

He stayed at the estate with his mother and shared their cook's delicious dinner, but Maximus felt uneasy. He usually enjoyed his mother's company, but not tonight. There was a nagging in the pit of his stomach that he just couldn't shake, and he moved the food on his plate from one side to the other.

"You don't like the squab?" his mother inquired, peering at his full plate.

He glanced down at the tiny fowl and shook his head. "It's fine. I mean, it's delicious."

"There's something on your mind. What is it, Max?"

Maximus glanced up at her. "Hmm…"

"It's the board meeting tomorrow, isn't it?"

His brow furrowed. "How did you know about that?"

"Just because I'm not involved in Knight Shipping doesn't mean I don't know what's going on. And it's your first meeting since your father died."

"True."

"And it's the first time that you'll find out just how bad you'll butt heads with your father's illegitimate spawn."

"Mother, must you call him that? He is my brother, after all."

"A brother you never knew anything about."

"And whose fault is that? All the adults in our lives made sure Lucius and I could never get to know each other. Maybe if we had we wouldn't be at each other's throats now." Maximus pushed back from the table and began pacing the floor. "This could have all been avoided if you, Father and Jocelyn, for that matter, had been honest."

Charlotte Knight rose from her seat in a flurry. "I'll tell you what it would have been like, Maximus. Your father would have left us to be with his other family, leaving me to raise you alone. That's what would have happened. I did what I had to do to keep my family intact, to make sure *my son* was on top."

Maximus sighed heavily. "And in the end it was all for naught, wasn't it? Because I'm not on top, Mother, and I never will be. I have to share the throne with Lucius."

His mother's head dropped down, and tears slid down her cheeks. "I'm sorry, Max. If I had any idea that your father would have done this, I would have…"

"Blackmailed him into keeping me as head of Knight Shipping?" Maximus snorted. "All that would have brought about is more hate and animosity from him, and I think I got plenty of that when he was alive."

His mother held her head in her hands and began sobbing. Maximus rushed over to her and pulled her into his arms. He held her until her sobs began to quiet. "I'm so sorry," she murmured against his chest. "I did my best."

"I know you did," Maximus responded softly. He couldn't be mad at her. She was the only family he had left. Or was she? He did have a half brother, but there was no way a relationship between the two of them was possible.

"And tomorrow—" she glanced up at him "—do you think the Armstrong girl will vote your way now that you've been seeing each other?"

Now there was a million-dollar question if ever there was one. He'd set out on a path to seduce Tahlia, and in the end it was he who'd been seduced by her, by her beauty and by her spirit. But tomorrow was judgment day. He'd shared with Tahlia his feelings about expanding Knight Shipping. She knew how much it meant to him. But he also couldn't ask her to vote with him. He wanted her to do it because she believed in him. But would she? Would Tahlia vote with him or against him?

Tahlia was uneasy as she prepared for bed. She'd been antsy all night, and even a cup of her favorite chamomile tea had done little to help calm her frayed nerves. She was on edge about tomorrow's board meeting. She knew the significance of the meeting and the possibility of brother-against-brother, and it weighed heavily on her mind. After leaving Kaitlynn, she'd thought she'd feel better. She'd spoken her feelings aloud. But she hadn't told the one person who mattered most: Maximus.

If theirs was a normal relationship, she might be willing to take the risk, but it wasn't. There was a thread linking the two of them together. A thread that threatened to destroy everything between them.

Tahlia was surprised when her doorbell rang. It was after 10:00 p.m., and she was getting ready for bed. She had on her favorite nightie and bunny slippers, and her hair was tied in an unattractive messy bun. She peeked through the peephole, and her breath caught in throat. Maximus was standing on the other side. What was he doing here so late?

He knocked softly on her door. "Tahlia?"

She didn't hesitate and swung open the door. He was leaning against it, looking sexy in jeans and a pullover V-neck sweater. "Max?"

He walked toward her, pulled her in his arms and kicked the door shut with his foot. Then he began kissing her with such masterful passion that she lost her breath. She reacted without question and curled her arms around his neck and kissed him back. Then she jumped into his arms, wrapping her legs around him. He caught her and carried her to the bedroom.

They didn't talk as they undressed each other. Instead, Tahlia merely lifted her arms so Maximus could remove her nightie as she kicked off her slippers. And he did the same when she pulled his sweater off and reached for the zipper on his jeans. She pushed them and his briefs down his legs, and he stepped out of them; his perfect body was completely open to her gaze. They met on the bed, falling back against the pillows. He tugged the clip in her hair free and glided his fingers through her tresses.

It felt good to have him touch her. And when he dipped his head to kiss her and she felt the stubble on his cheek, Tahlia was happy he'd come. They could have this one last night together before circumstances inevitably forced them to make a stand. When she felt his tongue darting through her parted lips, she went mad, kissing him back with everything she had. There was nothing more arousing, except maybe having him inside her.

She sighed with delight when Maximus left her lips and began to tongue her ear and nip at her neck. As he moved away and went lower, Tahlia shamelessly thrust her breasts at him, and he took the bait. He toyed with them first, playing with her nipples between his thumb and forefinger, and then his mouth was on her, laving her with hot flicks of his tongue.

When he finally suckled them, Tahlia bucked as the sensations he evoked ricocheted through her. But he didn't stop tormenting her. His path went downward to her belly. He teased her with light kisses and soft touches. His hands caressed the curve of her hip and thighs, but instead of going to the place she wanted him to, he flicked his tongue across the sensitive spot at the back of her knees and went lower to massage her calves and feet.

"Max…" He knew where she wanted him and the heat of his mouth. But he was deliberately drawing out the pleasure.

He glanced up at her. His eyes were heavy lidded with desire as he kissed his way back up her legs and thighs, stroked her belly, then paused, hovering over the place that ached for his touch, his fingers, his mouth. "You want me here?" he teased.

She nodded enthusiastically.

When he bent his head, she weaved her fingers through his curls and waited, waited for him to make her his, because she was. At the first flick of his tongue on her, Tahlia ground her hips into the bed as fire raced through her veins at the contact. Her every nerve ending was on fire waiting for his next action. Maximus teased the nub at the center of her with gentle flicks, stimulating her sensitive tissues, and when he darted his tongue inside her, Tahlia became unglued. She cried and keened as his clever tongue and fingers drew out a scream and her first orgasm surged through her.

Maximus lapped up all of Tahlia's sweet nectar but didn't stop tormenting her. After he'd left his mother at the estate, he hadn't known where he was driving until he'd ended up at Tahlia's doorstep. Tomorrow would bring their first real test, and he was afraid of what might happen. As much as he wanted to ask Tahlia to vote with him, he didn't. He needed to know if she'd do it on her own because she cared for him and wanted what was best for *him*.

Maybe deep down he knew the answer and that tonight might be potentially the last time he would ever have her. If so, he was going to make it count. He cupped her buttocks and thrust his tongue deeper inside her. Tahlia panted uncontrollably as he continued his determined assault. Her second orgasm came quickly, and she yielded every inch of herself to him.

It was only then that Maximus sheathed himself with the condoms he'd kept in his pants pocket since meeting Tahlia and slid up her sweat-slick body. He wanted to be inside her, but Tahlia pushed him backward and climbed on top of him. She took his erection in her hands and traced the length of him. Maximus hissed out a breath when both her hands encompassed his girth and she took him inside her mouth.

He heard a moan escape his lips as he felt her take him deeper into her moist, silky mouth. He reveled in the way her tongue swirled around his length and how she paid special attention to the crown, teasing it with light flicks of her tongue. He threw his head back and accepted her ministrations not only because it felt good but because he was with Tahlia, a woman he'd come to care about greatly and could possibly love.

When he could take no more, he flipped her over onto her back and kissed her. The sigh of pleasure that escaped her lips was cut off by Maximus entering her, possessing her, inhabiting her completely. He pressed his lips into hers and thrust his tongue inside her as the lower half of him did the same. Her answer was to roll her hips to give him better access. And so he moved deeper, and Tahlia accepted him greedily, hungrily, bucking and writhing underneath him.

That was what he loved about her, her openness, her lack of inhibition when it came to their lovemaking. She let him know that she enjoyed every minute of it. So he thrust into her more steadily, bringing both of them to the precipice, then easing back. He would make the moment last. He raised himself on his forearms and slowly thrust in and out of her. Tahlia splayed her hands across his chest and then upward to encircle his neck, urging him to pick up the pace.

He compiled and pounded into her over and over again. She gasped but clung to him as he built up their pleasure until finally the world turned on its axis and everything dissolved and pure bliss coursed through them.

Maximus fell on top of Tahlia, and she accepted his weight, holding him to her. When their breathing returned to normal, he slowly released her and lay back against the pillows. Tahlia curled up beside him, her head on his chest. It felt so natural to be with her that he drifted off to sleep.

Chapter 12

Maximus stood at the head of the table in the Knight Shipping conference room at the Wednesday meeting. He'd left Tahlia's in the early-morning hours to get back home and face the day. He hadn't wanted to disturb her. No, that was a lie. He was afraid to face her and see doubt or confusion in those brown depths, so he'd taken the easy way out and slipped out of bed while she was sleeping.

Now he watched the executive leaders and heads of departments enter the room. He'd asked them to attend so he could introduce them. The board meeting was being held in the next fifteen minutes, and neither Lucius nor Tahlia had arrived yet. It gave Maximus a few minutes to get his head on straight. Most of the meeting was routine and would require very little input from either one of them. However, there was one item on the agenda that required a majority vote.

He wanted to take the company public. Knight Shipping had come a long way, but in order for the company to expand and compete with the big boys, it needed to become global. He'd discussed it with his father before he'd passed, and Arthur had adamantly refused. He'd wanted it to stay a family business, but Maximus had disagreed. It had been a source of contention between them. Maybe that was why Arthur had decided to split his shares of the company with Lucius—to make sure it would never happen.

Maximus was hoping to convince Lucius and Tahlia that it was the right move. Lucius had to realize it was the right move. He'd seen for himself at the shipping yard that they were at capacity. Plus his own company, Knight International, was a publicly traded company, as was his fiancée's, and they'd both been quite successful. He wanted the same for Knight Shipping.

Lucius stepped into the boardroom several moments later. Maximus glanced in his direction. His older brother looked ever the businessman in a sleek gray suit and tie. His hair was neatly cropped as always. Maybe if things had been different they might have had a relationship, but now they were on opposite sides.

When Lucius saw him standing at the far side of the room, he strode toward him. He extended his hand. "Maximus."

Maximus was surprised he wasn't calling him Max again to rile him up. "Lucius." He shook his hand.

Lucius glanced around at all the people in the room. "Are all these people really necessary? Aren't you, Tahlia and I the only shareholders?"

"Yes, but I thought you'd like to meet some of the heads of the departments and see who works for you," Maximus responded smoothly. "Not all of them were on-site during your tour."

"Of course. Good thinking. Where's Tahlia?"

Maximus hated that Lucius was using her first name. He didn't know her like Maximus did, as *intimately* as he did. As if her ears were ringing, Tahlia entered the room just then in a stunning suit that Maximus suspected was new. She didn't usually wear suits. Her style was much more bohemian chic. He watched her long legs as they strolled toward him, and his mind went to the two of them in bed last night and how he'd taken her from behind just that morning.

She smiled at both men when she made it to their group. "Lucius, good to see you again." She held out her hand.

Lucius accepted and patted her hand. "Tahlia. You're looking well. Actually, might I say, glowing?" He glanced in Maximus's direction. "Life is certainly agreeing with you."

Tahlia blushed. "Thank you." She hazarded a glance at his direction. "Maximus."

He noticed that she called him by his given name and not Max, like when they were together. Did that mean something? There was also a question lurking in her eyes, like why hadn't he kissed her goodbye when he'd left?

"Tahlia." Maximus nodded his head and looked down at his watch. "We should get started." He moved away from the duo and toward the head of the table. He cleared his throat. "Good morning, everyone. I'd like to get started. I'm sure you'd all like to get back to work."

There were several laughs and guffaws, but eventually they all took their seats. Lucius flanked Maximus's right while Tahlia opted to sit at his left. When he glanced in her direction as he sat down, she gave him a tentative smile.

"I'll call this board meeting to order," Maximus

stated and looked at his assistant, Elena, to record the time since she was taking the minutes.

The next hour went by quickly, with Maximus reviewing typical business matters and introducing the executive team and key department heads. Lucius asked questions occasionally while Tahlia was silent and wrote notes in a folio she'd brought with her, but Maximus knew it was the calm before the storm.

"Now on to new business," Maximus said. "As many of you know, Knight Shipping has had an excellent last decade, but our reach within the United States and abroad has reached its full potential. In order to go after new contracts, we need to expand, but as good as we're doing financially, we just don't have the working capital for a project of this magnitude."

"I'm in agreement. Expansion is always good," Lucius stated. "I mentioned as much during the tour. But why is this on the table now? I'd thought I'd have time to review your proposal beforehand." He eyed Maximus suspiciously.

"There's a multimillion-dollar deal to transport luxury vehicles that's come across my desk, but the only way we can go after it is if we expand."

"What do you propose we do?"

"We need to go public."

"Pardon me?" Lucius asked in a chilly tone.

Maximus turned to stare at him. "You heard me. If we go public, we can raise the capital we need to expand Knight Shipping and finally reach our full potential."

"But Knight Shipping is a family company, is it not?" Tahlia inquired, finally speaking for the first time.

"Yes, it is," Lucius stated, glaring at Maximus.

"Don't dismiss this out of turn," Maximus replied. "Going public makes sense. Elena, will you hand out the prospectus? This will show what impact transporting the additional goods will have on our bottom line."

His assistant rose from her post at his side to hand out packets to each person at the table. Maximus watched Lucius and Tahlia look over the materials. The room was silent as they both absorbed the material. Maximus knew some of it was over Tahlia's head, but she was bright enough to catch on, and if not he'd explain it to her, make her see how good this could be for the company.

It was Lucius, however, who spoke first. "Looks like you've done your homework, Max."

Maximus bristled. He'd resorted to calling him by his nickname. He took it to mean he'd gotten his older brother's ire, which wasn't a good sign of things to come.

"Yes, I have, and the name's Maximus."

"How long have you been working on this?" Lucius inquired. "You couldn't have come up with all this—" he pointed to the prospectus on the table "—in the last couple of months. So how long?"

"Does that really matter?" Maximus responded.

Lucius spun around in one of the executive chairs. "Yeah, it kind of does. Because if you've been working on this for months, it means you'd have brought it to Arthur's attention, and if you did, this would already be in the works. But since it's not, it leads me to believe that he shot you down."

"Is that true?" Tahlia asked softly from his side.

Maximus glanced at Tahlia. The look she gave him was both inquisitive and suspicious. He knew because he'd seen all of her looks, or at least he thought he had, until now.

She was silent as she waited for him to respond.

"Yes. I had mentioned this to my father."

"You mean *our* father," Lucius asserted.

A horrified gasp echoed from around the table.

"I mean, my father," Maximus repeated determinedly, "but he was too shortsighted to see what going public would do for our company."

Lucius stared at him. "Going public would mean we—" he pointed to both of them "—would have to put up our shares. What exactly is your intention here, Max? To have me put up all my shares and leave me with no stake in the company?"

Maximus snorted. "As I said, I presented this idea to my father well before I knew of your existence."

"But you're presenting it now, why?"

"Because it's an excellent idea."

"I don't think that's why," Lucius responded, folding his arms across his chest. "It's because you want to get rid of me and dilute my shares so that you end up as majority shareholder."

"That's not true," Maximus stated.

"Is he right?" Tahlia inquired, peering at him incredulously. "Is that why you're bringing this up now? I mean, we've hardly had time to process the fact that we're shareholders. And I know how badly you want to expand, but you want us to make this decision now."

"Time is of the essence, and we need to start moving on this."

Silence ensued at the table for several long moments.

"I'm inclined to agree with Arthur. If he didn't want this for his company, why should I go against his wishes?" Lucius inquired.

"You didn't even know him," Maximus stated vehemently.

"Through no fault of my own," Lucius returned

evenly. "And I'm not going to get into that right now. So my vote is no."

"You haven't even given this due consideration," Maximus replied. "This is a good deal. It will create hundreds of jobs and make Knight Shipping a force to be reckoned with. If this were one of your other companies, you wouldn't hesitate to pull the trigger. You're voting no out of spite just to see me fail."

"You have no idea how I feel," Lucius said. "And perhaps in time I'll change my mind, but at this moment the answer is no. And since your vote is undoubtedly yes, that leaves you, Tahlia." He looked at her from across the table. "Where do you stand?"

Maximus wanted to know the same thing and looked at Tahlia. His eyes pleaded with hers to trust him, to believe in him that he knew what was right for Knight Shipping and that he'd never lead them astray.

Tahlia glanced at Lucius and then at Maximus. He could see she was torn. This was a big decision. No, it was a monumental one. Because not only was she voting about whether to take Knight Shipping public, she would also be voting *for* or *against* Maximus. One outcome would mean they could continue on and flourish in their relationship knowing they were of one mind. The other outcome, the more treacherous one, possibly meant the end of a good thing. A good thing Maximus didn't want to let go, but ultimately it was Tahlia's decision. Same as it had been when they'd become involved.

"My vote is no," Tahlia finally said quietly.

"What was that?" Lucius asked. "Because I don't think everyone heard you. For the record, please, if you could speak up."

Tahlia looked at Maximus as she spoke. "My vote is no."

Maximus felt his heart closing in on itself, but he refused to allow his outward appearance to belie his inner turmoil and that his heart was breaking. "All right, let the record state that the vote is two to one and with fifty-one percent of the voting shares. This issue of going public is tabled. I believe that concludes new business, unless anyone else has anything else to add?"

As he looked around the table, he could see the disbelieving looks of his executive team, who knew going public was a solid move. "Then the Knight Shipping board meeting is concluded. Thank you, everyone, for attending."

Maximus closed the folder on the table that contained all the work he'd been diligently working on over the last year to convince his father and now Lucius and Tahlia to vote his way. But he'd failed once again. He rose to his feet and headed for the exit.

"Maximus, wait!" Tahlia caught up with him at the double doors. "Can we talk?"

"Not now, Tahlia," he said firmly, his mouth a grim line. "Not now."

Tahlia stared at Maximus's retreating figure and moved aside as the other meeting attendees left the conference room. She could feel tears stinging her eyelids, but she had to keep it together. She couldn't cry in front of them.

"Are you all right?" Lucius asked from her side.

Tahlia shook her head and felt him softly grasp her arm and pull her inside the now-empty room. Before she knew what was happening, he'd pulled her into his embrace, and she finally let out the tears she'd been holding in.

"There, there," he calmed her as if she were a small child as she cried into his no-doubt designer suit.

When she finally lifted her head, Lucius was looking down at her. "Come, sit." He guided her to a nearby chair, and once she'd sat, he offered her a handkerchief from the inner pocket of his suit jacket.

"Thank you." Tahlia sniffed, accepted the hanky and began blowing her nose. Why did she have to break down in front of Lucius of all people?

"He'll get over this," Lucius stated.

She glanced up at him. "Who?"

He smiled knowingly. "My brother."

"I don't know what you mean."

"No need to be coy, Tahlia. I know you and he are involved," he responded.

Her brow furrowed. "How?" Was she really that transparent?

He shrugged. "It's not hard to figure out after your reaction to him leaving just now. But to be frank, I noticed Maximus's interest in you from day one when we were at the estate and again during the tour. And from what I've heard, it's only progressed since then."

"Have you been having us followed?" She was horrified at the prospect.

Lucius shrugged. "Suffice it to say, I've been keeping an eye out on my baby brother. And I can see how much he's come to care for you and vice versa."

"You can?"

Lucius grinned, and Tahlia could see why Naomi had fallen for him. When he wasn't annoying Maximus, he was quite attractive. Of course, she had eyes only for Maximus, who now was so angry with her he didn't even want to talk to her, much less look at her.

"I can because I know it's how I felt when I fell for

Naomi. My grandmother said it was written all over my face, and I can see what she means because it's written all over yours."

Tahlia attempted a laugh. "It won't do much good now. Maximus hates me."

"He doesn't hate you. He may be angry with you. He may even feel a bit betrayed by you since you sided with me about going public, but he doesn't hate you."

Why hadn't she thought through her vote? She'd cursorily glanced over the expansion prospectus without giving it due consideration. She'd been so focused on honoring Arthur's wishes and projecting her own opinions and views about the man who'd been a father figure to her that she'd neglected to take into account Maximus's feelings. "What do you suppose I do?" Tahlia inquired.

"Ah." Lucius leaned back in his chair. "That's where you have me at a loss. I wish I knew my brother better to offer you some sound advice, but I don't. I only know how I would feel in this instance, and I would say to give him some time to settle down and let cooler heads prevail."

"Why are you telling me all this?" Tahlia inquired. "I'd think you'd want him to be unhappy."

He frowned. "Why would you think that?"

"Because," Tahlia responded, "you don't miss a chance to antagonize him. Get his goat. You know you do."

Lucius grinned mischievously. "I suppose I do sometimes, but isn't that what big brothers are supposed to do? Give their little brothers a hard time?"

Tahlia stared at Lucius for long moments, and then it hit her. "You want a relationship with Max, don't you?"

Lucius's mouth compressed and he was silent, and

Tahlia wondered if he was going to answer her, and then he said, "Yes, I do. I grew up an only child, Tahlia, and I've always wanted siblings, and now I have one but he doesn't want me." His eyes drifted to the closed door beyond which Maximus was down the hall in his office, probably seething with fury at what he considered her betrayal.

"I think he wants it, too," Tahlia said. "He's just afraid to admit it." She knew she was revealing a confidence, but maybe there was a way she could finally bridge the gap between these two proud and powerful men. So she continued. "Just because Arthur acknowledged him doesn't mean Maximus had it easy growing up, Lucius. Arthur was cold and distant with Maximus. Constantly pushing him to excel but never showing him affection. And in the end, giving you, us—" she pointed back and forth between them "—half the company he'd worked so hard for. He has a right to his anger. But I also know he doesn't blame you about your parentage. In fact, he's been angry with both your mothers and father for how they all handled the situation. You both could have known each other, grown up together, been a family if they'd all let go of their individual agendas."

"I couldn't agree with you more," Lucius said. "About our parents, that is. And thank you for sharing with me about Maximus's childhood. Being acknowledged as Arthur Knight's son wasn't all it was cracked up to be. I'd always thought the grass was greener on the other side. Clearly, I was wrong."

"I need to go to him." Tahlia rose to her feet. She couldn't just wait and see what happened between them. She had to know now, make him see that her vote today had nothing to do with her feelings for him or what he meant to her.

"Tahlia." Lucius touched her arm. "I know how much you want this, want my brother, but be careful. He's angry right now and he might lash out."

She nodded. "I understand." But she had to act. If she waited for the dust to settle, it might only push them further apart. She had to trust her instincts. He may not be ready to say he loved her, but deep down she knew Maximus would never hurt her.

Chapter 13

Maximus returned to his office after his epic fail of a board meeting and found Griffin waiting in his office. He frowned. "What are you doing here, Griff?" He tossed the folder with his proposals on the desk. He might as well burn it for what good it had done him today. He'd known Lucius would vote against him, but he'd been hoping against hope that he was wrong about Tahlia and that she'd pull through for him. For once, he needed someone to be on his side. But yet again, he'd been wrong. Why did everything have to be so hard?

"I thought you might need to see a friendly face," Griffin said. "When you texted me yesterday that today was the big vote, I wasn't sure how it would go for you."

"Well, it didn't." Maximus stalked to his desk. He reached inside his drawer and pulled out the bottle of bourbon he kept for special occasions to toast a good deal with the executives. But today was different. He *needed* it to take the edge off. He produced two small glasses. "Care to join me?"

"If it'll make you feel any better, then sure, I'll have

one." Griffin regarded him from the sofa, where he was perched.

Maximus poured two generous glasses and then walked over to hand one to Griffin. "Bottoms up." He didn't wait for Griffin and instead chugged the amber liquid back in one gulp.

"Take it easy, Max," Griffin said. "I know things didn't go your way today, but that doesn't mean it's over."

"Doesn't it?" Max's brown eyes stared at him. "It's over, Griffin. I'm tired of beating my head against a post and going nowhere. Maybe Lucius—" he pointed to the door, glass still in hand "—and Tahlia should see what it's like when there's no one at the helm. Let's see how they fare without me. I'm going on an extended vacation."

"To punish them for voting against you?" Griffin inquired. "Won't this hurt you in the process? You're a major shareholder, too, Max. Think about what you're saying."

"I don't care," Maximus replied, walking over to the bottle of bourbon and pouring himself another glass. He gulped down the second drink. "Damn my father for putting me in this position."

"There's nothing you could have done."

"Clearly, I didn't do a good job seducing Tahlia," Maximus said bitterly. "I should have never gotten involved with her when she was just a means to an unfruitful end. Our entire relationship was a complete and utter waste of time."

"Don't say that, Maximus, because I know that's not true." Griffin put down his glass and stood. "I've seen how you've changed since you've been with Tahlia.

You're more relaxed and carefree. Lighter even. She's been a good influence on you."

"I don't want to talk to her right now."

"Why not? Why can't you say how you feel about her?" Griffin inquired.

"Because she betrayed me today," Maximus hissed through clenched teeth. "She could have been on my side, but instead she sided with him."

"Your brother."

"My enemy."

"I don't believe that's how you truly feel. We've always been like brothers and you've always wanted a sibling. Well, you have one now. Maybe if you opened your heart, like you've done with Tahlia, and let love in. Then maybe…"

"Love has n-e-v-e-r done anything for me," Maximus responded bitterly, cutting him off. "Anyone I've ever loved has either lied to me, thrown it back in my face or betrayed me. I can do without that emotion, thank you very much."

"Fine. Then wallow in self-pity, Maximus, but I have to say the look of poor little rich boy doesn't look good on you."

Seconds later, he was gone, leaving Maximus alone. And this time, he truly felt that way.

Tahlia hid behind a planter as Griffin stormed out of Maximus's office. She'd heard more than she'd ever wanted to. And now her heart was breaking just like Maximus's. She caught sight of him sitting on the floor with his drink just as the door closed.

Tahlia swallowed the bile in her throat, and with as much decorum as she could muster after hearing that Maximus had purposely set out to seduce her, she made her way through the front doors of Knight Shipping and out to her car.

She sat inside for minutes, hours—she truly couldn't count because all she could do was hear Maximus's words reverberating through her mind. *I should have never gotten involved with her... Our entire relationship was a complete and utter waste of time.*

She was in stunned disbelief. He truly felt like getting involved with her was a complete and utter waste of time? Sobs took over her, bubbling over, and she cried until there were no more tears left. She knew people had to wonder why she was still sitting in visitor parking, but she physically was unable to move until the sobs subsided.

Eventually, Tahlia drove herself home. On the way, she called Kaitlynn, who promised to be there waiting for her. And she was. As soon as she opened the doors to her apartment, Kaitlynn was there, enveloping her in the warmest of embraces.

"Thank you, Kaitlynn." Tahlia clung to her baby sister as she closed the door behind her. Kaitlynn led her to the sofa, and Tahlia curled into a ball in the corner. She felt like such a fool for believing that Maximus had ever meant one word he'd ever said to her. *She was just a means to an unfruitful end.* Maximus's harsh words still stung hours after she'd heard them.

"Tahlia, what happened?" Kaitlynn asked. "You were kind of incoherent on the drive home, and I couldn't make out what you were saying."

That led to another round of fresh tears, and Kaitlynn stopped talking and merely held Tahlia as she let out the grief. "It was all a lie, Kaitlynn," she finally was able to say. "He was using me."

"No!" Her sister didn't want it to be true, and neither did she. She'd believed Maximus, *in him*, that he would never hurt her, that somewhere deep inside him, despite the trauma of losing his father and experiencing his indifference that he was someone capable of genuine feeling, but she was wrong. Maximus Xavier Knight was a cold, heartless bastard who cared about no one but himself.

"It's true," Tahlia responded. "He hoped that by seducing me, I'd be more pliable and would vote his way." She laughed, and her laughter turned to tears. "Of course, he got the shock of his life today when I voted against him, despite the fact that he'd made sure I fell for him. And I did, I fell hard for a liar. Are all the Knight men untrustworthy?"

Tahlia thought of Arthur and the years he'd lied to Charlotte and Jocelyn, to his sons, to himself. Maybe Maximus just didn't know any better. Look at his role model.

"I don't know what to say, Tahlia," Kaitlynn said. "I was rooting for Maximus. I was hoping that my sixth sense was wrong and that he was on the up-and-up. I'm sorry I was wrong and that I didn't do more to dissuade you from going down this path."

"Like you could have stopped me. I wanted Maximus from the moment I first saw him, and when he opened the door for a possible relationship, I walked right through it. Knowingly and happily."

"That still doesn't mean it doesn't hurt."

"Nope. It hurts like hell. It feels as if I'm literally being torn asunder." Tahlia held her stomach, which had been tied in knots since the board meeting. It had only worsened after she'd overheard Maximus's angry words.

"What are you going to do now?"

"At this very second?" Tahlia asked. "I'm going to

stay on my couch until the pain hurts a little less. And then tomorrow, I'm going to go into the gallery and run my business."

After Paul, she'd sat on the couch in her pajamas eating pizza and ice cream and in general feeling sorry for herself, but not anymore. She'd become stronger after him and knew that eventually the hurt of losing Maximus would ache a little less.

Kaitlynn smiled at her. "I'm proud of you, sis. If this had been Paul, you would never leave this house."

"Oh, I want to curl up in a ball and die," Tahlia said. At Kaitlynn's shocked look, she clarified, "Not literally, that is. But as much as I love Maximus, I can't change what's happened. Somehow I'll have to find a way to go on without him."

Maximus's head was pounding and his mouth tasted vile. He glanced around and realized he was at his penthouse and had fallen asleep on his sofa wearing yesterday's suit. The last clear memory he had was of being in his office yesterday with Griffin and having a bourbon. The room was spinning, so he laid his head back down, and that was when he recalled that his assistant, Elena, had called him a cab when she'd found him passed out in his office. He must have stumbled up to his penthouse on his own. Thank God he hadn't driven.

He sucked in a deep breath. Drinking hadn't changed the situation, it had only given him a hangover. Maximus vowed not to do that again. He was still in the minority at Knight Shipping, a company he'd always thought would be his someday. And now that he was no longer angry, he felt defeated. His father had set all of this in motion, but that still didn't mean that he wasn't hurt that Tahlia didn't believe in him, wouldn't stand by his side. She knew how he felt about Lucius, about the entire situation, and still she'd voted against him.

The more he thought about it, the angrier Maximus got. He needed to talk to Tahlia, if only to clear the air so he'd have no regrets. Gingerly, he eased himself off the sofa and headed for the shower.

Fifteen minutes later, he felt refreshed from the hot water and was dressed and ready to face the day. He thought about calling Elena or checking his email, but he'd been serious yesterday when he'd told Griffin he was taking a break from Knight Shipping. He'd let Lucius and Tahlia run the business in his absence. Instead, he spent the remainder of the afternoon making arrangements to take out his father's sailboat. Maximus had always loved the boat, and that was the one thing Arthur hadn't managed to give away during the reading of the will.

Once he had a captain lined up and arranged for provisions to be delivered to the sailboat for that evening, he packed a large suitcase because he wasn't coming back. At least not for a while. But before he could head to the marina, he needed to have a chat with a certain lady.

He took the Bugatti and arrived at Tahlia's apartment after 7:00 p.m. But he wasn't prepared for the reaction that greeted him. As soon as Tahlia opened the door and saw it was him, she slammed the door in his face.

Tahlia couldn't believe Maximus's nerve. He'd actually shown up on her doorstep after all the hideous things he'd told his best friend. What did he want? One for the road? A quick roll in the hay for old times' sake? She didn't want to let him in, but his incessant knocking and calling out her name was causing a disturbance to her neighbors.

She swung open the door but hung on to it. "What do you want, Maximus?"

His eyes widened at the use of his full name, but he didn't say anything. Instead he just stood there staring at her. "Can I come in?"

"Why?"

"Because we need to talk."

"We have nothing to say to each other. I heard quite enough yesterday."

His brows drew together in confusion. "I don't know what you're talking about."

"Does 'I should have never have gotten involved with her when she was just a means to an unfruitful end,' or, 'Our entire relationship was a complete and utter waste of time' ring a bell?" Tahlia inquired, her arms folded across her bosom.

His face clouded with uneasiness, and his dark eyes shuttered. "Tahlia."

He stepped forward, but she held out her hand as a defense mechanism. "Oh, no, you don't." She shook her head. "I'm not letting you in. So, what, you can sweet-talk your way out of this? I'm not that gullible, Maximus. You may have fooled me once, but not again. I won't be made a fool of for a second time."

"It's not like that," he replied. "You heard that conversation out of context."

She frowned. "By all means, explain."

"Not out here," he whispered when one of her neighbors passed by. "Let me in."

She glared at him and widened the door so he could enter, but she remained rooted to the spot. She wasn't getting comfortable. She would never be that way with him again, and that broke her heart after everything they'd been to each other. They'd been together only a short amount of time and it may not have meant anything to him, but it had meant everything to her.

"I'm sorry you heard what you did," Maximus said, turning to face her at the door. He stood rigidly in the middle of the living room as if afraid to come near her.

"No, I heard the truth, the unvarnished truth. And I'm thankful for it because now I know everyone was right when they warned me to stay away from you. My sister, hell, even Lucius, warned me to be careful, but I wouldn't listen. I had stars in my eyes where you were concerned." She shook her head in dismay. "What a fool I was."

"You're not a fool, Tahlia," Maximus replied. "Our relationship was real."

"*Was*, as in the past tense? So you admit it's over?"

"It's what you want, isn't it?" he inquired. "Because I don't see how we can go on. You're angry with me because of what you heard, and I get that. You have every right to be. I did intend to seduce you, Tahlia, to use you for my own gain, but somewhere along the line that changed and I abandoned that plan because I came to care for you. Truly care for you. But yesterday, you hurt me, too."

"What? You're going to put this on me?" Tahlia stared back at him in amazement.

"You knew how much I needed you on my side," Maximus stated. "How hard it's been for me growing up without my father's support. All I've ever wanted was for that man to believe in me. And in the end, he still didn't because he left Knight Shipping to not only Lucius, but you, too. He didn't even trust Lucius and me to figure out things on our own. He put you in the middle."

"That's not my fault."

"No, it's not, but you put yourself in the middle yesterday," he stated. "You asked me to share my world with you, and I did. I told you about how my father treated me with disdain, never showing me an ounce of the love or affection he so clearly felt for you. I shared my dreams for Knight Shipping and how much I wanted to expand, and yet you still didn't vote with me. And you didn't even have to vote against me. You could have abstained, but you didn't. You didn't support me, Tahlia. Instead, you shot an arrow straight through my heart by siding with Lucius, my enemy. You didn't even have the decency to read all of my proposal before you shot it down."

There was truth to Maximus's words. It was like he was shining a mirror on her faults, too, when she'd always thought she was on high moral ground. "I suppose you're right. I've failed Arthur and you. But Lucius doesn't have to be your enemy, Maximus."

But he wasn't hearing Tahlia. "He is, and because of him you've succeeded in mortally wounding me. I have nothing left to fight for. So you and Lucius can have the company. I'm done with it!"

"How dare you!" Tahlia shouted, rushing at him. "How dare you put this all on me! I admit I'm not perfect and I may have been on my high horse where Arthur was concerned, but *you* set out to seduce *me*! I didn't come after you. I only wanted to fulfill Arthur's wishes and see that you and Lucius got along."

"And I was wrong," Maximus admitted. "Am wrong," he corrected himself. "I shouldn't have mixed business and personal. And I take responsibility for my actions, and I'm truly sorry about that." He started toward the door.

Tahlia peered at him. "And that's it? That's all you have to say to me?"

"What more do you want from me, Tahlia?" Maximus asked.

I want you to love me, Tahlia thought. *Say you love me now and it might make it all better.* Then she could say those three little words back. She could admit she wasn't entirely blameless when it came to what went wrong between them. But he was silently staring at her, or should she say through her, as if she wasn't there. He'd checked out, checked out on her.

"There's nothing I want from you, Maximus. You can see yourself out." She spun on her heel and raced from the room.

When Tahlia made it to her bed, she threw herself down and clutched her pillow. Then Tahlia heard the click of the door as Maximus departed from her life forever.

Chapter 14

Maximus was enjoying his new carefree lifestyle. There was something to be said about letting go of all the entrapments that held him down and just being one with the sea. He'd been on the sailboat for two months and was enjoying the simple life.

He'd spoken to Griffin and his mother a handful of times, if only to assure them that he was all right. Otherwise, he kept his phone off. Occasionally, he'd turn on it and there'd be voice mails, texts and emails from Knight Shipping, which he'd promptly delete. It was time he started living life for himself instead of doing what was expected of him. It certain hadn't gotten him anywhere except with half a company and a broken heart.

Thanks to having so much time on his hand, Maximus had come to realize that he'd fallen in love with Tahlia Armstrong. He didn't know when it'd happened or how because he certainly hadn't been looking for it. It had just sneaked up on him. The knowledge didn't make him feel warm and fuzzy.

It felt bittersweet because their relationship had been

doomed from the start. Not just because he'd begun seeing her with the intention of seducing her, but because she held the key to something he'd desperately wanted but would never obtain. His father's love. His father's respect. Instead, all he'd ever gotten was his scorn. And a whole lot of confusion because if his father had never inserted that clause, Maximus might never have met Tahlia. And his life had been the richer for it, if only for a little while.

And so, he'd tuck his love for Tahlia away with the love he'd once felt for his father and had never had returned. Love had never been kind to him, so why should he freely give it again? Maybe if he stayed on the sailboat long enough he would finally forget about her.

Hell, he doubted it.

At night, Tahlia haunted his dreams. Deeper and sweeter than if she was with him in person. The smell of her perfume, the way she moaned when he was inside her or the giddiness she had when she'd just finished one of her paintings. He couldn't escape the images of her in his mind, so he stayed at sea hoping to rid himself of the memories. Memories he wondered would ever die.

"Your exhibit, baby girl, is everything," Sophia said as she and Kaitlynn admired Tahlia's art on display one Tuesday evening. Her collection was a mix of oil paintings, charcoal freehand artwork and several ceramic pieces.

"I'm with Mama on this one," Kaitlynn said. "You've truly outdone yourself, sis. I knew you were talented, but this is remarkable."

Tahlia beamed. "Thank you, guys." It was wonderful to receive praise from her family, but there was one person whose praise she desired most. Maximus. True to his word, she hadn't heard from him since he'd quietly left her apartment two months ago.

As the weeks had gone by, she'd begun to realize how incredibly unfair she'd been to Maximus. Forcing her view of Arthur on him and holding Maximus to an unreasonable standard, given all his father had put him through. Tahlia wanted to tell him that she'd *heard* him. No, that she *understood* his feelings and his disappointments about his father, his brother and even their relationship. Sure, she was mad as hell that he'd set out to seduce her, but she hadn't been an unwilling participant. She'd been crazy about Maximus from the moment she'd laid eyes on him. Her hope was that maybe one day they could wipe the slate clean and start again.

But he'd disappeared and left Los Angeles entirely. No one had seen or heard from him or knew how to locate him. They only knew that he'd chartered his father's sailboat and taken off for parts unknown. He'd left Knight Shipping without a word, forcing both Lucius and Tahlia to step in and handle day-to-day operations. Tahlia was learning more than she'd ever cared to learn about the shipping industry.

She'd much rather be here at the gallery in her element or painting, but being a shareholder in the business forced her to care about its goings-on. Robert Kellogg and the executive team were helpful, but she and Lucius were learning to lean on each other and becoming friends in the process. He wasn't half-bad, and Tahlia only hoped that one day Maximus would be able to see that, see that he could have a relationship with his older brother if he wanted one. Lucius was certainly open to it.

Despite all the upheaval, Tahlia was happy that her work was finally on display. She'd worked hard over the last few weeks finishing up the pieces. Everyone who was anyone in the Los Angeles art community and neighboring cities had been invited to the event. She was hoping for some positive press, which would encourage her to continue painting. Not that she'd ever stop. Painting was catharsis for her and was helping heal the wound that losing Maximus had cost her.

"Would you like some champagne?" she asked her mother when the waiter came around with a tray.

"Absolutely," Kaitlynn answered for her and reached for three glasses. She handed each of them a flute. "We have to toast the lady of the hour." Kaitlynn raised her flute. "To Tahlia—we hope all your dreams come true."

They clinked glasses and each took a sip of champagne. "Thank you, sis."

Faith rushed over to Tahlia. "Come, that indie magazine I told you about is here and would like a quote from you for their arts section."

"Excuse me for a second." Tahlia went with Faith to answer the journalist's questions.

Three hours later, the gallery was empty, and she and Faith were left to clean up after the caterers she'd hired for the event had left.

"Everything okay, boss?" Faith asked when she noticed Tahlia was introspective. "I would think you'd be smiling given the fantastic turnout we had and that half your pieces were purchased."

"I am very happy," Tahlia said, feigning a smile as she began turning off lights throughout the gallery.

"Why do I hear a *but* in there somewhere?"

Tahlia shrugged. "I don't know. Something's just missing is all."

"You wouldn't mean a curly-haired shipping magnate, would you?" Faith raised a brow.

"Am I that obvious?"

"Only to someone who's worked with you for three years," Faith responded. "I've never seen you as happy as you were when you were seeing Maximus. I hate that you've broken up. Do you think there's any chance you'd ever get back together?"

"That's doubtful, Faith," Tahlia responded when they'd finally made it to the front door.

"Just thought I'd ask." Faith squeezed her shoulder. "Stay strong, okay?"

"I will." But it was hard to do because deep down, although she wouldn't admit it to her family, Tahlia missed Maximus and wanted him back. But as long as she was a shareholder in Knight Shipping that would never happen. Tahlia took one final look at the gallery and then locked the door.

The seas were choppy. Maximus wished the sailboat was closer to dry land, but they were at least an hour out from the Los Angeles marina. After two and a half months at sea, he'd finally decided to come home, if for nothing else than to see his mother. She'd sounded lonely the last time he'd spoken to her, and Maximus had realized how selfish he was being by staying away when she had only him. So he was coming home. At least for a short visit.

He would stay for a couple of days during the week and be back on board by the weekend, but the weather was bad. Had been for hours. After putting on raincoats, he and the captain had battened down the hatches and were now waiting out the inclement weather inside the galley kitchen with some black coffee with a hint of bourbon.

"You sure you're ready to come home?" Roy inquired

when he glanced at Maximus. He'd shared some of what happened with the will, Tahlia and Knight Shipping with the captain. The older man hadn't offered any advice. He'd just listened to Maximus ramble on about losing his company and his woman. "I thought you were adamant about staying away."

"I was."

"What changed?" Roy inquired.

"My mother. She's missing me, and I kind of took off unexpectedly. I didn't even see her before I left, so I'm coming back for a quick visit."

"And then going back out again?"

"Probably."

"Just let me know. I'm at your disposal."

"No one you want to go home to?" Maximus inquired, raising a brow.

"Not at the moment, sir."

Maximus nodded. It was the opposite for him. He had his mother. And, of course, there was Tahlia. When he'd docked in Marina Del Ray, he'd caught sight of a Los Angeles newspaper and seen that she'd finally had her art exhibit. They were touting her as the next great artist. He was proud of Tahlia and that he'd encouraged her in some small way to achieve her dreams, even if he wasn't there to see it.

Just then, a loud knocking hit the portholes of the galley. "Maybe one of the sails came loose," Roy commented. "I'll go on out and take care of it."

Maximus shook his head. The man was nearly seventy years old, and even though he could more than handle himself on the sailboat, it would be easier for Maximus to maneuver. "You stay. I've got it."

Once he was outside, the rain beat down on Maximus, soaking him right through the raincoat he had on.

He was starboard when the one of the booms lurched at him. He tried to duck, but it was too late, and seconds later he was knocked unconscious.

"Tahlia, it's Lucius," a deep masculine voice said from the other end of the line early the next morning.

"Lucius, what is it?" Tahlia said as she rubbed sleep from her eyes. She glanced at her clock on her nightstand. It read 5:00 a.m. Her buzzer hadn't yet woken her to get up. "You sound funny. Is everything okay?"

"It's Max."

Tahlia's heart lurched as foreboding shot through her, and she sat straight up in the bed. "What's happened to him?"

"He's been injured in a boating accident and is en route to Cedars-Sinai Medical Center. I just thought you might want to know."

"I do. Thank you so much, Lucius. I'm on my way." Then she paused. "Are—are you going?"

"Yes, of course," he stated. "He's my brother."

The phone line went dead, and Tahlia rushed around her bedroom to find something to wear. As she threw on a pair of yoga pants and a T-shirt, Tahlia didn't know what to think. Lucius hadn't said much. She just prayed that Maximus was okay and that his injuries weren't serious.

When she arrived at the hospital twenty minutes later due to light morning traffic, Maximus's mother, Charlotte, Lucius and Naomi were already there.

Tahlia rushed forward. She glanced at Charlotte, but she looked so distraught as she sniffed into a Kleenex that Tahlia didn't dare speak to her. She went to Lucius, and he reached for her, grasping her hands in his. Lu-

cius looked equally desolate and not put together like
he usually was. He and Naomi both wore track suits.

"How is he?"

Lucius shook his head. "We don't know yet. They
just brought him and are assessing his injuries."

"What—what happened?" Tahlia could barely get
the words out as images of Maximus bleeding on the
floor of the sailboat assailed her.

"He was knocked over by one of the sails and hit
his head," Lucius replied. "We don't know much more
than that."

Tahlia nodded. "How's his mother?" She inclined
her head toward Charlotte Knight, who was sitting with
Maximus's friend Griffin.

"A wreck," Naomi answered her this time. "I thought
she wouldn't appreciate Lucius and my being here, but
when she saw us she almost seemed happy that she
wasn't going to go through this alone. I think she's
frightened of losing Maximus, too, after losing her
husband."

"That's understandable," Tahlia said. Her heart went
out to Charlotte even though his mother had been less
than kind to her previously. "I'm going to go sit with
her."

And that was where Tahlia remained for hours because the ER doctor had come out to inform them that
Maximus needed to go into surgery to repair the brain
bleed from the injury he'd sustained on the sailboat.
At the news, Charlotte had begun weeping uncontrollably, and it had taken both Tahlia and Naomi to calm
her down while Griffin and Lucius remained stalwart.
Eventually, Charlotte and Naomi dozed off. Unfortunately, Griffin had to depart because he was due in

court, but he promised to be back. So Tahlia stood to stretch her legs and to check on Lucius.

She found him outside the ER staring ahead of him—at what, Tahlia didn't know.

"Hey," she said, coming to stand beside him.

He looked down at her, and the despair she saw in his dark eyes startled her. Tahlia had known Lucius cared for Maximus, but she hadn't known just how much until now. Tahlia reached for his large hand and squeezed it.

"He's going to pull through this, Lucius. He has to."

Lucius glanced upward at the sky. "I don't pray, Tahlia. I never have, but I have been now. I can't lose…" His voice caught in his throat. "I can't lose my brother, too, not when I've never really gotten to know him."

Tahlia nodded as tears filled her eyes. "And you won't. *We* won't. He's healthy and strong. He'll pull through. You'll see."

Lucius sucked in a deep breath. "Thanks, Tahlia. Where's Naomi?"

"Dozing with Charlotte."

He nodded. "All right, we'll let them rest."

"While they're resting, why don't we head to the chapel?" Tahlia suggested. She wanted Maximus to have all the prayers they could both give. Knowing that she could lose Maximus and seeing how short life was had Tahlia reevaluating her feelings. When he woke up, maybe it was time to tell him just how much she'd missed him and that she loved him.

Maximus had a splitting headache. This was nothing like the hangover he'd had after he'd lost the vote at Knight Shipping months ago. This was much worse. Except this time, when he opened his eyes, he wasn't in his room or on the sailboat, which was the last place he remembered being. He was in a hospital room.

He blinked several times, trying to remember how he'd gotten here, but he couldn't. He could see, however, that someone's head was lying on the hospital bed beside him. He reached out and stroked the person's hair, and instantly the smell came to him.

Tahlia.

At his touch, she lifted her head and looked at him sleepily. Her brown eyes connected with his dark ones.

"Max?" she whispered. And then she blinked several times, as if she wanted to make sure she wasn't dreaming and that he was real.

"Yeah, I think that's my name," he said groggily with a half smile. His head felt foggy. Was he medicated?

"I'm so glad you're awake." She rose to her feet. "I have to tell your mother and Lucius." But before she could move away, he caught her arm.

"Wait. What are you doing here? What am I doing here? What happened?" He launched several questions at her.

She paused midstep. "You were in an accident on your sailboat on your way back to LA. You suffered a brain bleed and they had to go in and operate."

"So that's why my head feels so fuzzy?"

She nodded. "You've been out for almost twenty-four hours."

He glanced at the door. "Mother?"

"Lucius was able to get her to sleep in one of the empty rooms. Nearly browbeat every administrator he could for the privilege. I'll go get her." She started to move again, but once again, he stopped her.

"Are you coming back?"

Dared he hope?

"Yes."

Maximus watched Tahlia depart. So he wasn't dreaming. She was here and apparently had been at his bedside. For how long? How long would she stay by his side before circumstances inevitably forced her to leave him and he was alone again?

Chapter 15

Once outside the room, Tahlia clutched her hand to her mouth and allowed the sob of relief she'd been holding in to escape her lips. He was awake. Max was going to pull through. Her prayer—heck, all their prayers—had been answered. She'd wanted to jump up and dance, but the wary look Max had given her made her pause. She couldn't tell if he was happy to see her or not. But he had asked her if she was staying. Surely that meant something.

"Tahlia." Lucius strode toward her down the hall. "Is he okay? Is my brother still alive?" The fear in his tone was evident because Tahlia had felt the same fear herself over the last forty-eight hours.

Tahlia glanced up at Lucius. Tears winged her eyelashes, and she nodded. "Yes, yes." She clutched his muscled forearms. "He's fine. He's awake and asking to see his mother. I was just headed to find Charlotte."

"Oh, thank God." Relief flooded across Lucius's face as he rubbed his hands across his face. Tahlia could see just then what the threat of losing Max had done to Lucius. Worry creased his forehead, and his eyes were haunted. He'd been so strong holding it together for her and Charlotte, belying his own inner turmoil, but she could see now, when he let down his guard, just how scared he'd been.

"It's a miracle," Tahlia said with a smile. "You should go see for yourself." She inclined her head toward the door, but Lucius shook his head.

"No, he wants to see his mother first, not me."

"Lucius…" Tahlia stared back at him incredulously. "You've been at this hospital for two days, same as the rest of us. You have a right to see him."

"Do I?" Lucius asked with a grimace. "I'm not sure Maximus would agree with you. And I don't want to upset him, not now when he's recovering. I'll be around."

Her brows furrowed. "Are you sure?"

Lucius nodded. "It's enough that he's awake and stable. Come, let me take you to Charlotte."

Tahlia allowed him to walk her down the hall, but she glanced back at Maximus's door. What would it take to get the brothers to finally see the truth—that the family and love they'd always wanted was right there in front of them if they would only reach out and grab it?

"It's all right, Mama." Maximus had never called her anything other than Mother, but in that moment, seeing her break down as she sat on the edge of his hospital bed, it felt right. "It's okay." He patted her head as she bowed her head on his chest and wept. "I'm going to be okay."

"I—I—I just thought I was going to lose you," she cried into his chest. Maximus wrapped his arms around her as best he could with all the IV lines and drips around him taped to his hands and arms.

"You didn't," he stated firmly. "I'm here and I'm not going anywhere."

Finally, she lifted her gaze to meet his, and it was like Maximus truly saw her for the first time in years. And as he did, he could see she'd aged nearly overnight. Her usually coiffed black hair was in a ponytail, *a ponytail* of all things. Her eyes were puffy, red-rimmed with circles around them from lack of sleep. And she was wearing jeans with a cardigan sweater set. He'd never seen Charlotte Knight ever look so, so *casual*.

"I'm just thankful I wasn't alone," she said. "Your girlfriend, Tahlia, has been here with me this entire time."

"She's not my girlfriend, Mother. We broke up before I took off when she found out about my plan to seduce her when we first met."

"I beg to differ. That girl has been by your bed this entire time and by my side. She truly cares for you, Maximus. No, it's more than that." She shook her head. "She loves you."

"That may be so, but the circumstances that led to our breakup to begin with are still there, and that hasn't changed."

"Oh, honey." His mother's voice softened. "Are you sure there's no way to salvage your relationship? I admit I initially was angry with Tahlia for the fact that Arthur shared confidences with her that he didn't share with me, but I can't blame her for that. Instead, I've found her to be a warm and caring person, and I'm seeing what Arthur saw in her. She's a great listener. It's as if you can tell her anything without any judgment. It must be how he'd felt."

Maximus turned his head and looked away. "I don't

want to hear about Father now." Because she was right. It's how Tahlia made everyone feel, including him.

"And should I take it you don't want to talk about your brother, Lucius, either?" she asked. "Because he, too, has been at the hospital since he learned of your accident. He hasn't left this place, and he's made sure you've received the best possible care. He even flew in the best brain surgeon in the country to be on your case."

Maximus turned his head. "And where is he now?" he inquired caustically. "Why isn't he in here right now making sure I'm all right?"

His mother shrugged. "Maybe because he doesn't think he'd be welcome, and can you honestly blame him? You haven't exactly rolled out the welcome mat. But then again, neither have I. His very existence is a reminder of the failure of my marriage. Sometimes, it's hard for me to look at him because he reminds me of your father. He even resembles him."

"I can only imagine how hard that must be for you, Mama," Maximus said softly.

"It is." She wiped away an errant tear from her eyes. "But don't you worry about me." She lightly patted his chest. "I just want you to get better. That's what we all want."

"That's right," Tahlia said from behind her. She stood in the doorway carrying two foam cups with what Maximus could only assume was coffee. She walked toward them and handed one to his mother. "Charlotte, I brought this for you. Thought you might need it."

"Thank you, dear." His mother accepted the cup. "I did." She rose from his bed and patted the spot she'd vacated. "You sit and talk with Maximus for a spell. If you don't mind, I'm going to run home for a minute and take a quick shower."

"Of course." Tahlia nodded, smiling at her. "I'll stay here with the patient."

Once she'd gone and it was just the two of them, a silence fell over the room. Instead of sitting on the bed as his mother had done, Tahlia pulled up the chair she'd been sleeping in earlier and scooted it back toward the bed.

"I hope you don't mind the company?" she asked somewhat tentatively.

He shook his head. "No, I'm glad you're here."

"You are?" The hope in her voice was evident.

"I missed you."

She lowered her head as if she was fighting with herself, but eventually she lifted it long enough for him to see tears were shining in her eyes. "I missed you, too."

They both fell back into silence.

Tahlia was the first to speak. "You don't know how scared I was for you," she started. "I thought I might lose you. We all were scared to death. And it wasn't just me, Maximus. It was your mother and Lucius and Naomi."

"I heard he was here."

"He's been here this whole time," Tahlia said. "But that's a fight for another day." She inhaled deeply. "What I'm trying to say is…"

"Is what?"

Her brown eyes were misty and wistful, and Maximus's heart constricted. He wasn't sure he was ready for her next words, but they came all the same. "I love you," she whispered.

She stared at him, waiting for his reaction. Maximus didn't know if it was his brain injury or something else, but he was speechless for the first time in his life. He couldn't think of a single coherent thought. His mind was buzzing from Tahlia's confession.

"The thing is, having you nearly die has shown me life is too short, and I couldn't let another moment pass without telling you how I felt because I might not ever get another chance. I love you," she said it again. "I think I have since I first saw you at the gallery."

Maximus frowned. He didn't remember meeting her at the gallery. They met at the estate when she came for the reading of the will.

At his confused expression, she continued. "You didn't notice me back then. You were there for your father, and after speaking with him, you left shortly thereafter, but I never forgot you. And I suppose when the opportunity came for us to be more—" she paused "—I jumped on it. And I know that you seized on the opportunity to 'seduce' me, but it didn't take much doing"

"Tahlia."

"You don't have to say it back," Tahlia said, patting his hand on the bed. "I understand if you don't feel the same away about me, especially after I put Arthur's feelings and wishes above yours and voted against you. You had thirty years with the man to see his true character. While I only had a year to get to know him. Maybe I only saw what I wanted to see because I needed a male figure in my life and he fit that role."

At her words, Maximus's heart constricted in his chest. "You don't have to say that."

"Yes, I do. Because it's true. I treated you unfairly, and I was wrong. You had a right to your anger. He was your father, not mine. I'm not completely blameless in all this, and I know we were only together for a short time, but I just wanted you to know that—that it impacted me." She bunched her shoulders. "Anyway, I just wanted you to know, and I'll be here until you get better."

Tahlia's love was a gift he didn't deserve. After everything, Maximus didn't feel he deserved her or her love. She was too special of a woman to be with a man like him. Even knowing that he might not say the words back, Tahlia had still put herself out there and told him how she felt. While he sat in his bed, afraid to say the words back even though he felt the same way. He was cold, unfeeling and manipulative, same as his father. She needed someone better than him.

"Thank you," he finally said.

Consternation crossed her face. Had she been expecting him to utter the sentiment back even though she'd said otherwise? Maximus couldn't. He was afraid to. The last time he'd shown someone love, his father, it had been thrown back at him. He feared the same thing happening with Tahlia, and he couldn't bear it if she pushed him away, too. And that couldn't happen, because there was still a hurdle facing them. A hurdle neither of them was talking about.

"Yes, thank you," he said again. "You're amazing, Tahlia."

"But?" The sparkle and light that had been in her eyes a moment ago when she confessed her love had gone out.

"But I'm not sure I'm capable of loving you back," Maximus said finally.

"Capable of loving me? Or you don't at all?" Tahlia inquired.

"Does it really matter?" he said. "There's too much water under the bridge."

"I don't believe that." Tahlia rose to her feet and

peered down at him. Tears were streaming down her tapioca-colored cheeks. "I know we have something, Maximus. Please don't do this. Please don't push me away. Not again. Not after we almost lost you."

"I'm not pushing you away," he said. "You just deserve someone better than me."

"I don't want anyone else," she cried.

"Then you should!" he shouted back at her.

"Max..."

"Maybe you should just leave," Maximus said, turning away from her. "My head is starting to hurt." His heart broke as he heard Tahlia crying behind him, willing him to turn around, but he didn't look back. He couldn't. He was too afraid to take the risk. And so he heard her footsteps as she walked away and most likely out of his life for good this time.

Tahlia was stunned and leaned against the wall of the hospital corridor. She'd never expected Maximus to shun her after she told him she loved him. She slid down the wall into a heap on the floor, and her head fell forward as she sobbed.

She could hear people passing her by, but she didn't care. Embarrassment was the least of her worries. She couldn't move because this time Maximus had hurt her worse than before. This time, she'd put her heart and soul before him on a platter, and he'd just thrown it aside as if her love didn't matter one iota to him.

How could he be so cruel? So heartless?

She was still sitting on the floor when Lucius walked toward her. He crouched in front of her, an angry frown on his features. "What did he do now?" Lucius asked, glancing at the closed door of Maximus's room.

She shook her head.

"Here, let me help you up." Lucius reached for Tahlia, pulling her to her feet, and then his arms came around to embrace her as they'd done several times before. "I'm going to kill that little brother of mine, and right after I got him back no less."

"Don't," Tahlia cried yet again against Lucius's chest. She couldn't believe she was back here again. Not after Maximus almost died. In her worst nightmare, she'd never thought he'd turn his back on her, but he had. She lifted her head to look up at him. "He's made his feelings perfectly clear where I'm concerned. He doesn't want me, so—so I'm going to leave. Go home and get on with my life."

She started to move away from Lucius, but he touched her arm. "Tahlia. Don't leave. He's not in his right state. Maybe that surgery scrambled his brain somehow. He doesn't know what he's doing. He couldn't. Because if he did, he wouldn't let you go."

"He's knows exactly what he's doing, Lucius. You'll have to learn to accept that Maximus is somewhat of a prick. I have." Then as much as it hurt, she walked down the hall and away from Maximus, the love of her life.

"You stupid jerk!" Lucius barged into Maximus's room, startling him out of the haze of guilt he already felt for sending Tahlia away.

Lucius stabbed his finger in Maximus's direction several times. "You—you—you idiot!" he roared.

"What the hell?" Maximus yelled, covering his ears. "You do realize I'm in the hospital recovering from surgery." His head was still hurting something fierce, and none of the medications they'd given him had worked.

"Don't you dare go pulling the sick card," Lucius

said. "I've been talking to the doctor, and you're going to make a full recovery."

"That must really be upsetting news for you," Maximus responded with a snort. "I'm sure you'd much rather I'd disappear altogether."

"Jesus Christ, Max!" Lucius spun away from him for several moments. He was silent, and Max wondered what he was thinking. When he spun around, he said, "Can't you let up for a second?"

"Why?"

"Don't you get it?"

"Get what?"

"I don't hate you!" Lucius yelled, throwing his hands up in the air. At his words, Maximus was quiet. "I never have."

"Of course you do," Maximus said. "I was the son who grew up with Arthur as a father. I had everything in life handed to me on a silver platter, while you've had to struggle until you achieved success all on your own."

"So what? I've had it no harder than any other person out there," Lucius responded. "At least I had my grandmother and my friend Adam. And my mother occasionally, but she was too busy living her life and refusing to tell me who my father was. That's beside the point, Maximus. Why are *you* so angry? You'd think I would be. I'm the son he didn't acknowledge."

"You think you're the only one with a right to be angry?" Maximus asked, pressing the bed forward so he could sit upright even though his head felt like it was splitting into two. "Well, guess what, big brother. It finally occurred to me why I never had my father's love."

"Why is that?"

"Because I was always the stand-in for the son he really wanted. You. And despite everything I did, no matter how hard I worked, or how much I achieved, it was never good enough for Arthur Knight, because I could never be you, Lucius. So there. That's why I'm angry."

"Maximus." Lucius pulled up the chair that Tahlia had left closer to the bed. "What has that anger gotten you, huh? You've just let one of the best women I've ever met, other than Naomi, walk out." He pointed to the door. "And the only thing I can think of, other than you've lost your mind, is that you don't think you deserve her."

"You have no idea what you're talking about."

Lucius stared at him, and it was as if he could read Maximus's mind. "I think I do. Tahlia and her love for you has you running scared. And I get it, okay? I was scared, too, when I realized I loved Naomi, but I'm telling you, bro, having a woman like Tahlia in your life is the best kind of medicine you'll ever need."

The two men looked at each other, assessing the other. It was Maximus who finally spoke. "Why are you involving yourself in my personal life anyway? This is none of your concern. What's it to you if I'm alone or not?"

"I'm here because I *care*," Lucius stated evenly. "And I want you to be happy, same as me."

"Why? Why should you?"

"Because you're my brother." Lucius pounded his chest. "And that means something to me. I don't know what it means to you, but I grew up alone with no one other than Grandma, and I always wanted a little brother. And when I learned about you at the hospital, I wanted to go to you then, even when my world was shattering around me, and pull you into a hug and tell you everything was going to be all right because that's what a big brother does. But you looked at me with such scorn that I left."

Maximus remembered that night. The night when the world he'd always thought he'd known came crashing down, too. It'd been when he learned his father was a liar, a cheat and an all-around jerk. He'd seen Lucius and the stunned look on his face when he'd learned Arthur was their father. And his heart had gone out to him because he had no idea that he'd actually dodged a bullet. Arthur Knight had been a terrible father.

"You're right," Maximus said. "I was upset. And disillusioned. I'd always looked up to our father. That night I'd realized he was just a man. A fallible man with his own faults."

Lucius nodded. "We all are human, but the key is to learn from our mistakes and take a different path. Just because Arthur wasn't capable of loving you doesn't mean you're the same, Maximus. You can be a better man than him. I know you can be."

Maximus looked at Lucius, truly looked at him. And staring back at him for the first time in his life was someone who believed in him.

His brother.

"It's too late, Lucius," Maximus said, shaking his head. "I hurt Tahlia just now. There's no way she's coming back for more of the same. She told me she loved me, and I said thank you. I ruined everything."

"No, you haven't," Lucius stated emphatically. "While you were gone, we took care of Knight Shipping for you. We got to know each other, and I've never seen a woman more in love than Tahlia is with you. You can still fix this. It's never too late."

"I hope you're right," Maximus replied. He'd hurt Tahlia when he hadn't meant to. He just hadn't known how to love her, but having Lucius here to talk had helped. Helped him see that he was capable of much more if he was only willing to go out on the ledge and jump.

And for Tahlia he would.

Chapter 16

"Man, am I glad to see you," Griffin said when he visited the hospital later that afternoon. He leaned forward on the hospital bed to give Maximus a hug and took a seat in the chair across from him.

"About as happy as I am to see you," Maximus said, sitting up in his bed. "I missed you, Griff. Being out on that boat with a seventy-year-old man was starting to get lonesome."

Griffin shrugged. "You're the one who went on a self-imposed exile and kept all of us at arm's length, but let's not talk about that. How are you feeling?"

"Like crap," Maximus answered honestly. "My head is killing me. The doctor was here earlier and told me that's to be expected."

"Any complications from the surgery?"

Maximus shook his head. "No, the doctor said I should make a full recovery."

"Darn." Griffin snapped his fingers. "I was hoping to get that autographed baseball collection you have."

Maximus chuckled, but when he did, it made his

head hurt, and he rubbed his temples to ease the sharp pain from the laughter.

"Are you sure you're up for a visit?" Griffin asked, starting to rise from his seat. "I can always come back."

"For you, yes. And please stay." He patted the bed, indicating Griffin should sit down. "We haven't seen each other in a couple of months. Catch me up on what's going on with you. I could use the distraction."

Griffin's forehead creased. "I don't understand. Tahlia was here for days when you were injured and after the surgery. Even your brother, Lucius, was here causing a ruckus to make sure you got the best care. I just assumed circumstances had changed."

"They have, sort of," Maximus responded.

"Explain," Griffin said, folding his arms across his chest.

"Lucius and I are going to make an effort at this whole brother thing."

Maximus couldn't help but notice the wide grin that split across Griffin's dark features.

"That's great news, Max. I was hoping that would be the outcome. And Tahlia?"

"Ah…there's where I have a problem." He sighed as he remembered their encounter and how upset Tahlia had been. "I royally screwed up, Griff, and I'm going to have to do some serious damage control to get her back."

Griffin frowned. "What could you have possibly done from your hospital bed?"

"Push her away. She told me she loved me, and I knew she wanted me to say it back. And I wanted to say those words back to her, but I didn't. Instead, I told her there was too much water under the bridge between us and that we'd never work."

"You idiot!" Griffin rose from the chair he was sitting in and began pacing the floor. "After that woman stood by your side? How could you?"

"Please don't read me the riot act, okay? Lucius already did that. I know I have to fix things. And I will. As soon as I get out of here."

Griffin rolled his eyes upward. "You're on thin ice, my friend. If Tahlia gives you another chance, I would suggest you thank your lucky stars because you're not going to find someone who loves and cares for you more."

Maximus smiled. "Yes, I know that, and I promise you when I get out of here, I'm going to rectify the situation. I promise you. I will get Tahlia back."

"Do you really think you can let him go?" Kaitlynn asked Tahlia when she came on Saturday to help Kaitlynn pack boxes. She had helped Kaitlynn with the security deposit and first month's rent to move into a brand-new apartment complex with all the amenities, such as a fitness center and coffee bar. It was the least she could do since being owner of the gallery and a shareholder at Knight Shipping had given her extra cash in her bank account.

"I have no choice," Tahlia said. "Maximus rejected me, Kaitlynn. After I told him that I was at fault, too, and could have supported him instead of standing on my soap box and telling him about Arthur's feelings and wishes." She stopped putting tape on a box long enough to look at her sister. "I sat in front of him, face-to-face, and I told him that I missed him and that his accident had made me see that I couldn't go another minute without telling him how I feel, that I loved him. And you want to know what he said?"

"What?" Kaitlynn asked.

"He said, thank you. Thank you!" Tahlia repeated the words she still couldn't believe she'd heard, even though he'd said them days ago. "He acted as if I'd just given him flowers and a get-well card at the hospital, for Christ's sake. I told him I loved him."

"And you expected him to say it back?"

"I hoped," Tahlia responded with a shrug. "But at the very least, he could have said he cares about me. All I got was he missed me. Most likely he missed all the sex he was getting on the regular."

"It was like that, huh?"

Tahlia blushed and continued taping the box. "We had a very active sex life." But gosh, it seemed like that was decades ago when it had been only less than three months. Being with Maximus had been everything she'd ever imagined it would be. Her body had recognized being with his as if she'd come home, and now it craved his. But she'd have to get used to the fact that they would never be together again in any capacity except at board meetings.

That was when it hit her. And she stopped dead in her tracks.

"What?" Kaitlynn looked at her. "What is it, Tahlia? You look like you've been hit with some sort of revelation."

Tahlia nodded. "That's because I have." Why hadn't it occurred to her before? Maximus saw the shares of Knight Shipping as a stumbling block between them. He'd said so when they'd first broken up, when he'd accused her of not believing in him, of not supporting him and taking his side.

Maybe, just maybe, she had the key after all to salvage what was left of their relationship, if there was one. It was a risky move, but she had to try because if she didn't, she'd always wonder what if. She'd always wonder if they could have survived the drama if only she'd taken the chance.

"I'm glad to be getting out of here," Maximus said as he rose from the hospital bed and sat down in the wheelchair the nurse held for him.

"You and me both," his mother said from behind him. "I practically had to fight that brother of yours over which of us would be coming to pick you up and drive you home."

"Oh, yeah?" Maximus asked, laughing. It had surprised him, too, at the active role Lucius was now taking in his life. Ever since their talk a week ago, he'd made his presence known by visiting Maximus every day in the hospital. They would talk for hours about growing up, school, sports and, of course, women. They'd even played cards, and Lucius had taught him how to play poker. And slowly, Maximus was beginning to see the makings of a relationship with his brother.

"Yes," his mother harrumphed. "It was only when I'd agreed to have him and Naomi over for dinner that he'd finally relented."

Maximus glanced up at his mother. "Thank you. It means a lot to me that you're making an effort where Lucius is concerned."

She patted his shoulder, and then the nurse began wheeling him out of the room and toward the elevator. "Lucius and Naomi, yes, but his mother will never be welcomed in my home again."

He reached for his mother's hand and squeezed. "That's understandable. And I'm sure Lucius will understand. The only reason you allowed her the first time after the reading of the will was at my bequest."

"Thank you, darling," his mother replied. "And Naomi, she's such a lovely girl. Lucius is very lucky to have her."

Maximus gave her a sideward glance. "Yes, he is." Naomi had brought him a lovely get-well basket full of products from her men's line to make sure his stay at the hospital was more comfortable. He couldn't ask for a better sister-in-law.

"Makes me think of Tahlia and what a great addition she would be to the family."

"Matchmaking again, mother?"

"Me?" She touched her chest. "Never. You've told me time and time again to stay out of your love life. I was merely reminding you that Tahlia was at your bedside day and night when you were injured until you woke up."

"I know that." Lying in his hospital bed, he'd thought of nothing else but how he could get Tahlia back. What he could do to convince her to give him another chance. She certainly didn't have to give him one, not after he'd done the exact same thing his father had done to him. He'd thrown her love for him back in her face.

It was why he waited. He needed time, not only to heal, but to think of something grand. When he'd told Lucius of his idea, Lucius had given him some solid advice. *Speak from your heart.*

Would that be enough? Would Tahlia hear him when he told her he loved her and never wanted to live without her?

"I don't appreciate being summoned to meet you," Kaitlynn Armstrong said when Maximus arrived in a limousine to pick her up at her apartment complex at the beginning of the week.

"I'm sure you don't," Maximus responded. "I know I can't be your favorite person right now."

"That's right," Kaitlynn said. Her brown eyes turned to daggers when they looked at him. "You hurt Tahlia deeply *twice*. So I'm not sure what else you want, Maximus. It wasn't enough to have her madly and deeply in love with you?"

"Listen, Kaitlynn—"

"No, you listen. I've watched my sister pine for you for a year. And when she finally got a chance to meet you, she jumped right in with both feet and fell hard for you, Maximus Xavier Knight. While you, on the other hand, were only using her for your own agenda. It was despicable."

"You're right, Kat," he replied. "May I call you Kat?" He remembered Tahlia always used the nickname around her.

"Kat is for my friends, and I don't think you're one of them anymore."

Maximus smiled. She was tough, and he deserved it. "Maybe I can be, which is why I called you. I need your help."

"My help? To get my sister back? You must be joking."

"I'm not. You're right. I don't deserve Tahlia. I did have an ulterior motive when we began seeing each other, but all of that changed the more I got to know your sister. The more time we spent together, the deeper I fell in love with her."

Kaitlynn stared back at him. "Then why did you let her go, you big oaf!" She smacked his shoulder hard with her hand. "She stayed by your side in the hospital, admitted her shortcomings, and you still let her walk out that door."

"Because I'm an idiot!" Maximus said. "A complete and utter fool, but a fool who loves your sister. And you're right. I want her back, and I need your help to do it."

"I don't know how to help you. You're on your own." She shrugged.

"Oh, you can help me," Maximus said, stepping out of the limousine that had come to a halt. "Come inside and let me show you how." He held his hand out to her.

Kaitlynn glanced at him in bewilderment, as she clearly hadn't noticed the car had stopped. But when she exited the vehicle and saw their destination, she smiled at him. "You sly, sly devil. You really are as smart as they say you are."

Tahlia drove up to the Knight estate. Lucius had called her to inform her, *if she was interested*, that Maximus had been released from the hospital days ago. He knew darn well that she was interested.

Her love for his brother hadn't suddenly flown the coop in a week's time. But she did have news for Lucius. News he hadn't exactly been shocked to hear. It had taken her a few days to finalize the details, but she'd made it happen, and surprisingly he hadn't tried to change her mind or talk her out of it. Not that he could. She was adamant in her decision, and no one was going to talk her out of it.

She'd expected more of a reaction from him, but instead of trying to change her mind, Lucius had wished her good luck and said he hoped his brother finally saw the light, which was that she was a woman worth hanging on to. Tahlia thought so.

And so she'd taken a leap of faith by coming here. Maximus could very well turn her away and refuse to see her, but she was hoping against hope that he wouldn't turn her away.

Parking her VW Bug, she exited and headed for the large solid oak door of the Knight estate. She was greeted several moments later by a uniformed butler.

"Tahlia Armstrong," she told him. "I'm here to see—"

"Maximus," he said before she could finish. "I will fetch him for you. Please follow me into the sitting room."

He led her into a large room.

"Thank you," she said, taking a seat on a wingback chair.

"Can I get you any refreshments?" the butler inquired.

"No, that won't be necessary. I won't be staying long," Tahlia replied.

"That's too bad," Maximus said from the doorway. "Because I was hoping you'd stay awhile."

Tahlia's breath caught in her throat at the sight of him. He was *all right*. He was standing there looking like he'd just stepped out of a fashion magazine instead of a hospital bed. He wore jeans and a V-neck sweater, and he'd never looked more handsome to Tahlia. She swallowed the lump in her throat.

She'd come here with a purpose and she just had to get to it, but Maximus didn't seem to be in any hurry. Instead, he looked at his butler and said, "Can you bring us a pot of tea? Maybe chamomile? You'd like that, right?"

Tahlia smiled. He remembered that she liked chamomile tea and that it calmed her nerves. "Yes, that'll be fine."

The butler left the room, and Maximus took a seat across from Tahlia on the opposite wingback chair.

"I'm glad to see that you're looking well," Tahlia started. "How are you feeling?"

"I'm doing well," he responded. "Still a little weak and not where I'd like to be, but the doctor said that's normal after a couple of weeks in the hospital. He said once I exercise my muscles again that I'll be right as rain."

"Good, good." Tahlia nodded. "So…" Her words trailed off as she tried to figure out how to start the conversation. She'd never had trouble conversing with him, but this time was different. This time their entire relationship was on the line.

"So, I'm happy you came to see me."

Her brows drew together in confusion. "You are?"

He nodded. "I didn't like how I ended our last meeting."

"Neither did I," Tahlia said. "It was unpleasant, to say the least, but it's over and done with." She sat up more firmly in her chair. "It's actually why I'm here."

"Is that so?" Maximus scooted closer to the edge of the seat, and in so doing, their knees touched. The tiny action caused both of them to look up at each other.

Tahlia was surprised at what she saw there. Was that lust lurking in his eyes? Or was she imagining what she wanted to see there because she'd been unable to get Maximus out of her mind and her subconscious was manifesting itself?

She exhaled and tried again. "Yes. I thought you might want this." She reached inside her purse for the manila envelope and handed it to Maximus.

"What's this?"

"Open it. It's something you've always wanted."

Maximus was afraid to open the envelope and stared at it in his hands. What could Tahlia possibly be giving to him? And then it hit him, the only thing she could do to prove she believed in him.

He looked at her, and the depth of emotion on her face told him he was right. This had cost her, but she was doing it because she loved him and because she believed in him.

He handed her the envelope back. "I don't want this."

She frowned. "Why not? You haven't even opened it. You don't even know what's inside."

"I don't have to open it because I know what it says."

The butler returned, breaking the moment, and set the tray with the teapot, cups and cream and sugar in front of them on the settee. He went to pour it, but Maximus stopped him. "Thank you, I've got it."

Maximus reached for the teapot and began pouring, stalling for time as he prepared for the biggest speech of his life. The moment was here. Tahlia had come to him yet again, offering him everything she had in the hopes that this time he wouldn't reject her love.

He wouldn't make that mistake twice.

Maximus handed her the teacup and saucer and watched as she brought it to her delectable lips. And despite his injuries, his shaft sprung to life.

When she was finished sipping, she set the cup down on the settee. "Aren't you having any?"

He shook his head. He probably should have some tea to calm his nerves. He'd never told a woman he loved her before, so this was certainly a first.

"Tahlia…" he began, but she interrupted.

"Why won't you open that envelope?" she asked, inclining her head to the envelope sitting on the settee.

"I don't need to," he responded. "It says that you've signed your two percent share in Knight Shipping over to me."

Her eyes grew large in surprise. "H-how did you know? Did Lucius say something to you?"

Maximus chuckled. "So my brother knew you were going to do this and he let you?"

"Like he could stop me," Tahlia replied with a snort. "It's my stock to do with as I please, and I'm choosing to give it to you because it's rightfully yours and because it's what you deserve. Knight Shipping should have been yours to begin with. You earned it, but instead your father chose otherwise. And I'm here to tell you he was wrong, Maximus. He should have chosen you, because I do. And I always choose you each and every time."

"Oh, God, Tahlia." Maximus fell to his knees in front of her and clutched at her legs. "I don't deserve you. I never have, but I'm so glad you're here and that you'd do this *for me.*"

Tahlia's hands grasped both sides of his face, and Maximus thought he'd died and gone to heaven just to have her touch him again. How he'd longed for her! "I'd do anything for you," she said, "even come here again, not knowing how you'd react and…and—" Her words got choked from emotion, and she stopped, dropping her hands from his face.

"Not knowing if I'd reject your love again," he finished, glancing up at her warily.

She nodded as fresh tears formed in her eyes.

"I won't," Maximus said, shaking his head. "I won't ever again."

"You won't?" Her voice was hesitant and unsure.

He couldn't put his feelings into words as relief surged through him. Tahlia was one in a million. She was without guile and had every reason to hate him, to never want to see him again, but instead she'd come here with her heart in her hands asking for his love yet again. He wouldn't fail her.

Summoning all the courage he'd ever had, Maximus took her hands in his and raised them to his lips. He couldn't resist the forces any longer. She'd unlocked the door to his heart, a door he'd kept hidden because of his father, but she'd transformed him and set him free.

"I love you, Tahlia," Maximus said simply, remembering Lucius's words to speak from the heart. "And I'm sorry for everything. For foolishly thinking that I could seduce you into my way of thinking to vote for me when it was you who was seducing me with your every look, your every action and your every kiss."

Tears shone in Tahlia's eyes at his words, and Maximus was thankful that she wasn't pulling away from him. Instead, she was clutching his hand to her heart, and Maximus's heart swelled with love. He hadn't lost her!

"You're my every dream come true, Tahlia. You're the dream I didn't even know I was looking for, but I am so happy that I found you. I was a scared man before you came into my life. Afraid of love because I'd been rejected by my father so many times."

"I know that, sweetheart." She whispered the endearment.

"I was so afraid to let you in because I was afraid of being rejected, but what did I do? I did the same thing to you that my father did to me. In the hospital, I rejected your love even though you'd been there for me in my time of need, and I'm not sure if I'll ever truly forgive myself for hurting you that way. But I promise you that I will spend my every waking minute trying, trying to be the best man that I can be for you, the woman I love."

"Oh, Maximus!" she cried and threw her arms around his neck and began planting kisses on his neck and ears, but he pulled away.

"Wait, sweetheart. I'm not done yet."

"You're not? I thought that was really, really good," she said. "Can't you just stop there?"

"No." He shook his head. "Because there's so much more I have to say."

"Like what?"

"That you didn't have to give me your stock," Maximus said, glancing down at the manila envelope that sat on the table.

"Of course I did. I wanted to show you that I just want you. And only you. None of it, any of it, means a thing without you in my life."

"And you mean more to me than Knight Shipping. So much more. Do you have any idea how much you've enriched my life?" he asked. "You've helped bridge the gap between me and Lucius."

"I have?"

"Yes, we've been talking since I've been in the hospital, and I have to admit, I kind of like having an older brother. Someone to bounce ideas off of. And it's why I can't let you give away what's rightfully half his."

"But he doesn't want Knight Shipping," Tahlia said. "He just wants you to be happy."

Maximus grinned and playfully tapped her nose. "There you go again, ever the optimist."

She shrugged. "What can I say? It's who I am."

Maximus swung her into his arms, causing them

both to fall onto the floor. Tahlia ended up on the rug with Maximus hovering over her. He loved looking at her and knew he'd never tire of it. So he took his fill now. Tahlia was all he would ever need. "And I love who you are," he said, lowering his head until his lips were mere inches from hers. "Matter of fact, I love everything about you."

And then he did the one thing he'd wanted most, the one thing he'd missed over the last few months. Maximus finally kissed Tahlia.

Chapter 17

A kiss had never been sweeter to Tahlia than the one Maximus bestowed on her after he'd just professed his love to her. She'd taken a risk coming to the estate today, and it had paid off. Maximus now held her in his arms on the throw rug in his family's sitting room as he kissed her gently at first, stroking her hair.

Tahlia cried out in disappointment. She wanted more. It didn't help that the scent of his cologne was teasing her senses, and it made every part of Tahlia's body tingle, especially when she felt the jut of his erection in his jeans. Her nipples thrust toward him through the confines of her blouse, desperate for his touch. They hadn't been together in so long; she didn't want to wait a moment longer.

Tahlia began writhing beneath him even more so when he dipped his head and licked at the seams of her mouth, seeking entry. She parted her already moistened lips, and his tongue darted inside, possessively mating with hers until she was going mad for him. Her senses were roaring to new heights, and she arched into him for greater contact and was rewarded when she felt the hard ridge of his manhood pushing against her pelvis. But Maximus stopped her.

"We should, uh, take this to my room," he murmured huskily.

That was when Tahlia realized that they were still on the throw in the middle of his family's sitting room. He had aroused her to fever pitch, making her forget their location. She blushed beet red. "Yes, of course."

They left everything in the room, including her purse, exactly where it was, and she took the hand Maximus offered her and let him lead her to his bedroom. It was up a flight of stairs and down the hall, heightening the anticipation of finally being with Maximus after so long without him.

When they finally made it inside the room, Maximus closed and locked the door. Then they began peeling their clothes off, eager to feel the friction of body against naked body.

"I've looked forward to this moment for so long," Tahlia said as they met on the bed, and he slid down on top of her.

"As have I." Then he claimed her mouth with a hot, hungry kiss. Tahlia moaned as he kissed her with skilled mastery. Her entire body trembled with every thrust of his tongue inside her mouth. His tongue invaded hers, and all Tahlia could do was take, take more of him as he went deeper, giving her everything. And when his lips left hers to nip at her earlobe and then glide to her neck and throat, molten heat began to pool between her thighs.

Maximus had always made her feel this way, this hot, this aroused with him and only him. Then his hand slipped underneath her and downward to cup her backside, bringing his arousal against her belly and rubbing her *there* with his engorged tip. Tahlia wanted to drag him inside her to have every inch of his skin imprinted on her. She writhed in his hold, eager for him to reach her slit, but instead of driving into her, he slid her up and down the steel of his erection with slow, leisurely strokes.

"Enough of the foreplay," Tahlia whimpered. "Please… take me."

"Not yet," Maximus said and began molding and massaging her breasts before dipping his head to sample one and then the other. At the graze of his tongue, licking and swirling her breasts, corkscrews of ecstasy went through Tahlia, and she was forced to take a sharp breath.

But he continued his onslaught of her senses when his hands delved between her thighs and touched her exactly where she wanted him to, dipping and withdrawing, making her pant his name as he stoked the fire deep within her. She opened her legs wider to give him better access. And he took it, moving down her body.

His hands were no longer possessing. It was his mouth at her slick, hot core, milking every ounce of her satisfaction as he used his tongue and teeth to suckle her. She whimpered and keened as he licked his way in and out of her, pleading for him to end her agony as she bucked helplessly beneath his lashing tongue.

She was sweaty and delirious when she finally saw him pause long enough to put on a condom, and then he was back between her thighs, thrusting into her. He plunged inside her, into the very depths of her, then he withdrew and plunged in deeper until he was all the way inside her. Then he began moving, slowly, then faster and faster until she convulsed and shattered around him. Maximus's roar came next, and he stiffened in her arms, but he didn't stop ramming into her until her body gave way again and she shattered into a million pieces.

Maximus gathered Tahlia's exhausted and shaking body into his arms. He loved her so much and with everything in him. What they'd shared just now was more than physical. It transcended anything he'd ever felt. Time and space ceased to exist. And he knew he never wanted to let her go. He loved her.

When Tahlia finally began to stir, he found she was still awake. "Hello, beautiful." He stroked her cheek.

"Did I pass out?" she asked in disbelief.

He laughed. "Uh, something like that."

She poked him in the ribs. "Don't tease me. You just wore me out. I wasn't prepared for your exuberance."

Maximus thought about how he reveled in the taste of her sweet stickiness when he'd been between her thighs. Her sighs of pleasure as he'd licked her and she'd pleaded with him to take her. He liked that she gave herself so completely to him, but there was one final thing he hadn't done.

Maximus slid from the bed and reached for the nightstand drawer.

Tahlia saw his actions and held his hand. "Oh, no you don't, mister. My highly sensitized flesh needs time to recover."

He chuckled to himself. She thought he was reaching for another condom; he wasn't. Instead, he reached for the ring box he'd purchased yesterday, thanks to a little help from Kaitlynn, Tahlia's sister. After leaving the hospital, he'd called her and picked her up. He needed assistance because he wasn't sure what ring Tahlia might like. At first, Kaitlynn hadn't been too keen to meet up with the man who'd broken her sister's heart, but when he'd told her just how much he loved Tahlia and that he would make things right, she'd agreed. And they'd found a beautiful six-carat princess-cut diamond ring.

"Tahlia." Maximus kneeled at the bedside. "I know this might seem sudden to you since we're just getting back together, but you were right about something. Having a near-death experience changes you. And it changed me. It made me see life is short, and I don't want to miss a single minute of being with you." He opened the ring box. "Tahlia Armstrong, will you do me the honor of being my wife? Will you marry me?

"Wh-what?" Tahlia's eyes grew large with wonder. "You want to marry me?"

He nodded. "I was so lonely until you came into my life, but you've brightened up my whole world. You've changed my life, Tahlia, and I'm the better for it. So I want us to last a lifetime. Please—say you'll marry me."

Tears streamed down Tahlia's cheeks as she looked at him and nodded. "You've changed my life, too, Maximus. You've enriched it with your love and your encouragement. So yes, I'll marry you."

Maximus clutched her shoulders and kissed her. His lips parted hers with bold assurance, and his tongue slid firmly between them to explore her with an eroticism that left her trembling. "You've made me the happiest man alive, Tahlia." Then he slipped the diamond ring onto her finger.

"And I'm the happiest woman alive," Tahlia said. Then she pulled him into her embrace as she whispered, "Now I'm ready for round two."

Epilogue

"I never thought I'd see the day that Maximus and Lucius would be running Knight Shipping together," Tahlia said as she and Naomi set the table at Maximus's penthouse. Lucius and Naomi were joining them for dinner because she and Maximus had just returned from their honeymoon in Saint Bart's.

They'd had their wedding on the Knight estate on the great lawn surrounded by family and friends. Her mother had walked Tahlia down the aisle, and Kaitlynn and Griffin had been maid of honor and best man. Lucius had been groomsman and Naomi bridesmaid, along with her coworker, Faith. It had been a spectacular day, one that Tahlia would never forget.

"Neither did I," Naomi said. "That was no small feat you accomplished, sister-in-law."

Tahlia turned and stared at her husband while he and Lucius grilled steaks on the grill on the balcony outside. "I didn't do it alone. It took both of our strong, yet very powerful husbands to put in the work."

"True, but you were the catalyst."

"No." Tahlia shook her head. "In his own weird way,

it was their father, Arthur," Tahlia said. "Though I don't think even he could have envisioned this."

Tahlia smiled as the two brothers sparred over who was the better grill master and drank their beers.

"How was the honeymoon?" Naomi queried as she played with her curly fro. Tahlia wished she was like her sister-in-law and could rock the natural look.

"Oh, Saint Bart's was amazing," Tahlia said, "and somewhat exhausting. Your brother-in-law was insatiable."

Naomi giggled. "It must run in the family."

Later, when both couples were gathered at the table, Maximus opened a bottle of wine and began pouring each of them a glass.

"None for me," Naomi said, placing her hand over the rim of the wineglass.

"Are you feeling all right?" Maximus inquired as the foursome usually drank quite frequently together as they each had a love of wine bars.

Naomi beamed from across the table, and Tahlia instantly knew the truth. "I'm feeling fine." She patted her flat belly. "I'm just eating for two now, so it's best I avoid alcoholic substances for the next six months."

Maximus's eyes grew large, and he reached across the table and pulled Lucius into a one-armed hug. "Congratulations, bro. And you, too, Naomi." He looked at his sister-in-law. "This is wonderful news. I'm going to be an uncle."

"That's right." Lucius grinned from ear to ear. "My baby is having a baby."

"Aw, honey." Naomi smiled at his sweet words.

"Soon it'll be your turn, Max," Lucius stated. "You mark my words."

Maximus chuckled as he looked across the table at his gorgeous wife. "Well, it certainly won't be for lack of trying on my part. I kept Tahlia flat on her back for most of our honeymoon."

"Maximus Xavier Knight!" Tahlia blushed from across the table.

He grinned mischievously. "Sorry, babe." But deep down, he wasn't sorry. He couldn't wait for the day when Tahlia told him she was pregnant.

He told her so later that evening, after Lucius and Naomi had gone and it was just the two of them staring out at the Los Angeles skyline on the balcony of the penthouse.

"You don't want to wait?" Tahlia asked, glancing behind her. Her back was to him, and Maximus had circled his arms around her middle. "I'd think you'd want me all to yourself." She could feel the bulge in his pants. Her husband had a voracious appetite for her.

"I do," Maximus whispered, nuzzling her neck and planting soft kisses there. "But I can't wait to see your belly swollen with my child."

Tahlia spun around in his arms to face him. Her hands stroked the sides of his face as she peered intently into his dark eyes. "And I can't wait to be the mother of your children."

And she sealed her wish with a kiss.

* * * * *

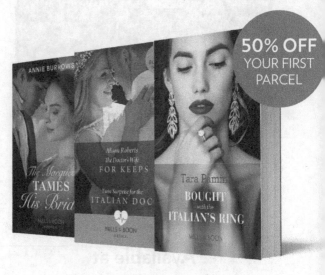

MILLS & BOON

MODERN

Power and Passion

Prepare to be swept off your feet by sophisticated, sexy and seductive heroes, in some of the world's most glamourous and romantic locations, where power and passion collide.

LET'S TALK
Romance

For exclusive extracts, competitions
and special offers, find us online:

f facebook.com/millsandboon

🐦 @MillsandBoon

📷 @MillsandBoonUK

Get in touch on 01413 063232

For all the latest titles coming soon, visit
millsandboon.co.uk/nextmonth